LORD SAVAGE

LORD SAVAGE

MIA GABRIEL

St. Martin's Paperbacks

This is a work of fiction. All of the characters, organizations, and events portrayed in this novel are either products of the author's imagination or are used fictitiously.

LORD SAVAGE

Copyright © 2016 by Mia Gabriel.
Excerpt from *Savage Nights* Copyright © 2016 by Mia Gabriel.

All rights reserved.

For information address St. Martin's Press, 175 Fifth Avenue, New York, NY 10010.

ISBN: 978-1-250-07680-9

Printed in the United States of America

St. Martin's Paperbacks edition / January 2016

St. Martin's Paperbacks are published by St. Martin's Press, 175 Fifth Avenue, New York, NY 10010.

10 9 8 7 6 5 4 3 2 1

ONE

❧

London, 1907

There are nights when a crowded ballroom can be the loneliest place on earth, when every happy face belongs to a stranger and every smile is meant for another, and love is as fleeting as the latest waltz.

I had not made the long voyage from New York to London to be lonely like that. Yet, that was exactly how I felt as the Honorable Eustace Smithson led me through the dance, his feet only slightly less plodding than his conversation.

"I trust you find our weather agreeable, Mrs. Hart?" he said, the words barely making their way past his thick bristle of a mustache. "To be sure, London must seem quite different from America, where you are accustomed to tropical climes and palm trees and such."

"Palm trees, Mr. Smithson?" I repeated, perplexed. I *was* trying to make the best of this evening, I truly was.

"Perhaps to the south, in Florida, but I am from New York, and we New Yorkers know nothing of palm trees and tropics. Our weather is much the same as yours here, except that it doesn't rain nearly as often, and we've never much fog to speak of."

"Ah." Mr. Smithson scowled and puckered his mouth beneath his mustache, clearly at a loss. "No fog and little rain. Well, well."

"Indeed, Mr. Smithson, it is so." I concentrated on keeping my smile bright and without the disappointment and dismay growing within me. "No fog at all."

I hadn't come to London to speak of the weather, either. Only a few weeks before, I'd at last put aside my dreary mourning for my husband and sailed to London with dozens of letters of introduction to the grandest ladies of English society. By New York standards, I'd traveled modestly: I was armed with only forty trunks of my most fashionable gowns and jewels, three maids, a private chef, and a secretary. The city's society pages had breathlessly (and a bit disapprovingly) reported all the details of my trip, but only I had known the true purpose for my escape.

An escape was exactly what it was, too, my long-overdue escape from the solitude that had been my too-constant companion. Here in England I hoped to find all the things my stultifying marriage had denied me: adventure, freedom, excitement, independence, and intrigue.

Especially intrigue.

Tonight was my first grand ball in Belgravia, at the home of the Viscount and Viscountess Carleigh, and I'd scarcely slept the night before from anticipation. Though the elegant company was brilliant with jewels and thick with titles, I had found myself trapped on the dance floor with one dull partner after another, a parade of gentlemen who saw me not as a woman but only as a prize.

"I say, Mrs. Hart," Mr. Smithson said, his pale eyes

popping as if struck with sudden inspiration. "I'd venture you've seen those palm trees yourself, haven't you? I'd venture you've seen a great deal of that enormous America of yours, what with your father's trains and all."

I smiled, even as the sting of his predictable words jabbed at me. Of course he'd mention Father's railroads. Everyone did, and they usually mentioned my late husband, Arthur, too. Arthur and Father together had created a vast fortune from iron and steel and other men's sweat, an empire proudly documented by the maps in Father's library in our Fifth Avenue mansion.

But to me the railroads represented only the impenetrable isolation of our family's great wealth, of being the solitary passenger in a private train car muffled in red plush and mahogany. Too well I remembered my life as an only child, with neither brothers nor sisters for company, and even Mama had died so long ago that I'd no memory of her for consolation, nothing beyond the stiff and formal portrait that hung in the drawing room of our Fifth Avenue house.

Father had spoken of the railroads as if they were his true family, his face lighting up in a way it never did for me. The intricacies of his ever-spreading empire were what had mattered most to him. If it hadn't been for the railroads, then Father wouldn't have forced me to marry his partner when I was seventeen and Arthur Hart forty years my senior. I hated the railroads and always had. Because of them, I'd never had a chance at being happy—until now.

"Railroads are the future," Mr. Smithson was saying, blissfully unaware of my thoughts. "You must be proud of your father's achievements for the betterment of your country."

"What you mean to say, Mr. Smithson, is that I should be proud of my father's money," I said, my voice tart though I smiled still. "That is your real reason for dancing with me, is it not? Not because I myself am of any true interest to you, but because of the dollars I represent."

Mr. Smithson's mouth fell open with astonishment. "Not at all, Mrs. Hart!" he protested. "You are most charming, ma'am, and such delightful company that I am honored to have this dance."

"Thank you, Mr. Smithson," I said. "But what a pity it is that I cannot say the same of you. Now if you will please excuse me."

I turned and left him, slipping gracefully between the other dancers. Some turned to look, surprised and curious, but I didn't care. I was twenty-five, and at last I was my own woman. I was done with pretending to be meek and obliging, and as I walked through the crowd I kept my head high and my expression serene. I'd no wish to return to the acquaintances who'd brought me to the ball, and instead I stepped through the tall open doors to the gallery that overlooked the garden. The shadowy figures of other guests were visible at the far end of the gallery, but they weren't looking for company, nor was I.

With a sigh of frustration, I rested my gloved hands on the stone balustrade and stared out into the moonlit formal garden.

Where were the handsome and worldly gentlemen whom I'd come to London to find? Where were the charming, seductive rogues whom I'd read of in novels, the dashing noblemen with generations of hauteur and breeding to give them the confidence not to be intimidated by the power of my wealth?

I'd hoped to find men who possessed the strength to match my own spirit, or even surpass it. Yet so far all I'd found were the same sorry breed of males that I'd left behind in New York, an uninspiring lot of self-centered dolts and impoverished younger sons who were attracted only to my fortune, not to me. Where was the adventure, the intrigue, the men, and (most daring of all!) the love that I'd so desperately hoped to find?

One man, that was all I wished for, but it was the single thing that all the money left by my father and husband couldn't buy. One man who'd be drawn to me for who I was as a woman, not as an heiress. One man who would become my friend, my partner, my lover, in every way that mattered.

I sighed again, slowly opening my ostrich-plume fan. I knew I should return to the ball. There was nothing to be gained by remaining here, alone in the dark.

Then suddenly I realized I wasn't alone. There was a rustling in the bushes in the garden below, the breathy little cries of a woman and the deeper voice of a man. Frowning, I shifted a few steps along the balustrade to see if I could discover the source of the sounds.

As soon as I saw the pair, I knew I should look away, and yet I didn't. I couldn't. I had never observed anyone else . . . *coupling* like this, and I was shocked and fascinated and oddly excited, all at the same time.

The gentleman—for from his impeccably tailored evening clothes, he surely was a gentleman—held his partner by her bare hips, her lace-trimmed petticoats thrown over her body and head. Her silk drawers were puddled around her ankles, and the jeweled buckles on her garters sparkled above her blue silk stockings. A lady, then, and likely a beauty, confident enough to be so daringly engaged. Bent over the back of a garden bench, her buttocks gleamed pearly white in the moonlight, and with her legs parted for the gentleman's convenience, the rosy petals of her most private self blossomed like a midnight rose. Her cries were soft and mewling, muffled beneath her skirts as well as by the strains of the waltz drifting through the open windows.

The lady's face was hidden and her identity with it, but I didn't care. All that mattered to me—all that I saw, really—was the gentleman. His face was hidden by the garden's shadowy branches, leaving me with only his back and arms to consider, well muscled and powerful even though shrouded by the civility of his evening coat.

I could hear him better now, too, not his exact words, but his voice, a low, deep rumble of desire and seduction to the woman beneath him. I didn't have to know the words to feel them, and the masculine mixture of coaxing praise and command that made me shiver.

He had remained clothed, only unfastening his trousers to free the magnificence of his cock. The moonlight spilled upon that, too, thick and strong as it drove hard into the lady, and glistening wetly with her juices. He fucked—for that vulgar word seemed so much more apt than the mealy *lovemaking*—her purposefully, masterfully, with an un-yielding rhythm, nearly withdrawing the full length of his cock, teasing her with the thick, blunt tip before driving deep again, making her cry out and arch with undeniable pleasure. He paused, buried deep, to let her feel his pres-ence, and with obvious appreciation swept his hands from the swell of her hips to the narrowness of her corseted waist and back, his thumbs tracing along her spine. He began to move again, thrusting hard, and impatiently he tossed his hair back from his forehead: black hair in the moonlight, as sleek as a raven's wing over the white collar of his shirt.

My lips parted as I watched, my quickening breath be-traying my own growing arousal. This was the kind of man I had imagined finding here in England, the kind of man who would think first of passion, not railroads.

My nipples tightened above the top of my corset, my breasts aching to be caressed as they pressed against the delicate silk of my gown. The gentleman's cock fascinated me, so ruddy and pulsing with virility. Restlessly I pressed my thighs together, feeling the heat growing in my own empty passage in sympathy, even envy.

The gentleman quickened his movements, not bothering to hide his groans of rising passion as he pounded against the woman. Arthur had always insisted on complete silence and tedious decorum in our bedroom, but this gentleman was shameless both in how completely he used and possessed his partner and in how he clearly did not give a damn if anyone saw or heard them together.

No wonder I leaned farther over the balustrade, desperately wishing I were the one he desired, the one bent over that bench, feeling his fingers holding tightly to my hips, bracing myself against the pounding thrust of that cock as he—

"Ah, here you are, Mrs. Hart," said the Viscountess Carleigh as she appeared through the tall doors to join me on the gallery. "I rather wondered where you had vanished to, but one of the footmen said he'd seen you go outside. Are you not enjoying your evening?"

Swiftly I left the balustrade, hoping the other woman would not realize that I'd been such an eager and shameless voyeur. Although as an American I wasn't required to defer to English nobility, I still sank into a graceful curtsey to the viscountess to be polite, and also to give myself another few seconds to collect myself.

"My lady," I murmured, keeping my head bowed until the viscountess motioned for me to rise, and to reply. "On the contrary, Lady Carleigh, I have been enjoying the evening immensely. But the company has been so brilliant that I became a bit overwhelmed, and required a fresh breath of night air to recover."

Lady Carleigh smiled, benignly accepting my social fib for what it was. Considered the epitome of aristocratic beauty, the viscountess had a flawless complexion and masses of auburn hair, but what most men noticed first was her voluptuous figure, which not even the strictest of corsets could fully subdue. She was a particular favorite of King Edward, and I'd heard rumors that she'd shared his majesty's royal bed. The viscountess was definitely part of the fast, fashionable set around the king, a lady who clearly did whatever she pleased, and exactly the kind of person that I had wished most to meet here in London.

"I did not believe New Yorkers were overwhelmed by anything," Lady Carleigh said, bemused. Lightly she fingered the thick dog collar of pearls around her throat. "Unless, perhaps, it was the number of eager young bucks you had surrounding you in the ballroom."

I smiled, too, one beautiful woman speaking nonsense to another.

"There was a crush of them, yes," I admitted. "Doubtless I am the novelty of the evening, the poor widow lady fresh from America."

Lady Carleigh chuckled, her gaze taking in my silk evening gown by Worth and the diamonds around my throat and wrists and pinned into my dark hair.

"You are too modest, my dear Mrs. Hart," she said. "There is nothing poor about you, as everyone knows perfectly well. You are the enchanting merry widow who has sailed among us on a wave of gold. True, you have youth and beauty to recommend you as well, but money is always most alluring to eager bachelors. You need only look at the success of the former Misses Astor and Vanderbilt. I've no doubt you'll be engaged to some dashing peer of your own by the end of the season."

"Forgive me, my lady, but you misunderstand," I said, determined not to leave such a grievous misconception hanging between us. "I have neither wish nor need of another husband, even one with a title."

"None?" Lady Carleigh asked archly, not believing me.

I shook my head. "My first marriage was not a love match, but an alliance for trade, contrived by my father to cement his business assets. My late husband was a distant, dispassionate gentleman, and I shed no tears at his death. Now that I have at last earned my independence, I refuse to be shackled to another tyrant in trousers. I wish for—for something more."

"Heavens, such a speech," said Lady Carleigh, more than a little condescending in the way that the English often were. She raised her brows as she openly appraised me. "You American women are so very frank."

"Indeed I am, Lady Carleigh." I wouldn't apologize for what I'd said. I'd only spoken the truth. I *had* been forced to sacrifice my youth and innocence to a much older man who'd no use for either quality, and I was determined to make up for the time I had lost in my loveless marriage. Once again I thought of the gentleman in the garden below, the man who was as tempting to me as the Devil himself.

"Your fortune-hunting bachelors are quite safe from me, my lady," I continued. "I have spent my first twenty-five years pleasing others. Now I am determined to please only myself."

Before the viscountess answered, the gentleman in the garden suddenly roared with his release, a deep, guttural sound of such purely male satisfaction that it made me gasp, more with longing than surprise. Lady Carleigh hurried across the stone flags of the gallery to lean over the balustrade in the place that I had discovered earlier.

"Oh, that must be Savage," the viscountess declared, peering into the shadows. "I would recognize his triumphant war cry anywhere."

"'Savage'?" I repeated, unable to keep from joining Lady Carleigh at the balustrade. Clearly I needn't have feared that she would find offense or mortification in the sight of the two lovers. Instead, the viscountess appeared as eager as I had been to glimpse the couple below. " 'Savage'? He is dressed quite like a gentleman, so I assumed that—"

"Hush, hush, there he is," the viscountess said eagerly, lowering her voice to a whisper and motioning for me to do the same. "That is the Earl of Savage, my dear, Savage by name, and likewise by inclination. There is *such* an air of danger about him that makes him quite irresistible, as any woman who has been *possessed* by him will attest. Ah, what a splendidly male beast!"

She spoke with such authority that I wondered if Lady Carleigh herself had been one of the women *possessed* by this same lord. In New York, such an appraisal would have been unspeakably shocking, but here it seemed only one more worldly observation. I had been presented to the viscountess only a few hours before, and now here I was being her confidante in a most intimate—and most fascinating—conversation.

I craned my neck to see over Lady Carleigh's shoulder. To my disappointment, Lord Savage had already tucked his member back into his trousers, and was standing to one side while his partner sat on the bench and attempted to put her disordered dress back to rights.

Finally the lady rose, still patting her hair. But no matter how many small repairs she made to her appearance, she wouldn't be able to change the expression of wanton satisfaction on her face, her eyes heavy-lidded and her mouth swollen with it. If she returned to the ballroom now, there wouldn't be a man or a woman who wouldn't guess immediately what she'd been doing in the garden. From the adoring way she was gazing at the gentleman, she didn't seem to care if all of London knew it.

He reached out and brushed back a stray lock of her hair, tucking it back into place. He said something that made her laugh, and then bent to kiss her quickly. She tucked her hand into his arm, and together they vanished into the shadows.

Lady Carleigh straightened, and nodded briskly.

"Lady Cynthia Telford, used and discarded once again," she said with obvious relish. "A sorry creature who grovels for male attention—completely unworthy of Savage. He knows it, too. Contempt mixed with carnality never makes for a pretty dish, nor one to be savored at length."

As my thoughts were still occupied with Savage, I said nothing. Lady Carleigh's dismissive comments surprised me. Savage hadn't appeared exactly contemptuous, considering the way he'd seen to Lady Telford's satisfaction as well as his own, nor had the lady acted as if she'd been either used or discarded. Far from it—so far, in fact, that I would have given much to trade places with her in a heartbeat. I wanted this kind of intimacy, this kind of trust, this kind of passion, with a man like Lord Savage.

No, I wanted it *with* Lord Savage.

"They are not lovers?" I asked carefully, not wanting to betray too much.

"Those two?" Lady Carleigh chuckled, still gazing into the now-empty garden. "Hardly. She was a passing amusement for him last summer, and it would appear she longs to renew their *affaire*. But it's clear that Savage has no interest in that, or in her, despite what we have just seen. He is a restless man, one who lives for the thrill of the hunt. It will take a far more interesting woman than Lady Telford to capture him."

A strong wave of relief swept through me, but still I needed to make certain I hadn't misinterpreted.

"You are sure, my lady?" I asked. "I thought Lord Savage seemed rather charmed by her ladyship."

"Oh, I am sure there is nothing between them, Mrs. Hart." Lady Carleigh turned away from the garden to study me shrewdly. "But tell me, my dear. Exactly how much of that little engagement did you witness? No false modesty, now. You were already watching when I found you here, weren't you? How much did you see of Lord Savage's, um, equipage? Enough to engage your own fancy?"

I looked evenly at the viscountess. There was nothing to be gained by denial, and yet my nature was to hold back, to retreat to the safety of privacy, especially from someone who was, really, still a stranger. To confide like this was a risk, and yet, if I didn't, this opportunity might be lost.

"What did I see of him, Lady Carleigh?" I repeated slowly. "Why, I saw . . . everything."

"*Quite* everything, my dear?" Lady Carleigh smiled, thoughtfully trailing her furled fan along the curve of her cheek. "A sufficiency to inspire you to long to see more?"

I opened my fan again, the ivory blades clicking softly one by one as the ostrich plumes fluttered apart. I was acutely aware of the significance of her answer. With the scandalous Lady Carleigh to lead me, doors to every kind of adventure—including those that I'd still no words to describe—might swing open to welcome me.

"I have been inspired, yes," I said cautiously, sharing more than I'd dreamed possible of myself, but far less than Lady Carleigh obviously expected. "But I am still such a newcomer to your country, and hope to be similarly *inspired* many more times in the course of my visit here."

Lady Carleigh laughed. "Oh, you shall, Mrs. Hart, you shall. I have taken an instant liking to you, my dear, and I am sure we shall become the fastest of friends. Now come with me, and let us see what manner of inspiration we can arrange for you this very evening."

We returned to the ballroom together, and at once we were both carried off to the dancing by eager partners. Yet, as one dance led to another, and a new partner with it, I became aware of a change in the gentlemen asking me to dance, and it was clear that my new friend Lady Carleigh had already kept her promise.

Gone were the callow bachelors my own age and younger, respectfully wooing me as a future wife and investment. In their place were a different kind of gentlemen, confident men in the powerful prime of their lives who made little secret of their desire not for marriage but for seduction. Each open look of appraisal, each suggestive whisper in my ear, excited me further. I had always thought the waltz a slightly insipid dance, but now I wished the orchestra would play forever.

"You must come riding with me in Hyde Park," my current partner was saying. He was an officer in a splendid uniform that emphasized his broad chest and the numerous medals that hung there. "You Americans do ride, eh, Mrs. Hart?"

"Of course we do, Colonel Roberts," I said, willing to acknowledge the obvious double entendre to his question. The colonel had potential, enough that I saw no harm in encouraging him. "I have always enjoyed the feel of a high-mettled steed beneath me."

The officer laughed heartily, his teeth showing beneath his clipped mustache. "I'd wager you do, Mrs. Hart. How I'd like to see you well mounted when—"

"Stand aside, Roberts," interrupted another man, tapping the colonel on the shoulder. "This is my dance with the lady."

To me this seemed the very height of rudeness, especially since I was enjoying the colonel's risqué banter. But as soon as I turned to confront the interloper, my rebuff vanished. I'd never seen this man's face before, yet I knew him immediately.

"Now, Roberts," the newcomer said, faintly bored, his manner belonging to a man accustomed to being obeyed.

"There are plenty of other ladies who will welcome your leaden style of flirtation."

The colonel scowled and glared, clearly considering standing his ground and defending it. But he, too, knew the other man's identity and his rank with it, both sufficient to take precedence over his own pride. The colonel had no choice, really. He bowed curtly in concession and backed away, abandoning me to the other man.

The other man: no, he was the only man, making all the others in the room fade away and vanish in my eyes.

He was taller than the colonel, tall enough that by merit of his height alone he would stand out in any gathering of ordinary men. His hair was black and sleek, his eyes hooded with ennui, and, ignoring the fashion for mustaches and beards set by the king, his jaw was so cleanshaven as to gleam faintly blue-black. His face was severe, all bones and hard planes, and in contrast his mouth was sensually full.

His features could be called patrician, and indeed he was by birth an aristocrat. But there was also a ruthlessness to his expression that did not belong on a man who had been born to wealth and privilege. Rather it was the rapacious look of a man who would take whatever he wanted, no matter the cost or the risk, and never be denied.

It was the look of the man that I had always desired without realizing it. Why not, when it felt as if I'd been waiting my entire life for this exact moment?

"Lord Savage," I murmured. "I am honored."

I began to dip into a curtsey. He, however, did not wish to wait for such a nicety. Now, I was neither small nor delicate, yet he swept me up into his arms and back into the waltz and the center of the crowded ballroom, leading me away with such authority that I'd no choice but to follow.

I felt both captured and captivated, and as I gazed up at his handsome face, I felt as dazzled as any schoolgirl. His eyes were pale, blue and gray and the color of mist, and ringed with dark lashes. Beautiful, mysterious eyes with a startling intensity, a gaze that could equally intimidate and fascinate.

"I must compliment you, my lord," I said, more breathlessly than I wished. Striving to recover my composure, I glanced down from his face to the beautifully knotted white silk tie at his throat.

The collar of his dress shirt sat precisely against his neck, with the black superfine of his evening coat tailored to perfection over his broad shoulders. To all the world, he was the epitome of a civilized English lord, yet as his large fingers completely enveloped my hand and I felt the heat of his palm through my gloves, I was reminded of what he'd done, what I'd witnessed, not an hour before.

"You are an excellent dancer, my lord," I said. "I am fortunate to have you as a partner."

He nodded in acknowledgment but did not smile. "I demand excellence of myself in all things, Mrs. Hart, no matter how trifling."

I smiled anyway, determined to charm him as I'd charmed all the others. "I can tell that of you already, my lord."

"How?" he asked. His voice was deep and rich, the kind of voice that could charm with only a handful of words. "From spying upon me earlier this evening?"

I caught my breath with surprise. "Did Lady Carleigh tell you that—"

"She did not," he said. "There was no need. I saw you myself, Mrs. Hart, leaning over the railing for a better prospect."

Speechless, I blushed furiously, looking away from his face to my white-gloved hand on his shoulder. I'd expected him to be angered by what I'd done, but instead he sounded almost amused, in a dry and very English manner.

"Is that how you entertain yourself?" he continued. "Watching, instead of participating? Is that what gives you the most pleasure? To be a voyeur?"

"I—I do not know what you mean, my lord," I stammered. In truth I had never before observed others making love, because I had never had the opportunity. This had been the first time, and though I had enjoyed it immensely, I was not going to confess that to him. "I had stepped out of doors for air, and heard, ah, curious sounds in the bushes."

"The sounds of a man taking a woman?" he said, bemused, as he deftly guided me through the steps of the dance even as my feet would have stumbled. His voice dropped a fraction lower, his words more confidential and meant for my ears alone. "As a married woman, Mrs. Hart, you must surely have recognized the nature of those 'curious sounds.' If you were drawn to them, then they must have intrigued you, and made you wish to see more. Perhaps you even imagined yourself making those same curious noises, unable to stop, nor wanting to."

His audacity stunned me, as did the frankness with which he spoke of such matters. I had wished for adventure, true, but I had not expected him—or any gentleman here tonight—to speak so directly to me, without the genteel gloss of a witty double meaning.

"I am sorry, my lord," I said, striving to draw the conversation back into my control, "but I do not believe that is a suitable topic for this company, in this house."

He laughed softly, a deep, rumbling sound in his chest that I found appallingly seductive.

"I can assure you, Mrs. Hart," he said, "that this house has been a haven to far, far less suitable pastimes, performed by this same company, than what you witnessed earlier."

"Does your assurance come from experience, my lord?"

I said defensively. "Was that scene in the garden only one of many in your past?"

"Is that what you imagine of me, Mrs. Hart? Is your fervid mind envisioning such a scene even now?"

Sharply I drew in my breath, for in fact I was imagining exactly that. Was I truly so—so transparent? He was toying with me, teasing me, twisting my words around for my own entertainment, and I did not like it.

"You flatter yourself, my lord," I said, "if you believe that I would devote my thoughts so exclusively to your—your dalliances."

" 'Dalliances,' " he repeated, faintly mocking. "I do not dally, Mrs. Hart. As our acquaintance grows, you'll discover that I am far more purposeful than that."

"Indeed, my lord." I swallowed, and licked my lips, which had suddenly grown dry. "But only if I cared sufficiently to make such findings."

He raised a single dark brow. "What a singular show of spirit, Mrs. Hart."

If having spirit meant I must challenge him, I'd do so. "I'm American, my lord. Spirit has been bred into me."

"I have met a good many American women, Mrs. Hart," he said, "and none of them have possessed what you call *spirit* to the degree that you appear to do. You are, in fact, not like any of them at all."

I couldn't tell if this was intended as a compliment or not. "You are exceptionally bold in your judgment of me, my lord, given that our entire acquaintance has been the length of this waltz."

"Not at all, Mrs. Hart," he said easily, ignoring the rebuff in my words. "Judgments, true judgments, can be made in an instant. I can see that you are not like the other American women, nor are you like the English ladies languishing in little groups about this room. You are not afraid of being alone. You are independent, a renegade, and you answer only to yourself. Is that not so?"

I caught my breath again, stunned that he had in fact assessed me with such accuracy. I'd never been a girl surrounded by a pack of giggling friends, and because of my solitary upbringing, I'd accepted my lack of close acquaintance, even embraced it as I'd grown older. Yet how had he guessed?

"You are silent, Mrs. Hart," he continued when I didn't answer. "You believe I have insulted you."

"No, my lord," I said, striving to recover. "Although to be called a recreant is hardly flattering to a lady."

"I called you a renegade, Mrs. Hart," he said. "A recreant acts from craven cowardice, but a renegade has made a conscious choice to exist beyond convention and expectations."

"I see I must choose my words with more care, my lord," I said, deftly avoiding admitting how correct his estimation had been. "You speak with a pedagogue's precision."

"I speak from experience, Mrs. Hart." His eyes were intent upon me, holding my gaze. "I consider myself to be a renegade as well. It is the reason we are drawn to one another. The Turks would call it *kismet*."

I shivered, feeling too vulnerable. To blame what I was feeling on kismet, on fate, seemed so easy and pat, and yet I had no better explanation myself for why I felt so inexorably drawn to him.

"I am disappointed, my lord," I said, determined to regain some semblance of control—of myself, if not of him. "Only the most callow of ballroom swains invoke fate as a way to win a lady's favor. Americans believe in plain speaking."

"Then speak plainly to me, Mrs. Hart," he said, unaffected by my reproof, "and I shall speak plainly to you.

Did watching me arouse you? Did your pulse quicken, your breath catch? Did your nipples stiffen and ache? Did your cunt tighten and grow wet with desire for my cock, Mrs. Hart?"

I stared into his pale eyes, shocked that he would dare say such words to me in the middle of a crowded Belgravia ballroom, the blunt vulgarities all the more potent in his aristocratic accent.

Yet what stunned me more was how my body was responding exactly as he described, now, as I danced with him. Beneath the layers of lace and silk petticoats, I felt shamefully wet, swollen, and empty.

My sex wept for his cock. There was no other way to describe it. With each gliding step I took, my now-damp thighs rubbed together, then released, a gentle friction transformed into an inadvertent caress that was growing increasingly unbearable. My breasts felt full and heavy as they pressed against the bones of my corset. As much as I was trying to assert myself against his arrogance, my body was shamelessly betraying the excitement that same arrogance roused in me.

"You are silent again, Mrs. Hart," he said, the most ordinary observation in the world under other circumstances. "What has become of your plain speaking now, I wonder?"

He was watching me closely beneath his dark lashes, seeing far more than I wished him to. Resisting the spell that he'd cast over me, I looked away to search for the acquaintances who had brought me in their carriage tonight.

If I parted from him now, the way I had earlier from Mr. Smithson, there would be a minor scandal and fuss, but it would be preferable to remaining here to listen to—

To what? The most devastatingly seductive man I had ever met, saying the exact forbidden things to me that I'd always wished a man would say? If his words alone could do this to me, what would it be like to feel those hands on my bare flesh and that cock driving its way deep into my body?

"Mrs. Hart?" I thought he sensed my wish to escape, as his hand tightened around my slender, corseted waist to hold me fast. "I await your reply, Mrs. Hart."

"Yes," I blurted out abruptly, yes to the truth, yes to everything he'd asked of me and other things he hadn't. I felt dizzy, almost light-headed, with my heartbeat thundering in my ears. Suddenly the waltz ended, leaving me wondering if he'd somehow planned it this way all along.

"Thank you, Mrs. Hart," he said, bowing like every other gentleman. "For the pleasure of this . . . dance."

For the first time, he smiled. His eyes lost their wolfish intensity, his expression softened, and he looked much younger. He offered me his arm and I took it, clasping tightly to his well-muscled arm as he guided me across the floor.

I supposed I was grateful for his support, considering how my knees wobbled beneath me. I could not begin to explain what had just happened between us, and I was conscious of how, for the first time all evening, no other gentleman stepped forward to ask to dance with me next. Instead they all hung back, watching me with Lord Savage, as if he'd made some kind of unspoken, primitive claim on me that the other men understood and respected.

And in spite of how warm I'd become from the dance and his nearness, I shivered again.

"Ah, Mrs. Hart," Lady Carleigh said, smiling over her spread fan. "How glad I am that Lord Savage has brought you back to me!"

Savage smiled in acknowledgment and slipped his arm free of my hand. At once I felt not only unsteady but bereft. Was the earl done with me, then? One dance and a single wicked conversation, and that was all?

"I was only now telling Lord Carleigh how much I enjoyed your company earlier, Mrs. Hart," the viscountess continued, waving vaguely toward her husband. "He suggested that I invite you to join us next week for a sojourn in the country. We intend to make a small party of it at Wrenton—that's our place in Hampshire. We all do what we please, with whom we please, and because we all swear one another to silence, it's all great fun, and no tedious regrets afterwards. No more than twenty, carefully chosen to exclude the bores."

"Oh, of course," I murmured. "Bores can be so—so boring."

"Exactly," said Lady Carleigh, chuckling. "Besides, I do detest a huge crowd. It destroys the intimacy of the country, don't you agree?"

I nodded. With the London season coming to an end, the nobility retreated to their country houses for the hunting season and for visiting one another's estates. I'd already received a small pile of invitations from other noble hostesses, but none was as intriguing as Lady Carleigh's.

"You must not hesitate, Mrs. Hart," said Lord Savage, his voice deep and confidential. "The viscountess's house parties are most extraordinary. You will not be disappointed."

I turned to face him. "Will you be a member of the party at Wrenton, Lord Savage?"

He held my gaze for a long moment—long enough to tantalize me. I understood, and so did he.

"If you will be there, Mrs. Hart," he said at last, "then nothing would keep me away."

Kismet, I thought, certain he was thinking the same. *Kismet.*

TWO

❧

"Seems as if I just had everything unpacked and settled into these tiny rooms, ma'am, and out come the trunks once again," said Hamlin, my lady's maid. "You've scarce been here in London a week, and now you're off again."

"Oh, hush, Hamlin." Unperturbed, I stood in the middle of my dressing room, staring off through the window without really seeing the view. I'd taken the best available suite of rooms overlooking the river here at the Savoy, but as lavish as the suite was, the space was still much smaller than my mansion in New York.

Even with Hamlin overseeing my wardrobe, the dressing room was nearly overflowing with silk, lace, plumes, and embroidered fine linen. Perhaps for once the maid did have reason to complain.

"I told you I'll only be taking two trunks with me," I

said, almost apologetically. "Even you can muster the energy for that."

Hamlin grumbled wordlessly, letting her disapproval simmer as she gathered up armfuls of lace-trimmed petticoats. The maid had been with me since I'd first been a bride, and Hamlin's loyalty over the years had earned her a certain right to speak plainly.

Not that I could have stopped Hamlin from offering her opinions even if I'd tried. The maid was a stout, prickly Bostonian with stringent notions of right and wrong, especially where her mistress was concerned. Hamlin was as watchful as a mother hawk, and her protectiveness had only increased since Arthur Hart had died.

"Two trunks, ma'am, only two trunks!" she repeated dolefully, shaking her head. "How are you to make do for a week in the country with only two trunks?"

"I shall manage," I said. "A great deal of clothing can be packed into two trunks."

"Not your clothing, ma'am, not at all," Hamlin said. "You'll need clothes for riding and clothes for shooting, ma'am, dresses for breakfast, luncheon, tea, and dinner, and I'm sure there'll be at least one grand ball. You won't be able to repeat a thing, either, or have those grand titled folk think worse of you. But I ask you, ma'am, how am I to put all that into two trunks?"

I smiled serenely. "Lady Carleigh was quite specific, Hamlin. It will be a small party of guests at Wrenton Manor, and she wishes everything to be informal and easy, without the usual constant parade of changes. Two trunks should be entirely sufficient for the dresses we discussed earlier."

"As you wish, ma'am," Hamlin muttered, making it clear that it wasn't what she wished at all. "But from what I've been hearing, ma'am, things might be more *easy* at this particular house than you might be expecting."

I turned to the maid, curious. I'd encountered a few raised eyebrows among my own London acquaintances when I mentioned that I'd accepted Lady Carleigh's invitation, but they'd all been too discreet to elaborate. "What exactly have you heard, Hamlin?"

"That this Wrenton Manor's called Wanton Manor on account of all the shenanigans that happen there, ma'am," Hamlin said, briskly rolling my silk stockings into tidy balls. "That having a noble title before your name's no guarantee of decency, if you understand me, ma'am. You can be sure I'll see that your bedroom door is locked each night, ma'am, to keep out the lechers and other rude gentlemen that prowl those halls."

"'Wanton Manor'?" I laughed, even as I thought of one rude gentleman in particular. "Oh, my, that is rich!"

"It's the truth, ma'am," Hamlin said with gloomy certainty. "Everyone here says so. It's a wicked, sinful place."

"Well, then," I said, "I promise you I shall be on my guard at all times."

I found Hamlin's gossip more exciting than cautionary, for servants often knew far more of their masters' habits than most realized. If the servants here at the Savoy said that the goings-on at Wrenton were wicked and sinful, then wicked and sinful they must be—and I could scarcely wait.

"I doubt I'll be in any true peril, surrounded by ladies and gentlemen," I continued. "And it's not as if I'm a fresh young debutante."

"A good thing you aren't, ma'am," Hamlin said darkly. "From what I've heard, an unmarried young lady would sooner spend a night in the stalls at Covent Garden than accept an invitation to Wrenton Manor."

I raised my brows with disbelief. "Really, Hamlin. Don't exaggerate."

"I'm not, ma'am, not by half," Hamlin declared, shaking her head. "They say the king himself has been a guest, all the way back when he was Prince of Wales, and he didn't bring the princess with him, neither. Actresses and other strumpets, that's his taste, low women eager for any sort of royal debauch, ma'am."

"His majesty has long been a friend to Lord and Lady Carleigh, Hamlin, so I'm not surprised that he has been their guest," I said, ignoring Hamlin's more salacious comments. "I'm certain her ladyship is an excellent hostess, one who addresses her guests' every comfort and need."

"I'll be the one looking after you and your good name, ma'am." Hamlin shook her fist to ward off imaginary libertines. "It won't be the first time I'll keep a cudgel by my bed, just in case."

"I appreciate your concern for my welfare, Hamlin," I said, "but I'm certain it's not necessary."

I paused, knowing that what I'd say next would not be well received.

"Besides, you shall not be accompanying me to Wrenton," I continued quickly, deciding speed was best. "Lady Carleigh has advised us to leave our own servants at home, and rely on her staff to attend us while we are her guests."

Hamlin gasped, stricken, her open hand pressed to her bosom.

"Not take me, ma'am!" she exclaimed. "Why—why, I have always attended you, ma'am! It's not proper for a lady of your station to travel alone, not at all. How can this Lady Carleigh expect you to—"

"Hamlin, that is enough," I said firmly. "You will remain here at the Savoy, while I will be making the journey to Wrenton by train, unaccompanied, the way hundreds of other women do every day without incident."

"But they're not you, ma'am," Hamlin insisted. "Not you."

"Hamlin, I am perfectly capable of— Yes?"

"These arrived for you, Mrs. Hart." One of my other servants appeared in the doorway, holding an enormous crystal vase of roses.

"How lovely!" I exclaimed, grateful for the interruption.

I leaned over the vase, breathing deeply of the flowers' fragrance. The roses were as lush as velvet, and so deep a red as to be almost black. Tucked among the stems was an envelope, and with my heart racing with anticipation, I slipped my finger under the flap to open it.

The roses could have been sent by any number of people—friends, acquaintances, even the hotel itself—but I dared to hope they'd be from one gentleman in particular.

Ever since the night of Lady Carleigh's ball, I'd played my dance with Lord Savage over and over in my head, wishing I'd been more witty, more charming, less shocked by all he'd said and done. I thought of myself as a lady who was always composed and in control, and yet in the course of a single dance he had ruffled me, unsettled me, rattled me in ways I'd never expected.

I couldn't recall another man who had radiated power and confidence in such a sexual manner, and I'd been drawn to him so completely that I almost felt as if I'd had no choice in the matter. He'd called it kismet, or fate, and though I'd tried to dismiss his words as the sort of pretty emptiness that men say while dancing, with him it had sounded like the purest truth. I scarcely knew him, and yet I felt as if we'd known each other forever.

When he'd guessed—for it had to have been a guess— that I was not a woman with scores of friends, I'd been stunned by his accuracy. A renegade, that's what he'd called me. If I were honest, I liked the sound of that, the hint of danger that he'd added to the word. But what

I'd liked more was that he'd confessed he was the same, a strange thing to share, and yet perfect because he'd said it.

I had always been alone, one more product of my suffocating, solitary childhood, and apart from the rest of my equals even as I'd stood among them. I'd also accepted that no one else felt the same. But to hear Lord Savage say the same of himself, a casual fact shared while we danced, had been exhilarating—yet almost frightening as well, because he'd made me feel dangerously vulnerable. It was as if he'd been able to look past my well-crafted, jewel-covered facade and see me as I really was.

There'd been danger in his sexual presence, too, a danger that had been equally irresistible. He hadn't been coy, and he hadn't been flirtatious. Instead, he'd stated his physical desire for me and frankly described mine for him. He had used words no gentleman should use to a lady, and yet from him they had sounded right, even as they'd shocked me, and excited me, too.

No, he excited me, shamelessly and without apology. Over and over, I'd imagined myself as the woman with him in the garden: her hips that he'd caress with a mixture of reverence and possession, her fingers clutching tight to the bench with her legs spread wide, the better to feel the full force of his cock.

I thought endlessly of how he'd pushed her hard against the bench with each thrust, how his fingers had dug into her hips to keep her steady, how she'd matched each of his primal groans with a cry of her own. Was it wrong to want that, too? He would be the one man who'd show me the kind of pleasure I'd read about in forbidden books, and had never felt with my husband. But Lord Savage would take me, claim me, ravish me, make me wild with joy, and then smile, and kiss me, and make me laugh softly, as if I were the only woman in his world.

No wonder I'd had trouble sleeping. He had behaved so differently from any other gentleman I'd ever met. I'd been thrown so off-balance by his sheer masculine arrogance that I'd been unable to measure his true interest, or if it came close to matching my own desire. Days had passed without so much as a word from him, and not once in my whirlwind of engagements did our paths cross. I'd despaired, fearing my obsession with him must be completely unrequited.

Yet as soon as I saw the embossed arms of the Earl of Savage on the card, I knew I had my answer. He'd written only a single word on the card, underlined with a bold, inky slash:

Tomorrow

That single word promised infinitely more than an entire book of flowery poetry because it had come from him. From *him*.

"Where shall I put the roses, ma'am?" Hamlin asked, seizing possession of the vase from the lower maid. "In the parlor?"

"On the table beside my bed, Hamlin," I said, keeping the card. "I wish to breathe their fragrance as I sleep."

Yet, Hamlin remained with the vase in her hands, clearly hoping I would reveal the sender's name.

"Quite the honor that is, ma'am," she said. "Whoever sent those roses would be mighty glad to hear you liked them so well."

But I only smiled, lightly tracing the embossed arms with my fingertip with anticipation. Hamlin didn't need to know; she would only disapprove. What happened next was between me and Lord Savage, and no one else.

Red roses meant passion and desire, and tomorrow—

tomorrow I'd begin to learn how deep that desire would run.

The next afternoon, I looked eagerly from the window as the train slowed for the stop. One glance at the sleepy little station, surrounded by green fields filled with cows, was sufficient to show that Wrenton was in fact in the country and far from London.

Yet, it was all part of the adventure that this trip had become for me. Before today, I had never once traveled unaccompanied, not even to cross the street. I'd first been with my father, and then my husband, and always surrounded by nursemaids and governesses, servants and porters, private secretaries to make arrangements, and security men with pistols beneath their jackets to keep me safe from the kidnappers Father had so feared. Long ago I had found a way to set myself aside mentally, to be alone in my head even with the others close around me, but they had always been there.

But today I had left my staff behind at the Savoy, with only Hamlin scowling on the platform at Victoria Station. I had chosen the viscountess's own compartment and had proudly handed the conductor my ticket myself, and in my purse were the chits for my two trunks.

These were ordinary experiences for most people, but for me they were rare, glorious signs of independence, as was the neat, fitted traveling suit of lavender serge that I wore with a large cream-colored hat and a heavy veil. I'd told Hamlin the veil was to protect my privacy, but covering my face had secretly made me feel worldly and mysterious, as if I traveled like this every day, and a bit wicked, too.

No, more than a bit wicked. Wasn't I even now on my way to join the gentleman who had feverishly occupied my thoughts and dreams ever since we'd met? If things went as I hoped, I'd soon see the man who would become my lover before this week was done.

My lover, I thought, thrilled to think of Lord Savage in that way. No wonder I was smiling as I stepped from the train, and for the first time since I'd left London, I lifted back my veil to breathe deeply of the country air.

"We'll have your things down in a moment, ma'am," the conductor said as the station's single porter wrestled my luggage to the platform. For me it was next to nothing: only the two trunks for gowns, three hat boxes, and several smaller valises and bags for the rest of my belongings.

I was disappointed to see that I was the only passenger to disembark at Wrenton station. Even though Lady Carleigh had promised that our party would be a small, select group, I had still hoped there would be others here to join me on the way to the manor house. I'd even dared to hope that Lord Savage himself might be on my train.

But I soon saw that I wouldn't be entirely without company. An elegant motorcar, accompanied by a horse-drawn cart, were waiting before the station, and as soon as I stepped from the train, the chauffeur threw open the car's door and trotted up to the platform. In his hands was a small introductory placard with my name neatly lettered upon it, a nicety made unnecessary by my being the only lady on the platform.

"Welcome to Wrenton, Mrs. Hart," he said, touching the front of his livery cap. "I am Simon, ma'am."

"Good afternoon, Simon," I said, smiling warmly at the chauffeur. It was impossible not to, really: he was a delicious young man with a ruddy face, bright blue eyes, and curling blond hair. His livery coat barely contained his broad shoulders and the rippling muscles of his arms and thighs, and he truly was the perfect model of a country-bred Adonis.

"Thank you, Mrs. Hart," he said, smiling in return. "My

only wish is to please you. Parker and I will see to your trunks."

That smile surprised me, and not just because of his dimples, either. I hadn't expected such—such *familiarity* from Lady Carleigh's staff. Simon was a servant, and servants were not supposed to smile like that at female guests of the household.

It was one thing for Hamlin to be impertinent, but another entirely for a male servant from another household to be so bold. Keeping my expression stern, I lowered my veil back over my face, determined to reinforce decorum.

Yet, from behind my veil I watched Simon and Parker—who was also quite handsome—as they loaded my belongings into the wagon, their breeches pulling snugly over their buttocks and thighs as they bent and lifted the heavy trunks and cases. In most houses, the servants with the responsibility of driving cars and carriages were seldom as young or as worthy of such regard as these two men.

At last they were done, and Simon opened the door to the motorcar for me, standing respectfully to one side. I walked briskly to the door, gathering my skirts to one side to climb inside the car.

"Permit me to assist you, Mrs. Hart," Simon said, taking me firmly by the elbow. "That step is a high one."

Although the step wasn't high at all, I simply nodded. But as I bent to climb into the car, I was shocked to feel the chauffeur's hand on the back of my skirts, lightly caressing my bottom as he guided me inside.

I gasped and quickly turned and sat, the audacity of his touch still burning on my flesh beneath my skirt.

Unperturbed, Simon reached down to push the hem of my skirts into the car, so that they wouldn't be caught in the door. As he did, he slid his gloved hand beneath my skirts and touched my silk-covered ankle.

I gasped again, but perhaps not quite as startled as I'd

been before, and when he slid his hand up my leg to my thigh, I didn't gasp at all. He did not stop until he'd reached the top of my stocking, his deerskin-covered fingers warm and sure on my bare thigh.

I'd never felt leather on so intimate a part of my anatomy, and to my surprise, it was not distasteful. It was . . . intriguing.

"Her ladyship wishes you to be pleased in every way, Mrs. Hart," Simon said, his gaze intense with promise and his fingers tracing little teasing circles on my skin. "While you are her guest, whatever you desire is yours."

Before I could answer, he withdrew his hand and gently closed and latched the door, then climbed into the driver's seat and started the motorcar. He said nothing further, but instead concentrated on steering along the narrow, rutted road.

Yet, as I sat in the backseat, studying the broad sweep of his shoulders before me and the delightful way the manly sweat had dampened his blond curls around the rim of his cap, I had no doubt that if I asked him to stop the vehicle and continue what he'd begun, he would oblige.

I couldn't deny that I was tempted. I knew other ladies who dallied with their male servants, confessing in breathless whispers as they compared the prowess of the French gardener at the Newport cottage, or the groom who looked after the ponies at the lodge in the Adirondacks. I had only listened, with no tales of my own to confess.

To be sure, there hadn't been any handsome young men among my own servants who might have tempted me—both Father and Arthur had made sure of that—but it was also a matter of being the mistress. Commanding a servant to perform held little appeal for me, and in my eyes such obedience seemed to diminish the men.

There would be no challenge to that, and ultimately little

satisfaction. As handsome as he was, it would be nothing more than an empty coupling without true passion. I wished instead for a man who was not intimidated by my fortune or position, but who would see me only as a desirable woman, not a wealthy one.

It could never be like that with the burly Simon, so I decided that for now I would decline a taste of what he was offering and keep my sights set on Lord Savage. Still, the very fact that Lady Carleigh had offered me the chauffeur for more than transportation was an excellent omen for the week, and I could scarcely contain my excitement.

Before long we reached the estate. We entered beneath an ancient arch that served as the gate and passed through a small forest and lush green fields before, at last, the house itself came into view beyond a lake that shimmered in the late-afternoon sun.

Whatever notorious reputation Wrenton Manor had acquired over the centuries, it remained breathtakingly beautiful. I was accustomed to enormous estates, but the ancient titles and blue blood that bolstered English manor houses like this one put them on a level of magnificence that no American oil and railroads could ever achieve.

The old Elizabethan house at Wrenton had been much enlarged in the last century, and made over into an elaborate brick-and-stone tribute to a medieval castle—albeit a medieval castle with all the most modern conveniences. The house bristled with stone crockets and gargoyles, and from the center of the house rose a tall tower that dominated the surrounding landscape.

At the very top flew a large red-and-yellow flag featuring the stags of the viscount's crest to show he was in residence. The rampant, flagrant maleness of the stags reminded me of Lord Savage, and as I gazed up at the bold red flag, I could think of no better symbol of the week ahead.

I was shown to rooms that were handsomely appointed, with white and gold-trimmed furnishings and pink-and-green scrolled wallpaper. Because it was a corner room, there were tall windows on two sides with splendid views of the rolling countryside.

As was the custom for house parties, whether in Britain or America, I wouldn't meet the rest of the guests or my host and hostess until they gathered to dine later that evening. I'd at least two hours to amuse myself.

To pass the time, I decided upon a leisurely bath, dreaming of Lord Savage, while the lady's maid assigned to me unpacked my luggage.

The maid was named Simpson, and, much like the two male servants I had met earlier, she had clearly been hired as much for her youth and beauty as for her skill at looking after ladies. Most lady's maids were dour, even plain, so as to offer no competition to their ladies, or temptation to their masters. Certainly Hamlin, left behind in London, fit that description.

But Simpson had a voluptuous figure more suited for a sultan's harem than a severe maid's uniform, and her corseted breasts seemed to test and strain her bodice's buttons as she reached up to hang my gowns in the wardrobe.

As I watched her from the bath, I wondered idly if Simpson, too, would be willing to offer herself for amorous play to the gentlemen guests. Or, perhaps, even to the ladies, and with my thoughts already simmering with Lord Savage, I let myself consider the shapely Simpson as she moved gracefully about her tasks, her full hips and breasts swaying seductively.

While I had never explored lovemaking with another woman, I had overheard other women in the cloakrooms at balls. They'd laughed and whispered to one another, teasing whispers that suggested such things were not only possible but pleasurable, especially with a woman like Simpson.

What would it be like to suckle at those full breasts, I wondered, to flick my tongue over those nipples until they puckered and reddened, and caused their owner to sigh with delight?

How would it feel to have another woman touch me instead, a woman's small, soft hands so different from a man's? How fascinating would it be to kiss and fondle a body that mirrored my own, a body whose responses I could share so intimately?

I chuckled to myself, sinking more deeply into the perfumed water to hide how taut and rosy my own nipples had become. The fullness of my breasts bobbed gently just below the water's surface, and I longed to have a gentleman here to admire them. Such lascivious thoughts for me to have! Wryly I decided that there really must be something in the very air at this house, exactly as Hamlin had feared.

But even the most interminable afternoons finally pass, and at last it was time to go downstairs for dinner. Whatever other qualities Simpson might possess, she was an admirable lady's maid, and when I paused one final time before the pier glass in the bedroom, I could only be pleased by my reflection.

My dress had been delivered to me only yesterday at the hotel, directly from the shop of Monsieur Poiret. The gown was so daring that I might have thought twice about wearing it in London, and in staid New York, ruled by conservative Mrs. Astor—no.

Like all of Poiret's chicest dresses, this one was deceptively simple, with a slender, draped skirt that seemed to pour like liquid silk over my hips and legs. The neckline was cut square and dangerously low, with only a breath of silk gauze, embroidered with glittering faceted beads, over my bare shoulders and upper arms. Most shocking of all was the color, or rather the lack of color: the gleaming silk was exactly the same creamy color as my pale skin. Even from a short distance, I appeared to be more nude than clothed.

Blurring the lines of decency further was the jewelry that I had added liberally, ropes of gleaming pearls that only contributed to the sense of excess. I'd had Simpson dress my hair in the latest fashion, pinning the heavy chestnut waves into a burnished cloud around my face and elaborate curls around a twisted knot at the crown. One final jewel—a glittering diamond star that was both a signature and a lucky piece to me—was pinned into my hair over my right temple.

I smiled at my reflection with satisfaction, slowly opening my black-feather fan. I was accustomed to being beautiful, for I'd been beautiful since I'd been born—a final gift from my mother—but I'd never looked so blatantly and shamelessly seductive. Dressed as I was, there was no possible way that Lord Savage could overlook me, or my intentions.

I forced myself to walk slowly down the stairs, the slight train of my dress slipping down the steps after me. I could already hear the voices of the other guests, assembled in the library before being called to dinner. I wasn't uneasy about entering such a gathering alone, for like all widows, I'd had much practice doing so since Arthur's death. I liked the attention I always drew, and it was a little game with myself to see how many gentlemen would look my way, and how many wives would not approve.

But tonight I did not wish simply to enter this particular room. I wanted to make an entrance that announced myself not to every male guest but to one in particular. I needed to be sure that Lord Savage saw me to be composed and confident and unquestionably desirable, without a hint of nervous breathlessness.

Which is exactly how I did it.

Conversation stopped as I paused in the arched doorway. There were perhaps twenty ladies and gentlemen in the room, and every one of them turned to look at me. The ladies stared, mostly with envy, a few with admiration.

But it was, as always, the gentlemen that I most impressed. I'd never seen such frank desire in so many male eyes, like a palpable force directed entirely at me.

I smiled slowly, pulling my train to one side in a way that deftly drew my skirt even more closely around my body. Although only one man in the room really mattered to me, I purposefully didn't seek him out first, keeping both my gaze and my smile general, to encompass them all. No matter what I was thinking, I refused to appear too eager. I was determined to let Lord Savage come to me.

"Welcome, Mrs. Hart, welcome." Lady Carleigh swept forward, taking my hands in her own. "How happy I am to have you join our little party!"

"How honored I am to be included, my lady," I said. "I've never seen a more beautiful house than Wrenton Manor."

"I would venture in turn that old Wrenton has never had a more beautiful guest, Mrs. Hart," the viscountess said, making a quick and approving study of my revealing gown. "I wouldn't be surprised if your mere presence is sufficient to rouse the ghosts of all my husband's most rakish ancestors."

"You are too kind, my lady," I murmured politely, letting my glance wander about the room. "Too kind by half."

"By halves or wholes, I've only told the truth," Lady Carleigh said. "But then I suppose you'll have more interest in the living than in long-dead ghosts. Let me present you to everyone you do not yet know."

The other guests paraded before me in a well-mannered blur. I wasn't good at remembering names on any occasion, but especially not now, with my thoughts roiling with Lord Savage. I'd glimpsed him already, standing near the fireplace and watching me as Lady Carleigh and I moved about the room with the introductions. Even without looking directly at him, I sensed his presence, his nearness, his gaze upon me as I made meaningless pleasantries.

Still I wouldn't look his way to encourage or even acknowledge him. I'd behaved like a foolish schoolgirl when he danced with me, and I wasn't going to do it again. He'd said we were alike; tonight I would make sure I acted like it. I might not have a title, but I *was* Evelyn Vanderwick Hart, and I did have my pride.

With my dress, I'd blatantly signaled my interest. Now it would be up to him to act upon it.

"One more introduction, Mrs. Hart, and then you shall be free to choose your own companions before we go in to dinner," Lady Carleigh was saying. "Lord Blackledge, may I present Mrs. Hart, of New York? Mrs. Hart, Baron Blackledge."

"Mrs. Hart," the baron said, swallowing my hand in his thick-fingered grasp and holding fast. "I have been fascinated by you from the very moment you appeared among us."

"I am honored, my lord," I said, trying to slip my hand free of his unobtrusively. The baron was a large man with a barrel chest and ginger hair above a ruddy face. His smile was more fierce than friendly, baring far too many teeth, as if he wished to devour me on the spot. "It is not easy to stand out in such impressive company."

"A woman like you would stand out anywhere, Mrs. Hart." He squeezed my fingers more tightly to keep me from escaping, then harder still until it hurt, all the while watching my face for my reaction. "In Bombay, they'd worship you like a goddess."

"The baron has spent considerable time in India, Mrs.

Hart," Lady Carleigh said. "He is so thoroughly at home there that I almost expect him to appear in a turban."

Resolutely I kept my expression even, not letting the pain he was causing show. I didn't know what sort of little test this was, but I would not give in, and finally he relaxed his grip enough for me to pull free.

That was enough for me. No matter how the baron flattered me, I resolved to keep clear of him for the rest of the visit. He was a bully, and one who clearly enjoyed inflicting pain, too, a most unsavory—and dangerous—combination.

"I have always thought India must be a fascinating place to visit," I murmured without a smile. "Such an exotic and faraway land."

The baron leaned closer with confidential relish. "It is the complete opposite of Britain, Mrs. Hart. True, the natives are a heathen lot, but in sensual matters they are entirely our superiors."

"Indeed, my lord." In my opinion, it would not have been difficult for anyone to surpass the baron himself. "I suppose you must draw your conclusion from the brothels of the cities?"

"No, no," he said, warming to his subject, and to me. "You will see models of fornication carved into the walls of their very temples, displaying postures and inventiveness that would astound even the most skilled English whore."

"On the walls of their temples, my lord?" I asked, doubting him. "That would be quite curious for a place of holy worship."

"Oh yes, Mrs. Hart," he said. "They are completely frank, and as free with their rutting as beasts in the wild. In fact, my dear, I have a book in my room filled with engravings of lewd statuary, if you should care to see it for, ah, inspiration. Nothing but cocks and cunts."

"Pray recall that Mrs. Hart is a newcomer, Baron," Lady Carleigh said, a note of caution in her voice. "You don't want to put her off on the first night."

But the baron would not be deterred; he leered openly at me. "I haven't forgotten for a moment that Mrs. Hart is a newcomer, my lady. Not for a moment. Later, when the entertainment starts and the Game begins in earnest, I mean to make her my prize. Eh, Mrs. Hart? You'd like that, wouldn't you? Consider what you and I could—"

"What the lady would like, Blackledge, is to have you step away," Lord Savage said, appearing at exactly the right moment. "She'll be fortunate to have any fingers left, the way you were wringing her hand."

"Lord Savage," Lord Blackledge said curtly, his fierce, toothy smile instantly becoming a grimace as he faced the other man. "You've a damn lot to say for Mrs. Hart's welfare. She's a newcomer, you know. She's fair game."

"Perhaps to you," Lord Savage said, his smile faintly bored. "Mrs. Hart is not a newcomer to me. We're old, old acquaintances. We have a certain . . . understanding."

A certain understanding: oh, I did like that, and I flashed him a quick smile of gratitude.

The baron's ruddy face turned a deeper red. "We shall see how long that lasts, my lord, once she—"

"Gentlemen, please," Lady Carleigh interrupted. "I note that it is time to go in for dinner. As is our custom here at Wrenton, we shall follow precedence for the last time tonight. Lord Savage, you shall take in Lady Winthrop. Baron, Lady Wessex. Mrs. Hart, I believe you will be with Mr. Gilbert."

Obediently we all began to find our appointed partners and line up according to their rank. It was always the same with the English, I thought, going two by two like well-bred animals heading into the ark.

I'd hoped that here in the country things would be less

formally determined, so that I might sit beside Lord Savage. As an American, without a noble title of my own, I would be doomed to be paired off with the only gentleman who was likewise as undistinguished, a stout banker named Mr. Gilbert. Even now I could see him bearing determinedly down on me, ready to claim my company.

Only a few steps away, Lord Savage stood waiting for his partner to finish a conversation, and quickly I seized this last opportunity to approach him, touching his sleeve lightly with the ivory blades of my furled fan.

"I must thank you, my lord," I said in a confidential whisper. "You were quite my gallant knight-errant to rescue me like that."

He glanced down at my fan, frowning.

"I did not act from gallantry, Mrs. Hart," he said without lifting his gaze from the fan. "My reason was not to defend you from Blackledge's attentions, but to mark you as my possession before the rest of the room. I do not like the tedium of petty rivals, Mrs. Hart."

"Your possession?" I repeated with surprise, and a bit of indignation, too. "Your *possession*? Lord Savage, I do not understand how—"

"You will," he said, and turned away to offer his arm to Lady Wessex, leaving me standing openmouthed with outrage.

"Mrs. Hart?" Mr. Gilbert said, his arm crooked for me to take. "Shall we join the others?"

"Thank you, Mr. Gilbert, you are too kind," I said, taking the banker's arm as I continued to glare at Lord Savage's back. "I am glad to discover there is at least one true gentleman here tonight."

My indignation continued throughout the long dinner. I was seated near the far end of the table, yet near enough to Lord Savage that he could have raised his glass to me in salute if he wished it, or even exchanged a word or two

across the arranged flowers and silver candlesticks. Instead
he devoted himself entirely to listening to Lady Wessex
as if she were the most fascinating of women, and if he
glanced at me even once during the course of the meal, I
did not see it.

But I saw him.

Through all twelve courses, I could not make myself
ignore him. Over the turtle soup and the salmon, the sad-
dle of beef and the roasted game birds, the molded *chau-
froid* and the sorbets, through champagne and Bordeaux
and cognac, my gaze kept returning to him.

The black-and-white severity of evening dress suited
him, setting off the sharp planes of his face in the candlelight. His dark hair was sleekly combed back from his
forehead, his angular profile fit for an ancient coin, and he
was as effortlessly seductive as any man I'd ever seen.

Perhaps he hadn't meant *possession* as I'd heard it, as
ownership. Perhaps he'd meant it in a sexual way, a pre-
diction of how he intended to make love to me.

My heart beat a bit faster as I considered this possible
explanation. Surely that was how he'd be as a lover, strong
and sure. Perhaps I'd reacted to the word—*possession*—
as an American—an American who was accustomed to
buying whatever I pleased, no matter the price. Perhaps
here in England, where words often seemed more layered
with subtlety, he'd intended something quite different.

I sipped my champagne, studying him. I had no wish
to be his possession as property, but to be possessed by
him—that was entirely different.

At last Lady Carleigh rose, signaling the end of the
meal. In most houses, the ladies would retreat to the drawing room and leave the table to the gentlemen and their
port and cigars. But at Wrenton, the expected things were
seldom done, as I soon discovered.

The viscountess smiled at her expectant guests. "We

shall now withdraw to the Egyptian Room, if you please. We have a small entertainment arranged for you, a brief entr'acte that will set the mood for the rest of the evening."

The Egyptian Room was aptly named. The walls were draped with red-and-gold-striped silk, gathered in the center of the ceiling to transform the room into a pharaoh's tent complete with nodding palm trees in brass pots. All the paintings on the walls were of Egyptian themes, mysterious pyramids and deities with the heads of animals, and the oversize mantel was supported by a pair of bare-breasted stone sphinxes. Rich carpets were strewn across the floor, and ornate gold benches, covered with pillows, replaced ordinary chairs. Tall torchères gave only a shadowy light to the room, and the heady, musky sweetness of incense contributed to the exotic atmosphere.

With the formal seating from dinner over, I looked for Lord Savage, but to my disappointment, he was nowhere to be seen. Across the room, the baron beckoned brusquely, as much as ordering me to join him. Pointedly I turned away and ignored him, not caring if saving myself meant wounding his pride.

"Sit by me, Mrs. Hart," the viscountess said, patting the cushioned bench beside her, and I happily obliged.

"What is the nature of the entr'acte, my lady?" I asked, imagining the usual kind of after-dinner entertainment: a singer from the opera, or perhaps a violinist. "From what others were saying around me at dinner, I gather your entertainments are much applauded."

Lady Carleigh smiled, preening a bit at the praise.

"My friends are most generous," she said. "I always strive for originality, you see, as a wise hostess should. I promised you'd never be bored at Wrenton, and I am a woman of my word."

"Mrs. Hart will not be bored tonight, Lady Carleigh," Lord Savage said, suddenly appearing behind us with the quiet stealth of a large, predatory cat. "I believe she will find your entertainment particularly enthralling, considering her predilections."

Without any invitation, he took the last place on the bench beside me. There was sufficient room, even for a man as large as the earl, but he still contrived to sit so close as to press his thigh against mine. He did it carelessly, as if by accident, and took no outward notice of how our thighs touched.

Yet, I was acutely aware of him there, the hard, lean muscles pressed against my softer flesh, the inky black of his evening trousers in sharp contrast to the luminous, blush-colored silk of my gown. I was sure I could feel his warmth, his energy, even through the layers of our clothes, and I almost longed for the older fashions that would have insulated me more completely beneath layers of wire hoops and lace petticoats.

I almost wished it, but not quite. Nor did I draw away from him, either. Instead I let him press his leg into mine, a gentle, insistent pressure that hinted at the other intrusions he would like to make into my body.

I slowly opened my fan, hoping he'd take no notice of how my fingers trembled.

"I did not realize, Lord Savage," I said, "that we'd become sufficiently familiar for you to identify my predilections."

"Sufficient for one or two observations," he said easily, resting his elbow on the bench's arm as he turned to face me. "I know that you find it acceptable to jab your fan into a gentleman's arm."

I frowned, tempted to do it again.

"I did not *jab* it, my lord," I protested. "I merely tapped it upon your sleeve to draw your attention, in a manner that is entirely polite and proper."

He smiled, but a chilly smile, with no humor to it, as

he glanced briefly at the small band of turbaned musicians settling in the corner of the room.

"Perhaps in New York, such bravado is considered polite," he said, "but in this country, gentlemen do not appreciate a lady who chooses to wield her fan like a bludgeon."

"You exaggerate, Lord Savage."

"I rather think not, Mrs. Hart." A single lock of his dark hair fell across his forehead, and he sleeked it back with his palm. The link on his starched white cuff was black onyx, framed by a tiny gold serpent and centered by a single diamond, as brilliantly hard and beautiful as he was himself. "Would you consider it another exaggeration if I reminded you how much you enjoy being a spectator?"

This time, I was ready. "Nearly as much as you enjoyed being the actor with an audience," I said, smiling. "You see, Lord Savage, I've observed a few predilections myself."

His smile warmed, the unexpected charm of it making me melt inside.

"Touché, Mrs. Hart," he said. "Then as performers and as spectators, we should both enjoy this evening, shouldn't we?"

"I intend to, my lord," I said, feeling that I'd somehow won this particular skirmish. His last comment about the performance we were to watch made little sense to me, but I let it pass. Formal entertainments like the one we would soon see were the purview of specially hired performers, not guests.

But before the hour was over, I would learn exactly how wrong—how very wrong—my assumption could be.

THREE

The music was unfamiliar to me, driven by small drums that a seated musician held balanced on his crossed legs. The two other men played some sort of flutes, their keening notes darting over and around the melody in a strangely hypnotic harmony. The primal pulse of the drums, created by the drummer's bare palms, was a rhythm far from the usual genteel Mozart or Handel heard in country manors, yet I found it irresistibly alluring, even seductive, especially in the incense-laden room. Lady Carleigh had indeed contrived a most original entr'acte.

Soon it became clear that the musicians were not the entire entertainment but merely the accompanists. The arched double doors opened, and a man and a woman entered together.

The man was swarthy and handsome, with a long black beard and a mustache that curled upward. He wore full

Zouave-style trousers of red silk and a long, open robe, richly embroidered with metallic threads that glittered and winked in the murky half-light. On his head was a turban, and large gold hoops hung from his ears.

I wasn't sure if he was a true foreigner, or perhaps only an English actor in swarthy paint, but it did not matter. He was wonderfully virile and menacing, making it clear that he would be more the villain than the hero of whatever tableau he and the woman would perform.

The woman was small in stature, but voluptuously proportioned. She, too, wore an exotic costume, though it was much more revealing. Her waist was tightly cinched with a wide leather corselet that supported her brazenly naked breasts, draped with jingling necklaces of brass coins. A thick line of kohl decorated her eyes, and her lips, cheeks, and nipples had been reddened with carmine. Her full trousers were gathered at the ankles, much like the man's, and bangles clattered up and down her bare arms. Fastened closely around her throat was an unusual necklace of gold beads and green gems that was so tall that it forced her to hold her head proudly high. Where the man was dark, she was ivory fair, her white-blond hair streaming over her shoulders and breasts to her waist.

"A harem scene will be presented," Lady Carleigh announced with relish. "In which the latest Circassian captive must please her pagan master to win his favor and his mercy to preserve her life."

She clapped her hands, and the tableau began. The man sank back onto a pile of pillows on the floor, the picture of indolence. The woman struck a brief, dramatic pose, her arms arched over her head to display her thrusting breasts, and then began to move, slowly, slowly.

She let the music dictate her movements, her torso twisting sinuously and her painted breasts quivering like ripe fruit on a tree. Still she kept her hands raised, twitching her head to make her hair spill like a fall of pale silk along her back.

Every motion emphasized the exaggerated roll of her hips and buttocks through the silk, and each step of her small white feet sent her gaudy jewelry jingling across her bare skin like another kind of music. In theory her dance was meant to entice the man, but she was aware of her larger audience, too, artfully turning and twisting to include every man and woman in the room.

Fascinated, I leaned forward on the bench. I couldn't deny that the music and the dancer were seducing me as well, and I felt the beguiling rhythm curling through my blood and deep in my belly. The costly dress that I'd earlier thought to be so revealing now seemed as heavy and dull as a nun's habit, and part of me wished I could throw it off and dance with the same freedom and abandon as the woman before us.

The music quickened, the drum more insistent. The woman threw back her head and kicked one foot high in the air, arching her back impossibly far.

I gasped. As the woman kicked, she revealed that her silken trousers were completely open both in front and in back, offering a provocative glimpse of her private self. What made her nudity all the more shocking was that she'd been shaved clean, revealing every detail of her full-lipped sex. Another kick, another glimpse, glistening red and wet.

One of the gentlemen swore loudly, unable to contain himself.

Could the woman have painted herself there as well? I wondered. At once I imagined the lubricious process of sitting before a mirror with legs spread wide, and the tickling sensation of a brush and paint gliding over my own sex. Or was the dancer simply so aroused by the dance that she'd blossomed like an open rose?

I'd certainly never shown myself in such a state to my

husband, Arthur. If I'd ever managed to become so visibly aroused, he would have been appalled.

But what if I looked like that to Lord Savage?

I stole a glance at him sitting beside me, curious to see his response to the woman's performance. He sat with his head resting on his bent arm and his gaze intent and focused.

But he wasn't looking at the performance. He was watching me.

My cheeks flaming, I looked quickly away, back to the dancer. He'd accused me before of being a voyeur, and I'd denied it. Now he had the proof that I enjoyed watching others, yet I found I did not care.

No, it went far beyond that: I was glad of it. For him to prefer to watch me watching (oh, it was so tangled!) and to concentrate on my reaction rather than on the lewd entr'acte was in itself wildly exciting, and enough to make my heart race even faster.

Yet, soon I was drawn back into the performance. For the first time the woman dropped her arms, and came to dance directly before the man on the cushions. Still shimmying, she bent her knees and parted her legs so that the open trousers fell open to bare her completely. She slid her hands over her hips and the juncture of her thighs, her fingers framing her seductive core. She arched close to the man, offering herself as blatantly as was possible.

"Enough," the man barked, quickly rising to his feet as the woman sank down to crouch on her heels. "Down!"

The woman shook her hair back over her shoulders and knelt before him. With deft fingers, she opened his trousers and drew his cock and balls free of the crimson silk. He was already erect, and his sizable cock eagerly sprang forward into her fingers. She parted her painted lips and took his cock into her mouth, her cheeks hollowing as she sucked him deeper.

The man closed his eyes and groaned with pleasure as he rocked his hips against the woman's mouth. He tangled his dark fingers into her pale hair to hold her head so firmly that she couldn't have pulled back even if she'd wished it.

I watched it all with breathless fascination. I'd heard whispers of this act, knowing it was practiced by the French, but to see it performed—ah, who would have guessed it would be so exciting?

How full the woman's mouth must be, even into her throat, and yet she greedily sucked harder. I tried to imagine how the man's cock must taste, how it must fill her mouth and press against her tongue. How powerful in turn the woman must feel, to be able to give this man such obvious pleasure!

The man was clearly approaching his climax, his eyes squeezed shut and his face contorted as his hips jerked more rapidly. I knew the pair were players hired by Lady Carleigh, yet this was not pretend. This was *real,* passion straining for release, and I could not look away. My own body was on fire, too, my breasts tight and my quim so wet and aching in sympathy that I surreptitiously pressed my thighs tightly together, hoping for some sort of relief myself.

Then, suddenly, everything changed. The man pushed the woman away and his rigid cock slipped free from her mouth. She bent down meekly at his feet with her head bowed, her hair falling around her face like a veil, and he shoved aside her hair to uncover the wide jeweled necklace.

He fumbled with the necklace, turning it around her throat until he found a loop that was part of the design, and then from his sleeve he withdrew a length of chain and fastened it to the loop. The woman was chained like a dog, the glittering necklace now a leashed collar, and she looked up at him like a dog, too, still crouching and waiting for her master's command.

"Kneel," he ordered curtly, and without hesitation the woman turned about on her hands and knees. Her hair briefly tangled in the leash, and impatiently the man wrapped the chain around his hand and snapped it back, jerking her head with it and making her yelp with pain. Apparently that was what he desired, for then he let the chain slack.

Swiftly she lowered her shoulders to the floor and raised her hips in the air, the open halves of her trousers sliding apart to reveal the perfect white moons of her bottom with her pouting, wet sex below. Yet, despite how the woman must have suffered, she was clearly aroused, her breathing so ragged that her whole body shook as she waited for the man's final assault.

I was shaking, too, not only with the shock of what I was witnessing but with the excitement it roused within me, forcing me to clutch my hands together in a tight knot in my lap to keep some manner of self-control.

How had I never known of such things? Why had I been kept so blindly innocent?

The man paused, breathing hard as he studied the woman's shameless presentation before him for a long moment. Surely he would take her now, I thought; she was nearly begging him to do it. Surely he would plunge that gleaming, purpled cock into her, and give them both what they wanted.

But instead he raised his hand and struck the woman hard across her offered bottom with the flat of his palm, so hard that he pushed her forward across the floor. Again he struck her, and again after that, the blows flying until her once-pearly skin glowed fiery red with the marks of his hand.

Only then did he fall upon her, twisting the chain around his wrist to hold her steady as he drove his cock into her greedy core. After so much delay, neither of them could last long, and over the music the woman's frenzied cries rose higher and higher until they reached a crescendo of need. When at last she spent, she screamed with her release, her whole body bucking and shuddering from the force of it. That was enough to fetch the man as well, who with his final thrust collapsed atop her, writhing together as she wrung the last drop of seed and pleasure from his cock.

Even before they'd finished, the audience began to applaud, with many of the gentlemen coming to their feet with cries of "brava, bravo." It was, I thought, exactly the same display of genteel approval that they'd grant the performers in an opera or a play on the London stage—not that a performance like this one would ever grace the boards at Covent Garden.

The couple slowly untangled themselves and rose to their feet, their hair and costumes plastered to their sweaty bodies as they took their bows hand in hand. As the woman curtseyed before Lady Carleigh, the opening in her trousers again slipped open, showing her partner's seed as it trickled wetly down her thighs.

Yet, for me, the spell of the performance was still not broken. My entire body felt on edge and unfulfilled, the tension almost unbearable as those around me laughed and chatted. I forced myself to take a deep breath, to swallow, to relax, to try to calm both my racing heart and the ache of desire within me.

Slowly I opened my clasped hands. My fingers were numb for having been so tightly clenched, and my palms were marked with white half-moons from my nails.

Finally I dared to look again to Lord Savage.

He was smiling. Smiling at *me*.

He didn't say anything, nor did I. His smile spoke more loudly of desire than words ever could, and anticipation raced through me.

"I hope you enjoyed my little entr'acte, Mrs. Hart," Lady Carleigh said cheerfully beside me. "Those two are wonderfully accomplished, aren't they?"

"Yes—yes, they are, my lady," I stammered, turning toward the viscountess. "It was most enjoyable."

"I am so glad," Lady Carleigh said. "Especially because that is only the beginning of our evening's entertainments."

Gracefully the viscountess rose, clapping her gloved hands twice for silence, and all her guests turned toward her.

"Very well, my dear friends," she began. "Half of you are already well aware of our next divertissement, and half of you are not, being newcomers to Wrenton. For your benefit, I shall explain."

She smiled, letting the anticipation build.

"With so many delightful possibilities for companionship in our company," she continued, "we have over time devised an amusing way to make the selection a bit easier. It's also a way for you who have visited here before to welcome those who've not yet had the, ah, *pleasure*."

Several of the guests laughed knowingly at that.

The viscountess merely smiled again.

"To begin," she said, "I ask that all of you lovely first-time guests—as well as those of you who have chosen to play that role again—return to your rooms. There you'll find entertaining costumes that I've had designed especially for you, my newest guests. I ask that you change your attire, and return to us here as soon as possible. Go now, my dears; the sooner you've changed, the sooner our charming festivities, our little game, will truly begin."

I rose, at last beginning to recover from the performance.

"Are we to have a masquerade, my lady?" I asked. "If I'd known, I would have brought my own costume. I've a most splendid one, a Russian fantasy by Monsieur Poiret."

"I'm sure you do, Mrs. Hart," the viscountess said easily. "Poiret does make beautiful things. I'm afraid the costumes I've provided won't be nearly as magnificent, but it is the only way to ensure that everyone is properly provided for. Otherwise there's always one or two guests who forget to bring a suitable costume of their own, and thus are left out of the Game."

I nodded. I understood the wisdom of the viscountess's thoughtful plan, but still I wished that I could have worn my own costume, enticingly covered as it was in crystal jewels and swirling gold embroidery. Nothing the viscountess provided could rival it, and there would have been no doubt I'd have captured Lord Savage's attention.

"Now, my dears, if you please," the viscountess continued. "Return to your rooms. Your maids and manservants will be waiting to assist you in changing, and then hurry back!"

"Yes, Mrs. Hart," Lord Savage said, smiling still as he leaned back against the bench. "Do hurry back. I'm not very good at waiting."

That was all the incentive I required. I rushed up the stairs to my room, eager to see the costume that Lady Carleigh had provided. The viscountess was known for her extravagant taste, and I was sure the costume would be exquisite, even if it wasn't by Poiret, and tightly laced, too. The viscountess did know how to dress herself to please gentlemen, and I was reassured by that. How could I not be, with Lord Savage waiting impatiently for me?

But when I entered my bedroom, the costume lying on the bed for me made me gasp with dismay.

It was the simplest of garments, a long shift of sheer white silk, untrimmed and without sleeves, and made to slip over the head without any fastenings.

"Simpson!" I called, and the maid appeared instantly from the dressing room. "Simpson, her ladyship said she'd sent me a fancy dress costume to wear tonight. Where is it? Or at least where is the rest of it?"

"That is the costume, ma'am," Simpson said. "And that is all of it."

"This?" I plucked the costume from the bed, holding it up. The silk was so sheer that I could see right through it—as would everyone else. "I cannot wear *this*. It won't even cover my corset!"

"It's not supposed to, ma'am," Simpson said, her face impassive. "You're not to wear a corset, nor anything else. Just the costume, ma'am."

"Nothing?" Appalled, I stared at the filmy silk in my hands. By comparison, the costume of the dancer I'd just seen was propriety itself. "I might as well parade myself naked as to wear *this*."

"Yes, ma'am," Simpson said. "That's rather the purpose, isn't it?"

"Don't be impudent," I snapped. "Why would her ladyship expect her guests to appear is such a—a state of nudity?"

"Not all her guests, ma'am," Simpson said. "Only the newcomers. The newcomer gentlemen will be wearing trousers of the same stuff, and without any drawers beneath, neither. Nothing's to be hidden, ma'am, not tonight."

"Nothing's to be hidden?" I repeated, my voice rising. Certainly nothing would be hidden if I were to appear in this—this costume. "Hidden from what?"

"From the Protectors, ma'am," Simpson said, as if this were the most obvious explanation in the world. "Forgive me, ma'am, but didn't her ladyship explain the Game to you?"

"No, she did not," I said. "Simpson, go to her ladyship and tell her that I must speak to her at once. At once!"

The maid curtseyed and left, and I sank onto the edge

of the bed, the costume still clutched in my hands. I looked down at it, seeing how the stones of my rings showed through the silk. Not even Arthur had seen me in such a revealing garment. I could not imagine appearing before a group of virtual strangers in such an indecent state.

It would be one thing to undress before Lord Savage, as a lover would in my bedroom, but not *this*. With a wordless exclamation I balled up the costume and hurled it across the bed.

"Mrs. Hart?" Sounding faintly wounded, Lady Carleigh stood in the door with Simpson hovering behind her. "I understand you are having some misgivings about my taste in costumes."

I came forward and shut the door behind the other woman, leaving Simpson in the hall. I took a deep breath to compose myself, and chose my words with care. I didn't wish to offend the viscountess, but I did need to make my misgivings clear.

"When I accepted your invitation, Lady Carleigh," I began, "I thought I would be attending a house party in the country. I'd no idea that you would be turning your house into a—a brothel, with your guests expected to parade about in next to nothing!"

"A brothel?" Lady Carleigh clucked with dismay. "Oh, my dear, it seems we do have a misunderstanding. When I met you, I believed you were an adventurous lady, full of spirit, and one who would contribute to my gathering."

I raised my chin. "I am spirited, yes, but that does not mean that I am a—a slattern."

"So what exactly does it mean?" The viscountess tipped her head to one side. "That you are a spirited prig? That you are too cowardly to explore the more interesting aspects of pleasure? That you are unable to trust another? That you are too fearful to give yourself over to delights so rich that you cannot even imagine them?"

I didn't answer, my head spinning with doubts. Explained this way, I did sound like a prude, and worse, a coward. Hadn't I left New York behind for exactly this kind of experimentation? Hadn't I wished to discover experiences that were far beyond my narrow past?

"Especially when that pleasure would be in the arms of Lord Savage," Lady Carleigh continued. "He has taken a great liking to you, you know. He is most particular in his choices of companionship, and I assure you that he was immediately drawn to you."

"He was?" I asked, pleased. "I was drawn to him as well. Though he has been somewhat—somewhat challenging."

"What man isn't?" said the viscountess, sweeping her arm through the air to encompass challenging men everywhere. "But Lord Savage is worth that challenge, Mrs. Hart. Entirely."

I sighed, thinking of him. If ever a man was worth a challenge—any challenge—it would be Lord Savage.

"Nor will our delightful little game be such a terrible ordeal," Lady Carleigh continued. "It's all in sport, you see, and great fun. You newcomers will now be called Innocents, because you are. Those of us who've visited here before become the Protectors, protecting and educating the Innocents in our ways. Surely you can find no threat in that?"

I said nothing. I didn't agree, but then, I no longer quite disagreed, either. After all, I truly *was* an innocent, in more ways than someone like Lady Carleigh could ever understand.

"As soon as all the Innocents return to join us downstairs, the next stage of our entertainment will begin," the viscountess continued. "Even now the Protectors are choosing the Innocents they wish to have under their, ah, tutelage, by submitting their selection by way of cards in a hat. It's my role to announce the pairings, and then the true amusement begins."

"I see," I said, reassured. With Lady Carleigh making the final decisions, there would be no question of my ending up with anyone other than Lord Savage. "What occurs after that?"

"Why, I cannot say," Lady Carleigh said, chuckling. "Each Protector will have a different method of instruction, just as each Innocent will have different inadequacies or failings that will need correction. All in sport, of course."

"Of course," I murmured faintly. "But the pleasure that you promise—"

"Oh, it will be there, I'm certain of that," Lady Carleigh said blithely. "For the remainder of the week, the Innocent must do exactly as the Protector bids. Having played the part of an Innocent myself—for I would never ask my guests to do anything without having experienced it firsthand—I can assure you that you will enjoy yourself."

"If you have done it yourself," I said slowly, "then I suppose it must not be so very bad."

"Not at all!" exclaimed the viscountess. "While the experience of being an Innocent may at first seem distressing, it is in fact quite, quite thrilling, and pleasurable. Especially if you draw a Protector like Lord Savage."

Slowly I retrieved the costume and smoothed it in my hands. It was not just the revealing nature of the costume that concerned me; it was also how it symbolized my lack of choice, and how I would be required to give up control to another, even if that other was Lord Savage. "Must I wear this?"

"I fear so, my dear," Lady Carleigh said. "To give wings to our little fantasy, it's necessary to strip away all our old misgivings and inhibitions. It is a costume, to make you believe more in the part you've chosen to play among us. That's all it is, you know: playing, and pretend."

I listened, trying to make sense of this explanation. "Playing" and "pretend" struck me as childish, yet the so-called Game that would be played would be nothing but adult.

Lady Carleigh lay her gloved hand on my arm to reassure me.

"Consider it all a way to entertain ourselves most pleasurably for the time we are here," she said, "and nothing beyond that. In your role as an Innocent, you must be dressed to reflect inexperience, even purity."

I shook my head as I looked down at the costume. "It's not my inexperience that I dread showing, my lady."

Lady Carleigh laughed. "You of all the ladies should have no fears on that count! You are exceptionally beautiful, and I expect the interest in you will be strongly contested."

Yet still I hesitated, and with a sigh, Lady Carleigh rose.

"If I have not convinced you yet, Mrs. Hart," she said, her voice and manner full of resignation, "and you still do not wish to play our game, then I shall send for the motorcar for you directly. You're not a prisoner here, you know. You're always free to leave at any time, and return to London, or wherever you wish."

The viscountess crossed the room, pausing at the door to smile sadly.

"Poor Savage!" she said. "He will be most grievously disappointed when I tell him you've changed your mind."

I considered the costume again, striving to imagine Lord Savage's reaction when he saw me in it. If I departed now, I'd never know for sure what that reaction would be, and all I'd be left with would be regrets. If I fled to London, then I might as well sail home to New York on the next steamship.

My grand, ambitious adventure would be done, finished before it had begun, and all because I was too much a coward to seize the opportunity—and the man—that I'd claimed I wanted. I'd always believed myself to be independent, but if I left now, I'd be letting my prim upbringing win, and I'd be acting exactly like every other proper New York widow would. I would not be the bold renegade that Lord Savage had called me. I'd be a sheep—a proper, obedient, boring sheep.

And at last I had my answer. I nodded resolutely, my mind made up.

"If you please, my lady," I said. "Send for Simpson, so that I might change my clothes."

Lady Carleigh smiled and clapped her hands. "Oh, I am glad, Mrs. Hart! You'll see. You will not regret this, not for a moment."

The viscountess summoned the maid, and left to return to her other guests. Simpson said nothing, but briskly began removing the many layers of my evening dress.

"Have you prepared other ladies to be, ah, Innocents, Simpson?" I asked as the maid unfastened the long row of tiny buttons on the back of my dress. "That is, before today?"

"I've done better than that, ma'am," Simpson said. "I've played the role of an Innocent myself, when there weren't enough fine ladies to match the gentlemen. Her ladyship told the truth, too. It is most exciting, having all those gentlemen gawking away at you like you was a right goddess."

"You weren't ashamed to wear so little?"

"What, you mean the costume?" Simpson said, unlacing my long corset. "Nay, not really. All the other Innocents'll be dressed the same, so that's a comfort. We're paid extra wages for it, too, plus what our masters give us. I've earned more in a week playing an Innocent than an entire year as a maid."

"That must be welcome," I said, thankful there'd be

no money involved with my performance. Having a gentleman—even Lord Savage—pay for my favors would be . . . distasteful.

"Extra money's always welcome, ma'am," Simpson agreed. "I won't deny it. But mostly it's the power of the Game, ma'am. Standing there before them gentlemen, displaying what God gave you, it makes you feel powerful to be a woman. Nothing to be a-frighted of, ma'am. You'll see."

She quickly removed the last of my clothes, leaving only my shoes and stockings.

"Gentlemen prefer a pretty pair of silk stockings to a bare leg, ma'am," Simpson explained briskly. "And the heeled shoes show your feet and ankles to better advantage than slapping along barefoot like a duck."

She held the costume up over my arms and dropped it over my now-naked body. The silk slithered and fell into place, clinging to my breasts and bottom like the merest whisper of a caress.

"You must take off your jewels, ma'am," Simpson said, already pulling the diamond pin from my hair. "You can't be wearing nothing that shows who you are, or were. Innocents don't have pasts, and they don't have futures. They can only live in the present, as their Protector sees fit."

I frowned. "That sounds rather like my own father and his endless rules."

"I'll warrant it is, ma'am," Simpson said, musing. "For aren't all fathers and husbands protectors?"

"I should not like my father to have seen me dressed like this," I said.

Simpson laughed, deeply and earthily.

"Nor my own da, either," she said. "I would've gotten a proper thrashing if he had. But Lady Carleigh's game is different, because it's pretend. You're not to address your Protector unless he addresses you first, or unless he gives you leave. He can call you whatever he pleases, but you can only call him 'Master,' even if he be a lord. You're supposed to be dependent on him for everything. That's part of the sport. There you are, ma'am. Have I pleased you?"

Taking a deep breath, I crossed the room to the tall standing mirror.

It was I, but not I. The woman staring back at me from the mirror was undeniably beautiful, but in a wild, untamed way, like some shameless forest nymph. On my body, the costume was like a magical mist, making me look more naked than if I'd been without it. Nothing was hidden, from the round fullness of my breasts to the dip of my navel, to the shadowy curls at the juncture of my thighs.

"Permit me, ma'am," Simpson said, standing behind me. She reached around to fondle my breasts and tweak my nipples. Startled, I gasped, and tried to squirm free.

"Nay, ma'am, you must trust me about this," Simpson said firmly. "The gentlemen do love the titties, and you've a wondrous pair of them. But you want to show yourself pert and ready. Rub them yourself before you enter the room so they'll be stiff, ma'am. Though as soon as you feel all them eyes on you, they'll go hard on their own."

But my nipples didn't need any further rubbing, from Simpson or my own fingers. The thought of the scene that the maid described—of standing like this before a crowd of lustful men—was more than sufficient to make my nipples into tight buds of excitement, and bring a flush to my cheeks as well.

"Thank you, Simpson," I said. "I believe I am ready. Will you escort me downstairs?"

We walked swiftly down the stairs and back to the Egyptian Room. Although the footmen we passed were too well trained to stare, I was still acutely aware of walking before them, the filmy costume drifting about my naked body and my uncorseted flesh jiggling with each step.

I told myself I was playing a role, and that I was now a different lady altogether from the painfully proper Mrs. Hart of New York. But then, hadn't that been a role as well, pretending in public that I was Arthur's loving and dutiful wife when there had never been a scrap of genuine feeling between us?

"How fetching you look, my dear!" Lady Carleigh exclaimed, slipping through the door of the Egyptian Room and into the hallway to greet me. "I'm so happy you decided not to leave us, with your Protector most grateful of all."

"It's Lord Savage, isn't it?" I asked eagerly, trying to see past the viscountess and through the barely cracked door. "Is he there?"

"Indeed he is," Lady Carleigh said, taking my hand. "But I must tell you that there has been a small bit of, ah, confusion."

"Confusion, my lady?" I asked, confused myself. "What kind of confusion? Doesn't Lord Savage wish to be my Protector?"

"Oh, he does, he does," Lady Carleigh assured me. "But it seems that another gentleman has also become determined to possess you."

"*Two* gentlemen!" I exclaimed with dismay. I'd been so focused on the earl that I hadn't even considered that he'd have a rival, nor did I wish him to. "But I thought Lord Savage was—"

"Yes, yes," Lady Carleigh said, pulling me forward. "It is rather irritating, is it not? But I have contrived a solution worthy of Solomon himself. I have asked the two gentlemen to bid for the opportunity of educating you, with the winning bid to benefit the local parish charity. There's no better way to test a gentleman's ardor than through his pockets."

"You're going to *sell* me, my lady?" I asked, stunned by this new twist.

"I suppose so, yes," Lady Carleigh said. "It's rather a brilliant idea, is it not? The gentlemen believe everything's been fairly done, charity benefits, and you shall have the delicious experience of being a prized houri, desired and fought over. Now come, my dear, and be as tempting as possible."

The footman opened the door more widely, and Lady Carleigh led me into the room. The air was thick with the heady scent of more incense, redolent of dark mysteries, while the musicians continued to softly play their exotic music. It did have all the feel of some sultan's palace instead of a country house, a seductive invitation that was impossible to resist.

My hesitation had made me late, and now I would be the last Innocent to be chosen. The chairs of the Protectors had been arranged in a close ring around a small bench, while the Innocents who had already been claimed stood obediently behind their Protectors.

It made for a shocking sight, the Protectors still in their full evening attire, while the Innocents were half dressed in the same kind of revealing costumes that I myself wore. Seeing the other women's thinly veiled breasts was unsettling, but far worse—or was it far more exciting?—were the male Innocents, gentlemen with whom I had conversed politely over dinner now with their upper bodies bare and their cocks and balls proudly displayed through the sheer fabric of their loose trousers.

I had never seen gentlemen—or ordinary men, either—show themselves so freely to me. Hastily I lowered my gaze, my cheeks burning.

"Climb up, my dear, climb up," whispered the viscountess, helping me step up onto the bench. "Do not be shy, but bold, even brazen, the way a true beauty should. Stand to the front where all can admire you."

I swallowed, unable to look up as I instinctively shielded my breasts with my hands.

Coward, I told myself, *coward,* coward! I had wanted excitement in my life, and surely there could be few experiences more calculated to make my heart quicken than this, to wear the merest scrap of clothing and stand in a crimson-draped room above the man I longed to have as my lover.

"A smile, my beautiful Innocent," purred the viscountess beside me, "a winning smile for your would-be Protectors, to encourage them to bid deeply for the privilege of educating you."

I was playing a role. I had to remember that. I was no longer Mrs. Arthur Hart, but an Innocent, a beautiful, brazen Innocent, desiring to please and be pleased by my Protector. I breathed deeply of the incense to force myself to relax, and slowly raised my chin.

And at once I met the gaze of Lord Savage, sitting directly before me.

I caught my breath, startled by the intensity of his pale blue eyes. Because I was standing on the bench, his face was turned up toward me, yet there was nothing of the supplicant about his expression, nothing worshipful. True, his full lips were curled into the merest hint of a smile, the smile of a gentleman agreeably happy with what he saw.

But his eyes betrayed that genteel smile. Instead of agreeability, his eyes were watching me with raw hunger and desire so great that I could feel it as surely as if he'd reached out and caressed me. His eyes flicked down over my body, appraising not only my voluptuous beauty but the depth of his own need. The intensity of his scrutiny made my heart beat faster and my skin glow with an un-expected warmth that had little to do with embarrassment.

His gaze stirred a restlessness in my body, and I fought the unexpected wish to press my thighs together more tightly, as if that would somehow ease the restlessness. His eyes promised that he'd explain, and make me understand. I wanted that knowledge from him; no, I *needed* it, with an urgency that I'd no words to describe.

I forgot the other Protectors and Innocents watching me, forgot Lady Carleigh, forgot the gaudy surroundings of the Egyptian Room. Every part of my awareness narrowed so completely that Lord Savage and I might have been standing alone in some vast, empty space. For me, nothing existed except him.

My lips parted on their own, and my breath quickened, and I could not have dragged my gaze away from his if my very life had depended upon it.

"Take your hands from your breasts," he said, startling me not with his request but with the rough, deep sound of his voice. "Show them to me."

I slowly dropped my hands to my sides, my earlier shyness forgotten. At once, too, I felt my nipples tighten against the sheer cloth, exactly as they had when Simpson had tugged them, except that now it was Lord Savage's hands that I longed to have caressing my breasts.

"Excellent," he said, drawing the syllables out.

It was all the encouragement I needed. I pulled back my shoulders and hollowed my belly to mimic the effect that my corset usually created. The result was to lift my breasts higher, as if I was presenting them to Lord Savage, the rosy tips pushing forward with a brazenness I had never realized I possessed, exactly as Lady Carleigh had advised me to be.

This time the earl said nothing, nor did his half smile change. But I saw the extra spark of interest and desire in his eyes, a hunger that was so predatory that an answering shiver rippled through my body.

"Surely she must be one of the most lovely Innocents ever to grace our party," Lady Carleigh said, her voice low and enticing. "How fortunate the gentleman who will be her Protector! Shall we begin the bidding, my friends?"

"A hundred guineas," Lord Savage said with such confident assurance that it was almost a drawl. "That will make for a fair start, yes?"

"Damnation, Savage," said the man beside him, his voice full of violent anger. "There's nothing fair about this devil's bargain. The bitch *will* be mine, no matter how far you empty your pockets!"

I gasped, my eyes widening. The seductive spell that had existed between me and Lord Savage had been shattered, and the reality of my situation was now harshly apparent.

Lord Savage was only one of the gentlemen vying for me.

The other was Baron Blackledge.

FOUR

In an instant the mood in the room changed. The sweet air of seduction and amusement vanished as quickly as the musicians stopped playing, leaving only the leaden anger of Baron Blackledge. Automatically I shrank back to the edge of the bench, and again covered my breasts with my hands—not so much to shield myself in modesty but as a way of protecting myself from the violence of the baron's outburst.

Slowly Lord Savage turned in his chair to face the other man, his half smile still in place. I sensed a sudden tension behind his outwardly relaxed features, something taut and dangerous that the baron would be a fool to ignore.

"I'll thank you, Blackledge," he said with deceptive mildness, "not to refer to Mrs. Hart with such crude vulgarity. She is a lady, and deserves to be treated as such."

But the baron shook his head, his face flushed and mottled above the stiff white collar of his dress shirt.

"If I buy her, then I can call her whatever I wish," he said bluntly. "Those are the damned rules of the Game, aren't they?"

"The rules, Baron, say that she is an Innocent," Lady Carleigh said gently, gliding forward to stand before me and the two men. "Pray recall, too, that you are bidding not for ownership of the Innocent's person, but merely for the right to her education whilst you are my guest."

"A welcome reminder, Lady Carleigh," Lord Savage said, and though his smile widened, the tension was still apparent in his handsome features. "You are wisdom itself."

Lady Carleigh feathered her hand before her in acknowledgment.

"You are far too generous, my lord," she said. "I'd thought I had explained the rules of our little auction sufficiently, but if Lord Blackledge has misinterpreted them, then I am the one at fault, for my lack of clarity. Is that not so, Baron?"

But Lord Blackledge was in no humor for reminders, or apologies, either.

"Two hundred," he said curtly, his gaze riveted to my breasts.

Savage's smile widened a fraction. "Four hundred."

"Five," answered Lord Blackledge.

"Ah, Blackledge," Savage said. "And here I thought we were doubling. A thousand pounds."

A thousand pounds. I was trembling, my heart drumming in my breast. A thousand pounds was nearly five thousand dollars, an enormous sum for a frivolous party game.

Because that was what it was, wasn't it? A game, and no more?

But what would I do if the baron outbid Lord Savage? I didn't like Lord Blackledge, and worse, I didn't trust him. Why did I sense that this had become a game I couldn't quit?

"Damn you, Savage," said Lord Blackledge. He was sweating now, the coppery little hairs at his temples curling damply. "Two thousand pounds!"

"You needn't take this course, Baron," Lady Carleigh said, coaxing. "There is another Innocent in need of instruction, a rare beauty I invited especially at your request."

For the first time I noticed the other young woman who was waiting to one side without a Protector. She hadn't been at dinner, and I guessed she must be one of the servants willing to participate, as Simpson had described. She was indeed a rare beauty, with luminous large eyes, pale gold hair, and heavy, full breasts beneath her transparent gown, but she looked disappointed, even petulant, at being ignored, like the last wallflower at a ball. Despite my uneasiness, I felt sorry for her.

"It's quite rude of you to ignore the other, ah, Innocent, Baron," I said. "Especially if you requested that she—"

"Silence!" ordered Lord Blackledge curtly, his eyes flashing. "No Innocent has the right to address a Protector without permission. You deserve punishment for that, and when you are mine, I'll make sure that you never dare open your mouth except to—"

"But she won't be yours, Blackledge," Savage said beside him. "Ten thousand."

"Ten thousand!" the baron exclaimed, his face florid and mottled with anger. "Damn you, Savage. Ten thousand for—"

"For this Innocent." Savage's voice was deceptively mild. "A round sum, yes?"

"You will counter, Baron?" asked Lady Carleigh hopefully. "Recall the wagers are for a charitable—"

"Blast the charity, and blast the wagers with it." The baron stood abruptly, his hands clenched into tight fists at his side. "You take her, Savage, and to the devil with you both."

He turned and crossed the room to the young woman he'd ignored, and seized her by the wrist.

"Come," he said, pulling her along to the door. "I've had enough of this company."

The girl followed him, stumbling a bit over the hem of her flowing gown. He swore, and jerked her arm to make her keep up.

Yet, despite this treatment, her smile was sly and knowing in a way that puzzled me. Perhaps the girl had done this before. Perhaps she was already familiar with the baron's temper and knew how to manage it to her benefit. Certainly she seemed unconcerned with the rough way Lord Blackledge was treating her, and with a little shiver, I thought how grateful I was not to be in the girl's place.

"Well now, I suppose that's done," the viscountess said, smiling at Savage as the other guests, Protectors and Innocents alike, began to leave the room to begin their own, more private, amusements. "While I thank you for your generosity," Lady Carleigh continued, "I must also accept your bid of ten thousand as final, since Lord Blackledge did not raise his offer beyond that."

Savage rose and bowed slightly. "I offered ten thousand, Lady Carleigh, and ten thousand it will be. Your little parish will undoubtedly spend it in a more Christian manner than would I. I'll have a bank draft sent to your attention."

Lady Carleigh chuckled, running her fingers lightly up and down her long strands of pearls. She was a Protector herself, and as she conversed with Lord Savage, a powerfully built and mostly naked young man came to stand respectfully beside her. Without looking at him, the viscountess idly began stroking the young man's bare chest, her jeweled fingers toying with his dark, curling hair and pinching his small, puckered nipples.

I knew I shouldn't be shocked, but I was; nor was the sight of Lord Carleigh escorting a giggling young woman from the room, with his hand firmly on her bottom, any less unsettling.

"My church wardens wouldn't dare accept that draft, my lord," Lady Carleigh continued with languid bemusement, "if they knew the half of how you spent your . . . money."

"Then you'd best not tell them," Lord Savage said, turning away from her to me, still standing on the bench. He offered me his hand, and I took it, hopping lightly down to the carpeted floor.

"I must thank you, too, my lord," I said warmly, still holding his hand as I gazed up at him. "That was most generous of you, and on my behalf, too. Ten thousand pounds!"

He turned his head slightly, regarding me with a side-long gaze.

"It is only money," he said, "and I would have thought that you, of all women, would know that money doesn't matter."

I blushed, surprised that he knew that much of my background. He was right, of course. If my life had taught me anything, it was that money in itself seldom brought happiness. "But you did it for me."

"I did it to keep you from falling into Blackledge's brutish hands, yes," he said. "I would have done the same to preserve a good horse or hunting dog."

"Ah," I said, surprised again, but not as agreeably as before. I wished he would smile at me as he had at the viscountess. "Still, I must say that you—"

"Mrs. Hart," he said, cutting me off. "As boorish as Blackledge can be, he was correct in one matter. You, as an Innocent, have no right to speak to a Protector without being first addressed. Weren't the rules of the Game explained to you?"

I nodded, trying to remember what Simpson had told me. "Yes, I suppose they were."

He frowned down at me, and I thought how much larger, how much stronger, he was than I.

"Recall that you are my Innocent, and I your Protector," he said. " 'Yes, Master' is the proper response, and the only response that is acceptable. Do you understand?"

I hesitated. Much of the reason I had come to England— and most of the reason I had come to Wrenton Manor— was to escape who I had been in New York. I'd thought I was done with deferring to men, and now here Lord Savage was expecting exactly that of me.

"Forgive me, my lord," I began, "but I cannot see why I must—"

"Because in this place, you are no longer Mrs. Hart," he said evenly. "You are only an Innocent, and you know nothing. You must be led and guided toward the knowledge of pleasure. You must trust me, or remain ignorant. Is that clear?"

It wasn't, and as I stood before him, I felt nothing but confusion. I was desperate to discover the kind of love and pleasure that the rest of the world experienced, but I didn't want to be ordered about like the lowest of half-witted scullery maids. If I'd any sense, I thought, I would leave this place now, in my own clothes and on my own terms.

And yet, and yet . . .

The longer I gazed up into Lord Savage's pale blue eyes, the more I doubted myself. This week might be a mere game to Lady Carleigh and her friends, but it felt like much more to me.

What if this truly was the one path left to me? In the ways of pleasure, I was every bit as shamefully ignorant as he claimed. That part wasn't a game—that was the truth. I knew nothing, really, nothing at all, while I didn't doubt that he knew everything.

As if reading my thoughts, Lord Savage suddenly smiled: not a wide, fool's grin, but a small, secret smile for me alone, as if hinting at all we'd soon come to share if only I'd agree to trust him, and obey.

"You will trust me?" he asked again.

"Yes, Master," I murmured, this time agreeing. *"Yes."*

He nodded, clearly pleased, and pressed my fingers lightly to show his approval. But when he lifted my hand to his lips, bowing over it with an unexpected, old-fashioned air, I nearly gasped aloud. No man had ever made so romantic and courtly a gesture to me, ever.

Of course I would trust him. How could I not, after that?

"Since you are now my Innocent, I will call you Eve, here in our little Eden together," he said. "You will answer to that, won't you, Eve?"

It was the perfect name for an Innocent, even as it was also a variation of my own name, Evelyn. I had never been called anything other than my given name, and I liked the idea that Lord Savage would be the only one to use this one, a special little endearment between us alone.

I nodded, then remembered how I was supposed to reply.

"Yes, Master," I said. "That is, my name is Eve, Master."

"Good." He smiled again, and released my hand, turning away. Most of the other Protectors and Innocents had already left the room. Lady Carleigh and her Innocent still lingered, as she offered a few final orders to the servants who had appeared to put the room back to rights.

Lord Savage beckoned to one of the maids.

"Show this Innocent to my rooms," he told her. "Barry will tend to her."

"Who is Barry?" I asked.

Savage wheeled around and frowned, his expression instantly as ominous as thunder. "I did not address you, Eve."

I blushed, embarrassed that I had already erred. This reminded me of the old children's game Mother, May I?, with much more at stake.

"Forgive me, Master, I didn't mean to—"

"You are not to speak until I address you, Eve," he said curtly, and turned back to the maid. "Show her upstairs at once."

He left me then, crossing the room to speak once more with Lady Carleigh. Though his back was to me, his displeasure was apparent in the squared set of his shoulders, and I felt disappointment well up within me—not with him, but with myself.

"I'll show you to his lordship's rooms, ma'am," the maid said, still treating me with the respect due to Mrs. Hart. "This way, ma'am."

As soon as we were on the stairs and out of Savage's hearing, I touched the maid's sleeve.

"Who is Barry?" I asked anxiously, fearing that the earl might be passing me along to a different Protector. "I don't believe I met any gentleman here with that name. Is he another guest? What do you know of him?"

The maid smiled, but I didn't miss the faint pity in her voice.

"Oh no, ma'am, Mr. Barry's not a gentleman," she said. "He's Lord Savage's manservant. I expect his lordship will have told Mr. Barry to look after you until he joins you. His lordship's rooms are here, at the end of this hall. He's such friends with the Lord and Lady Carleigh that his rooms here are almost like lodgings, with everything just to his liking for whenever he visits."

She rapped on the door, and the manservant answered so swiftly that I suspected he must have been waiting nearby.

"This is Mr. Barry, Mrs. Hart," the maid said. "Mr. Barry, Mrs. Hart is his lordship's new Innocent, and his lordship says you're to put her at ease until he comes upstairs."

"Good evening, Mrs. Hart," Barry said, opening the door more widely for me to pass inside. He was a small, wiry man with wisps of graying hair over a mostly bald head, and clearly proud of his impeccable manners. Not once did his gaze drop to my revealing costume, for which I was endlessly grateful.

Curious, I looked about, eager for more clues to Lord Savage. To my surprise, the rooms were lit not by gaslight but by dozens of candles, in wall sconces, in chandeliers, and in candle stands, that cast everything with an antique light, full of mysterious shadows.

"Is there no gas lighting in this part of the house, Barry?" I asked, keeping close to the servant. "I would have thought Lord Carleigh would have had it installed here as well."

"Yes, ma'am, there is gas lighting throughout the house," Barry said, answering one question and no more.

"Then why not use it here? Why candles instead?"

The servant's expression didn't change. "It is Lord Savage's preference, ma'am."

I nodded, for there wasn't much I could say beyond that, the perfect servant's reticent reply. But why would Lord Savage have such an outdated preference? I had always lived with the newest and most modern of conveniences. In New York, even gaslights had been replaced by electric ones. Why would a young man—for he could not be past thirty—wish to use such an old-fashioned and inconvenient light?

Not that Barry would volunteer an answer as he led me down a short hall and through a sitting room. The maid had been right: the rooms had the feel not of a transient guest's impersonal, if expensively appointed, quarters but of the more permanent lodgings of an individual with very definite tastes, and the soft light and shadows cast by the candles somehow made it all the more personal.

It was also clearly the place of a man with many interests that he avidly and actively pursued. I saw that at once. Despite my father's faults, he had worked ferociously hard, and in these rooms I could see the obvious signs of a similar temperament in Lord Savage.

There were newspapers and books everywhere, books that were read and marked, and not simply for show. An oversize desk dominated the sitting room, and scattered across it were notebooks and maps and the schedule booklets for trains and steamships.

Manly souvenirs of foreign travels decorated the rooms as well, from the stretched zebra skin used as a rug on the floor, to a miniature pagoda carved from Chinese ivory, to a white marble bust of some ancient Roman senator staring blankly from a column out into the room. Father had kept these sorts of curiosities about his office, too, the stuffed head of a moose he'd shot in Maine and a painted, feathered tomahawk from a Plains Indian that he swore (to my horror) had been used for scalping.

But then there were other things here in Lord Savage's rooms that would never have found their way to Father's office. Over the fireplace hung a large painting of a woman sprawled over a daybed, wearing only a small diadem and bright jewels that glowed against her pearly skin. She smiled shamelessly, proud of her nudity in a way that made me blush for her.

That was only the beginning: the terra-cotta statue of a muscular, goatish satyr with a nymph, their limbs intimately entangled; a small watercolor of two beautiful young women lying together in a bed, kissing and fondling each other; and, most stunning of all, an engraving of another woman whose head was thrown back in a frenzy of passion, mating with the sizable swan clasped tightly between her thighs. It was not only shocking to me but physically impossible.

But, to my astonishment, this engraving and the other artworks had the most curious effect on me, making my heart race and my blood warm in a way that overwhelmed my initial embarrassment.

It was much the same as when I'd first spied Lord Savage with the other woman in the London garden, and I remembered how he'd told me that I must like to watch. I'd been offended then, but now I merely wondered if he'd been right.

I'd come here to discover passion, hadn't I? Perhaps looking at explicit pictures like these were part of my discovery. Perhaps they were meant to be . . . inspiring. And if the artwork affected Lord Savage in the same way, then it was no wonder that he kept it here at Wrenton, where he came to participate in Lady Carleigh's sensual games.

Yet, I forgot everything when Barry led me through the last door.

"His lordship wishes you to wait for him in here, Mrs. Hart," Barry said. "Is there anything else, ma'am?"

"No, Barry," I said. "No."

I could scarcely wait for the servant to leave. I was standing in Lord Savage's bedroom, and the excitement I felt was almost unbearable. Unlike the exotic, erotic clutter of the sitting room, this was spare, even austere.

An enormous antique bed with elaborately carved posts dominated the room, the red velvet coverlet, pillows, and canopy glowing by the light from the candles and the fire in the hearth. Beneath my bare feet was an oriental carpet, thick and plush with swirling patterns of crimson and blue.

There were no pictures on these walls. The room's single ornament was the sweeping view of the surrounding countryside visible through tall windows without curtains. A single armchair near the window, two small tables flanking the bed, and a large, framed dressing mirror were the only other pieces of furniture in the room.

I ran my fingers lightly over the velvet coverlet, trying to imagine Savage himself lying against the piled pillows at the head of the bed. Before long, I wouldn't have to imagine, and a tremor of anticipation rippled through me.

Swiftly I drew my hand back as if it had been burned, curling it against my chest, and retreated to the chair beside the window to compose myself. The view was lovely, fields and ancient trees splashed by moonlight, and the dark blue skies overhead scattered with stars. It could have been a warm evening at my house in Upstate New York rather than here in—

"Are you stargazing, Eve?"

At the sound of Savage's voice, I immediately twisted around in the chair to face him. He was standing in the doorway to the bedroom, still dressed in his impeccable formal clothes from dinner.

In the candlelight, he was all black and white, from his starkly white shirt and black suit to his inky-black hair and the white teeth of his smile. It was more predatory than humorous, that smile, and all that spared it from pure wolfishness were his pale blue eyes with the thick, dark lashes.

He was such a striking, intoxicatingly male figure that all words and thoughts flew from my head, and I could do nothing but stare at him.

"There's no sin to looking at the stars, Eve," he said. "Even a beggar may look at a king, and the moon as well."

Slowly he began to cross the room. He unfastened his

tie, tugging it from beneath the starched collar, and let it fall to the floor without a thought. He shrugged his shoulders free of his coat and dropped that, too, followed by his white brocade waistcoat, leaving a soft, costly trail of discarded black and white behind him on the carpet.

I made a gulping little laugh, so much like a nervous schoolgirl that I winced. "I'm hardly a beggar, my lord. You know that. But the stars certainly are beautiful tonight."

He stopped, and frowned.

"Oh, Eve," he said softly, pulling the top pearl stud of his shirt to open the collar. "You've forgotten again, haven't you?"

"Forgotten?" I repeated uneasily, slipping from the chair to stand with my back to the window. "What have I forgotten?"

"Who you are," he said, sounding disappointed and almost sad. "Who I am."

"Oh, that Game foolishness," I said hurriedly, remembering now. "I didn't think it mattered when we were alone, my lord. I thought it was only for when we were downstairs, with the others."

"'That Game foolishness'?" He tipped his head to one side, his frown now one of puzzlement. "The Game's hardly foolish, Eve. At least it isn't to me."

"That is, it's not to me, either," I said quickly. I felt off-balance and uncertain, and unsure of what sort of answer he was expecting. "If it were, I, ah, I wouldn't be here."

"Very well," he said. He raised his chin a fraction, to unfasten another stud on his shirt, his gaze never leaving mine. "Then I'll forgive your forgetfulness, and permit you to begin again, as an Innocent. Will you agree to that, Eve?"

I swallowed, nervously smoothing a stray curl of my hair behind my ear. How could I think, with him undressing like this? As he took the onyx links with the gold snakes from his cuffs, his shirt fell open nearly to the waist, revealing that he wore no undershirt beneath, the way most gentlemen would. Instead there was only a tantalizing glimpse of his bare chest and the whorls of black hair upon it.

I'd never seen a gentleman's chest like this, not once.

"Eve?" he asked again, working the last of the onyx cuff links free. "If you do not wish what I can give you, then you are free to—"

"No, Master," I said breathlessly. "I wish it."

"You will obey me in all matters?" He tossed the shirt's studs in his palm like a gambler's dice. "You will trust me completely?"

"Yes, Master," I said quickly, as much to convince myself as him. *"Yes."*

"I am glad." He turned away and dropped the shirt studs and cuff links with a clatter into a porcelain dish on the mantel. With his back to me, he poured himself a brandy from the decanter on the nearby table.

He didn't offer the wine to me. Not that I wanted any, but I wasn't accustomed to not being considered, the way a gentleman always did with a lady.

But then I wasn't a lady any longer, not to him. I'd just agreed once again to be an Innocent, and the realization was at once both exciting and daunting. What would he expect me to do? What desires of his would I be obliged to fulfill?

And what in turn could I expect of him?

"So here we are, my pretty Innocent," he said, coming slowly toward me with the cut-crystal tumbler in hand. "We'll have a week to learn each other's ways, won't we?"

Instinctively I took a step back, away from him, bumping against the cool glass of the window. *Foolish,* foolish, I scolded myself. I needed to be bold and confident with him, not skittish as a cat. No, I felt more like the mouse, with him as the cat.

"Won't we, Eve?" he repeated, bemused by my unease.

"Yes, Master," I said belatedly. I had to remember that he expected an answer to every question.

"Good," he said. He dropped into the armchair that I'd been sitting in earlier and stretched his long legs out before him, making himself comfortable.

I, however, was anything but comfortable. I was standing between his chair and the window—trapped between them, really—and anytime he wished, he could reach out to touch me.

Or I could touch him, I told myself, glancing down to the black-clad leg so close to mine. The fabric pulled and stretched over his muscular thigh, and I longed to place my hand there to feel his strength, his power.

That's what a woman like Lady Carleigh would do, I thought. *She wouldn't be shy.* If I wanted this man as much as I claimed, then I should let him know with a seductive kiss or a caress. Likely he'd welcome it, even expect it.

But then Lady Carleigh would know exactly *how* to please a man, and I . . . I did not.

"You seem uneasy, Eve," he said. He didn't have to be a clairvoyant for that; surely he could hear the racing of my heart from his chair. "To prove how generous a master I am, especially compared to others in this house, I shall permit you to ask me three questions, just like a genie. Anything at all."

It was a precious opportunity to learn more of him, and an unexpected one, too. But, in the way of such moments, my thoughts went blank, and I blurted the first thing that came to my head.

"Why—why do you use candles instead of the gaslight?"

"Because I prefer them," he said easily. "I have an old

soul, Eve, and a romantic one. I find little to please me in the hasty vulgarity of modern life. If in this small way I can exist in former days, then so be it."

"But don't you own a motorcar?" I asked, in my astonishment unwittingly using my second question.

"I do," he confessed, holding the glass close to his cheek. "Several, in fact. One cannot completely escape one's life, no matter how much one wishes otherwise. But I much prefer a candle's warm light to the greenish glow of gas, the blood and urgency of a fast horse to a rumbling motor, and a painter's mastery to the chemical wizardry of a photograph."

No other man I'd known would ever have made such an admission, nor so poetically, and it intrigued me. "Then you are a true romantic, aren't you?"

"I am, and proudly so," he said, and smiled. "Which is why I am so intrigued by you. And that, Eve, was the last of your allotted questions for me."

"Oh!" I exclaimed with dismay. "I didn't mean to—"

"I don't care what you intended, Eve," he said, cutting me off. "All that matters to me is what you do, and what you will do now is what I say."

Reluctantly I nodded. He hadn't exactly tricked me, but the distraction of his mere presence had made me trip myself. If this was part of the Game, then I'd already lost the first gambit.

"Take your hair down," he said. "I want to see it loose."

Years had passed since I'd either dressed or unpinned my hair myself, especially without a mirror; Hamlin would never have permitted it. I hadn't been seen in public with my hair loose since I was fourteen. Likely, Savage was aware of all this, but I didn't wish to admit to being so helpless.

Instead, I reached up and began pulling out the dozens of pins that held my elaborately braided, curled, and puffed hair in place. I neatly tucked each pin between my lips, the same way as Hamlin did.

"Let the pins fall," Savage said. "Barry will gather them. I've far better uses for your mouth than that."

I took the hairpins from my lips and dropped them as he'd ordered. One by one they fell to the polished floor-boards with a little ping, like drops of metallic rain.

He watched me closely, sipping the amber-colored brandy as his gaze drifted from my hair to my breasts. His gaze was focused and intent and left no doubt of his appreciation. Of course: I hadn't considered it, but the act of lifting my hands to undo my hair also raised my breasts, swaying and shimmying against my filmy Innocent's gown.

I remembered how he'd watched and admired me this same way when I'd stood on the bench during the auction. Daringly I once again began to play to his interest, and as my confidence grew, I turned this way and that as I made a kind of dance of freeing my hair. I never would have performed like this before Arthur, nor would he have been anything but scandalized if I had.

But Savage clearly approved, his focused gaze never leaving me.

I was almost disappointed when the last pin fell to the floor. I shook my head from side to side to make the heavy waves of hair fall and settle over my shoulders and down my back, and began to rake my fingers through it like a comb.

"Leave your hair as it is, Eve," he said. "I like it like that, with an air of wildness."

I smiled, even as I was unable to keep from coquettishly twisting one errant lock into a curl around my fingers. It was a strange compliment, to be praised for being tousled and untidy, but because it came from Savage, I liked it more than any of the well-worn banalities I'd heard in ballrooms both in New York and London.

I gave my hair a little toss, embracing the wildness he'd seen in me.

"So you feel the freedom, my wild little Innocent," he said, chuckling. "I knew it was there inside of you, waiting to be released."

"Yes, Master," I said breathlessly, feeling happy as well as wild. It pleased me to please him, a roundabout benefit that I hadn't expected. "Yes, I do."

I watched the muscles in his throat work as he finished the brandy, the slight sheen of the skin under his jaw. He set the empty glass down on the table before he smiled at me again.

"Very good, Eve," he said. "I imagine that you'll now find it easy enough to remove that wretched garment."

"My costume?" Startled, I ran my hands lightly over the front of the gown. Earlier this evening I had despised this costume for being too revealing, and now it had become my last scrap of—of what?

The gossamer-weight fabric hid nothing. Dressed like this, I was as good—or as bad—as naked. He'd already seen most of me when I'd stood on the bench for the auction, beneath the bright gaslights. There were precious few secrets left to be revealed, yet still I hesitated, my last scruples clinging fiercely to my New York–born modesty.

"Yes, Eve, that tawdry foolishness that Lady Carleigh chose for the Innocents to wear," he said, watching me closely. "It's a damned tease. I cannot believe you are attached to so wretched a garment."

"I'm not, Master," I said quickly. "It's only that—that—"

"That you are shy? Is that it?"

I sighed softly. "Yes, Master, I suppose I am," I admitted. "Not even my husband saw me without my clothes."

"Then I am honored to be the first," he said, his voice low and coaxing. "Come along now, Eve. This is only the initial step if you wish to be free. Show me yourself in all your wild beauty."

If he truly wished me naked, then he could have torn the fragile costume from my body in an instant; as my master, I'd granted him every right to do so. But the fact that he wished me to make the decision to reveal myself—ah, that made it somehow much easier.

Before I change my mind, I grabbed the costume's hem and jerked it up and over my head, then tossed it to the floor with the hairpins. Perhaps it was remembering how Lady Carleigh had praised my figure that gave me confidence, or simply my own desire to be as wild as he urged me to be. Whatever the reason, I didn't shrink away, but stood straight and proud in my heeled slippers, almost defiant with my hair tumbling down my back.

Or maybe—no, most likely—it was seeing the flash of desire and hunger in his eyes as he studied me, infinitely more intense than when he'd watched me during the auction. He didn't try to mask it, either, the way some gentlemen would. He wanted me, and he wanted me to know it.

"You are a rarity, Eve," he said, his voice lowering to more of a growl. "From the first time I saw you in the garden, saw the excitement in your eyes as I fucked another woman, I knew it would come to this for us."

"I did, too," I whispered. What was it about such declarations that made them impossible to speak loudly? And why was it that when he said *fucked*—a word I'd never dared speak myself—I knew I had to have him fuck me as well? "I did, and I—"

"Hush, Eve, hush," he said, placing his forefinger across his lips as a more emphatic warning. "I ask the questions, and you reply. I give the orders, and you obey."

"Yes, Master." I was eager in my replies now, ready to follow wherever he led. He'd been right about shedding the costume. I did feel more free without clothing, and my body was warm and quivering inside with anticipation for whatever he'd propose.

"You're a widow," he said, a statement, not a question.

"You're a widower, too, aren't you?" Lady Carleigh had told me that Lady Savage had died several years before, tragically young.

His expression didn't change.

"Yes, I am," he said. "But you are not asking the questions, Eve. I am. No children, I presume?"

I shook my head. I'd wanted children, lots of children, to make up for my solitary childhood. But although I'd been a wife, I had not been blessed with motherhood.

"I thought not," he said. "Your body's too pristine to have suffered through childbirth."

I winced at that, the casual dismissal of my greatest disappointment, and because of it, my question in return was sharper than I'd intended.

"Have *you* any children?" I asked. "Legitimate ones, that is. Have you fathered a precious heir to your earldom?"

He frowned. "Eve, you forget yourself again. I ask the questions, not you. But yes, I have a single son, and yes, he is my heir."

He said it not proudly, the way most fathers would, but with a curious finality that made it clear that he'd volunteer nothing more about the boy.

"Now tell me, Eve," he continued. "Did your husband please you when he lived?"

"Arthur?" My husband's face rose up in my memory like an unpleasant, potbellied ghost, one I'd done my best to banish.

Savage shifted impatiently in the chair. "If that was your husband's name, then yes."

"He provided for me," I said carefully. "I never wanted as his wife."

"That's not what I asked." Savage tipped his head back in the chair so that most of his face was shadowed from me. "I want to know if his cock gave you satisfaction, if he made you desire him day and night, if he could make you come until you screamed with pleasure."

I blushed, more with shame for the unhappy marriage I'd endured than for the bluntness of his query.

And I wondered, too, how the late Lady Savage would have answered that same question. . . .

"No, Master," I said softly. "I was very young when I wed, and my husband was older. Too old."

"Did you take lovers to compensate for your husband's inadequacy?"

"No," I said. "Not until now."

His smile shone in the shadows.

"You honor me once again, Eve," he said. "And I give you my word that you will not be disappointed."

"Yes, Master," I whispered, my breath suddenly tight in my chest. Could he really make me experience what he'd described?

"Come here, Eve," he said. "Come here, and kiss me."

I nodded, taking the last steps to stand beside him, sprawled and glorious and waiting for me. I puckered my mouth, bent down, and closed my eyes. Quickly I pressed my lips against his, then drew back.

He stared at me, aghast, even angry. "My god. Is that dry little peck what you call a kiss?"

"Yes," I said defensively, for it was all I knew how to do. "My husband didn't believe—"

"Your husband has no place here, Eve," he said. "Not now."

He caught me around the waist to pull me forward, and with his other hand tangled his fingers in my hair to guide my face down to his. He slanted his mouth over mine and kissed me hard, seducing me with his lips. I was stunned by how hot, how insistent, how soft and then hard this kind of kiss was.

I broke away, gasping, but he wouldn't let me escape.

"*This* is how a man kisses a woman," Savage said, his voice low and rough. "This is how a man shows a woman how much he desires her, and wants to possess her."

And when Savage began to kiss me again, I understood exactly what he meant.

FIVE

Savage teased my lips apart and his tongue pushed into my mouth, wetly swiping against mine with sensual purpose. He tasted of the brandy, a hint of coffee from dinner, and of himself, masculine and dark. I could have pulled away again, but this time I didn't. Instead, I let myself be led, and found my own way as well. Tentatively I swirled my tongue against his, echoing and responding as he deepened the kiss.

How could I feel both scorched and drowning at the same time? It was enough to make me dizzy, and my legs felt so weak beneath me that I put one hand on Savage's shoulder to steady myself.

He must have sensed my imbalance, as he put it to his advantage. Deftly he slipped his arm around my waist and tipped me into his lap. My legs hung inelegantly over the cushioned arm of the chair, and the soft wool of his trousers with his well-muscled thighs beneath pressed against my bare bottom. I flailed my arms a bit, trying to figure how to settle myself, but he kept kissing me, and I soon decided that that mattered more.

Besides, curled against him like this with my bottom against the hollow of his belly was not such a bad place to be. He smelled good, a mixture of the starch from his shirt and faint lime from his shaving soap, mingled with the purely male scent of his skin. His body was warm and strong beneath mine, his power unmistakable.

Being naked while he was still dressed made me feel more than simply free. It made me feel wicked, sinful, passionate, all things I'd never experienced but was now learning to relish very much.

Because now I was kissing him, too, my mouth working hungrily against his. One of my shoes slipped from my foot and dropped to the floor, then the second, and I paid them no heed. I'd forgotten to be shy, or that this was new to me. I simply wanted more of this, and of him.

My fingers curled around the back of his neck and slipped into the black silk of his hair, while my other hand spread across his chest, and I felt his heart beating beneath my fingers.

"What man wouldn't want you, Eve?" he whispered fiercely, his breath warm on the shell of my ear. "You're so damned beautiful."

He pushed aside my hair and closed his hand over my breast, cupping and kneading the tender flesh. I gasped, startled by the heat and heaviness that instantly built within me. It was almost an ache, the finest line between pain and pleasure, and when he tugged lightly at my nipple, squeezing the tip and releasing it, I caught my breath with a shuddering sigh.

Shamelessly I arched against his hand for more. The pleasure shimmered through my body, centering low in my belly and between my legs, there in my sex.

"Do I hurt you, Eve?" he asked, again into my ear so that the words teased hotly on my skin. "Is it too much for you to bear?"

"No, Master," I said. "It's that—that I feel it in other places."

"Other places, Eve?" He shifted to my other breast, the same rhythmic caress centered with an intense pull on my nipple. His breathing had changed, too, quickening like mine. "Here?"

"Noooo, Master," I said, my words drawn out in a low moan. I drew my knees up higher over the arm of the chair and pressed my thighs tightly together, hoping that would ease my needing, but it seemed only to make it worse—or better.

"Then here." His hand slid down my belly and eased between my legs, lightly stroking the insides of my thighs until they traitorously slipped apart for him. Before I realized it, he'd parted my cleft and slipped a finger deep inside.

My back bowed and I cried out softly, startled not so much by the intrusion but by how impossibly good it felt.

"You're so narrow and wet, Eve," he murmured. "Wet for me, yes?"

I nodded, my eyes squeezed shut, and was too lost in what he was doing to answer. Moving against his finger was impossible to resist, easing the tension that was growing inside me and yet building it, too. He kissed me again, his tongue in my mouth echoing the pace of his finger inside my passage.

He added a second finger beside the first, pressing deep inside places of my channel that I'd never known were there, that begged for him to touch, to press, to stroke.

So good, so very good.

Fleetingly I thought of how I must look: naked and sprawled across his lap, my legs shamelessly spread as I writhed against his finger. My skin was starkly white against the black of his evening trousers. I'd hooked one leg around his calf and another over the arm of the chair, and as my hips rolled I had a glimpse of my calves in their shiny silk stockings, the brilliants on the buckles of my garters winking in the candlelight.

How foolish to think of such a thing, at such a moment. I felt tense and feverish, with all my being centered on his fingers.

"Such a greedy Innocent," he said. "Greedy for more, aren't you?"

"Yes." I gasped, panting, though I'd no real notion of what that "more" would be. *"Yes."*

"Then look at me, Eve," he said, his breathing now harsh. "Open your eyes, and don't shut them again."

In a haze of pleasure, I dragged my eyes open. His handsome face was strained, the hard planes so taut that even the candlelight couldn't soften them. I'd done nothing to arouse him, and besides, he was still dressed. Could touching me be enough for him? Did I really have that kind of power?

"There," he said, smoothing my tangled hair back from my face. "I want to know the exact moment when you spend."

With his fingers still caressing me within, he lightly stroked the pad of his thumb over a small nubbin of flesh and nerves near my opening. It was as if I'd been struck by lightning, if lightning were a bright and blinding strike of sensation.

I couldn't breathe; I couldn't think. My entire body was coiled around this tiny place between my legs, clenching around his fingers to draw them deeper inside. He let some of my moisture slicken his thumb, and stroked more firmly over the nubbin.

And in an instant, the tension in my body broke and my release came with it, so unexpected that I cried aloud from the force. Relief and joy together overwhelmed me, finally rolling away to leave me shaken and exhausted and gasping for breath.

All the time Savage had watched me, his gaze locked with mine, and his breathing ragged. I'd thought there was something predatory about Savage—and if I was honest, it was part of his fascination for me—but the pure masculine triumph I saw now in his pale eyes belonged on some primal creature, not on an English peer.

I felt bewitched, as if he'd created a spell over us both in this candlelit world. I couldn't look away. Even if my legs would have carried me, I couldn't think of escape.

Nor did I wish to.

"You've never had that before, have you, Eve?" he asked, his voice almost a growl, thick with lust. "Not like that?"

"Never." I'd never spoken more truthfully, either.

He swiped his hair, as black as a raven's wing, back from his forehead. "I've only started with you, you know."

"Yes," I said, all that I needed to say. *"Yes."*

He moved swiftly, scooping me into his arms and carrying me to the bed. He dropped me on my back in the center of the red velvet counterpane, my hair spreading in a tangle around my face as I sank into the feather bed. He pulled off my garters and my stockings and seized me by my ankles, his fingers surrounding my narrow bones like shackles. He pulled me forward until my bottom was on the very edge of the bed, then shoved one of the pillows beneath my hips.

I whimpered with excitement, my heart racing. I was still wet, still full and heavy with longing for him. I remembered the first time I'd seen him in the garden, when he'd been with the now-forgotten Lady Telford. I remembered the mesmerizing sight of his cock as it had plunged into the other woman, completely possessing her. Now at last I was the one who'd feel that demanding cock, and the power with which Savage used it.

I was wrong.

He knelt on the carpet beside the bed, and hooked my knees over his shoulders so that I couldn't close my legs. I wriggled, unsure of why he'd wish to be so close to that part of me, especially now when the honey of my first release still flowed.

But he wished to be closer, much closer. He kissed the insides of my thighs, the faint stubble of his beard rough against my skin. Slowly he worked his way along my thigh to my sex. To my shock, he eased open my nether lips with his thumbs and covered my slit with his mouth. He licked me first with broad, sweeping strokes that made me melt, then sucked and teased at that same nubbin that had already brought me such pleasure.

I was still swollen, still sensitive, and each teasing lap of his tongue made me whimper. My hips bucked, striving to find my rhythm, but he was the one in maddening control, torturing my cleft with the wet velvet of his tongue.

Whenever I felt myself nearing the edge of my desire, he drew back, gentling his caress to keep me poised there until I was panting and trembling and clutching fistfuls of the coverlet. Finally he circled his tongue around my nubbin and flicked it, and I arched and cried out as my climax came again, waves and waves of it washing over me.

With my eyes closed, I murmured his name as the last tremors of pleasure rippled and faded through my body. I was limp with it, drenched with sweat. When he rose and swung my legs back onto the bed, gently settling me back against the pillows, I let him. I was exhausted with pleasure, so sated I could scarcely move myself.

He had yet to find such release himself. His face was rigid with self-control, his breathing hard, and when I glanced down at his trousers, his cock was blatantly erect and ready for me.

I smiled, holding my hand out to him and expecting him at last to shed his clothes and climb into the bed with me for more. It was his turn now, and I meant to do my best to give him the same pleasure he'd given me.

But instead he pulled the sheets and coverlet over me, and retreated to pour himself more brandy.

Stunned, I sat up. "Won't you join me, Savage?"

"Recall who I am, Eve," he said, keeping his back to me. His voice was severe, even harsh, and so was his manner.

I could make no sense of it, or him, after what we'd just done. "You are cruel."

"I am your master," he said, turning back, "and your opinion doesn't matter to me."

"How can you say that?" I demanded, wounded. "You said yourself we'd just begun."

"We have," he said curtly. "But what happens next is my decision to make, not yours."

"Don't you wish to—to make love to me?" I asked in a small voice.

He emptied the glass. "Do not be so missish, Eve. I will never 'make love' to you. I will fuck you, and you will fuck me, but we will not make love."

I clutched the sheet tightly over my bare breasts, painfully aware of how he'd avoided answering my question. "But after the—the magic you just made me feel—"

"Your climax, Eve, your ecstasy," he said. "You spent. You came. You were tossed off. You felt the little death. There was no magic involved, and certainly no love."

"It's not about the *words*," I said tartly. "It's about the—"

"You must put aside this American arrogance, Eve," he said, his words clipped and condescending. "No matter how many dollars you have to your name, you cannot buy me, nor can you order me about. It is your choice now. You may leave this house and the Game, or you may stay and abide by its rules."

He was maddening, *maddening*. Standing there before the marble mantelpiece, with a crystal glass of expensive brandy in one hand and declaiming in his impeccable accent, he represented British civility at its best, and equally British superiority at its worst. Doubtless that was what he wanted me to see, the aristocrat facing down the crass American.

But I saw beyond that. That careful control was all a ruse. I saw the rumpled, unbuttoned shirt and the dark curls on his bare chest, the once-neat hair now tousled and falling across his forehead. I saw how the vein in his temple throbbed with tension, how the chiseled line of his jaw was rigid with it. I saw how his cock still thrust forward against the front of his evening trousers, and I knew my scent would be inescapable on his clothes, his hands, his lips.

He turned his head a fraction, the angles of his face sharp in the candlelight. "Your choice, Mrs. Hart."

Breaking character to use my formal name like that was hardly a subtle way to show that he believed I was the one at fault, and I'd no intention of listening to any more of it. I threw back the covers and swung my legs over the side of the bed.

I didn't have to look to know he was watching me as I walked across the room.

"Very well, then, my lord," I said, retrieving my costume from the floor. "If you wish to speak further, I shall be in my own rooms."

"No, you won't," he said. "You'll sleep here."

I pulled the costume over my head and smoothed it as

best I could. "Given how odious you find my company, I don't understand why I should—"

"Because even if you have abandoned Lady Carleigh's house party, the rest of the company has not," he said. "If you leave these rooms, you'll be fair game for any other master to claim and use. I can guarantee that none of them would be as respectful towards you as I have been."

"Respectful!" I felt scorned and humiliated and angry, but not in the least respected.

Yet, he was likely right about the other guests, and especially Baron Blackledge. I would rather wander unattended on a city street than chance meeting him in the hall.

"Sleep here," Savage continued. "In the morning, you may do as you please. Return to your rooms, return to London, return to New York."

A quick, bitter smile flickered across his face. "Or go straight to the Devil. Your choice. I'm sure you know the way."

"If I do, it's because you have shown it to me." I raised my chin and folded my arms over my breasts, striving to appear aloof and deny how much his words had stung my pride. "Good night, Lord Savage."

"Good night, Mrs. Hart." He set the glass on the mantel and bowed with undeniable sarcasm. " 'May flights of angels sing thee to thy rest.' "

I didn't answer. I was sure I'd heard that before, that it was a quotation from some famous poem or song, but the last thing I wished to do was reveal my ignorance, and let him dismiss me again as a vulgar American philistine.

Defiantly I pulled the costume back over my head and tossed it aside, letting him see exactly what he was missing. Then I returned to the bed, settling in the center of it against the pillows, pointedly not covering myself with the sheets. I hoped I resembled the woman in the painting over his desk, flagrant and without shame, and I hoped he'd think so as well.

Now it was my turn to watch him as he walked across the bedroom, and my turn, too, to admire him as he did. He moved with athletic ease, confident in his own self. I hated to admit it now, but I remained intensely attracted to him, and seeing his usually immaculate dress disheveled only made me more excited.

Even in the middle of this quarrel—which, I supposed, was what it was—he was in no hurry to leave the room, but walked at the pace that he chose, shoving his shirtsleeves back from his wrists.

But at the door, he stopped, and turned around to face me one last time, his pale blue eyes so intense that, again, I caught my breath.

"Believe me or not, Eve," he said softly. "But know that I'll be very disappointed if, in the morning, you decide to leave me. *Bonne nuit, ma chérie.*"

Then he closed the door, and was gone.

It was not the way I had expected the night to end, nor would I ever have wished it this way. I rose and slowly went about the bedroom, snuffing the last of the candles that hadn't already guttered out. Bright flames vanished into twisting wisps of smoke, the scent of burned wax and disappointment.

I slipped back into the bed and drew the covers up high. The sheets smelled of him, and with keen regret I buried my face into the pillow, remembering everything and breathing deeply.

It was a poor substitute for the man who'd left me.

Before I slept, I took care to shift to one side of the bed, leaving the side nearest the door open for him. I wasn't sure why, since I'd no real reason to expect Savage to change his mind and join me, yet still I did it.

And then, feeling weary and confused, I finally drifted off to sleep.

I was not by habit an early riser, and by the time I roused myself the next morning, the sun was streaming through the windows and across the bed. For a long time I hovered between sleep and full wakefulness, freely drifting back into unconsciousness. Why shouldn't I? The bed was warm, the sky was blue, and birds were singing cheerfully outside the window.

I smiled and stretched, content, and at last dragged my eyes slowly open.

I was not in my bedroom, not in New York or in any of my other houses. I was not in a steamship cabin, or a hotel that I recognized, either. There were tall windows with stained glass at their pointed tops, silver candlesticks with burned-down candles, and a view of rolling green fields and formal gardens.

And under the sheets, I was completely naked.

Disoriented, I swiftly widened my eyes and rolled over.

Sitting in the armchair before me was Lord Savage, wearing a carelessly tied silk paisley robe and nothing else beneath.

"Good morning," he said, the same nonchalant greeting he'd have used if we'd met downstairs in the breakfast room. "I trust you slept well?"

"I—yes, good morning," I stammered, pulling the sheets modestly high over my bare breasts. Now that I was awake, the memory of last night came racing back, and I flushed. Being naked in Lord Savage's bed by candlelight seemed very different from being in his bed this morning, with the streaming sunshine and the chirping birds in the branches outside the window.

I glanced at the pillow beside mine to see if he'd lain there while I'd slept.

"I kept my word, Mrs. Hart," he said, reading my thoughts. "I left you in peace to sleep alone."

"Thank you, my lord," I said self-consciously. For now, at least, he seemed to have put aside the Game, and I slipped back to using his title just as he'd used my married name.

He was newly shaved, his jaw gleaming and sleek, and he must also have just bathed. His hair was combed wetly back from his forehead, and even at a distance I caught the scent of the spicy lime soap that he favored. I'd never imagined any man being such a tempting sight so early in the morning.

But tempting or not, I'd no idea where I stood with him, or worse, where I wished to be standing. We'd both been furious when we parted last night. My temper had definitely cooled since then, but it was impossible to tell his mood from his demeanor.

Was he trying to coax me into staying, or was he simply being the well-bred host with the perfect manners before he escorted me back to my rooms to pack?

He wasn't making it easy for me, either, sitting there with his eyes half closed and just enough of a smile on his face to show one dimple. He shifted in the chair, making himself more comfortable, and the slippery silk of his robe slid farther open over his chest and across his well-muscled thighs. At once I thought of what else was barely hidden by the paisley silk, of the cock that I'd never had the chance to see last night.

No, he wasn't making this easy for me at all.

I smoothed a lock of my tangled hair behind my ear. I was acutely aware of how untidy and unwashed I was, especially in comparison to him, now well groomed by Barry. The trail of clothing that he'd discarded last night was gone from the floor, and the blackened and guttered candles had all been cleaned away and replaced.

My costume had been replaced by a new, fresh one as

well, folded and waiting for me on the bedside table, with my shoes side by side on the floor below and my silk stockings rolled and tucked inside with the jeweled garters. It was mortifying proof that the servant had also come in while I'd slept.

"I'm sorry to have inconvenienced you, my lord," I said tentatively. "I trust you slept well yourself."

"I didn't," he said. "I spent most of the night here, while you slept."

"You watched me?" I asked, unsettled by the intimacy of what he'd done. The last person who'd watched me while I slept must have been a nursemaid or governess when I was a child. Not even Arthur had spent an entire night in my bed.

He nodded. "I didn't watch you, Mrs. Hart, so much as watch over you. There is a difference."

"I, ah, suppose there must be," I said, though I wasn't sure there was. Did he really feel that I'd needed protecting? Had I been at risk from the other masters even here, in his bedroom? "A difference, that is."

"There is," he said firmly. "You say your husband did not satisfy you. Did you ever love him?"

I hadn't expected that, especially not so soon after I'd awakened. I considered dissembling, the way I'd always done with Arthur; really, our entire marriage had been a lie. But with Savage I felt drawn to tell the truth, especially about this.

"No," I said softly. "I never loved him, nor did he love me."

"Then why did you marry?" he asked. "You are an independent woman. I cannot conceive of you being forced to do anything."

I smiled sadly. "I was very young," I said. "Only seventeen. I liked the fuss, the excitement, of being a bride."

"But not a wife?"

"Not Arthur's wife, no," I said, and sighed. "There was never any excitement in that. But I'd no choice. My father made that clear enough. Arthur was his business partner, and our marriage was a way of cementing their assets between them. I know it must sound preposterous to you."

"Not at all," he said. "There are a good many English parents who will sell their daughters' souls for a title."

I hadn't expected that kind of sympathy from him, or the warmth of understanding in his voice. I'd been right to tell him the truth, right to confide in him as I had in no one else.

"Did you love your wife?" I asked.

"Oh, yes," he said, his expression clouded with melancholy. "I loved her more than was wise. I married her to save her. And I couldn't. No one could. But I was blinded by love, and suffered for it, too."

"I'm sorry," I murmured, all I could think to say after such a confidence. I wondered what had become of his wife, though the finality in his voice kept me from asking more. I understood that what he'd just told me was something he seldom shared, the same as I'd kept the truth of my marriage to myself as well.

Oh, Savage and I were alike, uncannily so. Each had let the other see a secret part of the past, of our private being, and in the process we'd drawn ourselves together a little more closely.

He shook his head, seeming to shake away the memories he clearly did not wish to revisit. He sighed, and rested his head on his hand.

"You understand now why I did not wish to let you slip from my sight," he said. "As beautiful as you were by candlelight, Mrs. Hart, you are even more extraordinary now."

From any other man, this would have been a simple compliment, but from him, after what he'd just told me of his wife, it felt far more complicated.

Then he smiled, sending a fresh jolt of desire racing through my blood, and things became more complicated still. When he smiled at me like this, I instantly forgot everything except how he'd kissed me last night, how he'd caressed my breasts, how he'd made me whimper with longing as he'd licked me into shameless, blissful oblivion.

Hastily I looked down at my hands, tightly clutching the sheet.

"Shall I call for my maid so I might dress for breakfast?" I asked. "I know it's late, but I'm sure Lady Carleigh will have some manner of repast waiting for her guests."

"Oh, she will," he said easily. "Her breakfasts are generally well attended. But if I were to appear with you at my side, Mrs. Hart, on the first morning, it would be a sign that I was either dissatisfied or bored with you. It would mean that I was willing to share you with the other Protectors, or at the very least to have you perform for their amusement."

I flushed again. "I do not believe I would, ah, enjoy that."

"No," he agreed. "Nor would I. But the true question is what exactly *would* you enjoy, Mrs. Hart? The choice is yours. Shall we forget the unfortunate close to last night, and begin the Game anew?"

So he was giving me a second chance. I doubted very much that I'd receive a third. I thought of the pleasure he'd given me last night, of how much he'd already taught me about my desires. But mostly I thought of how much more I had to learn—and how I'd never find another teacher quite like him.

Nor, if I listened to the desire thrumming through my body, did I wish for any other.

But before I agreed, there was a question that I needed to ask, and that he needed to answer.

"I am willing to forget the unfortunate aspects of last

night, my lord," I said carefully, "and recall only the more pleasurable ones—"

"Excellent, Mrs. Hart! I am—"

"No, my lord, I am not finished," I said swiftly, not wanting to be distracted. "I wish to know why you refused to—to lie with me last night."

"Why?" He stared at me, not understanding. "I told you. You disobeyed the rules. You were the Innocent, and I the Protector, and it was my decision to make, not yours."

"You didn't let the rules concern you when you were with Lady Telford in the garden!"

"No, because there are no rules in a Belgravia garden," he said, then smiled with male smugness. "So what really concerns you is not the rules, or the Game, but how you compare yourself to another lady."

My cheeks warmed. "I know it must appear that way, but I assure you that—"

"Mrs. Hart, let me make this clear to you," he said firmly, his smile fading and his eyes darkening. "Lady Telford means less than nothing to me, while you are the most extraordinarily desirable woman I have ever met. There is no other like you."

Desirable. No man had ever called me that. It was better than being beautiful, better than being rich, and best of all was hearing it said by Lord Savage.

No, not quite. Best of all was having him look at me like that when he said it.

"The most extraordinarily, sinfully desirable woman," he repeated, leaning forward in his chair with growing impatience. "In fact, Mrs. Hart, I cannot recall another woman in my life that I have wanted with such fervent desperation as I do you."

"Do you?" I breathed. How was it that his words alone could cause the arousal now flickering through me?

"I do," he said, his voice lowering to the near growl that

only made me hotter. "From the moment I saw you in that ballroom, I've wanted you. I've wanted to fuck you, fuck you so long and hard and well that you'd be overflowing with my come, and it still wouldn't be enough. I've wanted to fuck you so you'd never stop wanting me, or thinking of the next time we'd fuck again."

"I want you now," I said, almost dizzy with longing. How could I not be, when he promised so much? "I want you even though we haven't—haven't—"

"Say it," he said, teasing me. "Say it properly. Forget you're a lady, and say it like a woman who wants a man."

I swallowed. "I want you to fuck me, and do everything you say, my lord. And—and more."

He grinned. "Are you saying you will stay, Mrs. Hart? That you will be my Innocent, and accept me as your Protector?"

"Yes," I said eagerly, my last doubts evaporating. "Oh, yes, Master."

He folded his arms over his chest, the robe slipping over his muscled biceps, and leaned back in the chair. "I'm not sure I should believe you, Eve."

"No!" I gasped with dismay. Then I realized he'd called me Eve, and that he'd seamlessly begun the Game again. "That is, Master, I regret that you do not believe me."

His smile was slow and wicked. "Perhaps I should test your obedience, Eve, and judge for myself if you are prepared to be an obliging Innocent."

"Whatever pleases you, Master." I pushed my hair back from my face and sat upright, prepared to do whatever he might ask. I hoped it would be within reason, and even if it wasn't, I'd a reckless feeling that I would do it anyway. Savage had that effect on me.

"Very well, Eve," he said. "You must prove it to me. First I would have you stop clutching that sheet in such a show of empty modesty, and bare your breasts to me."

"Yes, Master." That was easily done, and at once I dropped the sheet and shoved it down around my waist. I straightened my spine to raise my breasts higher, and smiled proudly.

"A fair beginning." His gaze immediately dropped to my breasts. "Now I want you to rub your nipples until they're stiff."

I blushed again, and gingerly covered my breasts with my hands.

He shook his head. "Not like that, Eve. Don't be gentle. I want you to pinch your nipples, pull them, twist them until they're as hard and red as ripe cherries."

Still I hesitated. It was not so much embarrassment that held me back, but simply not knowing what to do, the same as it had been earlier with Simpson. When I was very little, I had a nursemaid who'd slapped my hands if she caught them beneath the bedcovers, and the training had stuck with me since then. I didn't touch myself anywhere.

Until now. I gave my breasts another uncertain squeeze.

"Harder, Eve," Savage urged. "Remember what I did to you last night, and do it to yourself. Think of me, and do it."

Thinking of him not only made it easier, it made me imagine his hands on my breasts instead of my own, his large, slightly rough fingers squeezing and tugging at my nipples and caressing the full, pillowy flesh around them. I remembered last night, just as he'd bidden, and how I'd twisted and arched with abandon on Savage's lap, on the same chair where he sat now.

I drew my nipples out and pinched just the tips, exactly as he had done to me, and gasped at how the pleasure shot straight through my body to my core. I lifted my breasts, cradling them in my hands and then crushing them back against my ribs, and in return my breasts seemed to swell in my hands, aching with sensation.

My lips parted, and my breath broke into a ragged

panting. I pressed my thighs tightly together because I couldn't help it, thankful that the sheets still covered me below the waist so he couldn't see how shamelessly I sought to ease the growing ache there, too.

Not once did I look away from Savage. I was determined to let him see that I could be as obedient as any other Innocent, and do exactly what he asked. Besides, the sight of him stretched there before me, watching me so closely, served only to feed my desires, as if he were the prize for my performance.

Though of course, after the last time, there were no guarantees.

"My greedy little Innocent," he said. He was trying hard to remain calm, a worldly, blasé observer, but his face was flushed and his breathing was growing as irregular as my own. "You like to have your tits squeezed, don't you? Even if you must do it yourself?"

"Yes, Master." I gasped, and my fingers spread widely around my trembling breasts.

"You're so beautiful like this," he said, his voice a growl. "You're on fire now, aren't you?"

"Yes, Master," I whispered hoarsely. "I—I feel it everywhere."

"Where?" he asked. "Tell me."

"In my—my lower parts," I said. "Like last night."

"Then make yourself come, Eve," he urged. "Don't stop. Remember last night, and frig yourself until you spend."

"Oh, Master, I do not know if—"

"You can, Eve, and you will." He reached out and yanked the sheet and coverlet from the bed, baring the rest of me to his view. "Your quim's so red and open already. You're nearly there now, aren't you?"

I nodded, not trusting my voice. Slowly I slid one hand down my belly and through the thicket of chestnut curls, to the part of me that I'd only truly discovered last night.

My *quim,* that was what he'd called it, another forbidden word I'd heard but never spoken. I was slippery and swollen, and I shuddered as I explored by touch and sensation.

I rocked forward onto my knees and spread my thighs, opening my lips and building the tension further. I found the small nubbin that had been so electrifying last night, and even the most grazing of touches was almost too much. Gently I pressed the pads of my fingers over it, making tiny dancing circles, and squeezed my eyes shut to block out everything else. I was shaking, shuddering, and gasping for breath, my entire core gathered and knotted and begging for release.

"Almost there, Eve, almost there," Savage whispered hoarsely, now close beside me. "Push your fingers inside and feel how tight you are, tight and ready for me."

His voice sent me over the edge, and everything that had been wound so tightly inside me flew apart. I cried out with release, my legs turning so weak that I toppled backward against the pillows. I gasped for breath and twisted voluptuously as the last contractions shuddered through me, lost in pleasure.

Lost, but not for long. I felt the mattress sink and dip as he climbed onto it beside me. Still breathing hard, I opened my eyes, not daring to hold out my arms in welcome again.

But this time there was no question of his leaving: I'd only to look into his eyes as he rose over me to see that. All semblance of gentlemanly restraint had vanished from his face. His usually elegant features were fixed and hard, his eyes dark with lust. He'd stripped away the robe, and as he loomed naked over me, he seemed at once harshly primitive and supremely beautiful.

My gaze lowered to his cock, the veined length as hard as if it had been carved from wood, the head broad and purple, and for a fleeting moment I wondered if I'd be able to accommodate him.

He kissed me once, his mouth slashing roughly over mine as if he wanted to devour me. I threaded my fingers into the black silk of his hair, and opened my mouth wide to deepen the kiss as he pressed me into the mattress.

Though my last climax had barely passed, I was desperate for him, my need and excitement making me tremble. I knew I was supposed to wait for him to lead me, but I couldn't.

"Please, Master, now," I whispered into his ear. *"Now."*

He made a wordless growl and nipped the side of my throat. Then he reared back, grabbing me by the hips to center me on the bed. I spread my legs wide in encouragement, and shamelessly offered my still-swollen and wet quim to him. He took his cock and guided it between my nether lips. He took one quick shove to settle himself in my notch, then buried himself deep, to the end of my depth.

I cried out, not from pain but from wonder. I was so slick that he'd entered me easily, stretching and filling me in a way that I'd never imagined.

It was what I'd wanted, what I needed, and what I'd never had, and, heaven forgive me, I never wanted it to stop.

I lifted my arms to encircle his shoulders, and he seized my wrists and pushed my arms over my head, pinning my hands there. Yet, I felt freed, not trapped, as if my whole being were now centered on the place where we were joined. He ground his hips against mine, and I answered instinctively by curling my legs around his waist.

"My god, but you're tight," he said, groaning as he slammed into me, filling me again and again. "I could fuck you forever."

"Then try," I said raggedly. "I—I wouldn't stop you."

"You wouldn't be able to," he said, his breathing harsh. "You're so damned hot, Eve, you've made me like a bar of iron."

He growled into my shoulder, still holding my hands

over my head as his cock worked inside me. With each thrust his cock dragged over my sensitized channel, and I felt myself tightening around him, drawing him deeper. I was close to spending again, and I couldn't keep back the sharp little cries that matched the rhythm of his strokes.

He'd been right: this wasn't lovemaking. This was too powerful, too demanding, too insistent for mere love. This was fucking, and I couldn't get enough.

He was moving faster now, harder, pounding into me as droplets of sweat fell from his chest. His handsome face was contorted with concentration and effort.

"Come with me, Eve," he said, thrusting long and hard with his climax. "Fuck me *now*."

My torrent broke an instant after his, squeezing and milking his cock as he spent into my core. I cried and twisted beneath him, riding the waves of pleasure to their end.

As good as last night had been, it paled beside this. Everything did.

"Thank you," I managed to say, panting beneath him. "Thank you, Master."

"No," he said, and that was all. Nothing more. It wasn't exhaustion that made him silent, or the way he still was laboring to recover his breath. I could see that. This was different. Something inside him had changed, leaving his blue eyes shuttered against me.

He released my hands and pulled free of me. I caught my breath as his still-hard cock slipped from my body, leaving an emptiness I hadn't expected. But there was no doubt that he'd come inside me: his seed mingled with my juices to spill from me, warm and sticky.

"Here," he said, handing me a handkerchief that he'd taken from the bed table. "Use that."

I wished he'd kissed me, or said some little endearment, but that, apparently, was not what a Protector did.

The handkerchief was the finest Belgian linen, neatly pressed and marked with his family's crest embroidered in one corner, and almost too good to use for such a tawdry purpose. There was a neat stack of them on the table, at least a dozen, a convenience I hadn't noticed last night. I supposed it was good that he was prepared, and yet somehow that tidy stack seemed like a little too much preparation. Did he truly plan to fuck me all day, and all night as well?

I cleaned myself as best I could. My wrists burned now where he'd held them, and I flexed my fingers to make the blood return to my hands.

"Are you all right?" he asked. He was lying on his back, watching me rub my wrists. "Did I hurt your hands?"

"Not much," I lied. "They'll feel better soon."

"I didn't intend for that to happen," he said, looking at my wrists and not my face. "None of it."

I shrugged, and smiled, trying to lighten his mood.

"I didn't mind, Master," I said. "In fact I rather liked it. All of it."

He smiled bitterly, but without any humor. "A rotten sort of master I've turned out to be, eh?"

"Oh, no," I said quickly. "Not at all."

"Oh, yes." He sighed, lifting up the sheet. "Lie beside me, Eve, so I may sleep."

"Yes, Master," I murmured. I shoved my tangled hair behind my ears and carefully laid my head on the pillow beside his.

"Not like some infernal stone effigy," he said, shifting to his side to reach for me. "Here. Beside me, so I'll know where you are."

He pulled me close, drawing my bottom against his hips and his cock and keeping his arm around my waist.

"Like this, Eve," he said. "Like this."

I couldn't tell if he was being affectionate, territorial, or protective, though I supposed it didn't really matter. Whatever the reason, I liked lying this way with him, liked feeling small and safe against his powerful body. I listened as his breathing slowed and the tension eased from his body into sleep. Carefully, so that he wouldn't wake, I slipped my fingers into his so our hands were clasped.

And then, at last, I slept beside him.

SIX

This time when I woke, I knew exactly where I was: in Savage's bed, with him still soundly asleep beside me. From the path of the sun through the windows, I guessed it must be the middle of the afternoon, and I smiled, thinking how wonderfully indolent and sensual it was to still be in bed with a man at this hour of the day.

Carefully I sat upright to gaze down at him. We'd separated as we slept, and he now lay curled on his side, away from me, with one hand flung out over the edge of the bed and the other pillowed beneath his cheek. With his face relaxed, he looked much younger, almost boyish, his features softened and his hair tousled.

He also seemed much larger, spread out across the bed and occupying most of it, and I remembered with what ease that large and beautiful body had bent my own to its will, and how pleasurable it had been. Simply admiring him like this was enough to launch the first fresh flickers of arousal low in my belly, and I thought ruefully how my body must be longing to make up for years without any passion.

He'd called me greedy last night, and I couldn't deny it. I was greedy for sex, yes, but mostly I was greedy for him.

But before I could think of coaxing him into any further acts in the Game, I'd something far more urgent to tend to. I eased myself from the bed, trying not to wake Savage. There was a light wool throw folded on the chest at the foot of the bed, and I wrapped myself in it as a make-shift dressing gown while I went to find the water closet.

I opened and closed the bedroom door as quietly as I could, my bare feet making no sound on the polished wood floor of the hallway. I hoped I wouldn't meet Barry, for talking with him would be sure to wake Savage. The first door I tried led to a storage closet, but the second one opened to a very grand bathroom indeed, with diamond-patterned windows, tall mirrors, gray marble walls and floors, and an oversize marble tub in the center of the room.

All in all, it was at least double the size of the bathroom given to me, perhaps even larger. I didn't object. The size and the quantity of marble made this bath a chilly, echoing place.

Swiftly I tended to my business. As I washed my hands and then my face, I couldn't help studying my reflection in the mirror over the sink. Of course my hair was a shambles and I'd no rice powder or rouge left on my face, but I hadn't expected to see how my lips were still swollen and red from his kisses, or the way my eyes were heavy-lidded with sleep and wantonness.

Did fucking always leave its mark like this? I'd never seen such a face stare back at me in the mirror, and it was so different from my usual demeanor that it was unsettling.

If I were strolling down Fifth Avenue and met Mrs. Astor or Mrs. Vanderbilt, would they be able to tell what I'd been doing?

I grimaced, wrinkling my nose, and tried to pull the tangles from my hair. Innocent or not, Savage would have to part with me long enough to let Simpson brush and dress my hair, or else—

From behind the bedroom door came the sound of shattering glass, of a crystal tumbler being hurled against a wall.

"Eve! *Eve!*" Savage shouted. "Where the devil is she? Barry, you dog, so help me if you let her leave!"

So much for not waking him, I thought, and quickly opened the bathroom door, meaning to go to the bedroom to reassure him.

But Savage was already there, pushing his way into the doorway as soon as I opened it.

"My god, Eve," he said, grabbing me by the shoulders. "What are you doing in here?"

I jerked free, backing away and clutching the throw around me as if it were armor. "What do you think I was doing?"

"I told you specifically to stay with me," he said, biting off each word. "I told you not to leave."

"And I didn't," I said defensively, mystified by his outburst. "You told me not to wander about the house, and I haven't. I didn't think I needed your permission to come here to—to wash my face."

He raked his fingers back through his hair, clearly struggling to control his temper. His expression was dark as storm clouds, his bare chest heaving with the force of it. Yet, anger wasn't the only emotion on his face. To my surprise, I was sure I saw something very much like fear there in his eyes as well. What could a man like this— powerful, rich, titled—possibly be frightened of?

"I didn't wish to wake you, that was all," I said, calming my voice to help soothe him. I'd had experience with intemperate men: my father had flown into rages for seemingly no reason, and I'd learned that quiet explanations worked better than raging in return.

"You said you hadn't slept last night," I continued. "I didn't want to disturb you."

He tied the sash on his robe with quick, purposeful movements. "You left me, Eve."

"I left the bedroom, not you," I said, "and I was coming back directly."

He kept calling me Eve, clinging to the Game. Perhaps that was the key. I longed to reach out and put my arms around him in comfort, but didn't. Despite the physical intimacy of what we'd shared, I sensed he'd still rebuff me, and so I kept to words instead.

"Wasn't I here at the door when you opened it, Master?" I continued, striving to sound reassuring. "When you opened it, didn't you find me on the other side, waiting for you?"

It was working. The anger had faded from his face, and what was there now was only a usual male fear of looking foolish before me.

"Barry!" he called sharply. The servant appeared instantly behind him, where he'd likely been lurking all along. "Barry, the lady wishes to bathe. Draw her bath at once."

"Very well, my lord." Barry eased his way past me and Savage, and opened the taps on the tub. The water rushed out, splashing noisily against the marble.

"If you please, Master," I said, raising my voice to be heard over the water. "I'd prefer to go to my own room to wash, where I have my own things. I promise I won't be gone long, and—"

"Barry, send for Mrs. Hart's maid," he said. "Tell her to bring whatever her mistress needs for bathing."

He ignored me, instead striding to the tub and thrusting his hand into the water as Barry left us alone.

"Perfect," he said, and at last he smiled. "I believe I'll join you, Eve."

My eyes widened. "You will, Master?"

"I will," he said with relish. "This tub is quite large enough for two."

I was surprised by how quickly his mood had turned around. I didn't object, of course, for Savage like this was much better company than a furious Savage.

Perhaps his bad temper had been only because he'd awakened abruptly, combined with an aristocratic expectation to have things his way. I could understand that, for most of New York society suffered from the same conviction. Perhaps I'd exaggerated his behavior in my mind because I hadn't expected him to act like that.

And perhaps I was simply thinking too much.

I looked from him to the tub, imagining us inside it together. It was tempting, very tempting. There was plenty of room, both for bathing and for whatever else he might have planned.

Still I hung back, keeping myself cocooned in the woolen throw. I'd always regarded my baths as a place of solitude, to relax and to daydream, and I was quite certain that wasn't what he had in mind.

"Come, Eve," he said, leaning against the side of the tub. Steam rose from the warm water around him, giving him an air of mystery that he didn't need. "You've no reason to be shy with me. Not now."

"I'm not shy," I said promptly. "That is, I'm not shy, Master."

He grinned, suddenly boyish again. "I didn't think you were, Eve, even for an Innocent. But something is holding you back, yes?"

I said the first thing that entered my head: "I don't wish to drown, Master."

He chuckled, and closed the distance between us. I was glad; we'd been apart long enough, and watching the dark silk robe glide over his obviously bare skin made the heat gather inside me.

He settled one arm around my waist, pulling me closer. He kissed me, slowly and deeply, the way I liked it, and deftly eased his hand inside my throw to cup my breast. His thumb rubbed over my nipple, making it instantly harden, and I couldn't keep back the small whimper of delight that vibrated between our mouths.

"You're not thinking about drowning now, Eve, are you?" He pushed the throw farther down over my arms to bare both my breasts.

"No, Master," I said, arching my back so that my breast pushed into his palm. "Though I do wonder if the tub will overflow."

"It's a very large tub," he said, tugging the throw from around my arms. "It would take less time to fill the North Sea than that tub."

I shimmied my hips to make the throw fall to the floor. He grunted with approval, sliding his palms along the curve of my waist to my hips.

"You're far too bewitching to be an Innocent, Eve," he said, more of a growl. "I'm supposed to be the one educating you, yet you're making me forget everything I know."

"Whatever I know, I've learned from you, Master," I murmured, my breathing quickening. He eased his fingers across my notch, and I widened my stance to give him more, resting my hands against his chest for support.

"That's a pretty compliment from an Innocent," he said. "You do know how to play the Game. My god, how wet you are already."

"You *inspire* me, Master," I whispered breathlessly. He'd never comprehend how much of this wasn't a game for me, but an amazing awakening. "I cannot help myself."

"I wouldn't want you to." His kiss now was less leisurely and more ravenous, like a man who was done waiting. I understood, for I felt the same way myself.

Daring, I blindly hooked one finger into the looped knot on his sash so that the robe fell open. His cock seemed to spring into my hand, thick and hard for me already. The skin was velvety soft and heated in my hand, and as I slid my fingers along its length, he sucked in his breath.

I pulled my hand away as if it had been burned.

"I'm sorry," I said, flustered. "I didn't intend to cause you—"

"You did nothing wrong, Eve," he said, breathing hard, "and everything right. Too right. You have that effect me."

I smiled, relieved and pleased. "Then may I please touch you again, Master?"

"No, you may not," he said. "Not until we're in the tub."

Before I realized it, he'd scooped me into his arms and carried me the last few steps to the tub, setting me down into the water. He'd been right: the tub did seem nearly as large as a small sea, curved at both ends with the taps flowing in the middle. I sank back against the curved marble side, luxuriating in the warmth of the water as I watched him toss aside his robe.

I thought I could watch him by the hour and never see enough. The steam had given his skin a slight sheen, burnishing it, and accentuating the flat planes of his abdomen and the lean, bunched muscles of his shoulders and biceps. His cock stood proud and thick, ready for me, and I smiled with anticipation.

He climbed into the tub, sending little waves rippling toward me as he sank into the water, his knees rising up like islands. He held his hand out to me, and I pushed through the water to join him.

I slipped between his bent knees and leaned forward to kiss him, my hair trailing behind me in the water like a mermaid's tresses.

He smiled at me, full of temptation.

"I expect more than a kiss, Eve," he said. "Climb on my cock, and give me what we both want."

"In the water, Master?" I asked, laughing. "Can that be done?"

"With ease," he said, dragging me forward. "Here, settle yourself over me, and you'll see."

With considerable splashing, I climbed over him as he'd suggested, and balanced on my knees over his cock. I spread the lips of my quim open with one hand and carefully seated the blunt head of his cock into my opening. As eager as I was, it felt awkward and somehow upside down.

"Don't stop now," he said, his jaw clenched. "Slide down to the end."

I nodded resolutely. With my hands braced on his shoulders for balance, I sank as he'd told me to do. With my thighs held apart, I felt him sink deep into my quim, stretching me with delicious friction.

I gasped, and he smiled. "You like that, don't you?"

"I do, Master," I said, tentatively lifting myself up and then sliding back down. "I like it very much. I'd venture you do, too."

"I do," he said, putting his hands around my hips. "But I'll like this more, and so shall you."

He raised me nearly completely off his cock, then pulled me back down, driving himself as far as he could inside me with a great splash of water.

I gasped again, and dug my fingers into his shoulders as I ground against him. He seemed even larger, even hotter this way, filling every fraction of my channel. It was just short of being too much, but with him I'd happily dance this fine line between the perfect amount and a surfeit of pleasure.

"I—I believe you've filled me as far as you can, Master," I said, tipping my head back as he rocked into me again. I pressed one of my hands low on my belly, beneath the water. "I'm sure I can feel your cock here, you're so deep."

"Do you know what it does to me," he said with a groan, "hearing you say that?"

"No, Master," I said, my grin lopsided. "Tell me, please."

"It makes me want to fuck you even more," he said with a growl, driving into me again, "until you truly can feel my cock in every inch of your body."

I arched my back to take him in even deeper, my breasts bobbing on the surface of the water and my wet hair slapping against my back with each jolting stroke. Being surrounded by the lapping warm water, with each motion amplified and returned by the waves against the sides of the tub, served only to make it better.

"Say it again, Eve," he ordered, his eyes reflecting the water. "Tell me what I'm doing to you. There are few things better than a lady who'll tell me how much she likes my fucking."

Now that the first shock of it had faded, I liked hearing him speak so frankly, too, using forbidden, earthy words. To speak them myself was undeniably exciting, and made me feel all the more wicked.

"I—I like how you fuck me, Master," I said breathlessly, his thrusting setting the pace for my words. "I like how you fuck me with your—your big cock, and I—*oh*!"

As I'd spoken, he'd leaned forward to take one of my nipples into his mouth. He was suckling hard, rolling his tongue around my nipple and then grazing the tip with the edge of his teeth. The intensity stunned me, streaking directly to my core and making me tighten around his cock.

"Tell me what I've done to you," he said. "Tell me what I'm going to do again, and where you feel it."

I closed my eyes to concentrate on what he'd asked me to do.

"Look at me, Eve," he ordered roughly. "Don't hide. Tell me what I'm doing, what it makes you feel."

I dragged my lids open to meet his gaze. I was perilously close to my own climax, and to judge from the tension in his features, he was, too.

"You're—you're fucking me," I said, the words tumbling out rapidly, "and I'm riding your cock, and—and it feels so good because you're so hard and hot and—oh, Savage, I can't!"

"You can, Eve, and you will."

He grabbed my right hand and plunged it into the water, and pushed my fingers to where we were joined. I touched his cock, marveling at how I'd stretched to take him, and as he began to pull out, I instinctively circled my fingers around his cock, brushing against his balls below.

Swearing, he rubbed his thumb between my widespread lips and over my pearl as he jammed his cock hard into me. I shook from the force of it, and at last spun out as the convulsions rocked my core. He held me as I cried out, his gaze locked on mine as he watched me lose myself, over and over.

Then he held back no longer and pounded into me as his own release seized him. His eyes were wild, even ferocious, his teeth bared in such a fierce show of possession that I would have been terrified if I hadn't seen it before.

He held me tightly by my hips and I clung to him, riding out each demanding stroke. Water crashed over the side of the tub in splattering torrents, and when he came at last with a guttural roar, the sound echoed against the marble walls.

His chest heaving still, he sank back against the curve of the tub. He pulled me with him, loosely holding his arms around my back, and I went to him gladly. He closed his eyes as I feathered light kisses across his face, across those sharp cheekbones and the nose that was fit for a Roman general.

I didn't dare speak, remembering how badly that had gone last time. Instead, I was determined simply to savor this moment for what it was, and no more. I felt weightless, as if I were floating, and it wasn't due entirely to the water, either.

I rested my head against his shoulder, enjoying the warmth and feel of his chest beneath me and his arm across my back. There wasn't nearly as much water left in the tub now as when we'd started, and what remained was turning chilly.

With his fingers on my jaw, he turned my face up to his and kissed me. I hadn't expected such tenderness from him, and it gave me an extra glow inside.

"It's the damnedest thing, Eve," he said softly, "but I want you again."

"Truly, Master?" I asked playfully. I thought he was teasing, that he wasn't serious.

But he wasn't, and he was, his expression turning darkly solemn. He took my hand down into the water again, letting me feel his cock for myself. He was almost hard again, and if he wasn't as thick as he had been before he'd spent, I could have sworn I felt him swelling under my touch.

"You see how it is with you," he said. "I can think of nothing else when you're with me."

I lightly caressed him under the water, taking pleasure in giving pleasure to him.

"I thought that was why we're here at Wrenton, Master," I whispered, leaning closer to him. I couldn't understand why he considered this a problem. "We only have six days left for my education, and I've so much more to learn."

He grunted. "Five days. Today is nearly over, and cannot be counted."

Warily I drew back my hand from his cock. "Are you counting the hours until we leave so closely?"

"It's a vile habit of mine, Eve, one I cannot help." At last he smiled, but it was a polite, distant smile, with his thoughts clearly somewhere else. "I would very much enjoy continuing your education this afternoon, and would do so, too, if we hadn't other obligations."

I frowned, and before he could push me away, I retreated to the opposite end of the tub, my arms crossed over my breasts. There was a distinct chill in the room now.

"What other obligations could we possibly have?" I asked. "I thought Lady Carleigh had told us that all we must do is please ourselves."

"For the most part, yes, that is our only task." He dipped his face under the water, then pulled it back, wiping his palms back over his face and sleeking back his black hair. Droplets of water beaded on his lashes, making his eyes appear even more intensely blue, and when he smiled again, I felt a little lurch inside.

I wished he hadn't called what he'd shared with me a task. And I wished he weren't such a ridiculously beautiful man, so that it stung when he'd said that.

"But our generous hostess does have one or two little amusements planned for us for which she'll accept no excuses," he continued. "I suppose they're almost traditions by now. Dinner tonight with the assembled company is one of them. Barry!"

Immediately the bathroom door opened and the man-servant came striding in. He bowed before Savage, deftly avoided stepping in the puddles, and with brisk twists of his wrists, turned the faucets back on to refresh the bath-water.

I gave a startled yelp and sank low beneath the side of the tub, covering my breasts with my hands. I'd lived with servants my entire life, but not with *this* much familiarity. Most likely Barry had already seen me without clothes last night in Savage's bed, but then I'd been asleep, which somehow didn't make it as bad as this.

"Don't concern yourself with Barry," Savage said, comfortably stretching his arms out along the sides of the tub, his biceps glistening. "He's a modest fellow, to be sure, but he has seen so many naked ladies in his time with me that he's completely immune to the sight of another one. Isn't that so, Barry?"

"Yes, my lord," Barry said. He left us briefly, returning with a long tray that he set across the tub before Savage as a specially designed tea table. Like a tea table, too, it was set with a small lace-edged cloth, napkins, a porcelain plate of sandwiches, and another with sweet biscuits.

Warily I watched from my end of the tub. Why shouldn't Savage have paraded other naked conquests before his manservant? He was a young, unmarried gentleman in his prime, and the aristocratic set centered by the king would not expect the earl to remain celibate. The very fact that Savage was so familiar with Lady Carleigh's rituals proved he'd entertained other Innocents at other Wrenton house parties before this one.

Of course, I knew all this. I'd claimed I wanted the same, too, a lover to give me the passion my life so sorely needed, without any awkward promises of fidelity to complicate the pleasure. I'd come here to Wrenton expecting that, and I'd gotten exactly what I wanted. I'd agreed to

play Lady Carleigh's game, and so far I'd enjoyed myself—
and Lord Savage—immensely.

And hadn't I set my sights on Savage in the first place
after watching him fuck another woman?

I'd absolutely no reason to feel unhappy, or neglected,
or wounded, or jealous, or whatever it was that was plagu-
ing me now.

None.

"Would you have tea, Mrs. Hart?" asked Barry. "Or
would you prefer sherry?"

"Sherry, thank you," I said without looking up as he
brought me a glass.

"You didn't say 'Sherry, Barry,'" Savage said, bemused.
"I'm disappointed. How could you resist?"

I wasn't in the mood for his teasing. "I resisted," I said.
"Apparently I've no ear for low poetry."

"Now, Eve, don't be sarcastic with me," he warned. "An
idle observation doesn't merit sarcasm."

I sighed. "Forgive me, Master. No more sarcasm."

"Thank you, Eve," Savage said, devouring a beef sandwich with obvious relish. "You should eat something too,
you know. You must be hungry. Unless you secretly crept
out to the kitchens, you haven't eaten since last night,
either."

"You know I didn't leave," I said, a little resentful if
not sarcastic. "You've been watching me the entire time.
Master."

"True enough," he said, unperturbed as he reached for
a second sandwich. "But you should be thankful that I'm
not a harsh master. There are some here who won't let their
Innocents eat at all as part of their education, or who will
make them eat from a dish on the floor like a dog."

I frowned. "That's dreadful."

He licked a spot of mayonnaise from his finger. "'That's
dreadful, Master.'"

"That's dreadful, *Master*," I repeated, wishing I could watch him lick the mayonnaise without imagining he was licking it from me instead. "You can't fault me for not playing the Game. I've done everything you've asked."

"You have indeed, Eve," he said. "Everything, and far, far more besides."

He smiled slowly, so devastatingly and wickedly that I blushed, unable to resist his charm. How could I, when he looked at me like that, making me remember everything we'd done together?

And I *was* hungry. With my water-puckered fingers, I took a sandwich from the plate as daintily as if I were sitting in a proper drawing room, and not naked in a marble tub with an equally naked, beautiful English lord.

"Some Protectors demand complete abjection and debasement," he continued. "For that matter, some Innocents wish it, too."

"I can't believe that anyone would wish to be made to eat like a dog, Master," I said. "That makes little sense to me."

As an experiment, I tried licking mayonnaise from my fingers, too, to see if it had the same effect on him. I did it slowly, dragging the flat of my tongue along my fingers and lingering on the tips, and never taking my gaze away from his.

It worked. Clearly interested, he was watching every movement of my tongue.

Beneath the makeshift table, I felt his foot gently rubbing against my calf.

"You tempt me, Eve," he said, his voice dropping low.

I slipped my finger into my mouth and sucked the last bit of the thick, white sauce from it. "Do I, Master?"

"You do, Eve," he said, "you wicked, winsome creature."

The way he said it made me quite sure that if I could look beneath the tray, I'd see he had a cockstand again.

But, to my regretful surprise, he didn't continue what I was sure we'd begun.

"If only we weren't expected downstairs," he said with genuine regret. "Then you'd learn the punishment for eating like that."

Disappointed, I raised a single brow. "What can be more important than my education, Master?"

"Oh, I'll guarantee your education will continue downstairs, Eve," he said. "Just not perhaps in the ways that you expect. Barry, has Mrs. Hart's maid appeared yet?"

"How will my education continue, Master?" I asked, more than a bit anxiously. It was one thing to be fucked by Savage in his rooms, but I wasn't sure I was ready—if I ever would be—to do so before the other Protectors and Innocents. "What will I be expected to do at dinner?"

He smiled. "You are not to question me, Eve. Only masters have the privilege. Remember that, especially when we are with the others. Ah, here's your maid now. Simpson, isn't it?"

With a basket of my toiletries on her arm, Simpson joined us with the same lack of embarrassment as Barry had displayed. The voluptuous lady's maid curtseyed, somehow turning this simple act of deference into a seductive little dance. Her smile—and Savage's in return—was much warmer than I could have wished, nor was Savage's blatant, unrepentant nudity before the maid reassuring, either. Had Simpson once served as an Innocent for him, too?

"Mrs. Hart requires her hair washed and dressed, Simpson," Savage ordered, as if I myself were incapable of asking the maid to do it. "No pins, mind you. Her hair must be loose."

"Yes, my lord," Simpson said, setting the basket beside the tub.

"See that she is ready within the hour," he said. "I do not like to be kept waiting."

"*I* will be ready, Master," I said, even though I wasn't the one he had addressed. "You are not the only one who believes in promptness."

"Eve, Eve." He smiled indulgently. "Didn't I warn you about speaking only when addressed?"

My smile was more of a challenge. "You forbade me to ask questions, Master. You said nothing regarding statements."

He sighed with mock dismay. "Perhaps I've been too lenient," he said. "But what I've permitted here in private will not be tolerated when we're with the rest of the company."

I raised my brows quizzically, making my unspoken question so obvious that he laughed.

"I will not tolerate it," he said. "It's for your own good. You must trust me, Eve. Stubborn or obstinate Innocents will not be tolerated, and the punishments can be . . . dramatic."

Completely unself-conscious, he rose dripping from the water like some ancient river god. He was almost shockingly beautiful, his skin ruddy and glistening, and, fascinated, I watched the play of his muscles and sinews as he stepped from the tub.

I was glad to see he was no longer aroused, his handsome cock at ease. While it was unlikely that even he would wish to appear that way before the servants, I also preferred that—at least for this week—he'd keep that delectable sight for me alone.

And I was also glad to note that Simpson wasn't gawking the way I was, but instead pointedly concentrating on the tangled knots in my hair.

Barry bustled forward with a towel, patting his master dry and then slipping the robe over his broad shoulders. Savage wrapped it closed himself, and came to stand over me in my end of the tub. Simpson swiftly stepped back to stand by the wall, leaving me with my hair frothed with soap.

I looked up at Savage through my lashes. Iridescent soap bubbles had escaped to float on the water's surface, drifting around the curves of my breasts. With him, I didn't try to cover myself or hide, but let him look his fill.

"I could stand here all day gazing at you, Eve," he said gruffly. "You're that beautiful."

"Then stay, Master." I purred, shifting my legs together provocatively beneath the water. "I thought you would anyway, to watch over me."

His eyes narrowed, and too late I realized that that might not have been the wisest thing to say.

"Do not cross me, Eve," he warned softly. "What I do is for your own good. I may not stay here to watch over you now, but I will be in the next room, and you will not go anywhere without me. Do I make myself clear?"

He was serious, deadly serious, the fierce, implacable intensity of his expression more daunting than his words. I couldn't imagine what danger threatened me so gravely here in this remote noble house, far from any city, but when Savage looked at me like that, I didn't doubt that it existed.

And that I'd be an utter fool not to do as he had said.

I curled a wet lock of hair behind my ear, pausing with my palm turned upward.

"Yes, Master," I said softly. "I understand."

He bent down and took my jaw in his hand, holding it so firmly that I'd never escape, and kissed me roughly. Energy and emotion and white-hot heat coalesced in my mouth, scorching me with such power that when he finally released me, I was shaken and trembling with a desire that had become alarmingly familiar.

Yet, he held my gaze for a long moment after that, keeping me under his spell, before he abruptly turned away.

"Be ready," he said curtly, and left, closing the door as he did.

Be ready for what? I wondered, dazed as I stared after him. Likely he meant only to be dressed and ready to accompany him downstairs, but I wasn't sure. With Savage I seldom was.

"Don't you worry, ma'am," Simpson said, returning to scrub at my hair. "I'll have you ready before Mr. Barry's done with his lordship."

"I'm sure you will, Simpson," I murmured, still looking toward the door he'd closed behind him.

My body was taut with wanting, twisting and tightening low in my belly, and I'd wager that if I had looked down, I'd have seen that my nipples had hardened for him, too. It almost frightened me, how strongly he could affect me with only a kiss.

Almost, but not quite, for the rest of me was so wildly excited by that same kiss that nothing else mattered.

"There now, ma'am," Simpson said with the forced bright cheerfulness favored by all lady's maids, even the voluptuous ones. "If you'll but tip your head back, then I'll rinse the soap away, and we'll be done."

Obediently I sank back into the warm water, sliding forward across the smooth marble, with Simpson's face upside down above me.

"Tell me, Simpson," I said as I sat up again, then stood. "How well do you know Lord Savage?"

"Oh, well enough, ma'am," she said blandly, holding a towel open for me as I stepped from the tub. "His lordship's a great favorite in this house."

I stood while Simpson dried me. "I mean what do you know *of* him?"

Simpson paused with the towel in her hands.

"I never did lie with him, ma'am, if that's what you're trying to say," she said bluntly. "He's not one of the gentlemen that don't bring a lady of his own to be his Innocent. He's no need of us servants, not when he can have any fine lady he pleases."

I blushed furiously, knowing I was now in that category. "Thank you, Simpson."

"As you say, ma'am." Simpson gave a skeptical sniff as she helped me into my dressing gown. "But if I had a man even half as hot-blooded as his lordship, I'd want to know which doxy's quim he'd been in the habit of sticking his peggo into before me."

"His lordship is hardly my man, Simpson," I said quickly, ignoring the rest of what the maid had said. "That is, for these few days he is my master, and I'm his Innocent, but that's only a diversion, a conceit, for the sake of Lady Carleigh's game."

"I'll not stop you from believing what you wish, ma'am," Simpson said firmly as she began to draw the silver-backed brush through my hair, lifting up each long stroke to help the hair to dry. "But how his lordship looks at you—why, it sends chills up and down my spine, ma'am."

"Simpson, please," I protested, even as I flushed again. This was like having Hamlin here with me—even though Hamlin would likely rather perish than speak so freely of quims and peggos. "Don't romanticize."

"I'm not romanticizing, ma'am," Simpson said. "I'm only speaking true. In all the years that his lordship's been coming here as a guest, I don't recall him ever treating a lady like he treats you, and that includes his poor lady-wife, too."

"Lady Savage?" Quickly I turned around to face her. "What was she like, Simpson?"

"A true lady, ma'am, and ever so beautiful," Simpson said. "But she was as high-strung as a racehorse, and impetuous, too. Her maid told such stories of how her lady-ship would carry on!"

"What kind of stories?" I asked, intrigued. It was almost impossible to imagine Lord Savage as anyone's husband, yet here it sounded as if his countess might have been every bit his equal. "Did his lordship bring her here with him to play the Game?"

"Oh no, ma'am," Simpson said, clearly surprised that I had asked such a question. "He would never have brought her ladyship here for that. The only times they visited here together was when there was no mischief. To be sure, her ladyship would've enjoyed herself mightily, but his lordship would not have liked watching it. Not that he was ever here himself for the Game before she passed, neither. 'Twas only after that Lady Carleigh persuaded him to come, and ever since, too."

I tried to turn my head to see Simpson's expression. "How exactly did Lady Savage carry on? Was she that scandalous?"

"Oh, that's not for me to say, ma'am." Simpson laughed nervously. "Forgive me, ma'am, how I run on! I've already told more than's proper about them that's my betters, not if I wish to keep my place here at Wrenton. If his lordship heard me . . ."

"No, no, Simpson, please," I said, pressing for more. "Is there something I should know?"

But the maid only shook her head. "No, ma'am, nothing. Your hair's nearly dry. I'll go fetch your costume."

"But, Simpson, I would—"

"I'll return directly, ma'am," the maid said, hurrying from the room and away from my question.

I sighed. Servants so often did this, offering a tantalizing scrap of information from belowstairs, only to draw back when pressed. Usually this was just tattle and whispered hearsay, without any value, as every good mistress knew. But sometimes there could be a kernel of truth in what had been overheard and gleaned, and though I knew

I shouldn't encourage servants to gossip about their superiors, I did wish Simpson had continued with whatever secrets she knew of Lord Savage's late wife.

More likely there weren't any. My own father had not liked to speak of my mother, who had died when I was born. Given how young Lady Savage must have been when she'd died, her husband probably didn't wish to be reminded of her death, either: a tragic circumstance, not a mysterious secret.

Besides, by the time the maid returned with my costume, the moment for confidences had passed. I dressed quickly in the same simple costume as before, with Simpson coaxing my long hair into loose curls over my shoulders and down my back, the way Savage preferred.

Simpson had also brought me a fresh pair of silk stockings and a different pair of evening slippers. These were among my favorites, black silk satin embroidered with silver lilies and accented with rhinestones, the heels curved and high. Most nights they would scarcely be seen beneath the long, sweeping hem of an evening gown, but tonight they'd be on display as my only ornaments, an extravagant contrast to the nearly transparent costume.

"There now, ma'am, you're quite the picture," Simpson said with satisfaction. "His lordship will have to look sharp to keep the other gentlemen from buzzing too close to you."

"His lordship says that Lady Carleigh has a special entertainment for us tonight," I said. "He said it was a kind of tradition with her. Have you any notion of what it is?"

Simpson rolled her eyes. "I do indeed, ma'am. They've already been preparing for it in the kitchen, and I promise you'll be righteous surprised. New guests always are."

But before she could explain more, the door swung open and Savage rejoined us. Few gentlemen wore evening clothes as well as he did, and I couldn't think of another man who gave them such a rakish, reckless air. The stark contrast of black and white suited him perfectly with his dark hair and pale eyes, and everything was cut and tailored to display his broad shoulders and athletic frame.

He was so elegantly, flagrantly male that I almost sighed at the sight of him, and knowing I would be going downstairs on his arm gave me a quick little thrill of excitement—an excitement that only increased as his gaze raked me from head to toe.

"Well done, Simpson," he said with approval. "And promptly on time, too."

He stepped forward and took my hand. "You make the perfect Innocent, Eve," he said with a smile. "You'll have all the other women in a rage of jealousy when they see you, and all the men in rut."

I laughed, but he only shook his head.

"I'm serious, Eve," he said. "I'll have to keep you locked to my side, or risk losing you to another."

"I don't think so, Master," I said. "What other gentleman could possibly win me away from you?"

"Hah," he said, his expression turning grim. "You will have nothing to say about it. If some other bastard wants you, he'll try to claim you, and it will be up to me to fend him off."

I glanced up at him suspiciously, not sure if he was teasing. "That sounds rather primitive."

"It is," he agreed. "But that will be the least of tonight. Whatever else happens, stay with me. Don't question me, or venture any opinions, or speak to any other masters. If you can do that, then you should be fine. If you can't, well, then, I cannot answer for what might happen."

He tucked my hand into the crook of his arm, a gesture that I found touchingly protective. I didn't doubt that he'd watch over me at dinner, since he already had been doing exactly that ever since he'd claimed me as his own. The least I could do was to follow his instructions.

"You will at least try to obey, Eve, won't you?" he asked. Now he looked more worried than threatening, his dark brows drawn together in such a way as to suggest he didn't believe my obedience was even possible.

The insecurity of it made me smile. No, *he* made me smile, this staggeringly handsome man on my arm.

"I will, Master," I said softly. "You need not doubt me. For you, I will do it."

SEVEN

Despite Savage's insistence on being on time, we were the last to appear in the dining room. It seemed far longer than a single night ago that I, too, had been the last to join the company, consciously wishing to make my entrance after everyone else had already appeared. I thought of how proud I'd been of the pale evening gown I'd worn last night, and how seductively revealing I'd considered it.

I came down the stairs now with the same assurance as I had last night, confident that I'd be the most beguiling woman in the room. Tonight, however, I was wearing not a costly Parisian gown but a wisp of a shift that was only marginally better than being completely naked. I had no jewels in my hair or on my person except the rhinestones on my shoes. My breasts, my hips, my bottom, and the dark thatch of hair above my quim were all on display through the sheer fabric, a blatant invitation to anyone who cared to look.

I was blushing—I couldn't help that—but I managed to stand proudly, my head high and my long, unbound hair rippling down my back. I'd shed the refined Mrs. Hart along with my Poiret gown, and embraced my role as the Innocent Eve. With a man like Savage beside me, why wouldn't I?

Although he'd said the rules permitted it, I doubted very much that any gentleman would be willing to challenge Savage for his rights to me. He was without question the most handsome and seductive gentleman in the house, but more important, he was also the most powerful in terms of rank and fortune.

Besides, he was taking his role as Protector very seriously. He had already proved to Lord Blackledge and the others how much he'd wanted me through the auction. Beginning my "education" seemed only to have made him desire me more, and he seemed determined to make it known.

When we came to the door of the dining room, he placed his arm around my waist, his hand casually brushing the underside of my breast, and I couldn't help but sway into his caress.

"Remember what I told you, Eve," he said softly, adding a quick nip to the shell of my ear for emphasis. "Every man in this room wants you, but I can't protect you if you don't obey."

"Yes, Master," I whispered. "Because there is only one man here that I want to fuck."

That made him smile, a quick smile of approval, and of the white-hot lust I'd hoped to inspire. He pulled me closer still, drawing my bottom against his thigh, and I rubbed against him like a cat—or a perfectly obedient Innocent—begging for more.

I was certain we couldn't have made our intimacy more obvious, or his possession of me more definite.

Until, that is, we took our seats at the dining table. Demurely I unfolded my napkin and laid it across my lap, and only then did I look around at the other guests.

To my left sat Mr. Henery, a stout, bearded mine owner from the north who was mercifully too engrossed in his own Innocent and his wine to pay any attention to me. Most of the masters and mistresses wore evening dress like Savage, but there were several who hadn't made the effort, coming directly from their beds in haphazardly tied robes and dressing gowns. All the Innocents were dressed in the same revealing costumes as last night, with a few variations.

At one end of the table, Lady Wessex sat on the lap of Mr. Parkhurst, my mild-mannered partner from last night's dinner. The front of her ladyship's costume had been cut away, with her sizable breasts jutting through two jaggedly cut openings. Mr. Parkhurst was now suckling one of these, noisily grunting like a piglet at a teat, while Lady Wessex happily ground her bottom against his crotch.

Directly across the damask cloth, Lady Carleigh sat beside her husband, the two of them locked in a voracious kiss. As a mistress, she wore a yellow silk dressing gown, which Lord Carleigh had shoved aside as he roughly squeezed one breast, his fingers digging deep into her soft flesh.

I was pleasantly surprised to see them together, especially since they'd both left with Innocents of their own last night. I knew that infidelity was a part of the Game, but it was still rather charming to see a husband and wife so obviously aroused by each other.

Then I glanced beneath the table, and realized that the Carleighs' Innocents were indeed present. The dark head of Lady Carleigh's Innocent was nestled between her open legs, his hands forcing her thighs widely apart as he lapped at her writhing quim. Lord Carleigh's Innocent was similarly engaged, his fingers tangled in her hair as she bobbed over his cock, taking him deep into her throat as she fondled and cupped his balls in her nimble fingers.

His lordship could not bear much more of this, and suddenly he broke away from his wife's kiss and held his Innocent's head still, not letting her pull back as he drove hard into her mouth. With a bellow he came, his face flushed and florid as he bucked in the chair. His Innocent—a woman whom I now recognized as the Honorable Mrs. Bilton—crawled up to perch on his thigh, grinning triumphantly as she wiped his spendings from her lips before she kissed his gasping mouth.

The sight of Lord Carleigh's climax must have incited his wife as well. She pushed back her dressing gown to squeeze a breast in each hand, and arched against her Innocent's mouth, finishing with a series of mewling cries before she, too, sank back into her chair. Mrs. Bilton then leaned over and kissed her, too, a kiss that the viscountess eagerly returned, their lips parted and their tongues busily engaged.

But Lord Carleigh was busy, too. Presented with Mrs. Bilton's bottom as she leaned forward to kiss his wife, he promptly flipped up the hem of her costume to bare the lady's bottom. He made a great show of licking his fingers until they dripped with his saliva, and then he thrust them deep into Mrs. Bilton's core. Mrs. Bilton didn't flinch at this assault, but merely spread her legs apart to ease it, her bottom squirming to accommodate the viscount's fingers more completely.

Up and down the table, other guests applauded this performance and cheered with profanity-laced encouragements. Meanwhile, the footmen, clad in formal Georgian-style livery with knee breeches and white stockings, continued incongruously to serve the next course, replacing one plate with another.

"Did you enjoy that, Eve?" Savage asked mildly, sipping his wine as if this were any other dinner. "I know you do like to be the spectator."

I stared at him, at a loss for what he'd consider a proper reply. For once, the truth failed me: I was too shocked by what I'd just witnessed to say whether I enjoyed it or not. I'd known that Lady Carleigh and her friends were considered the fast set—fast enough to have house parties like this one—but I still hadn't expected our hostess and host to be quite this shameless.

"This is only a portion of their amusements here, you know," Savage said when I didn't answer. "I'd guess they've been at it all day with Mrs. Bilton and whoever the male might be below the table. They've always been a sociable pair. Their bed is enormous, specially designed for such frolics."

For once I was certain that he wasn't teasing me. I'd just seen the proof across the table.

Nor did I wish to reflect on how he knew the exact dimensions of Lord and Lady Carleigh's bed, any more than I wanted to know exactly how sociable he'd been with this sociable pair.

"Yes, Master," I said finally.

I wasn't sure what I was agreeing to, but at least it was a safe answer. I looked down at the quail on my plate, floating in a rich puddle of rosy-pink Burgundy sauce, my appetite gone.

I'd believed that last night with Savage had changed me, that I'd become much more free by pretending I was Eve.

Evidently I'd been wrong.

"That's not the final performance by our fair hostess, either," Savage continued, eating his dinner with no difficulty. "I do not wish to spoil her surprise, but I will say that we anticipate it. Isn't that so, Lady Carleigh?"

"I'll never forgive you if you tell, Savage," the viscountess replied, though so merrily that I suspected she'd be perfectly happy if Savage did in fact reveal the great secret. She was dining with gusto, completely recovered from her earlier interlude. The young man who'd so recently been lapping between her legs now stood behind her chair, his hands behind his back. Clearly, the viscountess had chosen him for reasons other than any aristocratic lineage—reasons that were abundantly obvious through his thin silk trousers.

"I like my secrets, Savage," the viscountess continued. "Though I am delighted that my surprises have left such a mark upon you."

"My dear lady," Savage said, "they are a memory I will never forget."

"Exactly as it should be!" she exclaimed, smiling slyly across the table at me. "But tell me, how goes the education of your own sweet Innocent?"

I smiled in return. I opened my mouth to reply, then remembered at the last instant that this might be against the rules. Instead, I glanced at Savage, silently hoping he'd guide me.

"It's not necessary for you to reply, Eve," he said mildly. "The question was directed to me, not to you. But your excellent deference is answer enough. You see, Lady Carleigh, what progress I have made with my Eve."

"Eve?" Lord Carleigh said, his eyes widening with amusement. "Trust you, Savage, to give such a name to your Innocent! Tell me, Eve, would you like to entertain my serpent in your luscious garden?"

"She would not, Carleigh." Savage's expression remained pleasant, but the warning in his voice was unmistakable, or at least it was to me. "Nor would I."

Relief washed over me. The last thing I wished was to be forced to perform before the others as Lady Carleigh just had.

But the viscountess herself was unconvinced.

"Oh, please, Savage," she said, wheedling. "Your Innocent is here for experience, for adventure. She told me so herself, even before I invited her to Wrenton. What fun is it for her to be locked up with you the entire week?"

The edge sharpened in Savage's voice as he said, "I believe Eve is receiving her share of experience and adventure in my company, Lady Carleigh. Recall that she is mine to educate."

Lady Carleigh made a coy little moue of dismay.

"But Carleigh and I were expecting you both to join us in our bedroom later," she said, pausing to drink deeply from her wine. "I'd rather set my heart on it, Savage, and you know I don't like to be denied."

Savage shrugged. "Then it shall be a novel experience for you, Laura, won't it?"

I didn't miss how he'd used the viscountess's given name. Yet, while most times this would be a sign of fond intimacy, now it seemed unmistakably patronizing, as if he were addressing an overindulged child.

And, like a spoiled child, Lady Carleigh appeared not to notice.

"I don't know why you won't share with us, Savage," she said. "You've never been so selfish with your Innocents before."

"Perhaps because Eve is more deserving than the others were," Savage said, almost as if it had only just occurred to him. He glanced down at me, tracing the backs of his fingers up along my bare arm and idly across the top curve of my breast through the sheer fabric. "She's quite ignorant, you know. Her previous education has been so woefully lacking."

With my gaze lowered to watch his hand trail over my skin, I prayed the others wouldn't see how wildly aroused I was even by so simple a touch from him. His fingers slipped lower, grazing my nipple. At once it tightened and thrust forward, and without thinking I sucked in my breath as sensation rippled through my body.

"Look at her!" Lord Carleigh exclaimed, leaning across the table to peer hungrily at me. "You may think she needs more education, Savage, but I'd guess she's already learned more than a lesson or two."

"Oh, she has," Savage said. "But I've many more lessons to teach her."

The way he said it made me catch my breath again and try to ease the delicious arousal building inside me. It amazed me that Savage could do this to me with only words, and I longed to leave the dining room and race back upstairs with him to his bed.

But, to my dismay, others could see the effect Savage had on me, too—one other in particular.

At the end of the table, where I'd somehow overlooked him, Lord Blackledge rose from his chair and came to stand behind Lord Carleigh.

Following closely behind him was his Innocent, the petulant girl with the white-blond hair. She wasn't being petulant now, for a scarf of black silk was tied across her mouth like a gag, the silk pulled so tightly that it bared her teeth in a contrived grimace. Her wrists were also bound with silk and pulled behind her back, forcing her back to arch and her breasts to thrust higher. The last part of her ensemble was a close-fitting black leather collar with a gold link in the front. Attached to the link was a chain— a chain that the baron kept tightly wrapped around his fist like a leash to make her follow.

It reminded me of what the woman in the entr'acte had worn around her neck last night, and how her partner had also used the chain to jerk her into obedience. Yet, as uncomfortable as this must have been, the gagged woman didn't appear to be in any real distress. She wasn't fighting her predicament; on the contrary, in a strange way she seemed to be enjoying it, undulating against her restraints with exaggerated movements and batting her eyes at the other Protectors when she knew the baron wasn't watching.

I remembered what Simpson had told me, that many of the "extra" Innocents delighted in their roles, and were well paid for their performances, too. But I was still glad I wasn't one of them, and with a shudder I imagined the stocky baron in the same position as the performers, pounding his cock into the blond Innocent's quim as he jerked on her collar.

But now Lord Blackledge had little interest in his Innocent, instead staring so blatantly at my breasts and my rosy, thrusting nipples that it took all my self-control not to lift the napkin from my lap to cover and shield myself.

"We don't need your empty assurances, Savage," he said with a contemptuous snarl. "We all can see from here how primed you have her. How many times did you fuck her before you came downstairs? Two, three?"

Savage lowered his chin, an ominous look, and set down his knife and fork.

"Suffice to say that it was more times than you could muster, Blackledge," he said. "Not that it is any affair of yours."

"You know the rules." Blackledge's face turned red at the insult. "Just because you bought her in that trumped-up auction doesn't mean you can keep her to yourself."

"The rules say he can, Blackledge," said Lord Carleigh with a sigh. "It's part of being a Protector. But it would be gentlemanly if he at least shared some of the details of his Innocent's charms. At least have her bend over so we'd a peek at that luscious notch of hers, Savage."

"Why, I'd bet her cunt's still soaking wet from wanting more cock," Blackledge said. "I'd bet a hundred pounds that you could get her off in under two minutes, she's that close now."

Lord Carleigh's expression lit at the suggestion. "Yes, yes, Savage," he said. "You've never been shy with an Innocent before. Take her right now on the table with her legs in the air, and I'll bet Blackledge here two hundred that you can make her spend in less than a minute. If any man can make her scream for it, it's you, Savage, eh?"

With relish he pulled out his large gold pocket watch, flipped open the case, and set it on the table, ready to count off the minute. The others at the table roared at the idea of such a wager, and thumped the table with their palms so hard that the crystal danced on the cloth.

Even as Savage's fingers continued to graze my breast, I pressed into his arm, hoping he truly would be my Protector and continue to defend me against the others. I could imagine all too easily how Lord Blackledge would want to determine whether he'd won or not, and I wanted none of it.

Of course, there was no doubt that I *was* wet, with Savage beside me. He was ignoring the other men as if the question had already been decided, and instead was tracing idle little circles over my skin that were only inflaming me more. There wasn't much doubt, either, that he could make me spend in less than the required minute. How could I not when he did this to me?

But I didn't want either Lord Blackledge or Lord Carleigh pawing between my legs to discover the extent of my arousal, and as for having Savage fuck me here before the others the way Lady Carleigh already had done—no amount of pretending for the sake of the Game was going to change my mind.

I could only pray that Savage thought so, too.

In desperation I looked away from Lord Carleigh to his

wife, hoping the viscountess would stop her husband. But Lady Carleigh's chair was now empty, and, even more surprising, her Innocent remained where she'd abandoned him, standing beside her pushed-out chair.

The men—and the ladies as well—around the table seemed to sense my anxiety like any other pack of ravening jackals, and it served only to stir their excitement and anticipation.

"It's only sporting, Savage," called Lord Wessex from farther down the table. "All in the spirit of the week, don't you know."

Savage ignored him. Instead, he reached out to Lord Carleigh's watch and decisively snapped the case shut beneath the palm of his hand.

"No," he said. "No bets, not with Eve."

The others groaned with disappointment.

"Come now, Savage," Lord Carleigh coaxed. "Where's the harm in a little wager?"

"Then share her," Lord Blackledge said. His hands were already flexing and twitching with unpleasant anticipation, as if he couldn't wait to touch me himself. "You know you're going to fuck her again. Why not let the rest of us see how your Innocent spends?"

"I can find out how wet she is for you, my lords," offered Mr. Henery, seated beside me. His face and his courage were flushed with wine, his voice loud with it. "It's the work of a moment."

Before I could react, he'd grabbed the napkin from my lap, yanked aside my costume, and shoved his hand between my thighs.

Horrified, I struck at his hand and tried to pull the hem of my gown back down and twist away from him. All around me the others were laughing and shouting encouragement to Mr. Henery. Laughing at my reaction, he'd risen from his chair to stand over me, his face flushed above his beard as I pushed and flailed at his hands as hard as I could.

Abruptly Henery's mouth popped open with surprise as Savage grabbed him by the arm. He spun Henery around and away from me, and as Henery tried to regain his balance, Savage's fist caught him under his jaw. It was a single uppercut, powerful and efficient and without mercy, and more than enough to make Henery's head snap back. He staggered backward, reeling, and Savage followed, punching Henery again with such force that he toppled to the carpeted floor, his body following with a dull thud.

But Savage wasn't done. He threw himself down on the other man, and grunting with exertion, the two of them rolled across the carpet to the bare stone floor with the tails of their evening jackets flailing behind them.

I watched with my hands clutched tightly together and pressed to my mouth. Around me, women screamed and men swore, and everyone crowded together for a better view of the fight. A wineglass was knocked to the floor, splashing red wine across the pale carpet, and no one noticed. Even the servants clustered together in the doorway, unable to resist the rare sight of their betters fighting.

Finally, Savage pinned the other man to the floor with his legs and began to rain blows upon Henery's face. Henery tried to defend himself, blindly swinging his fists, but Savage's attack was so ruthless that Henery was soon using his hands more as a shield than as a weapon, curling his arms over his face. There was already blood from his nose splattered across his shirt front, bright red on stark white, and on Savage's cuffs, too, above the tiny gold serpents on his onyx links.

None of the others tried to stop Savage, not wanting to risk having him turn toward them. His expression was set and merciless, with only his pale eyes revealing the extent of his fury.

I had never seen a gentleman behave like this. No, I'd never witnessed *any* man so deliberately determined to punish another with such primal violence.

"For God's sake, Savage, enough!" ordered Lord Carleigh. "Stop at once!"

But Savage didn't stop, and the viscount curtly waved for three footmen to intervene. The footmen hovered indecisively to one side, torn between following their master's orders and the grave consequences that could result from laying their hands upon an earl.

Tears of fear and frustration slipped down my cheeks as I watched. I knew I wasn't supposed to speak, and yet how could I not? This was not the Savage I knew, the man who had kissed me tenderly as he'd introduced me to passion. This was madness, a terrible madness, and if no one stopped Savage now, I feared he might kill the other man.

"Stop, Savage, please!" I cried at last, my voice echoing oddly in my ears. "Please, please, no more! No *more*!"

At once he drew back, his head whipping around toward me as he still crouched over Henery. His black hair was disheveled across his forehead and his pale eyes were as wild as a wolf's, his chest heaving from exertion. A tiny trickle of blood glistened in the corner of his mouth where his lip had been split.

I brushed away my tears with my fingers and took a gulping hiccup of a sigh.

"Please, Master," I said, barely remembering to call him that. "I beg you, please—please stop."

He gave a quick jerk of his head, shaking his hair back from his face, then used both hands to smooth it back. He took a deep breath, visibly collecting himself, and rose to his feet in a single graceful motion that belied his earlier violence. He straightened the satin lapels of his jacket, and shot his cuffs, briefly frowning at the crimson bloodstains.

He didn't look back at Henery, who had rolled to his side, groaning, as the footmen now rushed to attend him. He didn't look at anyone other than me, coming to stand directly before me.

He was so powerfully male that I felt it viscerally, a primal desire to mate that was almost impossible to resist. It shocked me how much I wanted him now, splattered as he was with another man's blood, and yet I couldn't deny the wet, welcoming heat and fullness in my quim, longing to be filled by his cock.

There was a single bruise on his left cheek, more likely caused from striking the stone floor than any stray blow from Henery. As lightly as I could, I reached up to touch my fingertips to the bruised skin, a show of sympathy for so much more than the injury alone.

"You're mine, Eve," he said, his breathing still ragged and his voice gruff. "Only mine."

His threaded his battered fingers through my hair and closed them together into another fist, holding me fast as he bent to kiss me. His mouth ground against mine, hard and aggressive, and I tasted not only the metallic tinge of blood from his lip but the rawness of his need and the power that went with it.

That much I understood, for I felt it, too, roiling inside me like an undeniable force. I thought I'd been aroused earlier, but it was nothing—*nothing*—like what was twisting and curling through me now.

"Savage," said Lord Carleigh curtly. "A word, if you please."

Savage took his time ending the kiss, giving me one last small nip before he finally dragged his mouth away from mine. Although he let me turn to face the viscount, he kept his arm possessively around my waist; it was a small gesture that I welcomed, and was grateful for.

The others were beginning to return to their seats around the table, laughing nervously and chattering too loudly as the footmen refilled their glasses. All were pretending that nothing untoward had just happened, but every ear was listening to their host, eager to hear what he'd say to the earl.

What the viscount did first was clear his throat.

"Lord Savage," he began. "Mrs. Hart. I—my wife and I, that is—we can't have this sort of thing occur in our house."

"Nothing occurred," Savage said, his voice purposefully bland and a bit bored as well. "Henery was warned. He chose not to heed that warning."

Uneasily Lord Carleigh glanced over his shoulder, back to Mr. Henery. Henery was sitting (or had been propped) upright in a chair near the wall with a servant attending him on either side, his head tipped back with a bag of ice on his nose and a glass of whiskey in his hand as a restorative.

"He'll be well enough," Savage said dismissively. "His kind always is."

Lord Carleigh shook his head. "I know the man's in trade, Savage, but he is a guest of mine and I—"

"I'd say Henery's not the one to blame, my lord," interrupted Lord Blackledge, his gagged Innocent following him like a dog on a leash. "I'd say it's Lord Savage's Innocent that's at fault. She's the one who deserves a thrashing for what she's caused."

"She's not yours, Blackledge," Savage said sharply, his bored manner dropping away like a mask. "There's no fault with her."

"You've been too gentle with her, Savage," the baron said, goading Savage. "Education must include punishment, you know. It's the only way an Innocent will learn to be properly grateful to her master."

Blackledge's gaze raked over me. I hated having him look at me like this, having him picture me bound and chained like his own Innocent, and I shrank against Savage.

Automatically his arm tightened around my waist, drawing me closer. I felt the tension in him coiling more tightly, and I feared he'd lash out at Blackledge the same way as he had done with Henery.

The baron would be a much more challenging opponent. He wasn't drunk, and he was much larger and stronger than Henery. Worst of all, he was a bully, and he wanted to fight. Even as unworldly as I was in such matters, I couldn't miss the antagonism simmering between the two men, threatening and dangerous.

"I require no advice from you, Blackledge," Savage said, biting off each word. "She is mine, not yours."

Swiftly Lord Carleigh stepped between them.

"I'll have no more brawling in my house," he said firmly. "You are here at Wrenton as my guests for pleasure and amusement, not for this kind of common, alehouse bravado."

The baron bowed to the viscount. As the lowest ranking of the three men, he had no choice.

"Forgive me, my lord," he said to Lord Carleigh, though without so much as a hint of contrition to match his apology. "I intended no slight. I was merely following the rules of Lady Carleigh's game that permit one Protector to challenge another for the sake of an Innocent."

"You press too far, Blackledge," Lord Carleigh said. "I know as well as you do what your intentions were, and they have nothing to do with my wife's rules. Now I must ask you and your Innocent to return to the table, and permit Lord Savage to, ah, compose himself."

"As you wish, my lord." Blackledge bowed again, this time pointedly to Lord Carleigh alone. As he backed away, he vented his frustration on his Innocent, giving an extra jerk on her leash to make her stumble after him.

Reluctantly Lord Carleigh turned back to Savage.

"I'll thank you, too, Savage, to keep your temper in check," he said. "No more fisticuffs, eh? You're an old acquaintance. You know the rules of the Game. Laura will have my head if there's any of her precious bric-a-brac broken in a melee." Then he smiled weakly, trying to turn it all into a joke.

But Savage was in no mood for joking. "What are you trying to say to me in your ludicrously complicated way, Carleigh?"

Lord Carleigh's face reddened. "Only that you, ah, mind yourself and Mrs. Hart. Be a good chap, yes?"

" 'A good chap'?" repeated Savage, leaving no doubt that there were few things he'd be less inclined to be.

"Well, yes," Lord Carleigh said uneasily. "I'm glad you understand, eh? I do appreciate that—"

He was interrupted by a footman standing at the doorway, beating on a drum as a fanfare to gather everyone's attention.

"Let it be known," he called in a solemn, booming voice. "Her ladyship is served!"

Four other footmen entered the room carrying an enormous platter on their shoulders. Lying in the center of the platter was Lady Carleigh, completely naked and surrounded by a bed of succulent sliced strawberries.

Relieved by such an amusing distraction, her guests began to cheer and applaud the viscountess's audacity, rising from their chairs to see more—and there was so much of her pale, voluptuous body to see.

In place of clothing, the pastry cook belowstairs had piped elaborate curls and flourishes of whipped cream, accentuated with more strawberries, across Lady Carleigh's full breasts and the dip of her navel, which enhanced her charms far more than it hid them. The process must have tickled, too, since she was still laughing as the platter was carefully set down in the center of the dining table.

"Fine, fresh strawberries, fine, oh!" she cried gleefully, mimicking a street hawker's call. She beckoned to her guests, raising her hands with care so that the whipped cream wouldn't slide off. "Fine strawberries and cream for everyone! Come, come, Protectors and Innocents alike, and eat your fill!"

Eagerly the viscountess's guests swarmed around her, men and women, Protectors and Innocents, bending down to lick the cream from her body. She laughed and writhed with lubricious delight, clearly relishing the feel of so many tongues lapping at her skin.

I watched, wide-eyed. So this must be Lady Carleigh's grand entertainment, the one that Savage had said he'd never forgotten—and no wonder, either.

"Ah, you see my dear Laura calls," Lord Carleigh said with obvious relief. "Mustn't keep the viscountess waiting, eh?"

With a hint of a bow, he left Savage and me and hurried to join his wife. He pushed aside the others crowding around the platter and bent over to kiss Lady Carleigh. With husbandly devotion, he licked one of her nipples clean, giving the plump flesh an extra nip with the edges of his teeth, which made her squeal. Then he opened his trousers and pulled out his cock, already half erect. He scooped a handful of the whipped cream from Lady Carleigh's thigh and lavished it like frosting along the length of his stiffening cock.

Before he'd finished, his Innocent, Lady Bilton, had appeared and dropped to her knees before him. He thrust his cock between her open lips and she sucked it with greedy enthusiasm, the sticky whipped cream oozing from the corners of her mouth as she fondled his ballocks at the same time.

I watched, intrigued. After Savage had kissed and licked my quim until I'd climaxed last night, I'd wondered if there was an acceptable—and pleasurable—way for me to reciprocate. Here was the proof that there was, and my imagination raced as I considered the possibilities.

But Savage did not feel the same.

"I've seen enough," Savage said, his voice still curt. "No one will notice us if we leave now."

EIGHT

❧

Savage's hand closed firmly over my fingers, making it clear that I would be leaving the dining room with him. Not that I'd object; I'd no wish to stay with the others, either, with the prospect of being alone again with Savage before me.

He led me swiftly from the dining room and up the stairs toward his rooms. His stride was so long and determined that I was breathless with hurrying, half running in my heeled slippers to keep pace with him across the polished floors and thick carpets and past the curtseying parlor maids and bowing footmen.

He offered no explanation of his haste, no apology for his earlier behavior, not even any small talk. He didn't so much as look down at me at his side. His expression was dark and implacable, offering nothing, with his thoughts turned inward and away from the rest of the world, including me. I'd already realized that his reticence wasn't part of the Game, part of playing the role of a master, but instead was part of him. I recognized it for what it was, because it was part of me as well. I'd been alone with him all of the last night and day, and had done wicked, shameless, wonderful things with him that would once have made me blush, and yet I still knew next to nothing of him as a man.

Nothing. And that, I did know, was exactly as he wished it to be.

As my father would have said, Savage kept his cards close to his vest. It was an excellent attribute for a poker player, but the very devil of a challenge for me now.

But I couldn't think of it, or him, like that. I needed to focus not on what he wasn't sharing with me but on what he was, which was exactly the sort of reckless passion and excitement that I'd left New York to experience. I couldn't think of Savage like the ordinary gentlemen I'd known, who had ordinary families and homes and occupations. He'd already made it abundantly clear that he wasn't like that. I couldn't think of a future with him beyond Wrenton Manor and the Game, which had brought us together, or beyond the seven nights that were all I was guaranteed to have with him.

I knew all this because, although I might be inexperienced with men, I wasn't a fool. And yet, when at last Barry shut the bedroom door and Savage and I were finally alone together, I still said the one thing to him that I shouldn't have, simply because I was too polite to keep silent.

"Thank you, Savage," I said to his back as he poured himself a glass of brandy. "Thank you for stopping Mr. Henery when he became too—too forward."

He didn't answer, sipping the brandy in silence. Because the day had been warm, the bedroom windows remained open, and the yellow flames of the candles around them danced and jumped on their wicks, casting uneasy shadows across the walls that seemed to mirror the evening's mood.

I stood uncertainly, my hands hanging awkwardly at my sides. I wished he would reply to me, wished it quite desperately. When he didn't, I plunged on, feeling obliged to fill the silence that was stretching more and more widely between us.

"It was very unpleasant, having Mr. Henery touch me as he did," I said. "I didn't expect it, you know. I've scarcely said two words to the man, and then to have him act so—so rudely—"

"Is that all it was to you, there in the dining room?" Savage demanded, abruptly wheeling around to face me. "A bit of unpleasantness? Some fellow who was rude?"

Startled by his reaction, I drew back a step, folding my arms defensively over my chest. Even by the candlelight, his expression was dark and impassive, much as it had been downstairs.

"For me, yes, it was," I said finally. "It was only part of the Game, I know, but it frightened me."

He frowned. "You were frightened by a drunkard pawing over your leg?"

I shook my head, unsure how honest I should be.

"In part it was Mr. Henery," I admitted. "But what frightened me more was you."

"You were frightened of me," he repeated, incredulous. He drank the rest of the brandy in a single swallow and set the empty glass down so hard that the crystal rang in protest. "First you thank me, and then you say I frightened you. What in blazes am I to make of that?"

"I thanked you for defending me," I said quickly. "But it was how you defended me that was—was frightening. I've never seen gentlemen fight like that."

"Will you believe me if I tell you I've never lost my temper like that?" he asked, his voice filled with bitterness, and more than a little of his earlier fury, too. "I lost my temper. I dishonored my friends. I insulted their hospitality, and I attacked another man as if I were some brawling bastard from the dockyards. If I weren't who I am, I'd be in jail for it now. And do you know why I did those things? Can you guess? Or will you only stand there before me in judgment, like some damned sibylic oracle from New York?"

"I'm not judging you, Savage," I protested. "I never said I was."

Before I could react, he was with me, holding my face between his hands so that I couldn't look away. His pale eyes were hard and cold, even with the candle flames reflected in them.

"Answer me, Eve," he demanded roughly, his thumbs pressing into my jaw. "I want to hear you say it. Tell me why I acted like a madman."

I had no idea what he meant, or what he expected me to say. I stared back at him, my heart beating wildly. He was going to kiss me, I was sure of it, and then it wouldn't matter what I said.

"Tell me, Eve," he ordered in a harsh whisper, his face only inches from mine. "You know the reasons better than I."

I swallowed, the muscles of my throat working convulsively just beneath his fingers. At last I shook my head in the tiny fraction of motion that his grasp would permit.

His mouth tightened, his lips so tightly compressed that the little cut began to bleed again, a tiny, glistening trickle.

Abruptly he released my face, lifting his hands away with such suddenness and force that I staggered backward, off-balance. I hadn't realized how much I'd been swaying into him, so much that he'd been supporting me.

"Stubborn," he said, biting the word off. "Why won't you say what we both know?"

"Because I *don't* know!" I cried furiously. "You are making no sense, Savage, none. None!"

He'd begun to pace back and forth before me like some great jungle cat, caged and unable to keep still.

"I came to Wrenton for pleasure," he said. "Mindless, rutting pleasure. That's the whole point of Laura's little game, isn't it? I've done it before, with other women. I should be fucking you whenever it pleases me, and anyone else who pleases me as well. I should be making you suck my cock at the dining table, while I suck some other woman's breasts. I should be sharing you with Carleigh, or any other man who wants you, and be eager to fuck their women—their Innocents—as well."

"Then do it, if that is what you want," I said, shoving back my tangled hair. I hated how he was saying the word *fuck,* short and sharp and ugly, and nothing like what he'd done with me. "I won't stop you."

"But you already have, Eve," he said. "You have blinded me to all the others. I can think of nothing but touching you, smelling you, tasting you, fucking you, and I would kill any other man who tried to take you from me. I almost did with Henery."

I wasn't sure if he intended this as a compliment or not. To me, it wasn't. Inspiring a man to attack another did not strike me as very flattering, and automatically I glanced down at the bloodstains on his cuffs, the crimson now darkening to brown.

"Your voice stopped me," he continued, tugging apart the knot of his necktie and opening the throat of his shirt. "Only you could do that, because at once I thought of how much I wanted you. I wanted to throw you down and pound my cock into you with your legs around my waist. That's what you wanted, too."

I shook my head, not wanting to admit the uncomfortable link between his aggression and my arousal.

"Don't lie," he said. "I saw it in your eyes then. I can see it there now, too."

My face grew warm, and I looked down so that my eyes wouldn't betray me again. Daring, I closed the space between us and reached up to curl my palm around the back of his neck. His skin was hot beneath my touch and the tendons were tight as iron bands, and gently I rubbed them with my fingers.

"Do you want me in return?" I asked softly, already knowing the answer. I didn't have to look into his eyes: his entire body was tense with white-hot lust. No wonder I was trembling in response, poised and ready for him.

But not for what he said next.

"You are like a witch who has cast her spell over me," he said, his voice hoarse with the same fury he'd shown before. "With every other woman, once I'd had her, the novelty was done, and I was cured. I thought you'd be the same. But you're like a poison I can't resist, Eve, a poison that's claiming my life. I think of nothing but how I fucked you last time, and how I'll fuck you again. I don't know how you have done it to me in so short a time, but damn you, you have. You *have*."

I gasped, so shocked by what he'd said that I recoiled from him as if I'd been burned.

"How can you say such ridiculous things to me?" I cried, my anger swiftly flaring to match his. "How can you be so unfair? You *are* mad, to speak so! How can you call me poison? How can you fault me for your—your weaknesses? Why, you're no better than Blackledge, blaming me!"

He raked his fingers through his hair. "Blast you, Eve, I'm not Blackledge. I don't blame you. I said you were the reason. That's not the same at all."

"Isn't it?" I said. "It certainly seems so to me."

"It's not," he said sharply. "Not at all."

I couldn't bear this. He was leading me down a dark, twisted, turning road, and I didn't want to follow any longer.

"I'm leaving," I said, heading for the door. "There's no need for me to stay and listen to you insult me."

He stepped in front of me, blocking my path. He stood with his legs apart and his hands clenched loosely at his sides, a black-and-white wall of impossibly handsome, confounding maleness. Part of me warned that I should be frightened again, but I was too angry and hurt to care.

I placed my palms on his chest and tried to shove him aside.

"I'm not staying with you, Savage," I said. "I'm leaving."

"No, you aren't," he said. "Because I'm leaving first."

Before I could react, he turned and was gone, slamming the bedroom door behind him. With a wordless exclamation of frustration, I threw myself at the door. My fingers slipped on the polished brass doorknob and fumbled as I tried to turn it, certain he'd locked me inside. But then the door opened easily, and to my chagrin I stood face-to-face not with Savage but with an unperturbed Barry.

"Where is his lordship?" I demanded, quickly scanning the corridor. "Where is he?"

"He has certain matters to attend to, ma'am," Barry said, as mild as usual. "Is there anything you require, ma'am?"

I paused, my thoughts racing wildly. I could follow my first impulse and return to my rooms, praying that I wouldn't meet Blackledge or any of the other masters on the way. I could send for a car in the morning, leave Wrenton for London, and never see Savage again.

I could do all that, or I could stay.

I could remain here in Savage's bedroom, surrounded by scores of flickering candles, and wait for him to return. He would, too. I was just as sure of that as Barry was, because I was certain he'd expect me to be here when he did.

And he'd be right. I wasn't ready to end things with

Savage, at least not like this. I was realizing that as my anger cooled. I had been equally at fault, letting my pride get the better of me. It hadn't been easy hearing him describe me as a poison, and yet I understood, for he'd become exactly the same for me.

I'd become jealous of any time he spent with others, let alone being parted from him. I thought of nothing except him and his cock, and what he would do next to please them both. The more I thought about it, the more I realized I'd been almost incessantly aroused since he'd sat beside me to watch the entr'acte. Even the merest touch from him had that effect on me, and for the first time I truly understood what an obsession could be.

Oh, yes, he'd been right: I did want him. My whole body ached fiercely with wanting, my quim too empty and longing for him to fill me again.

And that need would humble my pride every time.

I took a deep breath, striving once again to look like the lady I'd been born, at ease with servants, and not a scorned Innocent in a rumpled costume.

"Thank you, Barry, no," I said. "I require nothing more."

He bowed, and I retreated inside the room, letting him close the door gently after me.

I rubbed my arms against the evening air, noting wistfully how my nipples now were tight from the chill, not Savage's touch. With a sigh, I pulled the costume over my head—I was sure he would want to discover me naked when he returned—and climbed into his bed.

The sheets had been changed since Savage and I had lain there earlier, the pillows plumped and the coverlet straightened, and in vain I tried to recapture some sense of how it had felt to have him beside me. The bed was too large for one person alone, and I curled into a tight knot in the very center of the mattress with the coverlet pulled high beneath my chin.

I wondered where Savage was now. Was he stalking through the manor's hallways or gardens? Had he retreated to the library to lose himself in a book? Had he taken a horse from the stables to ride hard across the estate's moonlit fields?

I prayed he hadn't returned to the others in the dining room, and wasn't party to whatever else Lady Carleigh had concocted for entertainment. I remembered all too vividly how earlier he'd called the viscountess by her given name, and how both Lord and Lady Carleigh had hoped he'd come join them in their bed with their Innocents.

I prayed he hadn't gone there, either, or to any other bed besides. There was only one bed where he belonged, and it was here, with me, and I smiled forlornly at how woeful and pathetic that small certainty, however true, would sound to anyone else.

Lying curled on my side, I gazed through the open window at the stars and the rising moon. He would return to me soon. He must. I remembered how upset he'd been when he thought I'd left him, and now that he was the one who was gone, I felt his absence with a keenness I'd never expected.

We only had a handful of days at Wrenton, days that should be spent together, not apart. . . .

"Hush, Eve, I'm here."

I stirred, still too deeply asleep to tell if I was dreaming his voice and the brush of his lips on my cheek.

Then the springs creaked and the mattress shifted beneath his weight, and I felt a slight breeze of cooler air as he lifted the sheet and coverlet to join me in the bed. I was still on my side, and he glided his hand along my body to follow the dip of my waist and the swell of my hips. The hour was late enough that all the candles had guttered out, but there was light enough from the moon.

Drowsy as I was, his caress was enough to wake me,

and I tried to roll onto my back to kiss him, or at least to see his face.

"Stay as you are," he said softly as he held me steady. "I want you like this."

He slipped his body close behind mine, fitting neatly against me like we were two spoons. He was naked, his skin warm, and I wriggled more closely to him, relishing his heat as much as the intimacy of our position.

But he wanted me. That was what mattered most.

Instinctively I pushed my bottom against him and felt his cock, already thick and hard against his belly. There was the proof of his desire, and my heart quickened in anticipation. Again I tried to twist around to face him, expecting him to take me like that.

"No, Eve," he said, keeping me on my side. "You'll like this, I promise."

His hand swept along my hip again, then raised my upper thigh, bending my knee and easing it slightly forward to open me. I was trembling with both uncertainty and eagerness, and when he stroked his fingers along my slit he found me wet, the lips of my quim pouting and ready like another kind of kiss. Still, I heard him lick his fingers, sliding his saliva across my opening to make me even wetter.

"Oh, please, Savage," I murmured as I pressed back against his fingers. "Please, don't torment me any longer."

He chuckled. "Do as I say, and I won't. Be easy, and let me lead. You're so tight, and I don't want to hurt you."

Instead of his fingers, I felt the blunt head of his cock pressing against my opening. I gasped, struggling to do as he'd said and not to push back, and he pressed his hand onto my waist to hold me steady. He shifted his hips to better his aim, then pushed into me. I gasped again as his cock opened me, sliding far into my passage. Two quick shoves, and he'd filled me completely, his balls pressed against my bottom.

Buried deep, he paused to let me grow accustomed to taking him like this. It wasn't the same, the angle making his cock fill me in a new and different way that stole my breath away. I loved how this position made him curve around me, his large, muscular body bending to fit mine.

I gave a small shimmy of encouragement, and at once he drew back and plunged back in, making me whimper with delight. I twisted my hands in the bedclothes, bracing myself to take more.

"I told you that you'd like it this way," he said, his voice a rough growl against my ear. He drew back so far he was almost free of me, only to plunge back in with shuddering force. "I knew you would."

"I—I do," I said, the last word drifting off into a groan of purest pleasure. "Ah, Master! How well you know me!"

I'd effortlessly slipped back into the Game. Not being able to see his face seemed to make the pleasure more intense, as if the way his cock was stretching me, pounding back and forth so deeply inside my channel, was all I could concentrate upon. I hadn't expected to be so excited by the feeling of his balls slapping against my anus, something so absolutely forbidden that I'd no words for it.

"I know you better than anyone, Eve," he said. He shoved the thick waves of my hair to one side so that he could kiss the side of my throat. "I know what you want and what you need, and I know how to give it to you."

I believed him. The sensations he was creating within me were unlike anything I'd experienced before. He did know what I wanted, what I needed, and as for giving it to me—ah, I was eager for everything he could offer.

"Say it to me, Eve," he whispered. "Tell me what I'm doing to you."

I struggled to put together the words he wished to hear—a small price in return for the pleasure he was giving me.

"You're fucking me, Master," I said raggedly, no longer amazed by the power of those simple words to send a shiver through me as well. I loved how completely he filled me, reaching the very end of my passage with a finality that was just short of too much. His strokes were long, nearly pulling out, only to push back into me in a steady rhythm that was rapidly bringing me toward my release. "You're fucking me, and I'm fucking you, and it—it's divine."

"Divine?" He grunted, almost a laugh. "Then it's my duty to make you see all the stars in the heavens."

"Stars, Master?" I asked breathlessly, not understanding. I couldn't make myself focus on anything but what he was doing to me, let along stargazing.

"Stars." He reached over my hip and between my legs until he found my pearl.

I whimpered as he began to massage that tiny, vital part of me in light little circles, timing the pressure with the driving of his cock. Unable to stop, my hips rocked against the double pleasure of his teasing fingers and his driving cock. I was shaking with the force of my building climax, clutching the sheets with feverish desperation.

I arched my spine with my head thrown back as the tension built within my core. My breathy little cries punctuated every one of his thrusts, until at last my release crashed over me and my quim convulsed around his cock in pure, wild joy. I fell limply against the pillows, gasping as the last tremors rippled through me.

But Savage wasn't done. Now that he was assured of my pleasure, he began to chase his own. He braced himself, moving lower to increase his penetration, and moved like a piston so relentlessly that I instantly felt another climax coiling within me.

Mindlessly I let myself go with it, with him. Our bodies were slippery with sweat, and his balls struck heavily against my bottom with each stroke.

He shoved aside the damp curtain of my hair to kiss my shoulder, a kiss that was so rough and passionate that it felt more like a bite, a primitive expression of mating at the moment his climax began. It hurt, and made me cry out with the unexpected pain, yet it excited me, too, to have his passion so beyond his control. He groaned and swore, shuddering with the raw impact of it.

His cock ground against me so hard that the force of it echoed within me and triggered my second orgasm. I bucked and cried out, exhilarating in the glorious moment when he filled me with his hot seed.

And then, at last, I understood about the stars.

Utterly spent, he sank back against the pillows, drawing me with him. I settled naturally against his chest, savoring how his arms circled me protectively and our legs were tangled. His chest still heaved with each breath, and beneath my fingers I both felt and heard how his heart continued to race.

I was amazed that his cock continued to fill me, awash as I was in his spendings. Yet, I liked that, too, even as I tried not to read more into it than he likely intended. I had to remember that the intimacy of our bodies had nothing to do with the intimacy of our souls and hearts, and that what we did here in this bed was intended for pleasure, and nothing more.

He didn't speak, and neither did I. As his breathing slowed and he relaxed more fully beside me, I suspected he'd fallen asleep. Finally his cock slipped free of my quim, but I didn't reach for a handkerchief, not wishing to disturb him. He shifted against the pillows and tightened his arms around me. I smiled, letting myself enjoy the warmth of rare happiness and contentment, and purposefully not thinking of what would come next.

He was the one who finally broke the silence, startling me there in the dark.

"I couldn't stay away," he said. He spoke in a low, matter-of-fact tone, as if discussing a topic as ordinary as the weather.

But I wasn't fooled. I'd already learned to my sorrow that even the mildest of words could turn treacherous with him. This didn't feel like another part of the Game, but I couldn't tell for certain. How was I to reply to such a statement? How much could I dare confide of my own thoughts?

I shifted to face him, resting my arms on his chest. In the moonlight his face was planed with shadows, his dark hair tousled against the white linens.

"I'm glad you returned," I said softly. "Truly."

He paused before answering, just long enough to make me fear I'd made another misstep and confessed too much.

"It was good to find you here," he said finally.

Relieved, I smoothed a stray tendril of my hair behind one ear. "I was lonely."

He grunted. "I would venture that loneliness must be an unusual condition for a woman as beautiful as you are."

"It's not," I said, trying to smile. "I believe I've been lonely my entire life. You guessed that of me that first night, when we danced."

"I said that you were alone by choice," he said. "Being alone is not the same as being lonely. And it wasn't a guess. It was a certainty."

"Because you are that way, too," I said. "You recognized me as a renegade, exactly as you are yourself."

"That must not have been easy for you," he said. "It's been my limited experience that New Yorkers are almost alarmingly social."

That made me smile in earnest. "They can be, yes," I agreed. "Mrs. Astor, Mrs. Vanderbilt, Mrs. Whitney—they are indeed alarming in their pursuit of social esteem."

"Then what of the beautiful Mrs. Hart?" he asked, curious. "What of her place in that teeming, tawdry New York society of parvenus and oil magnates?"

His playfulness took me by surprise, and made me drop my guard more than I'd intended.

"My place there among those ladies is secure enough, for as long as I wish it," I said. "They would never dare not invite me to their balls and parties. I'm too wealthy to scorn."

"Then you should never be lonely," he said easily. "Balls and parties are the very lifeblood of ladies. Even the renegade ones."

"Perhaps," I said warily. "But I—I am not adept at transforming acquaintances into friends. My father built his fortune by trusting no one, and he did the same with me. I was never permitted from our house unattended. Servants raised me. He had me taught at home, and I never was sent to school. He didn't believe any other children were worthy of my company, and thus I had none. He chose my husband, and I went from the schoolroom to marriage. Then Arthur died, and I became a widow, and that—that is my story."

I gave a little shrug of my shoulders, already regretting having said so much.

"What of your sisters?" he asked. "What of your mother? Why did she permit this?"

His unfeigned interest surprised me, yet reassured me, too.

"My mother died of influenza when I was an infant," I said, unable to keep the old sorrow from my voice, "and I have no brothers or sisters. There was only me. So you see why loneliness and I are old friends."

"I'm sorry," he said. He traced his fingertips along the curve of my cheek with such unexpected gentleness that tears stung my eyes.

"You needn't apologize," I said quickly, drawing back

a fraction from his touch. His tenderness was too much, too sudden, and guessing that it could not last made it unbearable. "You are hardly to blame for anything that has happened in my life."

His face suddenly turned guarded. "I never said it was. But things are different for women."

I couldn't begin to guess what that meant. "If you are implying that only women are lonely—"

"I didn't intend that, either," he said, the slightest edge of testiness in his voice.

"Although as a man, and a peer as well, you would never be lonely," I said, more wistfully than I realized. "The whole world is open to you, without any of the limitations that constrict women."

"Eve, Eve." He sighed wearily. "I meant only what I said: that loneliness affects women in different ways than it does men, and given the warm nature of most women, it must be more difficult for them to bear."

"So you have never been lonely yourself?" I asked, longing for him to share his past, his fears, with me as I had with him. "Not once?"

His guarded expression did not change, a wall carefully composed to keep me at a distance.

"Men are different, Eve," he repeated, and, to my disappointment, that was all.

I drew in a deep, shuddering breath, then let it out in a long sigh. He was not saying anything that was offensive or disrespectful or challenging. I was the one who'd rambled on and then turned prickly, and with no real reason, either.

And I was the one breaking the rules of the Game, too, yearning for more from him than sexual experience and pleasure. I was not only an Innocent but a fool as well. I was fortunate that he didn't climb from the bed and walk through the door again, and not return.

Yet, I'd feel like an even greater fool if I apologized now, directly after I'd told him he needn't apologize. Why was it that Savage and I did so much better when we were Protector and Innocent?

Confused and frustrated, I pushed away from him and sat upright, hooking my arms around my bent knees with my hair falling down my back. I rested my chin on my arms and closed my eyes, determined not to let my emotions spill over as tears. I'd never thought of myself as a weeper, but there was something about Savage that made me feel everything, good and bad, so much more vividly that I couldn't help it.

"Eve," he said behind me. "Look at me."

I shook my head. Even in the moonlight, he'd be able to see my tears, and I was too ashamed to let that happen.

"Eve," he said, his voice low and rough and faintly puzzled. "Please."

That was not the command of a master but a simple request from a man. It was also more than enough to make my eyes fill in earnest, and I buried my face against my folded arms.

He didn't try again. Instead, he reached out and swept the tangled mass of my hair to one side and over my shoulder, baring my back. I felt the mattress sink as he came to sit behind me and stretched his long legs on either side of my hips. Instantly I felt better; it had taken no more than the heat of his skin against mine, the rough hair on his legs against the soft skin of my hips.

I started when he put his hands on my shoulders, not expecting it.

"Be easy," he whispered, his breath warm on my cheek. "Close your eyes. Empty your head, and think of nothing."

How could I think of nothing with him so close? He began to massage my back, digging his strong fingers into my muscles. I hadn't realized how tense I'd become, my back as taut as an arched bow, yet the circling pressure of his thumbs was breaking it down, freeing me. I raised my head, letting it fall back toward my spine, and let my arms drop limply to my sides.

"There, there," he said quietly, calming me. "Be easy, and trust me."

I was unable to keep back my little moans of pleasure, for his hands felt that good as they kneaded my flesh. He worked all along my spine, up and down and back again, clear to the twin dimples at the top of my bottom. When at last he was done, I sank back against his chest, limp and blissfully at ease.

"You will be pleased to know I've had words with Lady Carleigh," he said, over the top of my head. "We've reached an understanding."

At once the pleasant feeling began to recede as I imagined him spending the time he'd been gone frolicking in the Carleighs' infamous bed.

"You have?" I asked.

"I have," he said, "or rather, Lady Carleigh and I have together. To avoid any further disturbances with Blackledge, you and I are excused from dining downstairs. Unless, of course, you wish it, Eve."

"No—ah, whatever pleases you, Master," I said. I was pleased, too; I couldn't deny it. "What of Mr. Henery?"

"He is of no consequence," he said, clearly believing exactly that. "It's Blackledge that wants you, and I won't put you in that danger again."

I smiled with tremendous relief. "Thank you, Master."

"You needn't thank me, Eve," he said. "I've told you before that as your Protector, I am responsible for your welfare as well as your education."

I nodded, and linked my fingers into his, grateful even if he wouldn't let me say it aloud. He slipped in and out of the Game so seamlessly that it was often difficult for me to tell when he was playing and when he wasn't, and whether it was the master's cock that was fucking me or Savage's.

"Did Lady Carleigh say anything else, Master?" I asked.

He sighed with resignation. "No questions, Eve, no questions. But no, she said nothing to me. Our exchange this evening was entirely written."

"You—you didn't go to her rooms?"

"No," he said, a single, glorious word to my ears. "My first concern was you, and after what occurred in the dining room, I would never leave you alone, not even here. I was in the front room while you slept."

Once again I was perilously close to tears.

I couldn't stay away. . . .

My first concern was you. . . .

I would never leave you alone. . . .

"What is this?" he said, gently turning my shoulder toward the moonlight. Lightly he touched his fingertips to the place where he'd bitten me in passion, leaving my pale skin bruised and swollen.

"It's nothing," I said quickly, even as I winced at his touch.

"I've marked you," he said evenly, an observation without any apology or sympathy. "Does it hurt?"

"Only a little," I lied. I bruised easily, and though I was sure in the morning the mark would be quite noticeable, I didn't care. It excited me to remember the circumstances of the bruise's origin, and I'd gladly suffer another like it if it came with the same pleasure.

He bent and kissed the bruise. "Don't leave me, Eve. That's all I ask. Don't leave me."

"I won't, Master," I whispered, twisting around to kiss him. "Never."

NINE

The voices were what woke me.

I opened my eyes, listening. It was morning, and the sun was already bright over the trees. Savage lay beside me, still soundly asleep, his large, glorious body sprawled beneath the sheets, exactly as it should be. For the last two days and nights, we hadn't left his rooms, and had scarcely left this bed, exactly as it should be, too.

But there—there it was again, coming from the lawn outside the window. A man's voice, curt, even angry, shouting at a woman who was pleading with him. Although their words weren't distinct, the tone of them was, and it was chilling. At so early an hour, the voices most likely belonged to servants engaged in some unhappy lovers' quarrel—such things were often overheard in great houses with large staffs—but the woman's distress still unsettled me.

Taking care not to disturb Savage, I slipped from the bed and wrapped the extra coverlet around myself. Swiftly I padded across the room to the open window to see if I could spy the pair.

I didn't have to look far.

There on the front lawn before the house were the man and woman. They weren't servants but guests: Mrs. Anson in her Innocent's costume with her long, dark hair trailing over her shoulders, and Lord Standage as her master dressed in ordinary clothing, a white shirt and light-colored trousers without a coat.

As I watched, he embraced her, kissing her hard, while she tried to break away. At last she did, and began to run from him, gathering the hem of her trailing costume in her hands to free her legs. Angrily Lord Standage shouted at her to stop, and still Mrs. Anson fled like some wild wood nymph with her hair flying behind her.

But the grass was wet with morning dew, and her bare feet slipped and slid, making it easy for Lord Standage to grab her by her hair and pull her back. Mrs. Anson wailed and struggled against him, while he held her fast with one hand and opened the buttons on his trousers with the other. Brutishly he shoved her down to the grass on her hands and knees, and tossed her costume back over hips, exposing her bottom and quim.

She begged with him to let her go, her voice shrill and filled with panic. He pulled out his cock and gave it a few quick shakes of his hand up and down the shaft to make it hard before he dropped to his knees behind her.

But once again she wriggled free and escaped, running from him with desperate, stumbling speed as he shouted after her to stop. That desperation, plus the panic in her begging, were finally too much for me.

I ran back to the bed and shook Savage by the shoulder.

"You must wake up, Savage, I beg you!" I exclaimed anxiously. "Lord Standage is attacking Mrs. Anson, and we must stop him!"

He rolled over, blinking and grouchy, his jaw shadowed with a night's worth of beard and his hair rough and unruly. "What in blazes are you talking about?"

"I told you," I said breathlessly. "Mrs. Anson is being attacked by Lord Standage, and she needs our help!"

I hurried back to the window, leaning forward to rest my elbows on the sill. Nothing had changed: the lady was still eluding her pursuer, but only barely. From the way she was panting, I judged it was only a matter of time before he'd finally catch her.

Savage joined me at the window, yawning as he came to stand behind me.

"Now what's all this great bother?" he asked, leaning over my shoulder.

"Down there," I said, pointing. "It's Mrs. Anson and Lord Standage. I know she's his Innocent, but he's being very rough with her, and it's clear she doesn't wish to be caught and—and raped. Oh, we must stop him, Savage!"

He watched for a leisurely moment, more interested in running his hand along my back than in what was happening outside.

"Oh, those two," he said, yawning again. "There's nothing new there. She leaves her husband behind in Northumberland, and meets Standage here, and in London as well. It's the way they choose to play the Game."

"*That's* part of the Game?" I asked uncertainly. It was hard for me to believe that Mrs. Anson would choose this, from the way she was trying so hard to escape. From a distance, her panic and fear seemed thoroughly genuine. "She wants him to chase her like that?"

"She's working rather hard at it, isn't she?" He slid his hand beneath the coverlet wrapped around me, and gently began rubbing and squeezing my upturned bottom as I leaned on the windowsill. "All that shrieking and running about is merely her way of catching his attention and rousing a cockstand out of the old fellow."

This, I thought, was clearly not a problem with Savage. Already I could feel the hot, steely length of his cock pressing against my bottom, ready to ease into me with the slightest encouragement. I was still swollen from last night's encounters, still half aroused as well. Having a man like Savage standing naked while he gently kneaded my hip would have that effect on most women.

"I'd wager she's been leading him around for a good hour or so," Savage continued. "Look at the grass stains on his knees! Likely she's let him almost catch her a half-dozen times or more. If she's not careful, he'll— Ah, he's caught her fairly this time."

"She's—she's giving up," I said, chagrined at having believed the pantomime was real. "She's surrendered."

Mrs. Anson had done exactly that. This time when Lord Standage had pulled her down to the grass, she'd stayed there on her knees. She'd stopped wailing and protesting, too, and had in fact spread her knees farther apart to welcome her master, wiggling a bit to entice him further.

"One can never judge another's tastes when it comes to sex," Savage said philosophically, as if his hand had moved to cover my quim completely of its own volition. "Personally I wouldn't care for so much hysteria, culminating in a public rutting on the front lawn, but those two are entirely welcome to do whatever pleases them. You're wet, Eve."

"I—I cannot help it, Master," I said. I let the coverlet slip to the floor, shamelessly arching my back to push against his hand. Yet, it wasn't entirely because of how he was caressing me. Watching the pair on the lawn was arousing, too.

Lord Standage's cock was a short, thick affair, and even with Mrs. Anson positioned to accommodate him, he still needed several forceful thrusts to bury himself. Grimacing, he held her tightly by her full hips, while she bent forward, pillowing her head on her folded arms to improve his penetration and pushing upward to meet his thrusts. With each thrust, she gave out joyful little yips of pleasure that echoed across the lawn.

There was now no doubt that Mrs. Anson was a willing participant, and no doubt, either, that the earlier game of elusive pursuit that Mrs. Anson had played with Lord Standage had served to increase their ardor.

Now, too, I understood what Savage had said about not judging others' pleasures. Before I'd left New York, I certainly wouldn't have believed I would find my current position so exciting. I never would have expected to enjoy leaning naked in front of the open window of a peer's country house while my quim was being fingered open by an equally naked gentleman, both of us watching another couple fuck on the lawn.

"I like how you can't help it," Savage said, lowering his voice to the special, slightly gruff but seductive level that made me shiver. "It means that you're already willing, already aroused, the way that a proper Innocent should be."

"I—I am a proper Innocent, Master," I stammered, just as he slipped one of his thick fingers inside me. He rotated his finger, pressing inside my channel's walls, and I gasped with the pleasure of it. "Oh, Master!"

"Stand steady, Eve," he warned, sliding his finger in and out. "Keep your eyes open. I don't want you to miss the excellent performance that Mrs. Anson and Standage are giving for you."

"Nooo, Master," I whispered, clinging tightly to the windowsill. I was slippery around his finger, inflamed by his maddening strokes. I needed the support of the sill, for my knees were shaking beneath me.

"I doubt we're the only ones watching, either," Savage continued. "That's what they wanted, you know, an audience, or else they would have kept to their own room. I expect these windows on the west front of the house must resemble the boxes at Covent Garden at present. Don't you agree, Eve?"

"Yesss, Master," I somehow managed to answer. He'd added a second finger to the first, the growing pressure delicious, and yet not even close to how his cock would feel inside me. And of course I'd soon feel his cock. It was only a matter of when Savage would do it.

"You're so wet around my fingers, Eve," he said. "I can't begin to tell you how beautiful you are like this, rosy and open and dripping for my cock. I like seeing you so inspired. But then, you've always liked watching from above, haven't you?"

I knew exactly what he was going to say next, how he'd remind me of that first night in London. I knew it, and I was right.

"That was when I first saw you," he continued, stroking me still. "You were leaning over that balustrade to watch me. Your face was rapt, your lips parted, and I knew you were as wet as you are now. Having you watch me fuck another woman was the best part of that night, knowing you wanted me as much as I wanted you. As much as you want me now."

I was breathing hard, close to coming—but not so close that I hadn't heard what he'd said. I was flattered and touched that he'd called me the best part of that first night we met, and I loved learning that he'd instantly desired me as much as I had him.

But I only wished he hadn't thought of it now when he had me in much the same position as Lady Cynthia

Telford had been. Lady Telford had been bent over a garden bench for him, while I was now bent over the windowsill, which wasn't much of a difference.

I longed for Savage to have better associations with me, memories that were separate from the forgotten Lady Telford or any other woman. I didn't want to be predictable. I'd surprised him by watching him that night in the garden, and I was determined to surprise him again.

Swiftly, before I lost my nerve and before he could react, I twisted free of his hand and his deliciously teasing fingers. I darted across the room and clambered up to stand on the bed.

"Catch me, Master," I said breathlessly, bouncing slightly on the mattress with my arms outstretched to keep my balance. His face was so astonished as he stared up at me that I nearly laughed aloud. "Catch me if you can!"

"Oh, I'll catch you," he said, his eyes gleaming. "And when I do, you'll wish you hadn't done this, you naughty Innocent."

Despite his warning, he was grinning, a wicked grin that showed me he liked the challenge.

"You'll have to catch me first, Master." Defiantly I smiled back as I shoved my hair back over my shoulders, my breath coming in quick gulps of excitement. He was staring at my breasts, at how they must be trembling as I stood unsteadily on the bed. I bounced a bit more to tease him. My body was still so sexually on edge that I felt wild and reckless and daring. "I'll be faster than Mrs. Anson, too."

"But I'm infinitely faster than his lordship," he said. "You don't stand a chance with me."

He grabbed his paisley robe from the chair and shrugged it on, his gaze never leaving me. I wondered why he'd bothered with the robe, then realized that he thought he'd be chasing me not only in this room but through the house and perhaps farther, as the other couple had done.

I hadn't thought that far ahead. I was naked, without even the dubious covering of my Innocent's costume, and I'd a fleeting image of myself in that state racing down the long halls of Wrenton with him in hot pursuit.

I should have been shocked by this prospect. Instead, I found it wildly exciting, even exhilarating. I'd no real sense of how fast I could run. In my ordinary life, I was customarily weighed down by so many layers of clothing, corsetry, and propriety that it was nearly twenty years since I'd last run at all. I suspected he *was* faster, exactly as he'd claimed, but I was eager for the chance to try to outrun him—nearly as much as I was eager to be caught.

"Are you going to bounce on that bed all day, Eve?" he asked, slowly circling the bed. He was moving like a prowling tiger, every lean muscle with a purpose, and making me feel like his prey. "You know I can come get you there, too."

"I will, Master," I promised, "when the time is right."

He chuckled, and shook his hair back from his forehead and narrowed his eyes. His silk robe slipped open, displaying the dark whorls of hair on his chest.

I wondered if beneath that flowing, patterned silk he still had a cockstand. From the way he was looking at me, I guessed that he did.

"What a willful little Innocent you are!" he said, almost proudly. "You'll regret speeches like that, you know. I fear there must be a suitable punishment after this."

So he was enjoying this every bit as much as I was, a certainty that served only to spur me on. He had worked his way to the far side of the bed, near one of the bedside tables. If I jumped down now from the bedstead, I'd have a moment or two as a head start to reach the door.

"I'm not afraid of your punishments, Master," I said bravely. "You asked me to trust you, and I do."

He tipped his head to one side, considering me. "You trust me to do what is best for your education?"

"I do, Master," I said. "I must."

"An excellent answer, Eve," he said. "I shall take it into consideration as I decide your punishment for willfulness."

I wrinkled my nose; not exactly defiant, but not exactly believing that there'd be any serious punishment, either. Thus far he'd shown me only kindness with a heady mix of passion, and I suspected his "punishment" would simply be another facet of the Game.

"Don't make faces at me, Eve," he warned. "I do not like impudence in my Innocents."

Without looking away from me, he opened the table's drawer, reached inside, and took something out. I thought at first it was a pair of bracelets, the brightly polished silver glinting in the sun. *A gift of jewelry,* I thought pleasurably. I did love jewelry, and it would be very nice of him to give me a piece or two, as a memento of this week. What manner of punishment could that be?

Then I noticed the thick chain linking the two wide cuffs together, and with a chill I realized that what Savage was holding were not bracelets but a pair of manacles, similar to the ones I'd once seen on prisoners being led off by policemen in New York. Except these manacles weren't made for large male prisoners. They were small, almost dainty, designed to fit a lady's wrists.

Like mine.

"What is the meaning of—of those, Master?" I said, my earlier playfulness gone in an instant. "When you spoke of punishment, I didn't think—that is, I didn't know—"

"You must trust me, Eve," he said firmly. "You were the one who was willful and impudent, and now you must trust me to know best how to punish you."

His voice was deep and low, resonant with seduction. Every other time, his voice alone had been enough to make me melt. But I had never considered silver manacles part of seduction. In truth, I'd never once in my life considered silver manacles in any fashion at all.

Panicking, I thought of Lord Blackledge, and how roughly he'd appeared to use his Innocent, trussing her and binding her and stopping her words with a gag. Could Savage intend to do those things to me, too?

I folded my arms over my breasts. "I'm sorry, Savage, but I don't believe that being chained up like a dog would be—"

"I would never think of you like a dog, Eve," he said, a little wounded, slipping the offending manacles into the pocket of his robe and out of my sight. "It won't be like that at all. It's only an amusement, a *petite plaisir*. Part of the Game. You'll see. You haven't found anything else we've done disagreeable, have you?"

I sighed uneasily. "You know I haven't."

"Then why should it change now between us?" he reasoned wryly. That was exactly how he presented it, too, pure male logic against my fluttery female fear of the unknown. "Why would I suddenly do anything you did not like?"

I didn't answer, my mind—or was it my conscience?— struggling to convince myself one way or the other. I'd already done so many things with him, things that would have appalled me in New York, and I didn't regret any of them. I'd trusted him this far. Why couldn't I trust him in this, too?

"Trust me, Eve," he said as if reading my mind. He was so powerfully, achingly handsome, standing there looking at me as if I were the only woman in the world. He held his hand out to me, to help me climb from the bed and join him. "Trust me as your Protector to do what is best for you."

This was what I'd come for—not just for amusement, but for him. For *him*. I wasn't going to be a coward and not play the Game to the end.

I took a deep breath, then another.

Then I turned away from him and with an excited little whoop I hopped from the bed, and raced to the bedroom door. This time I was able to throw it open in an instant, and I ran down the short hall, past the bathroom and Savage's dressing room and a mildly bewildered Barry, and into the sitting room.

I didn't want to waste the seconds it would cost me to look around, but I knew he was behind me, and with each step drawing closer. I could hear his footsteps, his breathing, and I forced myself to run faster still.

If I headed straight across the room toward the next door, he'd catch me. But if instead I ran first around the oversize desk and through the narrow space between the desk and the wall, where there wouldn't be room for him to follow easily, then I might be able to reach it before he caught me.

That was my only goal, to reach the door. I'd figure out the rest afterward.

At the last moment, I cut around the leather-covered armchair and darted around the desk, squeezing myself through the space. Breathless and laughing, I felt clever and lithe, and exhilarated, too, to have eluded him this far. The door to the next room was just before me, the polished gilt doorknob almost within my reach.

Except that Savage had gotten there first.

He hadn't followed me around the desk as I'd expected. Instead, he'd gone straight to the door and cut me off. He was standing there now, his back to the door to block my way. His smile was confident, even smug, and he wasn't even breathing hard.

"You did better than I expected, Eve," he said, "but I told you before you couldn't win."

I felt decidedly less clever, but I wasn't going to give up yet.

"You haven't won," I said, tossing my hair back over my shoulders.

His gaze flicked down to the desk between us. "You have to come out from behind there at some point."

"Perhaps I do," I said, raising my chin. "Perhaps I don't."

His eyes gleamed at the challenge. "And perhaps I'll come haul you out."

He took one step toward me, then another, his hand outstretched to me. "Or you could surrender, Eve. You know it's inevitable."

I shook my head, poised with my hands on the desk before me. "I know nothing of the sort."

"Oh, Eve." He inched closer, beckoning. "You're forgetting I'm your master. What kind of Innocent forgets that?"

"Apparently a very wicked one, Master," I said, teasing, almost taunting him. If I could only get him to come closer and commit to one side of the desk, then I'd have a chance of breaking free. "I can't begin to imagine how much punishment I'll need after this."

"I can," he said, and the knowing way he smiled made me shiver with anticipation. "Now come, Eve, enough of this. Out from behind that desk."

I edged slowly to one side, letting him think I was heading that way. He did. His smile widened with satisfaction as he stepped forward, his hand reaching out to me. My heart racing, I smiled in return to encourage him further, and then fled in the opposite direction.

I'd several glorious seconds of thinking I'd escaped again, and then his arm closed around my waist like an iron band. I struggled to break free one last time, my nails raking down across his arm. He swore, but held me fast, and finally I stopped fighting.

I twisted around to face him, my breasts crushed against his chest. I was breathing hard, almost panting, and so was he, his heart beating fast against mine. Only the silk of his robe separated us, a luxurious barrier that seemed to accentuate the heat of his skin, and how his leanly muscled chest pressed into mine.

"Surrender?" he demanded, his arms tightening around my waist.

For a long moment I simply looked up at his face, so close to mine. I couldn't look enough at his pale blue eyes with their thick dark lashes, his stubbled jaw, his sensuously curved mouth, with the only sound between us our own ragged breathing.

Then abruptly he kissed me, his mouth crushing down on mine as if he'd devour me. I parted my lips for him at once and took his tongue deep, the way I craved. I'd no doubt this was a Protector's kiss, and I loved the forceful possession of it.

I'd guessed right: the chase through his rooms added even more fire to our morning. He was kissing me with a feverish new intensity, and I could not get enough of it, or of him.

I circled my hands around the back of his neck to support myself, my hands slipping into the black silk of his hair. I arched against him to press my breasts to his chest, rubbing my sensitized nipples against the silk of his robe.

He made a growling sound of satisfaction that reverberated between our joined mouths. I could taste the heat of his desire, the power of it. He tipped me back into the crook of his arm, and as I felt my balance wobble, I clung to his shoulders to keep from falling backward.

"You're safe, Eve," he whispered, sliding a hand down

the curving sweep of my hip. "I will never let you fall. Not now, not ever."

As if to prove it, he leaned me back farther and scooped his other arm beneath my knees to gather me from my feet. I was not a small woman, and I'd never had a man literally sweep me away like this, as if I weighed no more than thistledown. I gasped and fluttered at the delicious novelty of it as he carried me back to the bedroom.

He didn't make a great show of his strength; it was simply there, one more thing about him that made me feel safe and protected and womanly and beautiful, all at once. But most of all he made me feel desired and treasured, and for now that mattered more than anything else in the world.

I stretched myself luxuriantly on the sheets, letting my hair fan around me on the pillow as I gazed up at him. I loved how he was looking at me, raw hunger in his eyes, and when he climbed over me to find my mouth again, I arched up toward him in welcome.

"I've never wanted any other woman like I do you, Eve," he said, his voice rough with it. His expression was dark, his eyes heavy-lidded and full of unspoken promise of what he wished to do with me. "No other has ever come close."

"Then show me, Master," I begged, blindly reaching between us to try to untie the sash on his robe. I was weary of all the toying and teasing that had occupied our morning. I was ready for his cock, and shamelessly sought it. "Fuck me. I've waited long enough for this fine prize of yours."

He brushed my hand away, shifting just far enough aside that his cock was out of my reach.

"Not yet," he said. "I'll say when, Eve, not you."

"But I wish it now," I said with a breathless little pout. "Let me become your perfect Innocent."

"Then trust me, Eve," he said, kissing me hard, "and you will."

He ran his hands slowly up my sides and over my ribs, his thumbs grazing the undersides of my breasts as he continued up to stretch my arms over my head. He held me that way, his body covering mine as we kissed. He let one hand go and I curled it around his hips, delighting in the flex of his muscles beneath my fingers as he moved over me.

I felt something silken loop around my wrist and tighten, and by the time I turned my head, it was too late. A thick cord of black silk circled my wrist, and the more I struggled to pull free, the tighter the knot became. The other end of the rope was secured to one of the turnings in the massive bedstead, and no matter how I tugged, it would not budge.

"What is the meaning of this, Savage?" I demanded, panicking. The cords were nearly the same color as the dark wood of the bed, but how had I not noticed them before? "What are you doing to me?"

He still held me trapped beneath his body, and as I struggled, he gently raised my other wrist over my head. He slipped a second loop of cord around that wrist, too, and pulled it tight.

"I told you there'd be consequences, Eve," he said, sitting up to straddle me with one muscular thigh on either side of my hips. "It's for your own good, you see. Even the most cherished of Innocents must endure punishment."

I fought against the cords, but the harder I tugged, the more the cords tightened like little nooses and made the silk dig into my skin. "But please, Savage, not like this!"

" 'Master,' " he said evenly. "I'm your master, Eve. You've been willful enough today without forgetting that as well."

"But this isn't—"

"Hush," he said, placing a single finger across my lips to silence me. I smelled the honey-sweet scent of my own arousal on his hands, a pointed reminder of what he was withholding from me now.

"I'll admit that you were wise to question the manacles," he continued. "Cold metal is not appropriate for you. The silk restraints are far more suitable, and the contrast against your skin is quite charming. Black silk against pale ivory flesh. Or are you the color of white damask-rose petals? I told you I was a romantic, didn't I?"

I could still move my head and I did, jerking away from his finger. "Being trussed like a roasting hen is not romantic, not in the least!"

He frowned down at me, more with disappointment than displeasure, and somehow very, very English.

"You're only making it worse for yourself, Eve," he said. "You need to learn the virtue of patience and selflessness. Both are most necessary parts of any true pleasure."

"How?" I practically spat the single word, my initial fear melding into anger.

"Because waiting and denial make the final reward all the sweeter," he explained. "Most learn that simple lesson in the schoolroom, but then you are not like them, are you?"

He was almost lecturing me, shifting his role as my master to one of a tutor—if any tutor would dare look at a student with such unabashed and blatant desire.

"Don't lecture me, Savage," I said sharply. "Untie me instead."

"I could," he said, "but then you wouldn't learn anything, would you? I suspect a woman like you has always had whatever she wished. Nothing must be beyond your purse. What is it again that you New Yorkers call yourselves— millionaires?"

"You're no better, Savage," I said furiously. I was glad

now to see how my nails had earlier left long red welts down his arm, glad that I'd hurt him. "You're every bit as wealthy as I am, *and* you're an aristocrat whose family has had their way for—for *centuries*! How dare you preach to me?"

"Because I'm your master, Eve," he said. "And you are my Innocent."

With an athlete's easiness he climbed from the bed, releasing my legs. At once I struggled to push myself upright to sit, twisting and kicking against the bed and the cords around my wrists.

But my partial freedom was short-lived. Savage pulled two more lengths of the same silk cord from the drawer that had also held the manacles. Returning to the bed, he grabbed each of my ankles in turn. Although I fought and tried to kick him, he soon tied my ankles as he had my wrists, and secured them to the other bedposts.

When he'd carried me earlier, I'd found comfort in his strength, but now when he used it to subdue me like this, I felt only resentment. I was spread and bound, and though the cords did not really hurt unless I pulled on them, the position wasn't comfortable, and already I felt the strain on my muscles.

But perhaps worst of all was the humiliating indignity of it, of having my legs spread wide for him to see every intimate detail of my quim. Of course he'd seen it before, but then I had shared myself willingly, not like—like *this*.

"There," he said, gazing down at me with satisfaction. "That should put you in a suitable position for a bit of repentance."

"What could I possibly have to repent?" I asked, incredulous. "What have I done to merit this treatment from you?"

"I told you, Eve," he said. "You've been impatient, willful, and stubborn. You forget who I am, and the respect a proper Innocent must show her Protector."

His robe had slipped open as he'd bound me, and now he undid the sash to lap the edges over and retie it. His cock was still as hard as when he'd pushed me away earlier, the shaft sleek and stiff, the head blunt—powerful proof that he wasn't nearly as unmoved by the sight of my widespread legs as he wished me to think.

"It doesn't matter how much you want this, Eve," he said harshly, catching me looking. "You don't deserve it, not now."

To reinforce the message, he closed his fingers firmly around his cock and began to slide his hand up and down, his balls tightening visibly. The shaft pressed up toward his belly, and the head grew purple, glistening at the tip. His face flushed and his nostrils flared as he worked his hand. His gaze never left mine, intent on watching his effect upon me.

I blushed, embarrassed not by his performance but by my own shamelessness. The sight of his erect cock made me imagine it nudging into me, pressing deep and filling my channel. I could almost feel it there now, and in response my nipples tightened into sharp points and I felt the now-familiar heat gathering low in my belly. I couldn't help writhing uneasily against my bindings, my hips moving in a rhythm of yearning.

Savage glanced down at my notch, doubtless seeing the moisture that surely must be visible on the dark curling hairs and full pink lips. I couldn't help that, either, or stop the little moan of frustration that escaped my mouth.

"Not now," he said again, and pointedly pushed his cock back inside the robe, tying the sash into a tight knot. "You know why. You've only to remember what just occurred, how you leaped off this very bed to run away."

"You chased me!" I exclaimed, twisting against the

cords. "And you were the one who suggested it, saying I shouldn't judge the pleasures of others until I'd tried them. Admit it, Savage. You enjoyed that as much as I did!"

He didn't like that, his face shuttering against me in a way that made my heart sink.

"I don't have to admit anything, Eve," he said curtly. "Not to you."

I let my head drop back and sighed with the very impatience he'd accused me of having. "Then how long do you intend to keep me like this?"

"That's for me to decide, Eve," he said. "But I promise you that by the time I do, you'll be thanking me for your education. It's all part of the Game."

"The Game," I said bitterly. "I don't believe I care for your game any longer, *Master*."

His jaw was set and clenched, the muscles twitching around his mouth as if he was deciding whether to speak one last word or keep silent. Silence won. He turned on his heel and crossed the room, obviously heading for the door.

"Wait, Savage, please!" I cried out, turning my head to watch him. "You can't mean to leave me like this!"

He paused, his hand on the doorknob. "I can, Eve, and I will. Please use the time alone for reflection, as an Innocent should."

"No, Savage, please, no!" I wailed.

My only answer was the click of the door closing after him.

I made a wordless cry of frustration, twisting hard against my bonds. I couldn't believe he'd done this to me, and worse, that he now intended to abandon me in this state.

Hot tears welled up in my eyes and slid down my cheek, tears that I couldn't wipe away because of my tied hands.

Just when I'd thought things were going so well with Savage, he'd done this to me to prove they weren't.

God help me, I'd actually begun to believe that he might care more for me than as simply one more Innocent. I was so woefully ignorant of love that I wasn't sure I'd recognize it if it finally came lurching my way in the handsome form of Savage.

There were little signs, of course. He'd treated me with affection, even regard. He'd defended me from the others. Despite his role as my master, he'd always taken care that I found my climax before his in a way that was unexpectedly gentlemanly. When we were alone, he would often let the Game slip aside, and treat me like a woman instead of an Innocent—a woman that he obviously found fascinating in bed and out of it.

In return, I'd dared to let my feelings for him grow. I hadn't come here expecting anything more than an adventure, a dalliance, with him, and he'd given that to me in spades. I'd never imagined I'd truly feel this way with any man, and the passion we'd shared was worth ten times the voyage from New York.

It was as if I'd been sleepwalking for the first twenty-five years of my life, going through my days in a genteel, empty haze. Like a prince in a fairy tale, Savage had kissed me and brought me to life. He'd made me aware of the joy to be found in my body, and the shimmering pleasures that had never been part of my lot before. All I wanted now was more: more pleasure, more adventure, more risk, more delight, and, of course, much more of Savage's cock.

All I wanted was . . . all.

And the longer I thought of it, the more clear it became to me—albeit reluctantly, and with chagrin—that he'd been right about my being impatient. Horribly, dreadfully right.

I did expect all the best things in life to be brought to me on a polished silver charger engraved with my monogram, exactly the same way as my butler delivered my mail to me each morning at breakfast at home. I never thought of the cost, or the inconvenience to others. I'd never had to. This was simply how it *was* for me.

Even my loveless marriage had been more about me as a bride than Arthur as my husband. Once the flurry of attention surrounding our wedding—my trousseau, my new jewels and house and staff and carriage, our wedding trip—had passed, I'd made my general disappointment with married life so clear to Arthur that he'd swiftly retreated back to his bachelor ways, choosing to live at his club among his cronies rather than with me—which had been exactly what I'd wished, anyway.

When I'd come to London to find passion and excitement, I hadn't doubted I would find it. I'd felt the same after spying on Savage with Lady Telford that night in the garden. There had been no question in my mind that I would somehow arrange to be fucked by him, too. My introduction to him, the invitation from Lady Carleigh here to Wrenton, how Savage had bid against Lord Blackledge for me, how Savage had proved to be even better than my long-imagined dream lover could be—all of that had seemed almost inevitable to me.

To put the best face upon it, I could claim that it was no more than the fault of fate, and that fate had always smiled upon me. But this fate was not the same as Savage's kismet. My version of fate was couched in money and privilege, while his kismet had seemed more mystical, more romantic, and less dependent on the dollars in my bank accounts. For if I was honest with myself, I was exactly as Savage had said. I was a spoiled heiress from New York who had always gotten what I wanted.

Except, now, for Savage.

My muscles and joints ached from being stretched for so long in the same position, and I'd tugged so much against the cords that, silken or not, they'd rubbed and chafed against my skin. I was thirsty, and now that my blood had had time to cool, I was chilly as well. I lost track of how much time had passed as the sun moved across the sky and the shadows lengthened as I stared up at the ceiling.

Yet, what I thought of most as I lay there in that elegant bedroom was not when Savage would come back, but if. I'd given him every reason to stay away, and very little to come back. He'd said he would when he was ready, but I didn't entirely believe him, now. It could well be Barry who finally appeared to untie me; I wouldn't be surprised at all if he did.

I was humbled and contrite, and if only Savage would return, I'd do all I could to prove it to him. Of course I still longed for him, my desire a fever only he could break; that hadn't changed. I wasn't sure if he'd called me willful, stubborn, and selfish only as part of the Game, or because he really believed it of me. The ironic part was that now I believed it of myself.

If only he'd come back. . . .

TEN

I trust you had an enjoyable time whilst I was gone, Eve?"
Savage said when at last he came sauntering into the
bedroom. "Only the deepest of thoughts, appropriate to the
contrition of an Innocent?"

Relief was my first thought, flooding through me with
rare joy. He'd come back. He was smiling. His black mood
had been replaced by one that appeared much sunnier. And
surely, now, he'd untie me and ease my aching limbs—or
at least he would if I could keep my new resolutions.

"Yes, Master," I said, determined to play the Game better than he'd ever expected. "I did, Master."

He stood beside the bed, his gaze sweeping over my un-
clad body. While I had been trapped here, he'd clearly
been riding. Not only was he dressed for it—a white shirt
that was carelessly open at the throat, with the sleeves
rolled back over his biceps, close-fitting breeches, and tall,

polished boots—but his cheeks were ruddy from the fresh air, his hair windblown, and he smelled wonderfully of horse, leather, and the outdoors.

I could have stared at him forever. Each time I saw him, I was again bowled over by his sheer presence, and yet he had never looked more powerfully virile, or more attractive to me, than he did now.

"You surprise me, Eve," he said, sounding pleased and a little surprised. "I didn't expect to find you still here."

It must be patently obvious that I was there because, bound as I was, I'd no choice but to stay. How could it be otherwise? Yet, that didn't matter now, not now that he'd returned.

"You wished me to be here, Master," I answered simply, "and I am."

"Yes, but I've wished many things regarding you, Eve," he said cryptically, "yet wishing alone has not made them so."

"Yes, Master," I murmured, worrying that this might not be the proper answer.

Fortunately, he seemed preoccupied, lost in his own thoughts. He ran his fingertips along one of the cords binding my wrist, testing to see if it still held fast.

"I am surprised nonetheless," he said. "I was convinced that by now you would have shouted bloody hell for Barry and demanded he untie you. He would have, you know. I gave him leave to do so."

I gasped. "Truly?"

"Oh, yes," he said. "You succeeded far beyond my modest expectations for you. I didn't dream you'd last this long without giving in to your regal ways."

While there was nothing particularly regal about being tied spread-eagle and naked across his bed, the realization that I could have escaped, yet hadn't done so, stunned me. He was right, too: Mrs. Arthur Hart of Fifth Avenue would have demanded to be released, and quickly. I felt as if I'd been tried and tested and had passed, and the approval Savage was showing me now was all the sweeter because I hadn't known I was being judged.

I'd earned his approval because, at last, I was worthy.

"Thank you, Master," I said softly, my aching limbs forgotten. "It gives me joy to please you."

"I am glad of it, Eve." He leaned over to trace his finger along my jaw. "Very glad."

I turned my head to try to kiss his finger as the only part of him I might reach, but he'd dragged his fingers lower across my body, between my breasts, and over my belly. At last he cupped his hand over my quim, his fingers tangling in my curls as they covered my entrance. He didn't caress me, and it took every bit of my newfound willpower not to arch up against his hand and demand more.

"I did promise you a reward," he said, closely watching my face for my reaction. "Do you think you deserve it now?"

I could control what I said, but not my body's response to him. If he pressed his fingers into me—only a fraction would be enough—he'd discover the moisture that I felt gathering inside me. Already my heart was beating faster and my breath was quickening as well.

I swallowed hard, struggling for control. "It's not my decision, Master," I said. "It's for you to determine what I deserve."

"I already have, Eve." He lifted his hand from my body, leaving me bereft, and sat in the chair beside the bed to pull off his boots. At least he didn't summon Barry, to my relief, but did the task himself, dropping each boot to the floor with a thump. "I promised that you wouldn't be disappointed, and you won't."

He pulled open the drawer of the bedside table—the

same drawer that had held both the silk cords and the manacles—and pulled out a small flask. He opened it and poured a generous pool of an amber-colored oil into his hands. Working the oil into his palms, he came back to stand at the foot of the bed, between my spread legs.

"You must be sore by now," he said, dropping his voice low. "This will help."

He bent over me and began to smooth the oil into my arms, pressing his fingers deeply into my aching muscles. I whimpered, amazed at how very good his touch felt. The oil contained some ingredient that warmed my skin, taking away the chill and making me feel as if I were glowing from within.

Gradually he moved from my arms to my torso, pouring more oil between my breasts. This oil, too, he massaged into my skin with deep, powerful strokes, and I closed my eyes, practically purring with pleasure.

He took his time with my breasts, rubbing the oil in ever-narrowing circles until he reached my nipples. He rolled the sensitive tips between his fingers, tugging and drawing gently but insistently until I couldn't help rolling up into his caresses, my skin and blood growing warmer by the second. I pulled against the bonds, caring not how the cords dug into my wrists but only how much I could twist and turn against his hands.

He did the same with each of my legs, smoothing and rubbing the oil from my ankles to my calves and kneading the tight tendons of my inner thighs, over and over. Yet, no matter how near his hands came to my quim, at the last moment they always drew away, purposefully leaving the part of me that longed most for his touch feeling empty and unfulfilled.

My whole body was feverish now with arousal, and the heat of the oil combined with the sure touch of his hands. I'd surrendered to it, panting and writhing against the silk cords, yet still he would not give me the release I so desperately craved.

"You're so beautiful like this, Eve," he said, his voice harsh. "You're on fire for me, on fire with desire. Your cunt's weeping from wanting to take me in, isn't it? You must be like hot velvet inside, hot, wet velvet that's like heaven to my cock."

I could see that cock straining hard against the front of his pale trousers. From the size of the bulge, he must have been wickedly uncomfortable and as desperate as I was myself. Surely now he would relent and untie me, and give us both what we wanted.

Instead, he turned back to the drawer. As aroused as I was, the object he returned with shocked me.

"What—what is that, Master?" I stammered in confusion. "What is it for?"

I knew exactly what it was—an ivory phallus, carved in such loving detail as to be nearly a twin to Savage's cock—but I didn't want to consider what he'd do with it.

"It's for you," he said, practically growling the words. "I want to know how you look when you come around my cock."

Quickly he poured a measure of the oil onto the dildo, slathering it along the sides to make it slick. Then with one hand he gently parted my lips, and thrust nearly the entire length of the dildo deep inside, back and forth three times.

I cried out, bucking my hips as much as I could against the restraints. I was clinging to the very edge of my climax, my body bowed and tense with release so tantalizingly near. He smoothed his fingers over my oil-slicked lips, pressing my taut flesh against the ivory. If he worked the dildo again, I would spend, yet still he kept me hanging.

"This is how you look when you take my cock," he said, his words coming fast. "I can see how your quim stretches to take me, how your lips plump and curl against me. You're so red and wet and swollen, Eve, so close, that I can see that fat little clit of yours trembling and needy. So beautiful, and so hot."

I couldn't answer. I had no words.

And when he pressed the pad of his thumb against my pearl at the same moment as he began thrusting the dildo again, I screamed, spinning out of control as pleasure rocked my body.

He didn't wait until I'd finished spending before he yanked the silk cords first from my wrists and then my ankles. I curled my arms and legs, crying out as the blood rushed back to my aching muscles, and I pressed my legs together, shuddering as he pushed the dildo deeper within my channel.

But Savage had seen enough. He tore open the front of his trousers and released his cock. He grabbed the dildo and pulled it from me, and before I could feel its loss he shoved and buried his cock deep within me.

I cried out again, gladly trading the hard ivory for Savage's heated flesh, and when he pushed my thighs back and hooked my legs over his shoulders, I sensed another climax building fast within me. I was stretched tight this way, his cock stroking me deliciously within as he pumped his hips against the backs of my thighs. I took my sensitized breasts in my hands, squeezing and pulling on my nipples in time to his thrusts.

"Look at me, Eve," he demanded raggedly. "Look at me!"

I dragged my eyes open, met the intensity of his blue-eyed gaze, and immediately spent again, the spasms clenching and ripping through me with dizzying force. I rode them out as, in a frenzy of lust, he pounded into me, and then he, too, found his climax, roaring with the force of it.

He dropped forward onto the bed, pulling me into his arms and holding me tightly against his heaving chest. I pressed against him to savor the closeness as we both recovered. This was the first time I'd spent twice in such a short time, and little aftershocks continued to reverberate through my body. I loved being naked and sated while he was still dressed, my warm, oil-sheened skin lying in wicked contrast to his elegantly expensive clothes.

Furtively, so that he wouldn't notice, I rubbed my thumbs lightly across my wrists where he'd tied the cords, striving to ease the sting. The skin was raw and tender, crisscrossed with small abrasions and fresh-blooming bruises. It was my own fault, of course. He'd tied the cords just tight enough to hold me, not to hurt me. If I hadn't struggled against them, I would have been fine. I'd done this to myself. He'd never want to harm me in any way. He was my Protector, wasn't he?

"Thank you, Eve," he whispered into my ear, kissing the side of my throat. "That was perfect. No, *you* are perfect."

I smiled, tears of happiness beading my lashes. "Perfect" was so much better than "selfish" or "willful" or any of the other things he'd called me earlier.

Being perfect for him was . . . perfect.

When I woke, the night sky was dark blue and the moon had risen, and Savage was lying on his side, watching me.

I smiled up at him, his dark hair falling around his face and his features shadowed in the night-filled room. He hadn't lit any candles—or had Barry light them—which meant he'd likely slept as well, and hadn't been watching me the entire time. In the beginning, his watching had unsettled me, but now I liked it, even cherished it as proof of how much he cared for me. It made me feel safe, protected, knowing he wouldn't let any harm come to me, as if he were my own guardian angel.

"Master," I whispered, my voice groggy with sleep.

He reached for my hand, raising it to his lips to kiss it, his lips and beard grazing the back of my hand. He turned it over and nipped lightly at my palm, making me sigh.

"You asked me if I was lonely," he said gruffly. "I did not know what loneliness was until I was apart from you today."

The way he said it tore at my heart. I slipped my hand free of his and reached up to lay my palm along the side of his face, cradling his cheekbone.

"You're not lonely now," I said softly, "nor am I."

He drew in his breath, held it, then let it out as a long sigh.

"My father sat on the boards of several trading firms," he said. "He had access to considerable information regarding incoming ships and their cargoes, information that he used to his own financial advantage. My uncle—my mother's younger brother—was an impulsive man plagued by ill luck and bad choices. From pity, Father shared some scrap of news about a new venture, and my uncle invested the last bit of his fortune in it. The ship was lost, bankrupting my uncle, who responded by blowing his brains out in the front room at White's."

"Oh, Savage," I said. I was surprised, but not shocked. My own father's world was sadly full of men whose fortunes rose and fell with terrifying speed, and for whom the only honorable solution seemed suicide. "How dreadful for your family!"

"Yes," he said, his voice leaden. "Mother blamed Father, and left him abruptly and fled to Paris, without bothering to say farewell. I was away at school; I never saw her again, for she died soon after of cholera. My uncle had been a popular man, and the scandal of his ruin and death broke Father. The doctors said it was his heart, but I know it was bitterness and the condemnation of those he'd loved and trusted most that killed him. When I became the seventh Earl of Savage two weeks before my sixteenth birthday, I also became absolutely alone."

"I'm sorry," I said, struck by the insignificance of words. "I'm sorry for you now, to carry that burden, and I'm sorry for the boy you were then."

His smile was more of a grimace.

"I survived," he said. "Day by day, I did what was required of me. But you can understand why I find trust a very difficult commodity to give, or to accept."

"We are two of a kind, aren't we, Savage?" I said sadly. "We're what others have made us. We did survive, yes, but at a cost. We *are* renegades, exactly as you said, outcasts apart from the rest of the world."

"Not apart from you," he said, his voice as dark as the night around us. "Never from you."

"Never from you," I repeated. I reached up with my other hand to cradle his face. "I'm here, Master."

I drew his face down and kissed him; it was less a kiss born of passion than a pledge of trust and understanding that was in its way far more intimate than anything else we'd done or shared.

He pulled me into his arms, holding me tight. "Stay with me, Eve," he said. "Don't go."

"I will stay, Savage," I whispered, blinking back tears of emotion as I curled as closely against him as I could. "I will."

The next day, I sat in Savage's enormous marble bath, basking drowsily in the steamy water while my maid, Simpson, washed my hair. Through the open bathroom door, I saw Savage behind his desk in the sitting room, reading and reviewing various letters from his bankers and lawyers that had arrived earlier from London, letters that needed replies. It made me smile to see him like that, all brusque business and orders for his secretary beside him, after so much pleasure with me.

Only I saw that side of him, and only I knew the true tenderness we'd shared. Holding that knowledge like a treasured secret, I happily sank a little lower into the water.

"Here, ma'am, don't drown yourself." Simpson fretted, pulling me back up against the side of the tub. "I'd never forgive myself if anything happened to you while you was in my care."

I laughed softly. "Nothing is going to happen to me, Simpson. What kind of person would drown in the bath?"

"Oh, it's happened, ma'am," the maid said darkly. "Happened plenty o' times, to plenty o' ladies and gentlemen, too, I'm sure of it."

"Then I appreciate your concern, Simpson," I said, closing my eyes. It was how lady's maids demonstrated their loyalty, fussing about like this. Hamlin could be much the same, treating me as if I were made of the most fragile porcelain. "I wouldn't wish to perish here in his lordship's bath."

Simpson leaned closer, lowering her voice. "There's others besides me thinking of you, ma'am. Lady Carleigh's worried sick, and that's the truth."

I frowned, and opened my eyes. "Why should Lady Carleigh be worrying over me?"

"Because, ma'am," Simpson said succinctly, "you're like a prisoner in these rooms, ma'am. His lordship's keeping you locked up tight as some poor traitor in the Tower, making you take your meals up here alone with him and not letting you out for anything. All the other guests, they're speaking of nothing else."

"What I choose to do with Lord Savage is not anyone

else's affair, Simpson," I said, a little testy. "Not Lady Carleigh's, or the other guests', or most especially yours. I can assure you, I'm hardly his lordship's prisoner."

"No, ma'am?" Simpson asked, vigorously squeezing the shampoo through my hair. "Then why don't he let you come down to dine with the other guests?"

"It's not that he doesn't 'let' me, Simpson," I said. "It's no mystery. He and her ladyship agreed that after the unpleasantness between him and Lord Blackledge the other night, it would be best if he and I dined in private, apart from the others."

"Then that would be news to her ladyship, ma'am," Simpson said. "She's fearing for you, wondering why you're keeping apart."

My frown deepened. This was becoming too much. "Forgive me, Simpson, but I doubt very much that her ladyship is confiding her fears in you."

"But her ladyship did, ma'am," Simpson insisted, "on account of me being the only one his lordship lets see you. Excepting Mr. Barry, of course, not that he's to be trusted, belonging all loyal to his lordship's household as he does."

"Then I believe you're mistaken, Simpson, or perhaps you misheard Lady Carleigh," I said. Why would a viscountess like her ladyship make a maid like Simpson into her confidante? "She and Lord Savage agreed to it on Tuesday night. I assure you, Simpson, that his lordship has only my best interests in the matter."

"As you say, ma'am," Simpson said, in a way that made it clear she thought that what I was saying was complete nonsense. "But while his lordship's taking such fine care of you, ma'am, has he ever spoken to you of his poor wife, of what became of Lady Savage?"

"Really, Simpson," I said firmly. "Now you truly do presume on my good nature. Lord Savage is not a modern-day Bluebeard. The tragic details of his wife's death should be of absolutely no concern to you at any time, and I doubt Lady Carleigh would approve of her servants gossiping about any of her guests in such a disgusting and lurid fashion."

But Simpson persisted. "It's not lurid, ma'am, but the truth. Lady Savage was a young and beautiful lady in her prime—just like you, ma'am—with no ailments or illnesses to speak of, and a loving mother to his lordship's little boy. Then all of a sudden, there she was one morning, dead as can be in her own fine house. What do you make of that, ma'am?"

"That you are an inveterate tattle and slanderer, Simpson," I said, disgusted. Like every mistress with a staff, I'd had to deal with gossiping servants, and I'd even sacked several for it. "My husband also died suddenly. Does that make you suspect me of foul play as well?"

"No, ma'am," Simpson said. "But you're not—"

"Is it your habit to warn every Innocent who has drawn Lord Savage as a Protector in Lady Carleigh's game?"

"No, ma'am," Simpson said promptly. "Because he's never behaved like this before when he's come to Wrenton to play the Game, not with any other lady. You can ask her ladyship if you don't believe me."

For the first time, I paused, letting my doubts creep in. Savage had told me exactly that himself, over and over, saying that I was unlike any other woman he'd known. I'd taken it as the kind of pleasing but empty flattery that gentlemen whisper to ladies, especially ladies they wish to seduce. I'd never let myself seriously consider that, with Savage, it might be true.

"Keeping you all to himself, ma'am, away from the others, being so possessive-like, picking that fight with Mr. Henery—that wasn't like his lordship, not at all," Simpson continued. "No one plays the Game like that."

"I wouldn't know otherwise," I said, striving to sound aloof. "I've found the way he has played it to be quite—quite enjoyable."

Simpson regarded me with a look that could only be described as pitying. Uneasily I remembered how the maid herself had been an Innocent before—perhaps even with Savage, for all that she'd denied it—and was far more knowledgeable about men and sex than I myself ever would likely be.

"Forgive me, ma'am," Simpson said, "but that's because you are the most innocent Innocent that her ladyship's ever invited here to play. Other ladies are more worldly-wise, if you understand. They would've noticed the difference in Lord Savage straightaway."

Abruptly I stood, scattering water drops, and Simpson hurried to wrap me in a towel. This conversation was making me increasingly uncomfortable, even insecure, and I felt that I was betraying Savage simply by having it. The sooner it ended, the better.

"I will admit that I'm not the most experienced of ladies," I said, "That is why I accepted Lady Carleigh's invitation. I wished to, ah, to broaden my education, and with Lord Savage I have done exactly that."

"Yes, ma'am," Simpson said, blotting my arms. "Forgive me, ma'am, but these bruises on your wrists—"

I jerked back my hands, tucking them inside the towel. I should have realized the maid would notice. My fair skin now wore wide bands of bruises like matching bracelets, black-and-blue and rubbed raw by the silk cords that Savage had used yesterday. My ankles were likewise marked, and there was a fresher mark on my shoulder from this morning, where Savage had nipped at me again in the heat of his fucking.

I didn't mind the bruises—in fact, in a way I'd become proud of them. I'd left my marks on him as well. They were all visible proof of how intense our passion for each other could become, and how, too, I became so abandoned to the pleasure he stirred in me that I hadn't been able to tell the difference between that pleasure and pain. It was all vastly complicated, jumbled together into an intoxicating brew, and I didn't want to change any of it.

Except having the lady's maid notice now.

"You are being far too forward, Simpson," I said. I stepped from the tub, wrapping the towel closely around me and tucking one end in to make it stay in place like a gown.

"Yes, ma'am," the maid said softly, wrapping another towel around my dripping hair. "You've lost flesh, too. Don't he let you eat what Cook sends up, ma'am?"

"Of course I've been eating," I said. I did eat; I just hadn't eaten much. I'd been so consumed with passion that my appetite for mere food had disappeared, but I hadn't realized I'd lost weight, too. Not for the first time, I was thankful that Hamlin hadn't accompanied me here. Hamlin would have spotted it in an instant, and likely tried to force-feed me as well. "I'm hardly starving, Simpson."

"No, ma'am," Simpson said, hesitating. "I know there's only two more days before the week's done and the Game with it, but if his lordship dares go beyond pleasure, you need only to call for—"

"How delectable you look, my dear Eve," Savage said, joining us. "Venus rising from the sea would be envious of you in my bath."

I blushed, both from the compliment and from wondering if he'd overheard any of my conversation with Simpson. Immediately Simpson stepped back, with her head bowed, dipping a quick curtsey to Savage as she made way for him to join me.

"I trust I'll smell more agreeable than if I'd landed at

your feet in a scallop shell," I said, smiling as I held my hand out to him.

He was barefoot, wearing loose linen trousers and a V-neck sweater of soft blue lamb's wool that was the exact color of his eyes. The fact that he wore the sweater without bothering with a shirt beneath it was thrillingly intimate to me—something that an earl would never ordinarily do, and something, too, that I guessed must pain Barry exceedingly. He'd dressed in careless haste and without the manservant's help, going from being in bed with me directly to the pile of letters in his sitting room, and the results looked like it. He'd lingered so long with me, too, that he hadn't left time to be shaved, which meant that his jaw remained darkened with ungentlemanly stubble.

But in my eyes, Savage had never looked more irresistibly handsome, his sleeves shoved up over his forearms and the deep V of the sweater's neck offering me a heady glimpse of his broad chest and the dark, curling hair upon it. Beside his properly dressed secretary in his stiff, starched collar and tailored suit, Savage didn't looked like an earl at all. He looked like a pirate.

As he took both my hands in his, his smile was roguishly piratical, too, his teeth white against his stubbled jaw.

"Very well, then," he said gallantly. "Not Venus rising from the sea, but my own Innocent rising from the sweetest of rose petals strewn across her bath."

I laughed, pulling the towel from my head and letting my hair fall over my shoulders in damp, unruly curls.

"No rose petals, either," I said. "Only some sinfully expensive French nonsense, poured into the water to scent it and me with it."

"Ever the American, literal to a fault," he said, laughing with me as his fingers linked into mine. "Where's the romance in your soul, Eve?"

"You have more than enough romance in your soul for us both, and a dozen others besides," I teased in return. It was true, too. He was the most romantic man I'd ever met, or perhaps the most romantic man who wasn't afraid to let it show.

"If I do, Eve," he said, "then I'll lavish my stock entirely upon you."

His laughter faded as he raised one of my hands to his lips. His blue eyes smoldered, white-hot, when he looked at me: I could express it no other way. With his gaze locked with mine, he kissed not my hand but the bruise circling my wrist. When he was done, he lifted my other hand and did the same, his lips tracing a protective ring around my wrist that reminded me all over again of everything we'd shared.

I didn't realize I was holding my breath until he finished. I sighed in a shuddering rush of delight, a sigh that blew away all the niggling little doubts that Simpson had planted, too.

How could I ever doubt Savage when he'd do things like that? How could I ever suspect him of anything other than being his own darkly irresistible self?

"Dismiss your maid," he said, still holding my arched wrist before his mouth. "I want you alone."

I nodded, unable to look away from him. "Simpson, that will be all."

I was vaguely aware of the maid curtseying, seeing from the corner of my eye only the final dip of Simpson's black-clad figure as she backed from the room.

Savage didn't wait until she'd closed the door before he slipped his hand inside my towel. He quickly found my bottom, spreading his fingers to caress the swell of one cheek.

I swayed into him and rested my hands on his chest, loving the feel of his muscles beneath the soft wool sweater.

I parted my lips and tipped my face up toward his, sure he'd kiss me now.

He didn't.

"What was your maid saying to you?" he asked. He was smiling still, but the warmth was gone from his eyes.

"Nothing of any importance," I answered. That much was true, and I hoped it would be enough.

"Really, Eve?" He turned his head slightly, cocking a single dark brow to show his incredulity. "Nothing?"

I shook my head, drops of water flicking from my tangled hair. I'd no reason to be nervous with Savage, and yet I was. My gaze dropped from his eyes to his mouth.

"That 'nothing' upset you," he said. "I could hear it in your voice."

I sighed. "It was nothing but backstairs tattle, the kind of nonsense servants are always whispering among themselves about their betters. But—but you're right. What Simpson said did upset me, because it was so preposterous."

"Then tell me." He continued to caress my bottom beneath the towel, arousing yet comforting at the same time. "If you're upset, I need to know, so that I can remedy the problem. I don't want you to keep things to yourself. A trouble shared is a trouble halved."

I smiled nervously. "Didn't Benjamin Franklin say that first? A wise American?"

"You're stalling, Eve," he said. "Tell me what Simpson told you."

I sighed again, and at last relented. "She said that Lady Carleigh and the others are worried about us. About how we keep to ourselves and don't join them."

"Ah," he said. His expression didn't change. "So they are worried about us being such hermits. Would you rather have played the Game with others?"

"Hardly." I thought of how grateful I was not to have

been forced into sex with Lord Blackledge, or Lord Carleigh, or any of the other men, really. I'd come here wanting only Savage, and nothing I'd seen downstairs had changed my mind even a little.

"You've told me you left New York to find sexual adventure," he said. "Perhaps Lady Carleigh is right to be worried. Perhaps I've narrowed your experience too far by playing the Game the way I've chosen."

"But you haven't," I declared without hesitation. "Not in the least. I wouldn't trade this time in your company for all the world."

He smiled suddenly, like the sun coming out from behind gray clouds. "Nor would I, Eve. Was that all Simpson had to say?"

I paused. I'd gone this far without a misstep. I might as well continue to speak the rest and not be burdened with a guilty conscience on account of the omission.

"They are worried about us together," I said, "but more specifically they worry about you. They believe you have changed since you've become my Protector."

He frowned. "Simpson dared say that to you?"

"She did." My smile was wistful. "Evidently Lord and Lady Carleigh and the rest of them miss the earlier version of Lord Savage. He must have been so very entertaining in company."

"Would you prefer to have him here as well, Eve?" he asked, a note of bitterness to his voice. "That other chap? You sound as if you would."

"I never said that, Savage," I said defensively, surprised. "Not at all."

"You didn't have to," he said. "It was clear enough from your face alone. You're a dreadful liar, Eve."

He tried to smile again, and failed. I glimpsed a flash of unexpected vulnerability in his eyes, a doubt that I'd never expected to see there.

I reached up to cradle his jaw in my hands. "Then you'll believe me when I say that I do not want any other man here with me now. Only you, Savage."

He pulled my hands away from his face, though he didn't let them go.

"I'm a different man with you, Eve," he said, rubbing his thumbs lightly across my wrists. "I've told you that before. I've never been so—so reclusive with an Innocent here at Wrenton. I've always shared, and I've both given and taken, for the sheer sport of it. Some weeks I've fucked anything that was in my path, because that was just what I did. Good old Savage the satyr, insatiable to the last."

I didn't want to hear that, and tried not to wince when I did. What kept me there was the turmoil I saw in his eyes, a confusion that he clearly understood no better than I did myself.

He gave his head a rueful little toss, as if to shake away whatever demons were gnawing at him.

"But I don't want to give away a moment with you, Eve," he said, "and even the thought of another man with you drives me mad. You saw what happened with Henery. You were there. I've never done that before, and it was all because he dared touch you."

"You defended me, Savage," I said. "I'll never fault you for that."

"No," he said, his voice heavy. "But you see, that's exactly it. You make me different, Eve, and I can't begin to know why or how. It's simply how it is."

But it wasn't simple. His emotions were written raw all over his face, warring within him.

"Which version of yourself do you prefer?" I asked gently. It was a risky question, but I had to learn the answer.

"Which *version*?" He grimaced. "You say that as if I have a choice, Eve, as if I can change back and forth like some penny conjurer's best trick."

"Are you happy the way you've been with me?" I asked, the same question in other words. "Or would you rather return to being that charming, lighthearted fellow who apparently hopped from bed to bed?"

"Don't, Eve," he said sharply, taking several steps away from me to put both physical and emotional distance between us. "There's no need for you to try to coax me into a better humor. You, of anyone, must know by now I'm not persuaded by empty words."

I hugged my arms around my breasts in the damp towel, suddenly chill without him to warm me. "Then why won't you answer my question?"

"Because it doesn't matter," he said curtly. "In two days the Game will be done, and we'll go our own ways. If you are satisfied with this week, then so am I, and that will be an end to it."

His words cut me hard, exactly as he'd intended. "But what if I—we—don't wish it to end?"

"It will end, Eve," he said, his dark brows drawn tightly together. "It must end. That's the entire point of the Game—a week for amusement, experimentation, for doing things here that we must not do in the greater polite world. You knew that when you accepted Lady Carleigh's invitation."

I did. But I also remembered how he'd asked me not to leave him, and I'd promised I wouldn't. Was that only part of the Game, too, or had he simply wearied of me since then?

"What became of all that romance in your soul?" I asked, tremulous. "I thought you wanted to lavish that on me."

He swung around, leaving me to stare at his back while he pretended to look anywhere but at me.

"Do not confuse romance with music-hall sentiment, Eve," he said, his voice raised as if to convince himself by volume as well as me. "We're both too old to believe in the foolishness of love songs. In two days, we'll part without any regrets or looking back, exactly as all the other Protectors and Innocents will. And it will end."

"And it will end," I repeated, unable to keep the sorrow from my voice. I'd known from the beginning that I'd have Savage for only a week, and I'd assured myself that that would be enough. I'd thought I'd become a changed, modern woman. I'd believed I was ready to live as carelessly as any gentleman, and take my pleasure without a thought.

I'd been wrong.

I stared at his broad shoulders wrapped in pale blue, his dark hair curling over the nape of his neck, and I couldn't begin to think of returning to London alone. How could I pretend that he'd never come into my life? How could I not look back, not remember all he'd taught me, shown me, given me?

How could I be too old for love songs when I'd never fallen in love before?

And yet Savage was right. This was the Game. This was what I'd agreed to, and what he expected.

No, what he *wanted*. I couldn't forget that. He was mine and I was his for two more days, two more nights. That was all, and I couldn't dare squander a second.

I took a deep breath, unsure of what to do next. I'd only one choice, really, and I took it.

"Yes, Master," I said softly. "Only two days are left for you to continue my education, Master. I still have so much more to learn."

I watched his head straighten, his shoulders square in the sweater. Slowly he turned to face me again. His handsome features were composed in what I now thought of as his master's face. His jaw was purposefully set, his mouth curved in the slightest of smiles, and his eyes were heavy-lidded, as if all the world bored him. With him, it was all as good as a pasteboard mask, calculated to hide his true feelings and to reveal nothing.

Only then did he kiss me, pushing my head back into the crook of his arm to grind his mouth against mine. It was supposed to be a master's kiss of sensual dominance, and it was. But I could also taste his uneasiness and the chaotic energy of the emotions he refused to acknowledge, all of it proof that no matter what he might say, he wasn't ready to part with me yet.

All he had to do was admit it.

Two days, I thought as I kissed him hungrily in return, *only two days more. . . .*

ELEVEN

"Look at that rain," Savage said, staring gloomily out the window. He'd pulled on a pair of loose, striped linen pajama trousers that were hanging perilously low on his hips, and was sipping a cup of the tea that Barry had brought in earlier. "Damn. And here I'd planned to show you the gardens this morning."

"Truly?" I said, surprised. I found my costume and slipped it over my head, pulling my hair free to fall down my back. I slid from the bed to go stand behind Savage, and looped my arms around his waist. We hadn't left Savage's rooms for five days. I hadn't objected, of course, but I had seen nothing of Wrenton's famed rooms or grounds. I'd have a great deal of inventing to do if anyone in New York ever asked me for details.

"Truly," he said, still staring at the rain driving against the windows. "To a certain degree, that meddlesome maid was correct. I have been selfish where you are concerned."

"No, you haven't," I said quickly, a note of panic creeping into my voice. "It's how I wished it as well."

"Be easy, Eve," he said. "I've absolutely no intention of sharing you with anyone else. In that regard, I am entirely selfish. No, I meant that the Carleighs' house is a pretty one, and you've seen almost nothing of it. The gardens are quite fine at this time of year, and there's a charming folly with a bathing pool tucked inside."

"That does sound agreeable," I said with relief. We'd enjoyed ourselves so much in Savage's oversize tub that I could easily imagine what we'd try with more water and space.

"It is," he said, sipping the tea. "Besides, this far into the week, I don't expect the place to still be overrun with nymphs and satyrs. By now their interest—and their cocks—are usually beginning to flag."

I smiled, resting my cheek against his bare shoulder. "I doubt anyone will be outdoors today."

The rain had turned the wide front lawns into a sea of murky green, and blurred the trees with the gray skies into a single soggy horizon. Silvery puddles collected like little seas in the long gravel drive. Raindrops splattered hard against the window glass, making me grateful to be snug indoors.

"Not without a raft," Savage said philosophically. "We'll simply have to find other ways to amuse ourselves inside the house, that's all."

"I've never known that to be a challenge, Master," I said, slipping my fingers down his flat belly and inside his trousers to close lightly around his cock. At once it began to stiffen and grow beneath my touch, a certainty I never tired of. "Not for us."

"Hardly," he said. He finished the tea, striving to appear

nonchalant as he put the empty cup and saucer on the table, but the porcelain clattered against the wood and his breathing was quickening. It was clear he was enjoying the easy rhythm of my strokes, and he pushed against my fingers.

"No, Master," I purred, pressing my breasts against his side. He'd given me so much pleasure that I loved the chance to be able to give it back to him like this, and watching for the subtle changes in his expression.

But, to my surprise, after a few moments he gently lifted my hand to stop me.

"Not that, not yet," he said, kissing the back of my hand. "I've other ideas for this morning."

"Have you now?" I asked, disappointed, yet intrigued. Whenever I thought we'd exhausted the possibilities of our bodies together, he'd always suggested some intriguing new position or technique. I wasn't sure whether it was his imagination or his experience that was so boundless; I preferred to think it was his imagination, inspired by me.

"I do," he said, again staring out at the rain. "There's plenty to entertain us in other parts of this house. I was considering the gallery on the upper floor. I trust you have an appreciation for art?"

"Of course," I said, a bit indignantly. I appreciated art as well as any lady in New York, and had accompanied my husband on the dutiful trudge through the museums of Florence and Rome on our honeymoon. And didn't I make my annual contribution to the Metropolitan Museum each year to prove it? "Just because I'm an American doesn't mean I'm a hopeless philistine as well."

"Then you are certain to enjoy Carleigh's collection," he said, smiling as he rang for Barry. "He and his ancestors have amassed a rather extraordinary group of pieces. A small group, to be sure, but choice. There's a selection of cinquecento engravings that I believe you'll find particularly . . . inspiring."

The gleam in his eye told me these would not be the same type of Italian pictures that were being collected by the wealthy gentlemen of taste in New York, the sad-eyed Madonnas and weeping saints.

"I promise you'll find me to be a model connoisseur," I said. I was curious, and determined not to be amazed or shocked by whatever it was he was going to show me. "You'll see."

"Indeed," he said, his smile widening as if he were party to some wicked secret. "Ah, Barry, here you are. Send for Mrs. Hart's favorite dressing gown. I'm sure her maid will know which it is."

"I'm to wear my own clothes?" I asked, startled. I'd become so accustomed to wearing either the filmy Innocent costume or—more usually—nothing at all that the thought of again wearing my own silk dressing gown, heavy with lace and rich embroidery, was almost shocking.

"Not real clothes," he said. "Only the dressing gown, with nothing beneath. I don't know who we may encounter in the halls, and while I'm taking you upstairs to the gallery, that is the extent of my generosity. I intend to remain thoroughly selfish where your person is concerned, and share not even a glimpse of you with another man."

"Thank you, Master," I said softly. He might have regarded his small gesture as being selfish, but to me it was another sign that I meant more to him than his role as my Protector required. "I am grateful."

"You might not be quite so grateful, Eve, when you learn what I've planned," he said, turning toward the table beside the bed. "I want you on the bed now, on your stomach with your legs spread as widely apart as you can make them."

Obediently I climbed onto the bed and lay on my stomach as he'd ordered. I'd become very good at obeying him. I'd learned that the consequences of disobedience were too painful to ignore, just as the rewards for obedience were so delicious that I'd have been a fool to run counter to his orders.

I could hear him digging through the table's drawer behind me, and my heart beat a little faster, trying to imagine what he'd find there this time. Could it be the ivory dildo again, or the oil that had heated my skin, or the handcuffs that he never had used, or some other plaything altogether?

"This won't work," he said, his disapproval clear. "You're not nearly open enough for me."

I tried to spread my legs more widely, stretching my hip joints, but that didn't please him, either.

"Not like that," he said impatiently, sitting on the edge of the bed. "Come here beside me."

I sat up on my knees and nestled beside him, smoothing my hair back behind my ears. In his palm were two perfect spheres of gold about an inch in diameter, connected by a length of gold chain.

"The Chinese call these ben wah," he said, holding them out for me to see. "I had them made especially for you."

I studied the balls in his hand, pleased that he'd thought far enough ahead to procure them. He'd even had my initials monogrammed on the side of each sphere, swirling letters etched into the gold. But what exactly were they for?

"Thank you, Master," I said, finally deciding they must be a gift of jewelry. Presuming that the chain was some kind of bracelet, I reached out to wrap it around my wrist, but he pulled it back, out of my reach.

"No, Eve," he said patiently. "The first place the balls must go is in your mouth. Open for me."

I opened my mouth and he popped the balls inside, where they lay heavily on my tongue. Tentatively, I shifted them against the insides of my cheeks, making them bump against each other. There was something shifting inside the balls that made them jostle and quiver when touched, and I felt the vibrations reverberate on my tongue.

"Make them as wet as you can, Eve," he said, watching the balls bulge against my cheeks. "You'll want them that way when I push them into your sweet cunt."

I couldn't smile, with my mouth so full, but my eyes brightened with anticipation. I doubted he'd have much trouble with my quim accepting the balls, either, whether they were wet with saliva or not. I could already feel the moisture gathering between my legs, the telltale warmth of arousal blossoming low in my belly.

He patted his thigh. "I want you here, Eve, with your face to the floor," he said. "Lie across my legs with your ass in the air."

With the gold balls still in my mouth, I draped myself across his thighs as he'd ordered, my bottom raised and my head forward, my breasts falling forward and my hair hanging down like a curtain.

He didn't like that, and impatiently gathered my hair in one hand and shoved it over my other shoulder so he could see my face. With his hands on my hips, he pushed me a little farther forward until I was at last arranged to his satisfaction.

"There," he said, his breath quickening as he flipped the hem of my costume up to bare my bottom and all else besides. "Now spread your legs for me."

I didn't need to be asked twice. I'd come to love being shamelessly open to him like this, displaying myself so that he couldn't mistake his effect on me. It felt like the most primal kind of seduction, without words or subtlety, as if Savage were not just my lover but my mate.

"Beautiful," he whispered, his palms gently easing my thighs farther apart. "There's nothing a man likes more than seeing a woman's sex like this. Red, aroused, juicy, like a ripe fruit begging to be tasted."

He slid his fingers along my seam, teasing me before he finally parted the lips of my quim. With the knuckle of his forefinger, he pressed lightly on my pearl, circling it with exactly the right amount of pressure. I gasped, nearly letting the balls drop from my mouth, and he chuckled.

"What a waste it is, Eve, for me not to take you when you're this close," he said, his voice low and rough with desire. "You're tempting me in every way possible, and there's nothing I want more than to bury my cock as deeply as I can in you. But not yet."

He cupped his hand beneath my mouth. "Give me the ben wah balls."

I opened my mouth and the balls dropped into his hand. I'd already guessed where they would go, but I wasn't prepared for the sensation of having him slowly push first one sphere and then the other deep inside me, with the chain left to dangle outside my body.

Although the balls slipped easily into my channel—they were much smaller than Savage's cock—he stirred them lightly with his finger, making them knock against each other. I whimpered as the vibrations rippled inside me, and automatically I clenched around the balls, my muscles striving to hold them tight.

He chuckled at my response. "You like those, don't you?"

"Yes—yes, Master," I stammered. "Although the feeling is—is unexpected."

"Then it's exactly right." He gently lifted me off his knee to stand. "Better?"

"You know it's not," I said irritably. Inside me the balls were not uncomfortable, but I was acutely aware of their weight and their jittery vibration as they shifted against the fleshy walls of my passage. "That is, no, Master."

He smiled. "You will grow accustomed to the sensations, I think, and then you'll come to enjoy them. Take care to hold the balls tightly, too. You wouldn't wish to have them drop out and roll across the floor, would you? Ah, here's Barry with your dressing gown now."

Barry bowed and entered, my pink dressing gown over his arm and my beaded, heeled mules in his hand. He began to come toward us, but Savage put his hand up to stop him.

"Eve, go to Barry," he said, rising and reaching for his robe. "Walk across the room to meet him."

It seemed a curious request, even from Savage, but I saw no harm to it, and began walking across the room. Three steps, and I stopped, startled. As I moved, the gold balls within me moved, too, like a tickling caress from within that I'd no way to ease.

"Go, Eve," Savage said, knowing perfectly well what was happening to me. "No dawdling. Fetch your dressing gown and slippers. Now that we've decided to visit the picture gallery upstairs, I'd like to go there directly."

With fresh resolve, I let Barry help me into my dressing gown. I slipped on my mules, and held my hand out to Savage, trying not to think of the golden spheres, and utterly failing.

Savage knew it, too. "Patience, Eve, patience," he said gently as he led me through the door. "The more you can control your own response, the more intense your release can be. Consider it as another test."

I sighed restlessly. "Yes, Master."

He stopped and kissed me. "You will do it for me, Eve," he said with unexpected gentleness, "and you'll do it for yourself. I'd never ask you to endure anything if I didn't believe you'd the strength to succeed."

I took a deep breath and nodded, determined not to give in to the vibrating balls but to do what Savage had said. I wouldn't fail him in something as simple as this. Besides, he couldn't expect me to endure this all day. At some point, he'd have to remove the torturous little spheres, and then reward me as well as himself—perhaps even in the picture gallery.

Yet, by the time we'd walked the length of several halls and up two different staircases, I was flushed and clinging tightly to Savage's arm. I hadn't realized the effort involved in keeping the shifting balls in place, or how I'd had to keep consciously contracting the muscles of my channel as I walked. My body ached with a kind of half arousal, desperately poised on the very edge of longing and frustration. I was grateful we hadn't seen any of the other guests, and only the occasional footman or parlor maid who'd discreetly turned away as we'd passed.

Now I stood with Savage in the arched doorway of a long, narrow picture gallery, and I was too on edge to care about a single one of the paintings that hung in heavy gold frames all along the walls. The rain that drummed on the leaded-glass skylights matched the relentless thrum of desire in my veins. With an agitated sigh, I sank onto one of the wide, cushioned benches in the center of the gallery and tried to pull Savage down with me.

"You wish me to be patient, Master," I said, unfastening the silk frogs that fastened my dressing gown. "You wish me to wait. But, oh, Master, I cannot wait, not when I have you beside me, and I can never be patient with these wretched toys of yours inside me."

Yet, he resisted, standing instead of joining me on the bench. "You must wait, Eve, and you must be patient, or I'll never give you what truly want."

"Then I'll pull them out myself," I said impulsively. "You can't torment me any longer like this."

I reached between my legs to search for the gold chain that held the spheres together, intending to yank them free. But as soon as my fingers found the chain, his hand closed tightly around my wrist to stop me.

"I decide when to remove the ben wah," he said, his face

so close to mine that I could see the darker flecks in his blue-gray eyes, and every lash around them. "I decide how long you will remain in this 'torment,' as you call it. You will be patient, Eve, and you will wait, because I wish it. Not you."

Not so long ago—only a matter of days, really—I would have rebelled. Now his dominance seemed not only right but undeniably arousing. Only Savage truly knew what was best for me, and only Savage cared this much about my pleasure.

"Yes, Master," I said, my voice husky with longing. "I will wait. For you, I will be patient."

He smiled, and kissed my forehead, gently, a gesture of tenderness, not mastery. "I knew you would, Eve. Because of that, I'll grant you a brief respite here, and permit you to regain your composure."

"Thank you, Master," I said. Sitting still, the balls quieted, and I felt less feverish. I could be patient, especially for him. "You are . . . kind."

"Kind?" He cocked a single dark brow. "Not so long ago, you damned me as cruel."

"I was wrong," I said simply. "You are most kind, Master."

Now he frowned, almost a scowl. "You would find very few, if any, who would agree with you."

"I only care for my own opinion, Master," I said. "And I—I believe you are kind."

Abruptly he turned away, going to stand before a painting as if it were the most fascinating artwork imaginable. But I knew better, because I knew him. From the way he was standing, his legs widespread, his shoulders slightly hunched, and his hands tightly clasped behind his back over the flowing silk of his robe, I was certain he'd no idea at all of the subject of the painting he was staring at so assiduously.

Earlier in the week, I would have been unable to resist going to him or putting my arms around his shoulders to try to comfort him. Now I knew better than to do that, too. He was far too complicated a man to find solace in a predictable hug, and I respected that in him. He would come back to me when he was ready.

Perhaps even more important was how my self-confidence had grown. Being his Innocent had made me stronger. I *knew* he'd come back to me, and I knew he wouldn't be able to keep away from me for long—any more, really, than I could keep apart from him.

I couldn't explain it, because I didn't really understand it myself, but there it was just the same. It bound us together as tightly as the silk cords that he'd used to tie my wrists and ankles: elegant, even beautiful, bindings that would not break or give way no matter how sorely they were tested.

Unconsciously I circled my thumb to meet my forefinger around one wrist, mimicking the feel of the cords as I remembered how he'd made me his prisoner. There was so much to remember between us now, and nothing I wished to forget.

"I've told Carleigh he should take down this wretched simpering Cupid," he said, perhaps to me, perhaps to no one. "It's not remotely a Titian, but an appalling copy from some hack of a studio, yet Carleigh insists on keeping it hung here."

So this was how he would draw back from me today, behind a lecture on art forgeries.

"Perhaps the subtleties escape his lordship's eye, Master," I said, striving to make my conversation every bit as bland as his. "Perhaps he sees no difference between a true Titian and a forgery, and takes as much pleasure in the one as the other."

"Carleigh wouldn't know a Titian from an orangutan's

ass," he declared with disgust. "He wouldn't even know what this rubbish was supposed to be if it weren't for the thoughtful placard one of his ancestors pasted on the frame. I could put this side by side with my own Titians, and no matter how he squinted and screwed up his face, he still wouldn't see the difference."

"You own a painting by Titian, Master?" I asked, thinking of the paintings that hung in his rooms here at Wrenton. I'd heard enough dinner conversations between dueling millionaire collectors at home to know that works by Titian—or any other of the Old Masters—were the prizes they all craved, and that they were almost impossible to find at any price.

"I own three," he said proudly, at last turning back to face me. "My great-great-grandfather bought them in Rome, spiriting them across the Mediterranean under Bonaparte's nose. They're not here, of course, but at Thornbury."

"Is that your country house?" I asked, unable to keep back my curiosity. It wasn't so much that his life was one vast secret—and it was—but that he volunteered so little to me, keeping everything locked tightly inside himself.

But this time, to my surprise, he nodded. "It is, and has belonged to my family for hundreds of years," he said. "Although we've made a few improvements along the way, of course."

"Where is it?" I knew that any question could make him withdraw abruptly, but still I couldn't resist asking.

"In Norfolk," he said, his expression brightening with genuine fondness. "Hardly convenient to anything, and wild as can be. Yet the house has a beauty that makes the journey worthwhile, and the pictures in the breakfast room alone put all these daubs to shame. I've paintings in my gallery that rival those in his majesty's collection, and he knows it, too."

He laughed in such a way that I knew it wasn't just an empty joke, that the king really did envy Savage's paintings.

"Journey or not, you must enjoy going there," I said. "It's a mawkish sentiment, but it's also true: there's no place like home."

His smile faded. "There's no place like Thornbury, that's true enough," he said. "But I seldom go there now. It doesn't hold the most fortuitous of memories for me."

I knew better than to ask why. "But surely when your son comes home on his holidays—"

"He comes down to London," he said briskly. "We both prefer that now. He has his own friends and amusements, and I have mine."

I made quick calculations in my head. I doubted that Savage could be more than thirty. He must have been at least twenty when he'd wed, and likely older than that. Which meant that his son—the son with his own friends and amusements—was still a young boy, and I knew all too well the loneliness of a motherless child with a distant father.

"You must be proud of him," I said softly. "Fathers always are of their sons. What is his name?"

"Lawton," he said, too tersely for a father. He'd shown far more affection for the house than for his son, though apparently he saw little of both. "Thus far he has done little to merit my pride, but I have hopes that he will in time learn to choose better companions, and apply himself to his studies."

"He's young," I said, my heart going out to the young Lord Lawton.

But Savage reacted as if I hadn't spoken at all.

"He has too much of his mother in him," he said, his bitterness so apparent that it seemed a kind of defeat. "I see it in his face, his speech, his lack of respect."

"But half of him is also yours," I protested, thinking

how the boy could just as easily have received that lack of respect from his father as from his mother.

"Not the half I see," he insisted. "Not the half he cares to show to the world."

I remembered how Simpson had described Lady Savage as high-strung and impetuous. Perhaps young Lord Lawton was as well, which could be enough to trouble his father like this.

But what was even more puzzling was Savage's reference to his dead wife. I had assumed he'd grieved for Lady Savage simply because they'd both been so young and because of the words that others used to describe her death— words like *tragic* and *poor lady*. He'd said himself that he'd wished to save her, though he hadn't mentioned from what. Now, however, I sensed that wasn't entirely the story of their marriage, or at least not from Savage's point of view.

"The boy is your son," I continued gently. "If you are willing to guide and love him as a father should, then he is certain to grow into the young man you wish him to be."

Savage lowered his chin a fraction, his expression almost sorrowful.

"If you intended that little homily to soothe me, Eve," he said, "then you have failed. The boy is what he is, and all your female fussing will not change him."

" 'Female fussing'?" I repeated. "Is that what you heard? A bit of empathy for a motherless boy is hardly—"

"Don't begin," he said wearily. "Please. Lawton is not your son. I come here to Wrenton to forget my private concerns, not worry them to death like a terrier."

It was the single word *please* that stopped me from saying more, spoken as a request between friends, not a master's order. Even without knowing the details of his marriage or why he was so distant toward his son, I understood. Hadn't I come to Wrenton to escape as well?

Besides, I wasn't going to achieve anything now by

pressing him further about his son. He had become too guarded, too defensive, and nothing I could say was going to push past that. For now, distraction would be the better course; it wouldn't help his relationship with his son, but it might ease the tension that was knotting his shoulders and standing like a wall between us.

Purposefully I shook my hair back over my shoulders, raising my chin so that my face was turned up toward him, my parted lips like an offering.

"You told me there were engravings you wished me to see, Master, as part of my education," I said, my voice low and husky. "Pictures that you promised would inspire me."

He didn't answer at first, making me fear I'd misjudged. Then slowly he held out his hand, the sleeve of his silk robe sliding back along his bare arm.

"They will impress you, Eve," he said, his voice deep, a seductive match for my own. "Even as an Innocent, you can study these engravings and learn much."

I took his hand, letting his grasp swallow my fingers as he drew me to my feet. "Are the pictures far from here, Master?"

"Not at all." He tucked my hand into the crook of his arm. "They're in a small chamber of their own at the far end of the gallery. Are you sufficiently composed for such a walk, Eve?"

"I am, Master," I said. The ben wah balls were still heavy and teasing within me, but my respite on the bench had made the sensation bearable. "And I am most eager to see the engravings."

We walked quickly past the long row of dour family portraits and murky landscapes and through the arch at the far end of the gallery. Savage had been right: this was less a room than a chamber or bijou, with eight gilded walls instead of four.

The skylight was in the shape of a hexagonal star, and

even the gray light of the rainy day was magnified by the long mirrors along every other wall. Framed in gold and topped with carved cupids, the mirrors must have been very old, for their surfaces were rippled and mottled along the edges, giving their reflections a mysterious, antique cast. Another cushioned bench sat in the middle of the room, while against one of the walls stood a large, tall-backed armchair, also gilded.

But the true focus of the little room were the oversize engravings that hung between the mirrors, and I saw at once why Savage had predicted they'd be inspirational. Each of them showed a couple having sex, in the most inventive—and most improbable—of positions, with their faces contorted with passion and their heads thrown back with abandon. In every one, the artist had captured the exact moment of penetration, with the man's large, vein-laced cock thrusting into the woman's welcoming cunt.

As old-fashioned as the engravings were, their explicitness was exciting. I couldn't deny it. The longer I looked at twisting, muscular limbs and exaggerated cocks and quims, the more aroused I felt myself becoming, and the more conscious I was again of the golden spheres shifting and vibrating inside me.

"Carleigh claims his grandfather bought the entire room in Venice, where it belonged to some lubricious old *principe* or another from several centuries past," Savage said, "and for once I've no reason to doubt him. Everything's marked with the same crown and cipher—though I doubt that's what you're inspecting so closely."

"Not at all," I admitted, leaning closer to study one of the engravings. "I'm not sure this is even physically possible."

He smiled as he came to stand close behind me, his hands settling familiarly on my hips. "Do you mean how the lady has kept her hair and her pearls so perfectly in place while the man works her like a stallion in rut?"

"You know that's not what I meant," I scoffed. "It's how she must have been an acrobat in the circus to balance on her hands with her legs in the air like that, especially when he's fucking her so forcefully."

"You don't believe it's possible, Eve?" he asked, pulling my bottom snugly back against his cock so that I could feel how hard he already was. "We could attempt it here to make certain."

I chuckled, slowly moving up and down against him, the ben wah balls reverberating inside me at the same time. Knowing that they'd likely soon be removed made the sensation not only bearable but pleasurable.

"We might attempt it, Master, yes," I said breathlessly. "But I fear I might break my neck in the process. I rather think it's a posture best left in the past."

"But the past is not such a charmless place to visit, Eve," he said. His voice dropped lower, to a confidential whisper, as he gently turned me to face the nearest of the antique mirrors. In the rippled reflection, we were now standing side by side. "You would have been a beauty then, too."

"Would I?" I asked archly.

"Oh, yes," he assured me. "You would have been every bit as extraordinary a woman then as you are now."

I blushed at the compliment. Even if it was only part of the Game, I liked being extraordinary in his eyes.

"You wouldn't be a lady," he continued, "but a grand courtesan, one who outshone all the other women in sixteenth-century Venice, and the one who was most famous for her wantonness. The jealous gossips would whisper that there was nothing you wouldn't do with a man."

I smiled seductively, following his fantasy. "Not any man," I said. "Only one who could match my own desires."

"Of course," he said, smiling slyly. "I'd be such a man, wouldn't I?"

"Oh yes," I murmured. "I can imagine no other in your place."

"Then imagine that I am the prince who built this room," he said. "As soon as I saw you, I'd want to try every one of these positions with you."

He smoothed my hair back over my shoulders and slipped my dressing gown over my arms, letting it hang in the crooks of my elbows. Then he slowly eased the neckline of my costume down lower, tugging it below my bare breasts to frame them and raise them slightly, like tempting, quivering fruit. Cradling my breasts in his hands, he gently pinched and rubbed my nipples between his fingers until they were taut and red, and I gasped as sensation rippled from my breasts to my belly, and my too-full quim.

"You have the most luscious breasts, *mia bellissima*," he said. "Perfect for my hands, and for my mouth."

I tipped my head back against his shoulder. I loved watching him caress me like this, seeing his hands move across my flesh and my response show on my face. With my lips parted and my eyes beckoning with desire, my reflection in the wavering glass really did seem as if we'd stepped from the twentieth century back into the past, as if I were some knowing, sensual Renaissance courtesan with my princely lover.

"There," Savage said, whispering close into my ear, his dark head bent beside my white throat. "That is how the prince would see you, and being a man, he'd want to fuck you at once. He'd cover you with the richest pearls from the Orient, like the woman in the engravings, pearls to remind him—and you—of the priceless little jewel at the mouth of your cunt. And then he'd claim you, and make you his with his cock."

I thought of the wide, cushioned bench behind us, no doubt placed there for exactly the kind of purpose that

Savage was describing. I could imagine it all so well, down to the pearls I'd wear.

Except that now I was planning a different ending, just for him, and, master or not, I doubted he would object.

I slipped away from him, turning gracefully and sinking into the lowest of curtseys, fit for royalty.

"My prince," I said. "Your highness. If you would but take your throne, so that I might display my fealty to you."

I wasn't sure if *fealty* was quite the proper word in the situation, but from the way his eyes gleamed, it must have been close enough.

"My throne, eh?" he said, glancing back at the gilded armchair against the wall. "I will, but only if you join me."

I bowed my head. "I will follow you wherever you lead me, your highness."

Immediately he sat in the chair, looking every bit the imperious prince with his legs spread before him. He smiled slowly as he watched me.

"Approach," he said, beckoning. "A shy concubine is of no use to me."

"Yes, your majesty," I murmured, joining him. "I assure you I will not be shy."

I knelt between his legs, my breasts still proudly bare and my dressing gown fanning out behind me across the floor. Before me, his cock tented the front of his pajamas, rising as if in salute. It was easy enough to free it and his balls as well, my fingers sleeking lightly down his length to the nest of dark curls. His shaft was thick and ready, with a glistening drop on the end of the blunt, ruddy head. The sight alone was enough to make my pulse quicken and desire pool low within me.

I licked my lips to moisten them, my mouth poised over his cock. I glanced up at Savage. His face was fixed with anticipation, his gaze, glittering and intent, solely on me.

"Demonstrate your fealty to me, Eve," he said, playing

my game. He reached forward to trace the shape of my lips with his thumb. "Open your mouth, and take me inside."

I widened my lips and, rising onto my knees, took him into my mouth. I relished the saltiness of his taste, and how his cock was soft and hot on my tongue, yet rigid as my lips closed around him.

He thrust deeply, surprising me. He slipped his fingers into my hair, positioning the angle of my mouth to accommodate him better.

"Relax, Eve," he ordered, his voice rough. "Relax your jaw, so you can take more."

I did, and he thrust again, reaching the back of my throat. Instinctively I swallowed, taking him deeper, and I felt him shudder beneath me. He pulled back a fraction, and when he again sank into my throat, I was prepared, working my lips around his thickness as he thrust forward.

He grunted and swore, and I felt the straining muscles in his thighs beneath my palms. If my mouth hadn't been so full, I would have smiled. I'd intended to please him, but the sense of power I felt from giving him pleasure also aroused me to a shocking degree, and I began to rock my hips to make the golden ben wah balls caress me from within.

Breathing hard, he pulled back, slipping heavily from my mouth.

"You're a wicked creature," he said hoarsely, his approval undeniable.

I grinned. "Yes, your highness," I said. "I am."

I leaned forward to grasp the base of his cock, steadying it so that I could lick and flick my tongue across the weeping little eye. Then I flattened my tongue and drew it slowly along the underside in long, teasing strokes. At the same time, I reached down to cup his ballocks in my fingers and stroked them lightly, the way I knew he liked.

"Take me back into your mouth, Eve," he said, tension making his voice harsh. "Suck me."

I took him deeper, drawing him in with my lips and tongue, and sucked him as he'd ordered. He groaned, and shoved his fingers into my hair to hold my head steady as he thrust into my mouth, once, twice, three times.

Abruptly he jerked out, the wet, purpled head of his cock bobbing before my face.

"Enough," he said. "I want to spend in your hot little cunt."

He grabbed me by the shoulders and dragged me onto his lap, spreading my thighs so that I'd no choice but to straddle his cock.

"Wait," I said breathlessly, kicking off my heeled slippers. "The ben wah—"

"I haven't forgotten." He reached between my legs and hooked his finger into the chain and tugged. One by one, the gold balls—glistening with my pearly essence—slipped from my channel, making me gasp at the sudden, aching emptiness.

But not for long.

"Put me in, Eve," he ordered with urgency, holding his cock steady by the base for me. "Fuck, do it *now*."

Bracing my hand on his shoulder, I slowly lowered myself onto his cock. I loved that first moment when he entered me, how he could fill me so completely, and when he drove in hard to my depths, I couldn't keep back my cry of satisfaction, of delight at this utter repletion.

"Ride me, Eve," he demanded. "Fuck me hard."

I didn't need to be told. With my knees on either side of his hips, balanced on the chair's cushion, I raised myself nearly off his shaft, only to let my weight carry me forcefully back down. His fingers sank into my hips to guide my rhythm as I clung to his shoulders.

I caught a glimpse of how we were reflected over and over again in the mirrors, my back arched and my breasts bouncing as I rode him, his handsome face contorted and

his fingers digging deeply into my white hips and bottom
as he bucked beneath me. It was as if we'd become the
amorous couple in the engravings, connected over time
by sex.

After the long torment of the ben wah balls, I spent for
the first time almost at once, my quim clenching in delicious spasms around him as I climaxed.

"I'm not done," he said as I sank against his chest.
"Neither are you."

He continued to thrust into me, and I felt the first tremors of another orgasm. I began moving again, determined
to match him this second time. He kissed me hard, his
mouth devouring mine, and squeezed my nipples with
each thrust. I clung to him again as the sensations built,
the goal within reach now for him as well. I felt flushed
and feverish, my skin burning and my heartbeat thump-
ing, and it still wasn't enough.

"I—I can't, Savage," I stammered, writhing against his
chest. With each thrust he seemed to grow thicker and
harder, stretching me further. "It's too much."

"Not yet it isn't," he growled. "I want you with me to
the end."

He slipped his fingers down to where we were joined
and my quim's lips were spread around his cock, and
lightly pressed against my pearl. Now each time I rose
along his cock, I felt the double pleasure in my core, almost unbearable as I trembled around him. I was so sensitive, so close, that it was like a spark to tinder, and I
thrashed and cried with the intensity of it, yet still somehow held back, waiting for him.

Panting, I watched him, watched the wild look in his
face grow as he pounded into me, watched him give in to
the need with an animal intensity, watched his eyes lose
focus as he raced toward his release.

And when at last it claimed him, he came with a

mindless fury and a guttural roar, driving his cock and his seed into me with such primal force that I plunged into the depths with him. Through it all he watched me, never looking away from my face, as if at that moment he could see into my soul. I was swept along on the wave of my climax, forgetting everything else, and as it faded I shuddered and clung to him with tears in my eyes, as if my very life depended upon it, and him.

In that moment, perhaps it did.

I'd never felt so vulnerable, at once both lost and found, as I now did sprawled half naked across Savage in this foolish throne-chair. His strength was my solace, my comfort, and there was nothing better than hearing the beating of his heart beneath my ear.

What was it that Simpson had told me that first night? Innocents didn't have pasts or futures. They could live only in the present. Could any words be more true?

He held me tight, his arms wrapped around me and his unshaved cheek pressed close to my temple.

"Eve, Eve," he whispered hoarsely against my hair. "Don't ever leave me."

I went very still. He'd said that to me before, but it had only been part of the Game. But this—this felt different.

Slowly I raised my head from his chest, twisting so that I faced him. "What did you say, Savage?"

His expression was guarded and unsure, as if he feared he'd already said too much. Instead of replying, he turned my face up to his and kissed me, as if that would be answer enough. It was, yet it wasn't, and with a small sigh that was lost between our mouths, I closed my eyes and kissed him in return.

"Savage?" Lady Carleigh's voice was unmistakable, calling from the larger gallery. "Mrs. Hart? Are you in here, my dears?"

TWELVE

At once Savage broke away from the kiss, his arm still protectively around me. "Why the devil is that damned woman here now?"

But I wasn't going to wait to find out. Hurriedly I slipped free of Savage and the chair, and retrieved the gold ben wah balls from the floor, tucking them into the pocket of my dressing gown. I swiftly pulled up my costume once again over my breasts and retied my dressing gown for good measure.

Yet, one glance in the surrounding mirrors showed me how futile such small gestures were. My face remained flushed, my lips were bruised-looking from the fervor of Savage's kisses, and my hair was tangled and matted from our combined sweat. My feet were bare, and I'd no idea where my slippers had landed when I kicked them off. No one—especially not Lady Carleigh—would doubt for a moment what I'd been doing with Savage.

Nor would it help that he seemed in no particular hurry to dress himself, either. He'd scarcely closed the front of his pajamas when Lady Carleigh appeared in the arched doorway, a tall footman at her side.

The viscountess was also wearing a peignoir, thick with ruffling layers of French lace. Her apricot-colored hair was as elaborately dressed as if for tea with a duchess in Portman Square, and diamonds circled her wrists and throat.

In comparison, I was acutely aware of how unkempt—how *ravished*—I must look. After Simpson had been so inquisitive in her last visit to Savage's rooms, I had not asked the lady's maid to return. I hadn't worried about how my hair was arranged and neither had Savage; we'd been too lost in each other to care.

But with Lady Carleigh now before me as a reminder of what was proper and expected for ladies of our station, I realized that I must look like an unkempt slattern. Even now I could feel Savage's seed sticky and trickling down the insides of my thighs, and I pressed my legs together to keep from having it drip shamefully onto my bare feet.

Fortunately, the viscountess chose to take no notice.

"Here you two are!" she said brightly, not at all embarrassed at disturbing two of her guests. "I'd heard from the servants that you were walking upstairs, and when I remembered how very much you like the gallery, Savage, I knew—I *knew*—I'd find you here."

"So you have," said Savage. He rose slowly from the chair, tightening the sash on his robe, and came to stand beside me with his arm around my shoulders. "Though to be honest, Laura, I rather wish you hadn't bothered."

"Oh, pish, Savage," Lady Carleigh said, talking too fast. "Don't be such a boor. Tell me, Mrs. Hart. Are you enjoy-

ing my husband's collection of fine art? Has Savage shown
you the choicest pieces in the lot? Have you—"

"Enough of this nonsense, Laura," Savage interrupted
wearily. "As interfering as you can be, it's not your general habit to come badger your guests like this. What is it
that you really want? Why are you here?"

"Why? Why?" Lady Carleigh clasped her hands before
her as she gave an indignant little toss of her head. "I shall
tell you why, my lord Savage. I sought you both out because I am not accustomed to having my missives ignored,
especially when, as your hostess, I have only your own
welfare in mind. Perhaps it is because you are American,
Mrs. Hart, and do not understand the finer points of social etiquette, but I can assure you that it is barbarously ill
bred of you to leave my notes unanswered as you have."

I stared at the woman, taken aback. None of what the
viscountess was saying made any sense.

"I am not ill bred, my lady," I replied defensively, "nor
does being American have anything to do with my manners. I can hardly reply to notes that I have never received."

Lady Carleigh gasped. "Are you doubting my word,
Mrs. Hart? Are you questioning my veracity, when all I
wished was to inquire—"

"Why don't you simply ask her now?" Savage suggested.

"Yes, please, do," I said. "What were your inquiries, my
lady?"

Lady Carleigh blinked with embarrassment. "I would
rather ask you in private, Mrs. Hart."

I felt my cheeks grow hot, too. Clearly, whatever the viscountess was asking had to do with Savage. Now I also
realized something else: the tall footman that she'd brought
as an escort was one of the ones who'd intervened when
Savage had attacked Mr. Henery. Why had Lady Carleigh
felt it necessary to bring such an escort here?

Savage must have sensed my discomfort, though not the reason for it. He took his arm from around my shoulder with a small bow. "If you wish me to leave you alone, then I'll—"

"No!" I exclaimed, more sharply than I'd intended. I took his arm to draw him back. "That is, no, please, do not leave. Whatever her ladyship wishes to say may be said before you."

Lady Carleigh frowned. "Are you certain of that, Mrs. Hart?"

"Of course," I said, as Savage once again slipped his arm across my shoulder. I was glad that he did, linking my fingers into his as well. We were united and together, and I saw us that way, reflected over and over in the mirrors around us. "Please continue."

The viscountess's discomfort was obvious, and she hesitated just long enough to show that she'd thought better of her original question, whatever it might be.

"Very well," she said. "Will you and Lord Savage be joining us for the final dinner tomorrow evening?"

"Indeed we shall," Savage answered for us both. "Why shouldn't we?"

"Because you and Mrs. Hart have kept entirely to yourselves this week, Savage," the viscountess answered curtly. "Because this—this withdrawal is not your usual custom, nor is it how our little game is ordinarily played. Because we began to wonder if such an absence was agreeable to both of you, or the forceful design of only one."

Savage drew in his breath so sharply that I felt it. "Are you asking whether I've made Mrs. Hart into some sort of *prisoner*, Laura?"

"I'm not asking you, Savage, but Mrs. Hart," she said, pointedly looking at me. "You haven't played with the rest of us at all, ma'am. Has that been through your choice, or Lord Savage's?"

"Recall that by your rules I am her master," Savage said, his voice tense, "and—"

"I asked Mrs. Hart," Lady Carleigh said, "not you, Savage, and even if I—"

"Forgive me, Lady Carleigh, please," I interrupted, holding my hand up for silence and peace as well. "There's no need for quarreling, and no reason for it. I have not been forced, or coerced, or compelled to do anything—*anything*—that I did not wish to do. Not once."

The viscountess studied me, her lips pressed tightly together with skepticism. It was clear that she did not believe me, and equally clear that nothing else I might say would change her mind.

And the worst part was not that Lady Carleigh, or any of the others, doubted my word. No, the worst was that they dared question Savage.

I tightened my fingers around his, offering comfort and reassurance as much as seeking it for myself.

"Are you satisfied, Laura?" he asked evenly, an evenness that did not fool me at all. "Did Mrs. Hart give you the answer you sought? Or would you rather you'd had the chance to damn me again?"

Lady Carleigh gasped and fluttered her hands in front of her in ladylike distress.

"Never, Savage, never," she said quickly. "You know that Carleigh and I regard you as one of our oldest and dearest friends. We'd thought you were finally returning to your old self and at last recovering from Marianne's death, but when we saw—"

"This conversation is finished, Laura," he said, biting off each word. His hand squeezed mine. "Come with me, Eve, if you please. There is no need for us to remain here."

His handsome face was set and implacable, his expression so hard that it might have been carved from stone. Of course I left with him, my bare feet hurrying to match my strides to his. He did not so much as glance at Lady Carleigh, let alone say anything further. He kept his gaze straight before him, and did not speak another word as we went through the long halls back to his rooms, walking so quickly that we were nearly running.

He threw the door open and went striding past Barry, pulling me with him until we reached the bedroom, and slammed the door shut after us. At last he released my hand, and took a step backward, purposefully keeping a distance between us.

"There are things you should know of me, Eve," he began. He was breathing hard, struggling to keep some manner of composure, and I saw in his eyes the effort it took. "I had never intended to burden you with my troubles, but it is better you hear this from me instead of some misguided falsehoods from servants or—or others."

I nodded, with no notion of what might be coming. With Savage, it could be nothing, or it could be beyond my wildest imagining. Yet, because it *was* he, I would listen, and in silent sympathy I reached out to him.

He would not accept my hand or my comfort. Instead, he took another step back, his hands in fists at his sides.

"Listen first, Eve," he said heavily. "I loved Marianne— my wife—when we wed. I was young, and I believed her to be the most perfect woman in the world. But before long I discovered the flaws in her loveliness. I knew she'd been unhappy with her parents, and I wanted to rescue her from the misery she blamed on them. But her troubles were far deeper than I'd realized. Her mind was unsettled, her behavior erratic and unpredictable. I never knew what to expect from her, and with each day she grew a little worse."

"I'm sorry," I said softly, once again the only thing I could think of to say. "I'm sorry."

But he shook his head, shaking aside even that small

solace. His face was marked by suffering, by the burden of his grief.

"I took her to doctors of every kind, both in London and on the Continent," he said. "I agreed to every treatment, praying for a miracle, and kept her at Thornbury, far from London, where she could be tended with care. When our son was born, I dared to hope his young life might be a fresh start that could bring her back, but she demonstrated as little interest in being a mother as she did a wife. I had to send our boy away to be tended by others, from fear she'd harm him."

So many little mysteries were now fitting together: why Savage had had no wish to speak of his wife, why he avoided his house at Thornbury, why he was distant from his son, why he feared the boy would be like his mother—it all made heartbreaking sense to me now.

"She was only twenty-two when she died," he said, coming at last to the inevitable end of his story. "It was the madness that killed her. For the sake of the boy, I've tried to keep the details of her illness and death as quiet as I could, but there are always whispers, and not just among the servants, either. Not even friends can resist the temptation to draw the darkest of conclusions. You saw that for yourself."

"Even those who mean well can often be cruel when they don't know the truth," I said softly, longing to take him in my arms and share the pain with him. "I'm sure Lady Carleigh did not intend any hurtful slander—"

"I'm not hurt," he said bluntly. He turned and charged from the room, leaving the door ajar. Hesitantly I followed. He was standing over his desk, ransacking the top drawer. At last he found what he was searching for: a small handful of sealed notes.

He thrust them out to me. "There," he said. "Read them yourself. God only knows what she's written of me."

I stared down at the notes, seeing how his hand shook. "I don't understand," I said slowly. "What are these?"

"They're the notes that Lady Carleigh wrote to you," he said. "One, sometimes two, a day. They were all delivered here."

"The ones she mentioned while we were in the gallery?" I asked, though it was already obvious that they were. I recognized the viscountess's handwriting, and the coral-colored wax that sealed each letter.

"Yes," he said. "Take them."

I did, aligning their edges into a neat stack in my fingers while my thoughts ran wild. I knew what I had to ask, even as I dreaded his answer.

"Why didn't you give them to me when they were delivered?" My voice was small and uncertain. "That wasn't part of the Game. It couldn't have been. Oh, Savage, why did you keep them from me?"

"Why," he repeated. He tried to smile, and failed, his eyes filled with bitterness. "It's obvious enough, isn't it? I didn't want to share you."

I shook my head, confused. "I didn't wish to be shared, either," I began. "But that has nothing to do with—"

"I must go," he said, already moving toward the door. "There is someone I must see directly."

"No, Savage, wait!" I cried, following him. "I need to know why—"

"Read what Laura wrote to you, Eve." He paused, his hand on the doorknob, and looked at me as if he might never see me again. "Then, if you still wish it, we will talk further."

Before I could answer, he closed the door and was gone. I could have followed; for once he hadn't forbidden it. But he'd made it clear enough that he wished to be alone, and the way my head was spinning from all he'd told me, so did I.

It wasn't a good solitude, either. I hurt because he had walked out like that. How could I not? His scent was all over me, reminding me keenly with every breath of the hot, urgent sex we'd just shared in the gallery. I stared down at the envelopes in my hand, wondering—or was I dreading?—what messages they contained.

"May I bring you tea, Mrs. Hart?" Barry asked, appearing from nowhere as he always did.

"No, Barry, thank you," I murmured. "I believe I will wait for his lordship in the bedroom."

"Very well, ma'am," the servant said. "I do expect him to return shortly."

"You do?" I asked, my voice trembling with fragile hope.

"Yes, ma'am," he said confidently. "His lordship is wearing his dressing gown. He has not been shaven yet this day. He cannot go far in such a state."

"Ah," I said, feeling foolish for expecting more. "No, he cannot. Thank you, Barry, that will be all."

Barry hesitated, lingering longer than was proper. "Forgive me for speaking out of turn, ma'am, but I also believe his lordship will return because of you."

I smiled. Barry had been with Savage most of his life, and would be intimately acquainted with all his master's humors and habits, and his past as well. If Barry said that Savage would return because of me, then he would. He *would*.

"Thank you, Barry," I said softly. "Thank you very much."

He nodded, and quickly withdrew. With Lady Carleigh's notes in my hand, I retreated to the bedroom. I wanted Savage to find me there, the one place that had become so special to us that it was almost impossible to imagine us together anywhere else.

Sitting in the chair beside the window, I frowned down

at the sealed notes. Part of me wished I could simply burn them, sealed and unread, and be spared their contents. But Savage had specifically told me to read them, and so with a sigh I began to open the notes, one after the other, and arrange them by date on my knee.

Each was only a sentence or two long, the kind of little note that every good hostess sends to her guests to make them feel welcome at a house party—except that Lady Carleigh was referring not to a standard dinner or hunt but to the Game.

The first must have been written and delivered soon after Savage had won me in the auction. Less than a week had passed, and yet it already seemed a lifetime ago.

> *My dear Mrs. Hart,*
>
> *Didn't I promise you that all would fall into place as planned? I trust at this moment you are enjoying the most rapturous kisses & caresses from your delectable MASTER!*
>
> *Fondly,*
> *Lady C.*

The next must have been the following morning.

> *Dear Mrs. H.,*
>
> *How disappointing not to see you & Lord S. at breakfast, but I can only assume you are finding such rapture in each other's arms that you cannot be parted as yet. You must tell me all when we dine this evening.*
>
> *Lady C.*

But there hadn't been any time for confidential little conversations at that dinner—not after Savage had flown at Mr. Henery. Lady Carleigh herself hadn't witnessed that—she'd been in the kitchen at the time, being bedecked with strawberries and cream—but clearly she'd heard from her husband and others what had happened.

> *My dear Mrs. H.,*
>   *How dismayed I was to learn of the disturbance,* le désaccord, *if you will, between Lord S. & Mr. Henery this evening! To be sure, it is flattering to have so chivalrous a champion to defend one's virtue, as he did yours, but the degree of the defense was* très outré *for our little company.*
>   *Lord S. has been known to let his temper run wild before—truly he can be the* beau sauvage!—*but I had believed that such outbursts were well in his past. If you can, & in the sweetest way possible, urge him towards sobriety & genial behavior for the remainder of our time together. Pleasure is our only goal, yes?*
>
>   *You're a lamb,*
>   *Lady C.*

This note worried me. Not the part about Savage's temper—all men had tempers if they were crossed—but the French phrases that were sprinkled throughout. English-speaking ladies resorted to French only when they were especially upset, as if using the other language softened things they'd rather not be saying at all. Lady Carleigh was not happy with Savage, and her unhappiness grew with the next note.

> *Mrs. H., my dear,*
>   *It seems that Lord S. has made quite the hermits of you two. Please dine with us this evening, or at the very least join us for the later entertainments. If he is the reason you are staying away, please do*

*your best to persuade him otherwise, & tell him he
must answer to me. You are sorely missed,* ma chère.

À *plasir,*
Lady C.

But evidently Simpson had gone to her mistress after she'd seen my bruises in the bath, and in Lady Carleigh's next note both the playfulness and the French were gone.

> *Dear Mrs. Hart,*
>   *I have just now spoken with Simpson, who is much concerned on your behalf, as am I. Simpson suspects that things are not as they should be between you & Lord S. Please come to me in my rooms at once, or at the very least send word to me that you are well & unharmed.*
>
> *Lady C.*

I sighed impatiently. What real reason did they have for their concern? I preferred Savage's company to the licentious goings-on among the others, and he preferred mine. We'd been invited here to play the Game, and this was how we'd chosen to play it, that was all. I was hardly his prisoner, or whatever else they were imagining. I could have left him at any time. I'd simply chosen not to.

As for what we did together, that was no one's business but our own. These last days with Savage had been happier and more exciting than any I could recall in my entire life. That was all that mattered, wasn't it?

Certainly there was nothing in Lady Carleigh's notes for Savage to dread, and nothing that would turn me against him. Wishing he would return, I cracked the seal on the final envelope.

Dear Mrs. Hart,

*I beg you not to ignore these words as you have
ignored all my others. Lord Savage may be an old
& dear friend, but I fear that he has influenced you
in an unfortunate & desperate manner. I do not wish
to alarm you, but I worry that he may have lapsed
into past habits of unpredictable violence. There, I
have spelled it out plainly. I fear for your safety, my
dear. At the time of poor Lady Savage's death, there
were many questions asked about his role in her de-
mise, & none answered. Thus I urge you to take
care of his temper, & guard yourself against any further outbursts.*

*If I do not receive a reply, I shall be forced to
come seek you out, to reassure myself of your well-
being.*

In perfect sincerity,
Lady C.

I read the note over twice, then slowly refolded it to set
aside with the others. At least I now knew why Lady
Carleigh had appeared so suddenly in the gallery, and why
she'd brought the tall footman with her, too. And I was
thankful that Savage had explained to me about his wife;
if he hadn't, I might indeed have wondered what dark
things Lady Carleigh was hinting at.

Instead, it was all sadly easy to decipher. These mysteries around Lady Savage's death would be due to his desire to keep her last illness private. What the world
perceived as his uncontrollable temper, I realized, was his
way of protecting me in the same way he'd tried—and
failed—to protect his poor wife.

It was so unfair of the Carleighs to suspect him of
worse. He'd never turned against me, nor had I ever feared
for my safety in his company. Instead, with him I'd always

felt safe, secure, even cherished. We had played the Game of Protector and Innocent, but behind it was an unspoken understanding, an empathy, between us that went much deeper.

It would be difficult to describe in words, because words had often been secondary to our deepening trust. Lady Carleigh might claim a long friendship with Savage, but after only a week, I felt sure I was the one he trusted more, the one who knew him better.

I glanced up at the ormolu clock on the mantel, surprised to see that he'd been gone only fifteen minutes; it seemed like much longer. As far as I was concerned, we would have little to discuss when he returned. There were no great revelations in the viscountess's notes, and nothing that merited his uneasiness. All I wished now was to reassure him, and make our last hours together as memorable as possible.

I thought back to the gallery and how he'd wanted to see me draped in pearls. I could do that for him. In my room were the long, costly ropes of pearls I'd worn the first night; the pearls, like the rest of my jewels, were kept in a special strongbox built into the base of one of my trunks, and only Hamlin and I knew its precise location as well as the combination to the lock. I didn't trust Simpson enough to send for her to bring them back, nor was there time.

But if I was quick, I could run to my room and get the pearls myself. Then, when Savage returned, he'd find me in his bed, waiting for him in pearls and nothing else.

I tossed aside the notes and headed for the door, wrapping my dressing gown more modestly about my body. I managed to avoid Barry, and swiftly hurried down the long hallways to my own rooms. My bare feet made no sound on the polished floors, and I saw no one beyond a few servants. It was strange to return to my rooms, and to see all my belongings neatly arranged exactly as I'd left them last week. I'd grown so accustomed to my insular time with Savage that I felt as if I were somehow looking back a great distance over time, with my clothes and other things representing an Evelyn Hart that no longer existed.

I was glad there was no sign of Simpson, and I quickly found the necklaces, taking the long ropes of pearls from their silk-lined cases and tucking them into the pocket of my dressing gown. The pearls clinked softly against the gold ben wah balls that I'd forgotten were in my pocket, too, and I smiled wryly. What better symbols could there be of the old Evelyn bumping against the new version?

I closed the door gently and began back to Savage's rooms. Down this hall, turn left, and to the end of the next. A pair of parlor maids with trays curtseyed, and I bowed my head, not wishing to make eye contact with them any more than they did with me. I quickened my step, turned the last corner, and nearly ran directly into Baron Blackledge.

"My lord!" I gasped with surprise and dismay, and stumbled backward, barely saving myself from falling. "Forgive me, Baron, but I did not see you."

"Not at all, Mrs. Hart." He caught my arm to steady me, and kept hold of it. "We don't want you to take a tumble, do we?"

He was dressed for an afternoon in the country, in a tweed suit with a Norfolk jacket and a gaudy argyle-patterned vest beneath, and if I had sensed I was underdressed earlier in comparison with Lady Carleigh, I now felt as good—or as bad—as naked before Lord Blackledge. His gaze raked over me as if he could see straight through my dressing gown and my costume. I remembered that look from the auction, the raw hunger in his eyes, and it took all my will not to shrink away from him.

"Thank you, my lord, but I am quite recovered," I said,

trying to pull my arm free. "Where is your own Innocent, the blond girl? Why is she not with you?"

"We parted. She was far too . . . obliging, shall we say? No challenge. Not as you would be, Mrs. Hart."

He held fast to my arm, clearly delighting in my discomfort.

"If you please, my lord," I began again. "Please let me—"

"Hah, how I love to hear a lady beg!" he said, leering as he cut me off. He glanced past me, down the hallway. "Where's Savage? He's kept you locked up so tight this week that I can't believe he'd let you out of his sight, not like this."

"I'm hardly Lord Savage's prisoner, my lord," I said, wishing now there was a footman or two to summon for help. "Now if you'll excuse me—"

"You should thank your stars you're not, Mrs. Hart," he said, his fingers tightening around my arm. "He did that to his wife, you know, locked her away until she went mad. Some say he even pushed her to her death, from the window of their bedroom."

I gasped, shocked. Savage himself had told me his wife had died from her illness, but nothing of a fatal fall. Was it too painful to mention, so painful that Savage had purposefully omitted her death from his telling, or was Lord Blackledge simply repeating more audacious, unfounded gossip?

Pleased to see the effect his story had had, Lord Blackledge nodded, his eyes glittering.

"You understand now why you'd be much better off with me, Mrs. Hart," he said. "I'd show you how a real Englishman treats a woman, and you'd thank me for it."

"Thank—thank you, no," I stammered. "Now if you'll please excuse me, I must return to his lordship's rooms."

"Not yet." With a little jerk, he pulled me closer, his

broad face red with excitement. "Tomorrow night, I mean to claim you, Mrs. Hart. You'll be mine for next time, and Savage won't be able to stop me."

He pushed me to one side to throw me off-balance as he bent over me, determined to kiss me. I twisted sharply in his grasp and fought to break free, and turned my face away to avoid his mouth.

"Let me go, Baron," I ordered, fighting my panic to sound as stern as I could. I didn't want to cause even more of a scandal and scream for help, but I decided that if he persisted, I would. Surely there must be someone else in earshot, even in this cavernous house. "Let me go at once!"

"Release her."

Savage's voice was deceptively calm, but I recognized the steely tension coiled in every word. He had come up behind us, silent and barefoot, and he stood with his feet slightly apart and his hands knotted into fists at his sides.

One wrong word from Blackledge, and he'd strike. It was as simple, and as obvious, as that.

I didn't want them to fight over me. Blackledge wasn't like Henery. He was broad-chested, stronger, and with a bully's bravado. But that wasn't all. If Savage gave in to his temper again, I feared that Lord Carleigh might actually summon the local constable to have him arrested. Both men must have realized it as well—how could they not?—yet still Blackledge didn't release my arm.

"She's tired of you, Savage," he jeered. "Look at her! Why else would she be trolling the halls dressed like this, eager for a man who could satisfy her the way you can't?"

"That's a wicked lie, my lord!" I cried furiously. "You know I was returning to Lord Savage's rooms, and yet you trapped me!"

Savage's pale eyes flicked from Blackledge to me, revealing nothing. He couldn't believe Lord Blackledge, could he? Didn't he trust my word against the baron's?

"She's always wanted me," Lord Blackledge continued, goading Savage. "She never wanted you. You paid for her, but she wanted me more."

"No!" I shook my head, desperate to defend myself against such an outrageous lie. "I have never wanted you, not even for a second!"

"Then why were you coming to my bedroom?" he taunted. "Why had you left Savage for me, and—"

"Let her go, Blackledge," Savage interrupted curtly. "See which of us she chooses."

"Why should I leave the decision up to a slut like this?" Blackledge said, but after a moment's hesitation he released my arm, adding a shove for good measure. "Go on, decide."

I fled to Savage, darting to safety behind him. "You're an evil, manipulative man," I called back to Blackledge. "I would never choose you, not under any circumstances."

But Blackledge only laughed, and wagged a fat finger.

"You say that now," he said, "but you'll change your tune fast enough when you finally get a taste of my cock. Tomorrow, Mrs. Hart, tomorrow and you'll be mine."

To my relief, I felt Savage's arm circle my shoulders, drawing me close. Yet, the gesture seemed more possessive than protective, and definitely not affectionate, which tinged my relief with uneasiness.

"Come with me, Eve," he said, his voice still curt as he led me away, his fingers locked with mine. "You—we— have no place here."

If I'd expected a fiery outburst from him, none came. Instead, as soon as we'd returned to his bedroom, he dropped my hand and retreated to stand alone beside the window. He pretended to stare out at the lawn; I knew he saw nothing.

"When I returned," he said finally, "you were gone."

"But only for a few minutes," I protested, joining him at the window. "I intended to be back here to greet you."

He was so skilled at making his face blank, hiding everything deep inside.

"But you weren't," he said. "Did you read what the viscountess wrote of me? Was that what made you run away?"

I retrieved the notes from where I'd left them earlier, handing them to him with the most recent one open on top.

"Read them yourself," I said. "There is not a single word there that would make me leave you."

He scanned the notes so swiftly that I wondered if he was looking for some particular word or statement.

"You see," I said. "Nothing."

He stared down at the last note in his hands, holding it so tightly in his fingers that the stiff card was bending. "You are not frightened of me, as Lady Carleigh says you should be?"

"Why should I, when you have given me no reason to do so?" It was so hard not to go to him, to throw my arms around him and reassure him the way I longed to do. But I couldn't—not until he was ready. "You must challenge me more than that, Savage, if you wish to drive me away."

"That's the furthest thing from my mind," he said, a fervency in his words that I hadn't heard before. He was watching me closely, ready to pounce on any hesitation or doubt. "But I wish to be certain, Eve, and I wish you to speak only the truth. There is nothing you have heard or read today that has made you distrust me?"

I didn't pause, even proudly raising my chin. "Nothing."

"Rubbish." He tossed the notes onto the sideboard and sighed. "I've told you before, Eve, that you were not born to tell lies. I heard what Blackledge said to you about my wife, and I heard you gasp when he did."

"No, Savage, please!" I cried. "It was because I could

not believe he'd repeat such a dreadful story about you— about her!"

His eyes seemed emptied by sadness, his expression bleak with resignation. "Don't you fear that you'll be next, Eve? Everyone else does. Don't you worry that I'll shove you from this window to break your pretty neck on the drive, too?"

Tears of sympathy, not horror, stung my eyes, and I clasped my hands together at my waist to keep from reaching out to him.

"Tell me what happened, Savage," I whispered urgently. "I did not believe the baron, but I will believe you. Tell me the truth."

He closed his eyes and bowed his head, his dark hair falling across his forehead.

"I had had her nurse bring her to my library to dine with me, the two of us alone," he began in a hoarse whisper. "It was her birthday. She seemed happy enough, laughing and teasing the way she had when we'd first married, and I dared to think she was improving. Fool that I was, I turned my back, and that was all she needed. She ran to the window, and before I could reach her, she jumped. That was how she left me, in an instant and without good-bye. She left me, and she was gone."

"Oh, Savage," I said softly. His mother, his father, his wife, all gone without farewell. No wonder he was so haunted by the past, when his past harbored such sorrow.

"I let them all believe she'd fallen," he continued, his voice as heavy as lead. "The nurse, the doctors, the police, the magistrate at the inquest. I didn't want to damn her memory with the truth that she'd taken her own life."

"But you told me."

He nodded, and slowly raised his gaze to meet mine.

"I did," he said. "Because I knew you would be the only one who believed me."

I went to him then, slipping my arms around his shoulders as if they were meant always to be there, drawing him close. With a sigh, he buried his face against my hair, his beard bristling against my throat, and clung to me like a drowning man. I murmured little scraps of words and nonsense over his head, and gently stroked my hands along his arms and back to comfort him as best I could.

I couldn't begin to imagine what he'd endured by keeping such a secret locked so tightly within him. He'd acted from love, protecting his wife in death as he had in life. In their aristocratic world, madness was unacceptable enough, but suicide was far worse. Her name would forever have been tainted—damned, as he'd said himself—and no minister would have buried even a countess in sanctified ground if it was known that she'd taken her own life.

Instead, he'd let the rumors circle around him, whispers of what a dangerous man he was, and how he'd pushed her to her death. He'd endured the scandal and rumors, saying nothing and telling no one, for the sake of his lost love.

At last I understood why, whenever he was most unguarded, he'd been so desperately insistent that I not leave him. His poor, mad wife had fled from him, in the most final of ways, and he could not bear for me to abandon him, too.

It hadn't been part of the Game. It was part of his life. And now, so was I.

THIRTEEN

I wasn't sure how long Savage and I stood there together. Three minutes could have passed, or thirty. What mattered was that by the time he finally separated from me, the bond that existed between us had strengthened and deepened.

Although it was curious to think that this had come about because of his late wife, in a way it was inevitable. His Marianne had made him who he was, just as my Arthur was a part of me, too. The past couldn't be changed, it could only be accepted as it was, and I was touched and honored that he'd trusted me with so intimate a part of his. I'd trusted him from the beginning. Now I knew—now I believed—that he trusted me in return, and that was a bond that would not break.

"Eve," he said softly, rubbing his thumb across my lower lip. His features had lost their tension, and though the sadness remained, the despair had left his face. The greatest difference showed in his pale eyes. The haunted introversion was gone, replaced by a clarity that was for now focused entirely on me. "What would I do without you?"

"Nor I without you," I said breathlessly, my heart tight in my chest. "Once, you told me that a trouble shared is a trouble halved. It was, and is, most excellent advice."

"Indeed it was, and is," he said. "And you are the most exceptional woman I have ever known."

He kissed me then, his lips gliding over mine not in passion—that was sure to come—but to seal his words.

I smiled and slid my hands inside his dressing gown to lay on his bare chest. His skin was warm, his heartbeat steady and measured beneath my palms.

"I will always listen to you, Savage, whenever you wish me to," I said. "Just as I would never wish to hear another deceitful word from Lord Blackledge. Not one!"

He grunted, displeased by the very mention of the baron's name. "Then why didn't you stay here, where you'd be safe?" he asked. "Why did you put yourself in his path like that?"

"I didn't," I said. "Not willfully, anyway. I went to my rooms, and as I was returning, he was also in the hallway. It could not be avoided."

He frowned. "What could possibly make you go to your rooms? If you wished anything, you could have sent Barry, or had him summon Simpson. There was absolutely no reason to put yourself at risk as you did."

"But there was," I insisted. I stepped back, untying the sash on my dressing gown. "I wanted to surprise you when you returned."

His gaze slipped down to the shadow between my breasts, unable not to.

"I wanted to finish what we'd begun in the gallery,"

I continued, fishing for the pearl necklaces in my pocket. I shook my hair back, and let the silken dressing gown slide from my shoulders to the floor. One by one, I reached up and dropped the necklaces over my head, the pearls sliding and falling heavily across my bare breasts.

"There," I said, my voice low and husky. I expected him to fall into the familiar pattern of fantasy, exactly as he had earlier in the mirrored gallery. "This is how I wished to surprise you, my lord."

But while his gaze remained on my pearl-draped breasts, he didn't join the fantasy. "That is where you went? To find those necklaces?"

"Yes, my lord, I did it for you," I said. I cupped my breasts with my hands, offering them to him through the sliding curtain of the pearls. "Isn't this what you desired?"

"Take them off, Eve," he said. "All of them."

"Truly?" I exclaimed, disappointed. "I thought you'd like them."

He wasn't smiling any longer. "They were given to you by other men, weren't they?"

The question bewildered me, since I was certain he knew the answer. Ladies didn't buy jewels for themselves, especially pearls.

"My father and my husband gave the necklaces to me, yes," I said, reluctantly beginning to lift the first necklace over my head. "But I do not see why I cannot—"

"Because I want you to wear these instead." He took a flat jeweler's box from the mantel and handed it to me. "For you, Eve. From me."

I recognized the distinctive red case from Cartier, and I took off the last of the other necklaces before I took the box from him. Slowly I opened the lid, prolonging the moment, and then caught my breath.

Curled in the silk-lined case was a long rope of the most exquisite pearls I'd ever seen, large and lustrous and perfectly matched. They were nearly identical to the ones worn by the woman in the engravings, and more than worthy of being a gift from a Renaissance prince.

"For you," he repeated, lifting the strand from the box and wrapping it around my neck. It was long enough to loop three times around my throat and still drape gracefully over my breasts.

He led me to the dressing mirror, standing behind me in the reflection. The iridescence of the pearls made my skin glow in comparison, and I blushed with pleasure.

"They're so beautiful, Savage," I said, running my fingers lightly along the strand. I couldn't begin to imagine its value.

"*You* are so beautiful," he said. "I wanted to give them to you in the gallery this morning, but the man bringing them from London was delayed."

I turned to face him. "That was why you went downstairs, for this necklace for me?"

He nodded, studying our reflection. "Apparently at the exact time you were gathering up those other pearls to surprise me. I much prefer these."

"I do, too," I said. I kissed his stubbled jaw, then trailed my lips along his throat. "Because they came from you."

"You will think of me whenever you wear them," he said, sliding his hand beneath the pearls to caress my breast. "Only me, Eve."

"Only you, Master," I whispered. "Always you."

"Yes," he said, sweeping me to the bed. "Exactly as it should be."

We spent the rest of that day and the next in his bedroom, and scarcely left the bed. In the back of my mind, I was acutely aware of the final dinner we'd agreed to attend, looming before us. I remembered all too well what had happened the last time Savage and I had joined the others in the dining room, and I dreaded another outburst—particularly one involving Lord Blackledge.

Yet I said nothing of it, and neither did Savage. It was a sign of how determined we both had become to savor each moment we had together, and to think of neither the past nor the future, nor of anything else beyond that single room. But the moments that remained were dwindling fast, and finally it was Savage who broke our self-imposed spell.

"I want you to dress for dinner tonight," he said. We were lying together on the bed with the golden sun of late afternoon spilling around us, I on my back and Savage on his side next to me with his head propped against his bent arm. He was lazily playing with the pearls, trailing them slowly around and over my nipple to tease it into puckering attention.

"Dress in what manner?" I asked, dragging myself back from drowsiness to reply, though not far enough to open my eyes. "My Innocent costume?"

"No," he said. "I do not wish to offer you as temptation to the buffoons. You need not wear the costume again."

"Thank you," I said, more relieved than he could have known. "What will the other ladies be wearing?"

"I care only for you," he said, more as a matter of fact than gallantry. "Surely you brought another dinner dress with you."

I had in fact brought nine, so that I might have choices. "Do you have a favorite color?"

He smiled lazily. "My favorite color is whatever you choose to wear."

"Then you shall be surprised."

"I suppose I'll have to give you up to Simpson soon," he said with philosophical regret. "I know how long it takes for ladies to dress."

"But not yet." I didn't want to think of the tedium of

being formally dressed, while I was in his bed. I arched up to kiss him, a leisurely, seductive invitation.

"And the pearls," he said. "You must wear the pearls."

"Of course," I murmured, smiling warmly up at him. I had worn the pearls ever since he'd given them to me, and I had no intention of taking them off for tonight. "Only you and I will know of all the things we've already done while wearing them."

"As it should be," he said, but his smile was enigmatic as he leaned forward and kissed me again. "I want you to think only of me whenever you wear them."

He deepened the kiss and I linked my arms around his shoulders. He rolled over me and I shifted beneath him, parting my legs in welcome. I was still wet from the last time, still swollen enough that he had to push his thick, heavy cock hard to enter me, and I caught my breath at the overwhelming sensation of being fucked open, and instantly filled.

He took me with the long, measured thrusts that I'd come to associate so completely with him, and I curled my legs high over his driving hips to take him deeper still. The necklace slipped and slid across my body, the pearls rolling over my skin and warmed by it. Each rhythmic stroke of his cock into my sensitized core pushed me a little closer to my release, yet still he held me just on the edge, building my pleasure with his own as he pounded his hips against me.

There was nothing like the need he could send licking through my body, the hot desire that scorched me. I could not resist him, nor did I want to. I rocked up to meet his thrusts, all sinuous energy to match his fire.

"My god, Eve." He groaned, making a guttural demand of my name. "You're so damned *perfect*."

I understood, for I felt the same about him. All I wished now was to lose myself completely with him, in him, and when he angled his hips to stroke the crown of his cock inside my passage, it was almost more than I could bear.

"Oh, Savage, please," I gasped, writhing against the pillows. *"Please."*

"Then come." His voice was raspy, his handsome face contorted in concentration. "Come with me now."

I came hard, crying out as the waves of release rippled through my body. He shuddered as he pumped into me, over and over, his head thrown back in his own ecstasy. He'd said I was perfect, but the truth was that we were perfect together. Completely, utterly perfect.

We lay together for a long time afterward, our limbs still intimately tangled and sheened with sweat.

"I can never get enough of you, Eve," he whispered, dragging his lips along my jaw. "You've ruined me completely."

I smiled, burrowing against him. "You've done the same for me."

He pulled his arms more closely around me. "What a pair that makes us, yes?"

"Yes," I said, the word a long whisper of contentment. I had never been more satisfied, or happier, either. In my mind, I'd begun dividing my life into the time before I'd met him and the time after. It didn't matter that I'd known him only a matter of weeks. By comparison, the time with him cast everything else into dull gray shadows of discontent. He'd changed me forever, and I wished never to go back.

"Yes," he repeated quietly. "Quite the pair."

I hadn't expected the sadness in his voice, almost a melancholy, with regret mixed in as well. Perhaps he was thinking of his wife, and I kissed him again in wordless sympathy.

"Ah, Eve," he said, smoothing my hair back from my face. He smiled, but it was bittersweet, and colored with the same sadness. He held me for a moment longer, then sighed. "I could lie here forever with you, but if I did, Barry would have an apoplexy."

"Hang Barry," I said. "I'd rather stay here."

"So would I," he said, turning his head to see the clock by the side of the bed. "But it's past time I gave you over to your maid to make you presentable for dinner, and Barry must do the same with me."

He eased away from me and swung his legs over the side of the bed. At once I felt his absence, and I reached for the blanket, pulling it up over my shoulders as I watched him put on his robe.

"Don't make yourself too comfortable," he said. "We must go."

I curled myself up more tightly under the blanket, relishing the last bit of warmth his body had left on the sheets. "Why?"

"Because we owe that much to our host and hostess," he explained. "I promised Laura that we would be at dinner, and we will. Come, Eve, out of the bed."

I couldn't understand how swiftly he'd changed his manner, becoming almost brusque. Clearly, his thoughts were already elsewhere, away from me, and the ease with which he'd made the transition wounded me.

"You didn't care about any of the other dinners," I said, reluctantly sliding from the bed. "Why should this one be so special?"

"Because it's the last one of the Game." He handed me my dressing gown. "I'll walk you to your rooms."

He was already opening the door for me by the time I'd tied my sash, and though he smiled as I joined him, I could sense the distance growing between us. He offered me his arm as we began down the hall, but I claimed his hand instead, linking my fingers into his to pull him closer.

"Will we see our hostess on a bed of fruit again to-night?" I asked, striving to be playful.

His smile was perfunctory. "Oh, I doubt it. There will be some sort of hired entertainment, yes, but by the end of the week, most of the guests are too spent for much more mischief. I doubt most of the men could muster a decent cockstand among them now."

"You could," I said. "*We* could."

He grunted. "Yes, but we're not about to show them, are we?" he said. "After dinner there will be a short ceremony—a kind of graduation, if you will—where the Protectors will each stand and sing the praises of their Innocents and what they've taught them, and pronounce their educations complete. Then other Protectors can offer to take on any of the Innocents for future schooling, a tidy way of deciding who will be paired with whom for the next time."

"Then that is what the baron meant when he said he'd claim me," I said with a shudder, remembering how Blackledge had grabbed me in this same hallway. "I'd never agree to be his Innocent."

"It's easy enough to avoid," he said. "A word or two to the viscountess, and she'll arrange it. Although I suspect she's already aware of your dislike for Blackledge."

"I'm sure she is," I said. We'd come to the door of my rooms. I turned to face him, slipping my hand inside his robe to place my open palm on his bare chest. "She should also know by now that there's only one master I'd ever want, and that's you."

"Me?" He seemed pleased, though more surprised than anything. "As flattering as that is, Eve, it cannot happen. The rules of the Game are that no Protector can have the same Innocent twice."

"But no other man could ever follow you, Master," I said, looking up at him from beneath my lashes. I slid my hand lower, loosening his sash so that I could curl my fingers around his cock. At once he began to harden, coming to life in my hand, and with a little thrill of excitement I wondered if he'd take me there, against the door, with the risk of being discovered at any moment. "You will always be my only master."

He didn't smile, and worse, he drew back from me, retying his robe. "Then perhaps you'll return as a mistress instead, ready to educate some callow youth as your own Innocent. I'm sure Lady Carleigh will provide one for you."

I gave my head a little shake of incomprehension. "Savage, you're making no sense."

I reached for him again, and he caught my wrists, gently pushing me away.

"I fear I'm making too much sense, Evelyn," he said softly, "and more than you evidently wish to hear. Tonight's dinner is a farewell of sorts, you know."

"A farewell?" I echoed. "What manner of farewell?"

"It's how the Game always ends, Eve," he said. "We all make our good-byes, and we go our own ways, and what has happened here at Wrenton is never spoken of again, no matter where or how we may meet in the future."

I stared at him, incredulous, searching his face for a truth that must be different from what he was saying. He was trying to be kind—kindness mixed with pity that I neither understood nor wanted.

"Are you saying good-bye to me, Savage?" I asked, unable to keep the panic from my voice. "Is that what you're doing?"

Having heard our voices, Simpson opened the door behind us, and I nearly toppled backward. Savage still held my arms, holding me fast.

"Oh, forgive me, Mrs. Hart," the maid exclaimed with dismay. "I'd no notion you—"

"Never mind, Simpson." My words tumbled over one another in desperate haste as I clutched at Savage, shamelessly trying to draw him back. "We must talk, Savage. Come inside with me, where we won't be disturbed, and—"

"No, Evelyn." He was already distancing himself from me; I could see that his eyes weren't even focused upon my face any longer. "You knew the rules from the first day. I'm sure Lady Carleigh explained them all to you."

"But we haven't followed the rules all week, Savage," I protested, flailing as he held my wrists. "Why should that change now? I want to know. I want to hear you explain. Why is this so different? Why do you suddenly care so much for *rules*?"

But he only shook his head, as if he'd already explained everything that needed explaining. "I'll come back for you in an hour, and we'll go downstairs together."

One by one, he raised my hands to his lips, turning them so that he could kiss my palms. Then he bowed, and left me.

And just like that, he was gone.

FOURTEEN

"Come inside, ma'am, if you please," Simpson said softly, taking my arm to guide me into the room so that she could close the door. "No use in making a scene. These great folk swear they won't talk about what mischief they've done here, but they will speak of you weeping and wailing in the hall, if you give them reason for it."

I sank onto the sofa, bending in half with my arms wrapped tightly together. I felt stunned, blindsided, overwhelmed by what Savage had just told me.

Most of all, I missed him, with my heart, my body, and my soul.

Why, why hadn't I known it wouldn't last? Why had I so willfully blinded myself? Why had I forgotten that inconstancy was one of the stipulations of visiting at Wrenton, and agreeing to play the Game? That was how Lady

Carleigh gave her guests the freedom to do what they pleased, by promising them an honor-bound discretion.

I had accepted that condition along with every other guest, and I'd enjoyed the same freedom. It was entirely my own fault that I'd chosen to forget those rules.

Savage had never once made any promises to me that he'd now broken, and though he'd trusted me with confidences, he'd always been careful not to speak once to me of love or a shared future. I realized that now, thinking back. Not once. I was the one who'd foolishly let myself care too much for him.

And now I'd be expected to put on the bravest of faces and go down to dinner. I'd have to listen as he reviewed my accomplishments as an Innocent to the others, and then smile and blithely say good-bye, as if he meant no more to me than any of the other guests.

Or worse: as little as I must mean to him.

"Are you too poorly to go downstairs this evening, Mrs. Hart?" Simpson asked with concern. "I have your bath ready, but if you'd rather lie down for a bit, then—"

"No, Simpson, I am fine." With a shuddering sigh, I stood, determined to gather myself. Blindly I felt for the pearls around my neck, the pearls Savage had given me, hoping they'd give me some small comfort. They didn't.

But if Savage could be distant, then so could I, at least on the outside. I came from a long line of tough-minded New Yorkers: it should be in my blood to be strong. Later, when I was back in London, there would be plenty of time to weep alone in private. Tonight I'd do my best not to let anyone—least of all Savage himself—know how very much his summary little farewell had wounded me.

"Excuse me, ma'am," Simpson said, "but you don't look very well."

"I assure you, Simpson," I said, taking a deep breath, "I am perfectly well."

Slowly I lifted the necklace over my head, coiling it into my hand. I held it there in my palm for a moment, the pearls pooled and warm with the heat of my body, and perhaps still a bit of Savage's as well. Then I resolutely handed the necklace to the maid and went to the bathroom and my tub, dropping my dressing gown behind me as I went.

I didn't wait for Simpson's assistance but began to wash myself as soon as I sank into the warm, scented water. It wasn't just that I wished to be ready; I was determined to scrub away every trace of Savage on my body, as swiftly as he seemed to have been rid of me. Yet, when Simpson began to wash my hair, I closed my eyes, and the fresh memories of all we'd done and shared came rushing back, no matter how much I wished to stop them. How much easier it was to clean my body than to scrub his memory from my thoughts and my soul!

"Should I send back to his lordship's rooms for your Innocent's costume, ma'am?" Simpson asked.

"No," I said with finality. "I won't be wearing that any longer. Lay out the red gown instead, Simpson."

Like all my evening gowns, the red one was new. But that was only part of the reason why I hadn't yet worn it. Quite simply, the dress was the most daringly brazen and modern I'd ever owned, and I hadn't had the courage to match it. Savage had not wanted me to tempt any of the other male guests by wearing my Innocent costume again, but I was sure to accomplish much the same effect in the red dress, and if I tormented Savage, too—what was the harm in that?

A short time later, after my hair had been brushed and pinned up into a crown of soft waves around my face, I stood before the mirror as Simpson dressed me. I had spent the past week wearing next to no clothes, and it felt chillingly oppressive to be covered once again in layer after layer of confining lace-trimmed fabric, chemise and corset cover and drawers and petticoats and garters and stockings. I'd worn a corset since I was a girl, yet now as Simpson began to tighten the strings I felt as if I were being laced back into my old self, as if the last week with Savage had never happened.

And I rebelled.

"Take all this—this off, Simpson," I said, already tugging at my undergarments. "I'm going to wear the dress without anything beneath."

"Oh, ma'am," Simpson said, full of doubt. "I don't know if the dress will fit proper without them."

"Monsieur Poiret's dresses aren't boned like the old Worth ones," I insisted. "I wish to try it that way."

Soon I was wearing nothing but my stockings. The instant Simpson slipped the dress over my bare shoulders, I knew I'd done the right thing. Or perhaps the very wrong thing, which was exactly what I wanted.

The dress wasn't merely red, it was scarlet, and if sex and passion had a color, then this would have been it. The silk was cut in the most modern style, draping over my body like a shimmering liquid. Without any petticoats beneath, it clung to my body and accentuated the swelling curves of my hips and breasts as well as the narrowness of my waist. The jet beading swirled over the bodice and skirt in an oriental pattern that served only to delineate my figure further, drawing the light with every movement.

But most shocking of all was the bodice, low and square and made entirely of black lace. Even with a corset and chemise beneath, it would have been scandalously revealing. But the way that I was wearing it now, my breasts were scarcely veiled by the lace and my nipples were clearly visible, and yet the lace also made the entire effect infinitely more seductive.

"Oh, my, ma'am," Simpson said with admiration, looking over my shoulder to my reflection in the mirror. "You'd stiffen the cock of a dead man in that dress. His lordship don't have a chance."

"I'm not sure he deserves one, Simpson," I said with a quick smile for my reflection.

"No, ma'am," Simpson said, grinning. "Shall I fetch your jewels, ma'am? Those diamonds you wore the first night would look splendid with all that black and red."

I considered, then shook my head. "I think the dress will be sufficient without additional ornament," I said. "Except, of course, the rope of pearls I was wearing earlier. Bring that, if you please."

Quickly Simpson retrieved the necklace, and with something close to reverence she draped it around my neck.

"Three times, Simpson," I said. "I want the pearls to fall over my breasts."

"Yes, ma'am," Simpson said, making the adjustment. "Forgive me for saying so, ma'am, but you must've been mighty pleasing to his lordship for him to give you pearls like them, especially after all the suffering he gave you, too."

"That's enough, Simpson," I said, but mildly. I couldn't fault the maid for thinking the pearls were a kind of payment for services rendered. For the women like Simpson who'd been Innocents, that's what an extravagant gift from a Protector surely would be.

From Savage, however, I wanted to think it meant a bit more, my thoughts drifting back to the morning in the gallery. Though perhaps it didn't. I had thought we'd grown close in these last days, and believed that there was a rare understanding between us, but the reality had turned out to be something altogether different.

I shoved aside the thought, and the first sting of tears in my eyes, too. The last thing I wished was to appear

before the others—before *him*—with swollen eyes and a
red nose. I took a deep breath, holding up my skirts
while Simpson slipped on my beaded evening shoes.

I walked away from the mirror, then turned and walked
slowly back toward it. The heeled shoes gave a sway to my
walk, and the scarlet silk slipped and slid seductively over
my body. The glittering black beads seemed to draw special attention to the tantalizing juncture of my thighs, even
hinting at my most private parts. Savage's pearls did the
same for my breasts, swinging gently over my lace-covered
nipples with each step.

I thought back to the first night here at Wrenton, how
I'd felt so seductive in the heavy cream-colored gown,
when I'd really known nothing at all about sex, let alone
seduction. Because of Savage, I'd become not only seductive but sensual as well, and my only regret was—

But no. I'd have no regrets, no regrets about anything.
I smiled one last time at my reflection, took my black-lace
fan from Simpson, and turned toward the door.

"Will you be expecting his lordship to take you down
to dinner, ma'am?" Simpson asked, following me.

"No, Simpson, I am not," I said, waiting for the maid
to open the door. "That is, he will likely be coming here
for me, but I will not be waiting for him. I am going downstairs myself."

I left quickly, before I could waver and change my mind,
and before Savage could appear and change my mind in
an entirely different way. The way my heart was racing, I
realized I almost hoped he would.

When I reached the library, I swiftly glanced about the
room to see if he was there. To my relief, he wasn't, and
neither was Lord Blackledge, but most of the other guests
already were. At once Lady Carleigh appeared, seizing me
by the arm to kiss her cheek in welcome.

"My dear Mrs. Hart, how absolutely ravishing—and

ravishable—you are tonight!" she exclaimed, looking me up and down. "That must be a Poiret, is it not?"

"Thank you, it is," I murmured, languidly opening my fan as I pretended to ignore the attention that my dress was drawing from every male in the room. Even the footmen were staring at me. "Monsieur Poiret has such a rare genius, doesn't he?"

"He does when the lady possesses a figure like yours," Lady Carleigh said. "You have made every man in this room forget all else besides his cock."

I smiled. "Which is, of course, not the case if I'd been clad entirely in whipped cream and strawberries."

Lady Carleigh laughed. "Touché, my dear! Quite true, yes, quite true. But then I did not have a bulldog like Savage to protect my, ah, virtue, either. Where is he? What have you done with him?"

"I expect he should join us soon." I forced myself to smile. "We've already said our good-byes."

The viscountess raised a single painted brow with surprise. "I cannot believe he would part with you an instant before he had to, considering how possessive he has been before this."

"I assure you, my lady, I am quite free." I shrugged, hoping I conveyed exactly the right degree of nonchalance, and not even a hint of the unhappiness Savage's cursory parting had brought me. I glanced around the room, forcing myself to survey the other gentlemen with a fresh eye.

"But you're not quite free yet, my dear," Lady Carleigh cautioned. "It's true that you can indicate a choice for a future week this evening, if someone in particular has caught your eye, but you may not act upon it quite yet."

Her perpetual hostess's smile faded, and she rested her hand lightly on my forearm. "Forgive me if your master has not been all he should this week, my dear. When I brought you and Savage together, I had no notion he'd act towards you as he has. It's inexplicable, and unforgivable, and I am very sorry you suffered from his unconscionable behavior."

"But I didn't suffer, my lady," I said. After our encounter in the gallery, Lady Carleigh's words shouldn't have surprised me, but they did. "I have few regrets or complaints where Lord Savage is concerned."

"Few?" asked Lady Carleigh, pouncing on the single word of doubt.

"None," I said firmly, correcting myself. My only complaint—if it could be called that—was of my own doing, not his, forgetting that our week together was meant to be that time, and no longer. "I have no regrets nor complaints, and if I were to make the choice again, I would without doubt once more choose Savage."

The viscountess tipped her head to one side. "This is the truth? You aren't simply being polite?"

"I wouldn't do that, my lady, not about Lord Savage," I said, more wistfully than I could have wished. "He is an . . . an *unforgettable* man."

"You intrigue me, Mrs. Hart," Lady Carleigh said, her curiosity apparent. "When we have more time and are at our leisure, I shall expect you to tell me more of your experiences with his lordship. Much more."

"Yes, my lady," I said. It was the only acceptable answer, even though I knew such a conversation with the viscountess would never happen. To make idle gossip of what I'd shared with Savage would be a kind of betrayal that I wouldn't commit. There were things that were too private, too special, too rare to confide to anyone else, and this last week with him was one of them.

"Yes, yes, yes," said Lady Carleigh, licking her lips with anticipation. "But I must ask you one more favor tonight, my dear. Please do your best to see that Savage keeps the peace. The last thing I wish tonight is more violent unpleasantness among the gentlemen. My nerves—and my furnishings—cannot bear it."

"I'd no intention of inspiring any violence, my lady," I said, remembering all too well the ugly scene with Mr. Henery.

But the viscountess remained skeptical. "In that dress, Mrs. Hart, you could inspire the entire country of males to riot and go to war. Pray limit yourself to conversing tonight, and let us all try to survive the night unscathed, yes? Ah, Lord Blackledge, we were just speaking of you!"

The baron bowed to both of us, but his gaze never wavered from my breasts.

"I trust you haven't forgotten what I told you, Mrs. Hart," he said, his smile too wide. "I *will* be claiming you tonight."

"Yes, yes, Baron, so you have told us all," Lady Carleigh said, hooking her arm into his. "But our lovely Mrs. Hart is not yours yet. You are absolutely forbidden to cause any mischief over her with Lord Savage, or else I shall have you both tossed out of my house like the curs that you are. Now come with me, and leave this lady in peace."

With Lady Carleigh tugging on his arm, Lord Blackledge had no choice but to follow, and as soon as they left me, several gentlemen immediately joined me in their place. Clearly, they'd been warned to behave as well, for although they stared at me with unabashed lust, their conversation was as bland and respectful as if I'd been their elderly maiden aunt.

And while each was perfectly presentable as gentlemen went, not one of them inspired an iota of desire in my blood. How could they, when they'd be following a man like Savage?

I was only half listening when I heard the footsteps coming down the hallway. I knew whom they belonged to, even without turning to see, and when he took my arm, his touch was so achingly familiar that I nearly gasped aloud.

"We must talk, Eve," Savage said, his voice rough and urgent. "Come with me."

"No, my lord," I said, pulling my arm free. I took a step apart from the other gentlemen, not wanting them to over-hear whatever Savage might say. I wanted and needed to be strong. He'd wounded me once already this day, and I wasn't going to let him do it again. "You've made it clear enough that we've nothing left to say."

"Nothing, Eve?" he asked. "When I've barely begun?"

Although he was impeccably dressed for dinner, his jaw shaved and his hair sleeked back, his expression was rav-aged and haunted, his pale eyes as desperate as a wild animal's. I hated seeing him like this, and it took all my will not to give in.

"There's nothing left to say, my lord," I repeated as firmly as I could. "You made that clear enough to me earlier."

He shook his head, his lips pressed tightly together. "The only thing that's clear is that you misunderstood me. I went to your rooms, only to have your maid tell me you hadn't waited. You left without me, Eve. I never believed you'd do that, not to me."

He was looking at me with a mixture of raw longing and despair so palpable that it shocked me.

"Please, Savage," I said softly. "I know the rules of the Game, too. I understand everything ends today. You don't have to explain them again."

"You wore the pearls," he said. "*My* pearls. You remem-bered. You're remembering now."

I blushed. I *was* remembering, one glorious memory of us together crashing into the next, and with the same in-tensity of our sex.

"Please don't, Savage," I begged. "I'm not a fool. Don't make me look like one now."

"You're never a fool, Eve," he said, that almost-hoarse voice that could hypnotize me. "Never."

No matter what he'd said before, the connection remained between us. I felt it, and I was sure he did as well. We might have been the only two people in the room instead of two among twenty.

He reached out and lightly ran his fingertips down the inside of my arm, letting the back of his hand graze over the side of my breast. My gaze followed his hand, unable to look away; he was wearing the black onyx links in his cuffs, and the diamond eyes of the coiled gold snakes seemed to wink at me as his fingers trailed down my arm. It was the lightest of caresses, yet still I shivered, the familiar desire beginning to build in my body.

"Not here, Savage," I begged, yet I didn't pull away. "Please."

"Then where, when you wouldn't wait for me?" he said, his hand dipping in between my arm and my hip to settle around my waist. "Why not here?"

"Because—because everyone is watching us," I stammered, leaning closer to him. The silk of my gown was so light that I felt the warmth of his hand through it, finding the narrowest part of my waist and holding me there, *there*.

"Do you think I give a damn about these other people?" he asked, demanding. "Do you think I'd let them keep me away from you?"

I closed my eyes when I shook my head, thinking that that would be enough to shut him away. But instead of making it easier to ignore him, the image he'd painted for me became more vivid, and infinitely more difficult to resist.

"I want you badly, Eve," he continued in a rough whisper meant only for my ears, "so badly that I want to pull up your skirt and take you here, now, with all of them watching, an audience to shock. You'd like that, too, wouldn't you? To put your legs around my hips and ride my cock as fast and hard as you wanted, your beautiful tits bouncing and your head thrown back until you came, screaming my name?"

Swept away by his words, I made a broken little cry when he finished, and pressed my hand across my mouth.

"Mrs. Hart, are you unwell?" asked Lady Carleigh, her face full of concern as she touched my hand. Beside her stood the tall footman, and beside him was Lord Carleigh, with the rest of the guests clustered around them.

"Forgive me, my lady," I said, blushing with confusion as I separated from Savage. "I am perfectly well. His lordship had just told me something that, ah, startled me."

The viscountess was not fooled, and her gaze shifted suspiciously to Savage.

"My lord," she said formally. "I do not wish any further misadventures in my house tonight, especially not involving you and this lady."

Savage took a deep breath, dragging his gaze away from me to collect himself. If he hadn't, I doubted he could have done it—nor could I.

"You have my word, Laura," he said at last, sleeking his hair back from his forehead. "No misadventures. All I wish to do now is take Mrs. Hart in to dinner."

At that moment, the butler struck the dinner gong. Two by two, the masters and the mistresses and their Innocents began to walk to the dining room. Savage offered his arm to me, and I took it gingerly, letting him lead me in to the table with the others.

I didn't speak, and neither did he, and I could only wonder if he was as confused as I was myself at that moment. He had made it abundantly clear earlier that this was good-bye, and yet neither his words nor his actions now were those of a man who was soon to be free of any attachments.

What could he hope to achieve by playing the last-minute role of a desperate lover? What was the point of stringing out our farewell over the entire evening, when the outcome would still be the same?

He led me to my place beside his at the table, waiting as the footman pushed my chair in for me before he sat as well. In the midst of the general fuss and conversation as everyone sat and settled, he squeezed my hand beneath the table, his fingers strong and sure around mine, and leaned close to my ear.

"You are incomparable, Eve," he said, his breath warm upon my ear. "Remember that. To me, no other woman can ever come close to you."

I turned my face toward his, and he kissed me, fast and hard, and yet with a subtle, unexpected sweetness, too. Afterward he held my gaze for a long moment, then turned away to answer the footman who was offering him wine.

I stared down at the damask napkin in my lap, surprised by the quick sting of tears that his kiss had brought. It could well have been our final kiss, a possibility that was suddenly unbearable to me. But I would not cry—I could not—and with a great effort I composed my lips into a smile, and raised my face to look around the table.

As Savage had predicted, they were a much less exuberant company this evening than when they'd assembled that first night. Only one or two of the Innocents still wore their costumes, which, after a week's wear, were looking decidedly bedraggled. No one seemed particularly interested in sex now, either, and there wasn't any groping or fondling or diving beneath the table.

To my eye, my fellow guests instead seemed as if all they desired was a good night's sleep in their own beds, and I remembered how Savage had predicted there wouldn't be a stiff cock among the lot. I'd have to agree.

Except, of course, for Savage and me. Having him

beside me was the most exquisite torment, as if my body could still sense and react to his by proximity alone. I could not put from my mind what he'd said to me in the library, and in my thoughts I kept playing the erotic scenario that he'd described, over and over. If he shoved back his chair now and seized me and fucked me there on the dining table, I would have been as eager for it as he claimed to be himself.

I forced myself to dip my spoon into the soup plate of vichyssoise before me, raise it to my lips, and swallow. *Yes,* I thought, *that's what I must do. Concentrate on the dinner, and try to forget the man beside me.* Through course after course I persevered, and though Savage would occasionally smile at me or brush his hand against mine, he didn't speak directly to me, nor did I to him. Twice, Barry appeared to whisper in Savage's ear, which seemed to please him, but he did not share his news, and I didn't ask for it.

At last Lady Carleigh rose, tapping her spoon against her water goblet for order as she smiled around the table at her guests.

"I must ask your attention, my dears, if you please," she began. "As you know, this is our last time as a party together, and it's the final act of the Game for the Protectors to describe how their Innocents have fared under their tutelage. From that, we shall decide if the Innocent is ready to progress to become a master or mistress, or must return to our next gathering for further education with a different Protector."

She turned to Lord Carleigh, seated beside her. "Please be first, Carleigh. I know you've much to say about your Innocent."

"Indeed." The bleary-eyed viscount dragged himself to his feet. He was one of the more worn-looking Protectors, and the perkiness of his Innocent, the Honorable Mrs. Bilton, popping to her feet beside him, only accentuated his exhaustion.

"I present my Innocent, whom I call Blossom," he said, putting his arm around her shoulders. "She has much to recommend her. She has become highly skilled in sucking cock, and will take a stiff cock wherever it is presented. She has a special talent for ass fucking, too, and has no shyness for sharing her master with another."

While those around the table applauded, the Honorable Mrs. Bilton beamed, as if this were the greatest compliment a woman could receive. I was silently horrified: not that I cared one bit for what was said of Mrs. Bilton, but I cared very much for what Savage was going to say about me.

Lord Carleigh held his hand up to silence the applause. "Yet, as estimable as this Innocent's accomplishments are, I recommend that she receive further training with another master. Do you agree?"

The loud chorus of "ayes" left no doubt. Clearly, this was part of the Game, and Mrs. Bilton looked so pleased by the decision that I was sure she'd been consulted.

Unable to keep quiet any longer, I leaned close to Savage. "Did you know this would happen? That it's decided who must remain an Innocent?"

"Oh, yes," he answered, nonchalant. His earlier agitation seemed to have passed and his mood had grown calm, or maybe he'd simply drunk enough wine that he'd become resigned. "It's always the same."

"But you haven't asked me which I preferred," I whispered.

He shrugged, and smiled. "I didn't feel it was necessary. I already have a good idea of what you would wish."

"But you don't *know*!" I was sure he didn't know my mind, because I didn't myself. Neither choice seemed particular agreeable to me, with any of the other gentlemen at the table. How could it be, after Savage?

"I believe I do," he said with maddening certainty, and turned away to speak to the man on his left.

Lord Carleigh was smiling, holding his hand up. "Very well, then. Are there any masters—or perhaps a mistress, since Blossom does need education in Sapphic skills— willing to accept her for training in our next session?"

"I'll claim her," called Lord Wessex.

"Then she's yours, Wessex," Lord Carleigh said with a benevolent wave of his hand. He gave one last, smacking kiss to Mrs. Bilton, and then pinched her bottom for good measure, making her squeal. "Good-bye to you, sweetheart. Go off to your new master, there's a good girl, and happy fucking to you both."

Happily Mrs. Bilton darted around the table to join Lord Wessex, who promptly pulled her onto his lap while the others applauded and cheered.

"An excellent resolution," Lady Carleigh said. "Mr. Parkhurst, will you be next to review your Innocent?"

My anxiety grew as I watched and listened. The other guests were beginning to enjoy themselves more, and the cheering and the catcalls were growing louder and more obscene, enough to make my head ache and my heart race with dread.

I thought that perhaps I should simply excuse myself and leave now, before it was my turn. I could retreat to my rooms, change my clothes, order a car, and leave. I'd already said good-bye to Savage, or rather, he'd said good-bye to me. There was no reason to remain and be humiliated with a public cataloging and dismissal, and given over to another man that I did not want—

"Lord Savage!" Lady Carleigh's voice rang out from the end of the table. "Will you please present your Innocent for review? Eve, isn't it?"

Savage took my hand and rose slowly to his feet, pulling me unwillingly with him.

"Please don't make me do this, Savage," I whispered, pleading, my fingers wrapped tightly into his. "To have to hear you say good-bye to me again will—it will break me."

His smile was slow and warm, which only made it worse, not better.

"Be brave, Eve," he said softly, cradling my cheek with the palm of his hand. "I promise this will all go exactly as you could wish."

Then he winked, a true conspirator's wink that took me entirely by surprise.

"Come, come, my lord," Lady Carleigh chided. "The time for private instruction is done. Please tell us of your Eve's lessons, and what devilish skills you have taught her."

"Oh, I have taught her a great many things, Lady Carleigh," he said, raising his voice so that everyone could hear him. "And in turn she has taught me as well. Never underestimate the talents of the American people."

"Enough of your damned drivel, Savage," Lord Black-ledge called. "You needn't go on any further. I'll take her next."

"No, you won't!" I exclaimed. "I don't care what the rules of this foolish game might be, I will not go—"

"You will not go anywhere," Savage interrupted calmly. "Unless you go with me. You see, I have decided that one week is not nearly sufficient for this lady. It has been only the beginning for us both. Instead, I intend to take her with me tonight, to London, to continue her further education there."

I gasped, too stunned for words. He didn't want to leave me. Instead, he wanted to leave *with* me, now, just the two of us.

"To London!" cried Lady Carleigh as the other guests burst into a babble of confused outrage and oaths. "Savage, you cannot do that. What of the rules? What of the Game?"

His smile widened, for he was so obviously enjoying every moment of this. "My dear lady, where Mrs. Hart is concerned, the rules exist only to be broken. That is, of course, if she agrees to come with me."

And at last he turned to me, lifting my hand to his lips.

"My car is waiting," he said, over the back of my hand. "My house is ready. God knows I'm ready, Eve. All you need do is say yes."

"You are sure of this?" I asked, unsure myself. He was an easy man to take to bed, but he was not an easy man. Far from it. Yet, after only one week with him, I could not now imagine my life without him in it. We belonged together.

"Give me seven more days, Eve," he said. "One more week. That's all I ask."

I took a deep breath. *One week, seven days.* I smiled, a giddy, daring smile for him alone.

"Seven more days with you, Savage," I whispered. "Seven days, and seven nights, in London. And I cannot wait for it to begin."

Coming soon…

**Look for the next novel in Mia Gabriel's sensational
Savage series**

SAVAGE NIGHTS

Available in February 2016

From St. Martin's Paperbacks

1907: On the road to London

Y ou're not frightened, are you?" The seventh Earl of Savage leaned closer, curling his long arm around the back of my shoulders in a gesture that could have been protective, or something else entirely. "If you've any regrets—"

"None," I said swiftly, determined to show no hesitation, no doubts. "And if I shiver, it's from excitement, not fear."

He smiled slowly, and if I hadn't shivered before, I did then. Desire did that to me, and I'd never desired a man as I did Savage. Wild, reckless, burning desire, desire that I'd never dreamed possible or ever wished to end: that was what I felt for Savage.

We sat on the curving back bench of his Rolls-Royce, racing through the inky darkness of the Hampshire country-side toward London and away from the house party at

Wrenton Manor. There were no stars, no moon, and the only light came from the car's headlights and silver carriage lanterns. Sitting on the other side of the curtained glass, Savage's driver clearly had orders to carry us to London as quickly as possible; we traveled at a breakneck pace, heedless of anything save each other in our luxurious haven.

"You shiver from excitement," Savage repeated. He eased aside the front edge of my sable coat to find the red silk of my evening gown. I'd daringly worn nothing beneath it—no petticoats, no chemise, no corset—and as he lay his hand upon my thigh, I felt at once the heat of his palm and his fingers through the slide of light silk.

He heard the little catch in my breath, and his smile widened. A flash of reflected light briefly lit his face in the darkness, a glimpse that was exactly long enough to remind me of how seductively, impossibly handsome he was. In that flash, his face was all planes and shadows, hard in all the ways that a man's should be, and framed by hair as black as his evening clothes. Yet his mouth was sensuously full, and his pale blue eyes could glow with a white-hot intensity that weakened my knees whenever he looked at me, the way he was studying mc now.

"You *are* excited, Mrs. Hart," he said. "You're almost feverish. It's rather obvious, isn't it?"

"To you it is," I said breathlessly. "Because of you."

"How very scandalous," he said with mock severity. "Were all the widows of New York society as eager as you?"

"The past doesn't matter." I didn't need to be reminded of the loveless, stultifying life I'd left behind. In my head I'd already begun to divide my life into the time before I'd met Savage, and the time since I'd become his. Impatiently I shrugged my shoulders free of my fur coat, too heated now for either its warmth or its ostentation.

"Seven days together in London," he said, his voice low. He pushed up the hem of my gown and slid his hand beneath it, roaming higher across my silk stockings and above my jeweled garters to the heated skin of my thigh. "That's all I offer."

"That's all I want," I said. "You, for seven days, and seven nights."

"There will be talk, you know." He pulled me onto his lap, where at once I felt the hard, blunt thrust of his cock through his trousers pushing against my bottom. "It means nothing to me, but to you—"

"Let them talk," I said, full of bravado. I meant it, too. Considering the dramatic exit we'd just made together from a house party that had included some of the England's best-bred society, I would be surprised if there wasn't gossip. I ran my palm across his chest, over the immaculate white linen of his shirt and the hard muscles beneath. "They will anyway."

"A brave declaration," he said as if he didn't believe me. He hooked one finger into the deep neckline of my gown, slowly pulling it down to bare my breasts. I arched toward him, relishing the feel of the silk sliding over my skin. Framed by the red gown and the dark fur, my skin was as pale and luminous as moonlight, and even in the shadows, he must have seen how my nipples were already tight and hard, aching for his touch. "Words may not be the only risk."

"I told you before," I said quickly, perhaps a little too quickly to be convincing. "I'm not afraid."

"You never are, are you?" He was tracing the full underside of one breast with the pad of his thumb and purposefully ignoring my aroused nipple. "Not even when you should be."

"Savage, if you are trying to—"

"Hush," he said, pressing his fingertip to my lips. "All

I ask is that you do not forget the obvious: that whatever happens between us cannot be undone."

"I'd never wish that." Restlessly I parted my legs with a whisper of silk, feeling the smooth wool of his evening trousers against my bare thigh. I was offering myself to him, wanting him to take me there in the car. The speed, the darkness, even the driver on the other side of the glass served only to heighten my desire. With Savage, I was shameless; he'd made me like that.

"But you wish for many other things," he said, glancing down.

"It's been hours, Savage," I said breathlessly. "That dinner was interminable, sitting there beside you and not being able to touch you. I want you now, here. I *need* you."

His hand stilled on my breast. "You're being forward, Eve. Bold, even brazen. That's not how an Innocent should behave with her master."

A guilty flush spread over my face, and I was thankful for the half-light in the car that hid it. He was right, of course. How soon I'd forgotten what he'd spent this last week teaching me!

"No, Master," I murmured, instantly as obedient as he expected me to be, and as I'd come to expect of myself as well. "I forgot, Master."

"You forgot." He sighed, cupping my breast in the palm of his hand and running his thumb lightly over my nipple. "You should be punished for being so forgetful."

"Yes, Master." I held my breath, not daring to show how much his torturous little caress was affecting me. "I deserve to be punished."

"The most obvious punishment, of course, would be to deny you what you most crave." He shoved the hem of my dress over my hips to bare me below the waist. He slipped his fingers through my dark curls to find the opening of my sex, and pushed one thick finger inside. The moisture of my blatant arousal made it easy for him to thrust deeply, finding the place inside me that was most sensitive. I gasped, unable not to, and arched my back to take him deeper.

"There," he said, his voice growing rougher. "That's what you crave, isn't it?"

"Yes, Master," I said, the two words breaking along with my self-control.

"Yes," he repeated, adding a second finger to stretch and stroke my swollen, greedy passage. "Yet if I were to deny you this, then I would also be punishing myself."

"Yes, Master," I said, my sex tightening around his fingers. "That is, no, Master, you do not deserve the same punishment as I."

"What a perceptive Innocent you are, Eve," he said, his own breath growing ragged. "You've redeemed your earlier impulsiveness."

"Thank—thank you, Master," I whispered, my body trembling, taut and straining for the release that he was building within me. From experience I knew he could keep me poised here on the torturous edge as long as he wanted to, and I knew, too, that he'd do exactly that if I couldn't prove myself worthy.

He smiled, a devil's smile in the half-light. "What would you like as a reward, Eve?"

My fevered quim begged for him to finish what he'd begun, and set me free. But that wasn't the answer he sought, and if I begged, he'd only deny me more.

"Your reward?" he asked again. "Surely there's something you would like, something that would please us both."

"Your—your cock," I managed to say. "I would like your cock, Master."

"Exactly." His smile widened as he drew his fingers from my sex, and I shuddered at the sudden emptiness. "It's yours to take."

Quickly I turned on his lap, sitting with my knees on either side of his legs. With shaking fingers I undid the row of black buttons on his trousers, and at last freed his cock: hard and ruddy and as eager for me as I was for it. I pulled my gown over my head, leaving nothing between us except the long strand of pearls he'd given me yesterday. I loved that he was still clothed with such formality, while I was not.

With a kind of reverence, I took his cock, heavy and hot and hard as granite, in my hands, and he groaned at my touch. Bracing one hand on his shoulder to steady myself against the swaying motion of the car, I poised to lower myself onto his cock, rubbing my honey-sweet on its head and prolonging this last delicious moment of anticipation for us both.

"Now, Eve," he ordered harshly. *"Now."*

And with a shuddering sigh, I sank down and took him as deeply as I could. . . .